AN ORDINARY YOUTH

WALTER KEMPOWSKI (1929–2007) was born in Hamburg. During World War II, he was made to serve in a penalty unit of the Hitler Youth due to his association with the rebellious Swingjugend movement of jazz lovers, and he did not finish high school. After the war he settled in West Germany. On a 1948 visit to Rostock, his hometown, in East Germany, Walter, his brother, and their mother were arrested for espionage; a Soviet military tribunal sentenced him to twenty-five years in prison, of which he served eight at the notorious "Yellow Misery" prison in Bautzen. In 1957 he graduated high school. His first success as an author was the autobiographical novel *An Ordinary Youth* (1971), part of his acclaimed German Chronicle series of novels. In the 1980s he began work on an immense project, *Echo Soundings*, gathering firsthand accounts, diaries, letters, and memoirs of World War II, which he collated and curated into ten volumes published over twenty years, and which is considered a modern classic.

MICHAEL LIPKIN is a translator and scholar of German literature. His writing has appeared in *The New Left Review*, *The Times Literary Supplement*, *The Nation*, and *The Paris Review*, among others. He is currently a visiting professor of German studies at Hamilton College in Clinton, New York.

OTHER BOOKS BY WALTER KEMPOWSKI
PUBLISHED BY NEW YORK REVIEW BOOKS

All for Nothing
Translated by Anthea Bell
Introduction by Jenny Erpenbeck

Marrow and Bone
Translated by Charlotte Collins

AN ORDINARY YOUTH

WALTER KEMPOWSKI

Translated from the German by
MICHAEL LIPKIN

NEW YORK REVIEW BOOKS

New York

THIS IS A NEW YORK REVIEW BOOK
PUBLISHED BY THE NEW YORK REVIEW OF BOOKS
207 East 32nd Street, New York, NY 10016
www.nyrb.com

Original German edition first published in 1971 as *Tadellöser & Wolff*.
First published as a New York Review Books Classic in 2023.

The translation of this work was supported by a grant from the Goethe-Institut.

Library of Congress Cataloging-in-Publication Data
Names: Kempowski, Walter, author. | Lipkin, Michael, translator.
Title: An ordinary youth / by Walter Kempowski ; translated from the German
 by Michael Lipkin.
Other titles: Tadellöser & Wolff. English
Description: New York : New York Review Books, [2023] | Series: New York
 Review Books classics
Identifiers: LCCN 2022037445 (print) | LCCN 2022037446 (ebook) | ISBN
 9781681377209 (paperback) | ISBN 9781681377216 (ebook)
Subjects: LCSH: Kempowski, Walter—Childhood and youth—Fiction. |
 LCGFT: Autobiographical fiction. | Novels.
Classification: LCC PT2671.E43 T313 2023 (print) | LCC PT2671.E43 (ebook)
 | DDC 833/.914—dc23/eng/20220930
LC record available at https://lccn.loc.gov/2022037445
LC ebook record available at https://lccn.loc.gov/2022037446

ISBN 978-1-68137-720-9
Available as an electronic book; ISBN 978-1-68137-721-6

Printed in the United States of America on acid-free paper.
10 9 8 7 6 5 4 3 2 1

CONTENTS

Dedicated to Detlev Nahmmacher

All details completely made up

I

In the morning we were huddled together, drinking coffee, perched on grey packing crates (did the things inside still belong to us?). Light patches fell on the darkened tapestry and the big oven, and I remembered how it once blew up. At noon we would be eating in the new apartment.

We gave the potted palm to the gardener, as there was no place for it any more. It was wonderful, how it had grown all these years. We'd decided to bring the walking stick – 'the Yellow Uncle' – with us, though; we jousted with it now and then. It would be magical in the new apartment. A charming view from the balcony. The central heating was a plus; there wasn't a stove that we'd have to stock with coal to heat.

When I arrived at our new home from school, I saw the furniture wagon from far away: the horses with rust-red tarps and brass plates on their reins.

We had been at Bohrmann's, of course. The grand piano was still standing inside the wagon, so I hadn't missed anything. The movers wore belts around their waists, and had fitted hooks underneath the piano. They unscrewed its legs and heaved it up the steps on a sledge. It weighed seven hundredweight. Their veins were bulging. My mother asked whether a few strong men from the neighbourhood could be enlisted to help.

A fat man slid by the movers and looked up the stairwell, lost in thought. Light came down from above, through a pebbled-glass window. The man was called Quade, he'd built the house.

It was a second-floor apartment and spacious, as Aunt Silbi had noticed from the beginning. The wardrobe was painted red. My father's targets and sabre were hung above the oak chest. ('The blade needs whetting, my boy.')

To the right was a cabinet containing reports from the Wolff Telegram Company, *Poisonous Fish and Fish Poisons*, and countless issues of *Kosmos Bändchen*.

My brother was stretched out in front of the mirror.

'The apartment's pretty all right. Real Goodmannsdörfer. Don't you think?'

'Yes.'

'Well, be happy then.'

We bought new lamps for every room. The lampshades in the living room were held by eagle talons. The light in the bedrooms flowed through alabaster. In the dining room, a bell that you pulled to call the girl hung down over a sprawling paper screen. No lamp was bought for the kitchen; there was already one in there.

Kröhl, a retired tax officer, mounted the lamps. He played the viola in a quartet (playing violin was like bringing sand to the beach), and he was glad for a chance to make himself useful.

'Would you mind hitting the light? The bottom switch. Thanks.'

Back when he was working, he'd once said to my father: 'Obviously this is all wrong.'

'What do you mean, "obviously"?' my father had shouted at him. 'And how can it "*all*" be wrong?'

My mother was pleased that the kitchen wasn't tiled. Tiles are so cold under your feet.

In the washbasin, the water leapt up like a spring from a divot. The tap was button-operated. ('Marvellous.')

All of the windows in the apartment opened inward.

'We'll figure it out,' said my mother. But she never did. Every time she opened them, she had to move the flowerpots.

Across the street, the butcher had an eagle made of tallow in his window, along with roses made of bacon. The pharmacist was next door to him. Everything was nearby. Around the corner was the boutique Vienna Fashions.

They were installing a new traffic sign at the intersection that read STOP.

On the spacious balcony enclosed by a glass ceiling, we put Jew's-beard geraniums and rat-tail cactus on the ledges.

The trees were still bare, but we'd have a lovely view over to the green tower of St Jacob's with the garden in bloom.

'Children, how pretty it is!' my mother said, clasping the geraniums.

To the left was a yellow-painted split-level building. Margarine crates filled with spring onions sat on the iron balconies that ran along its cleft rear wall. Next to it, you could even make out the little spire of the Catholic church, whose bell rang with real force.

*

In the evening my father came home from the office. He wore salt-and-pepper knickerbockers. He hung his felt hat on a red wardrobe hook and sang:

> How quietly all
> The dead are resting . . .[1]

My mother called it 'the Lodge song'.

'I'll pay you back later,' he said to Kröhl and shook his hand; 'for now, my utmost thanks.' He looked at the lamps. 'All wrong,' he muttered.

Then he sat down at the piano, leaned back and played Mozart's 'Sing Songs to the Great Pasha'.

A picture of Rostock harbour hung over the instrument in a thick gold frame, a wedding present from Consul Discher. It wasn't cheap, apparently.

My sister, Ulla ('What lovely braids you have, my child'), seven years older than me, got the attic room.

'Ahoy!' she cried, carrying vases upstairs. She wore a rust-coloured wool dress embroidered with garlands.

I shared a room with my brother Robert. He was six years older than me, with blond hair that lay in thick waves, like those of the Sea of Galilee that Jesus walked on in our illustrated Bible.

He often claimed that I gave off a 'pestilential stink'. He would suck his breath in and hold it, as though he were winding himself up. He liked to wear bow ties, and tied them patiently. When he was done he lay stretched out, as though to say, 'Well, don't I look magnificent?'

'Well, squirt?' he said, when we saw each other in the corridor.

My mother claimed that she came from a long line of Huguenots: the de Bonsacs.

'Our family was ennobled in the sixteenth century,' she said. As the cup bearer, her ancestor could supposedly distinguish between good wine and bad in an instant. A coat of arms showing a chalice and grapes had been handed down to our family; it now hangs in Wandsbek, with the engraving

Bonum bono, good things to the good man

When she said goodnight, she laid her hand on my forehead. ('Doesn't she look like a countess?') Then she recited her long prayers, and her eyes would slowly fill with tears.

'Oh, dear God, see how powerless we are before You. Be merciful; help us through the distresses of our bodies and our lives, so that goodness comes into us. Make us Your children. Help all men through Your all-powerful, all-moving, all-seeing goodness,' and so on. This often went on for a long time, and I tried, by stretching and straining, to show that I'd had enough.

Then she sang:

I'm tired, time to rest . . .[2]

All four verses. She had a beautiful voice. Finally, she bent over me and I was permitted to kiss her. ('But not on the mouth.')

'Tadellöser and Wölff!' my father would exclaim while leafing through the *Evening Post*. He would then play piano for a long while. I could hear him clearly through my open door – 'The Rustle of Spring' from Sindig or Schumann's *The Dances of the League of David* – played 'with humour and just a little foolishness', as he said.

Grooved panes of glass were set in the door to our room. If you leaned in from the end of the corridor, you could see right away whether I was still reading after I'd been told to go to sleep (Wolf Durian's *Kai from the Crate*). I always had my finger on the switch, in tense anticipation. My mother never caught me. ('Do you swear?')

But my brother Robert was craftier: he would sometimes creep up on me, and check whether the light bulb was still warm. 'Come on, aren't you ashamed of yourself?'

He himself read until the early morning (Lok Myler's *The Man Who Fell from Heaven*).

Robert had a hard time waking up ('Up and at 'em!'), but he had been tasked by our superstitious father with sentry duty at the window each morning, to keep an eye out for a young girl. When Robert saw one, he'd cry:

'Come on, Father, come quick!'

He'd come running: he'd be doubled over as though he couldn't hold himself up, half shaved, with dangling trousers and slapping slippers.

'Fine and dandy.'

If the first person you saw was an old woman, your day was ruined, or so the custom went.

Breakfast was always harmonious.

'What's going on with my skin?' my father asked, stretching out his neck to us. He had been gassed in Ypres.

'Wonderful,' we had to say, 'no bruises or peeling.' Otherwise, the day would be ruined.

Whoever came last was greeted with 'Ah! The sun rises!' The latecomer spent a long time looking for his buns, which – 'Hot!

Cold!' – had been hidden somewhere (usually in my mother's lap).

> Whoever comes to breakfast late,
> Eats what's left upon their plate.

Meyer's Historical Geographical Calendar lay next to my father's plate, detailing the national holidays.

> 1916 – The Storming of Fort Douaumont

He always had a harmless joke ready for me. I'd be sitting at the end of the table, and he'd test my Low German:

'What does *Kohlöppvehnah* mean? Answer me! Quickly!'

'The cow runs after the steer,' I had to answer. 'Good, fine,' was the reply.

My father bought himself a new bicycle. The old one, with its long axle you stepped on to climb up, was rusted. He also bought an old Klepper coat, whose tails could be buttoned up.

'I look like a Frenchman,' he said.

My mother reupholstered the armchairs; she couldn't look at the old velvet any more. For the balcony ('Oh, this view!') she bought wicker chairs.

A light-blue dress was made for her at Vienna Fashions. The upper part was cut like a pelerine, with three buttons down the chest. Knife pleats ran out from the buttons in all directions.

I got a so-called Hamburg suit, with a jacket that could be buttoned to the trousers.

My siblings were allowed to join the yacht club. They didn't want to join the rowing club; they weren't galley slaves, after all.

If Ulla had had an accordion she would have tormented us with the latest hits. She did, however, play the harmonica.

> On the bright beaches of the Saale,
> Stand castles so proud and bold.[3]

Her recitals annoyed my brother. When he started acting out, they were both grounded to the parlour. He wasn't a proper boy, she thought (and said). Proper boys came home with bruised knees and holes in their trousers. They climbed over every fence.

'Could you please let me know what fence I should be climbing over?' asked Robert.

Once they started sailing, my father would stand at the top of the stairs, watch in hand, waiting for them to get home.

'Where have you been?'

They were in for it now.

Ulla also had riding lessons. For 5 marks an hour the stable let her trot around the ring. She complained about having to wear tracksuit trousers, when Kati Rupp had a riding suit.

'Then you have to find yourself another father. I can't pull the money out of my ear.'

We watched her from the shadows of the bleachers. My father laughed when the horse broke wind.

At one event, she knelt in the saddle. 'That was a nail-biter,' she said afterwards, before telling us that she'd felt quite dizzy.

Another time, a stirrup banged her forehead.

'Going cuckoo?' asked Robert when she showed up with a lump on her head.

She took photos of horses with her Agfa box camera. The photos went into the family album.

The good comrade she wrote underneath each of them.

The whole family was photographed: Mother in her pelerine dress, Robert sailing, and me in my Hamburg suit. Even Father, in his SA uniform, standing under a birch tree.

2

Woldemann, a well-off, well-liked timber merchant, lived below us, on the first floor. He wore his black hair – shiny as patent-leather shoes – with a sharp middle parting, and had a ring with a blue stone on his little finger.

'Well, you scamp?' he said to me in a deep voice, and grabbed one of the open wine bottles that were standing everywhere. He drank without a glass, in long pulls.

He had a parlour, the 'Men's Room'. He had overstuffed armchairs in there, with knitted cushions that were more comfortable than those in our apartment. The rug was also thicker, and went well with the pictures in the room. Next to a smoking table was a black, commode-sized gramophone, which had a kind of gate in front, to let the music out.

> Isn't she sweet, isn't she lovely,
> Isn't she nice, Fraulein Gerda . . .[1]

Under the celluloid cover, a wax figurine decorated the gramophone. She wore a lace dress.

'Filigree,' my mother said.

In the mornings Woldemann sat at the coffee table in his housecoat.

He let the rotating plate containing the marmalade and honey spin while he ate his egg with a silver spoon. ('Egg with silver? But that tarnishes it!') He slurped the droplets off the milk jug with a smack, but ate his roll with a knife and fork.

> Everyone was happy, everyone was proud,
> If he had her, Fraulein Gerda.[2]

His wife was young and eager to talk. 'Woldi', she called him.

She went in and out of the apartment while the gramophone blared, went from one box of pralines to another, curled her hair, and wiped off the Copenhagen figurines with a feather duster.

'Your father is always screaming his head off. Which one of you is the "snot-nosed brat"?'

Their daughter, Ute, was nine, like me. She had a pageboy haircut and dark blue eyes. We were together all the time, and would sulk when we were apart. Mostly I lay on the carpet and she sat on my stomach. It was lovely and warm and cosy. I even pulled my legs in, so that she could lean against them. Then she rocked back and forth a little and dug around in my nose. (The first time she did it, I defended myself, ripping the upper part of my Hamburg suit away from the trousers.)

This way, I got to know the furniture from below: the coffee table with the legs crudely attached by the carpenter; the armchairs made of a leather that was the same hue as the movers' belts; the waste-paper basket, which always smelled rotten because someone had thrown in apple peels.

We had an argument once about which gender was more important, male or female.

The father, *der Vater*, was outranked by the government, *die*

Regierung, she said, and the continent, *der Kontinent*, by the earth, *die Erde*.

But the world, *die Welt*, is outranked by God, *den Gott*, I answered: He was masculine.

> All the people suddenly stand still
> To watch the sweet young lady.[3]

We jumped away from one another whenever we heard her mother coming around the corner,

'. . . Or we'll both be in for it,' she said.

*

Behind our building was a seltzer-water factory that belonged to our landlord.

> Whether out in the woods or snug in your den,
> Enjoy Dr Krause's Mineral Water.

We went on a visit where we sat in crates and rode on the conveyor belt: it went through dark sheds and past bays containing empty bottles.

We jumped off in a tiled workroom where the water was being bottled. Workers with rubber aprons stood at the conveyor belt and watched as the bottles jerked along in a row, before being filled up by the machine, corked, turned upside down, labelled and rolled into crates.

A padded lever turned the bottles upside down, and a second one came up from below to gently receive the bottle. Now and again a bottle would burst with a dull pop and rain shards.

The full crates were kept in the basement. It was cool there. We would drink a bottle all in one gulp – 'Let's see who finishes first' – and burp.

In the office, it smelled like tobacco and peppermint. Here Fraulein Reber, with her ski tan, signed off on the receipts with lightning speed. She pointed out that 'Reber' read the same backwards. Her brother, a pilot with the Legion, was even named Otto!

She gave me a songbook as a present and asked if I wanted to join the mighty Hitler Youth. Ute got *Lobunddank the Spinner: A New Songbook for Girls*.

> The morning has rung,
> The night is shattered.
> Up, heart, to new days
> Calls the new-born light.[4]

'I want a litre of corn schnapps,' said a drunk who had just come in. A picture of Clausewitz hung on the wall.[5]

We weren't allowed to meet Dr Krause. He strode across the courtyard in his riding breeches. To demonstrate the benefits of his mineral spring, he filled a zinc bucket with water ('Clear as crystal') and put some Rostock tap water next to it. It was a limey, brown broth.

'You've practically got vomit swimming in the tap water,' he said.

Witschorek, who drove for the Berthold-Otterstädt-Bremen Company, was always trying to chase us out of there. He came from Czechoslovakia, the Sudetenland.

'Egerlanders stand together,' I sang once, as a joke. The man began to cry.

We were however always welcome at Boldt's stables. He was the coachman, and would whistle contentedly as he mixed oats and chaff, and poured in some apple soda. He made 26 marks a week. My father gave me stubbed-out cigars for him.

Dr Krause had brought Max, a horse, back from Galatia. He hung a sign that read WAR COMRADE above the stable. Underneath it was an Iron Cross made of cardboard. During the World War, ships could also receive the Iron Cross, as could guide dogs.

We avoided Max because he bit. Nora the fat mare was harmless though, and she pulled better than Max.

In the evening, once we'd had enough to drink, we went inside. We played hide-and-seek in the dark and lay on the carpet again. The lights of the cars driving by played over the ceiling. A gurgling in the belly.

> Isn't she sweet, isn't she lovely,
> Isn't she nice . . .[6]

Ute rocked herself back and forth. Listen. See if the adults are coming ('. . . or we'll both be in for it'). We debated whether her father outranked my father, and then who ranked higher, her father or Dr Krause.

'My father wins both contests, naturally,' she said.

'Boy, why do you look so pale?' my mother asked at dinner. 'Like buttermilk and spit.'

'Oh, oak tree, how they've pruned you,' Robert said, shaking his head. But the Teewurst pork sausage tasted quite good to me just the same.

3

My father loved the city he was born in. Everyone said this about him. He was a member of the Society for Rostock Antiquities and regularly attended their lectures: 'The Religious Exercises of the Civil Guard' or 'Rostock's Soldiers in the Thirty Years' War'. He'd managed quite well with his Low German in Flanders.

On Sundays, while my mother basted the roast, he went walking with us. His right hand at his back, his left guiding his walking stick, now ahead of him and now behind. Since he knew a lot of people, he was always tipping his hat.

With business people he spoke about courtage, tonnage, and dividends; to women he said 'my most gracious lady' and kissed their hands. He himself was usually addressed as 'Herr Kempowski' or 'Körling'. While he was busy talking we stood by the gutter and tried to see whether we could make out a pale face in the prison's grated windows.

'Take me with you, Herr Kempowski,' a man with a cleft lip called, waving from the other side of the street. It was Dr Heuer.

'This again,' said my father. 'Well, how's it going?'

One time a drunken sailor started talking to him. He kept his gloves on.

'You never know what these people have touched,' he said. Once as a young man he'd had to settle up for a captain at a bordello. They'd stripped off the captain's trousers because he couldn't pay.

People said that Rostock was lesser than Lübeck and Hamburg, but greater than Wismar and Stralsund. A city that terrible architects botched for hundreds of years. It was amazing that despite everything the city still had certain charms. The Stone Gate, for example, which stank of men's piss: when the tram drove through it, the overhead cable had to squeeze through. ('Just like the soldiers here before who had to beat the drawbridge down.') Or the Kröpelin Gate, built in the Gothic style, with towers and arches, as well as the benches where old men played skat. ('An' I shoulda played the ace.') They had rubber rings around their pipes to keep them from falling from their toothless mouths.

Near by, nestled in the bushes on the ramparts, a wandering child made of granite was captured reclining: a bit like *Goethe in the Roman Campagna*, but more rustic.

The church towers were either overbearing or too small. St Mary's was a bulky monstrosity with an enormous west front. It was big enough to support three towers, each of which was topped off hastily and shoddily with a spire shaped like a rooster head. ('Like a hen with its chicks.')

St Peter's, on the other hand, was a church that consisted almost entirely of a single tower. You couldn't build something like that today, they said.

*

In the main post office my father emptied out locker 210. This had been his regiment number too. ('Do you want to be a hero?') He looked quickly through the letters and stuffed them in his pocket.

The post office stood by the Rose Garden. It was a ruin of the ramparts; another Gothic façade. A sloping path used to lead inside. When they got rid of the path and blocked off the garden, people climbed over the barriers in protest.

Next to the post office stood the Soldiers' Memorial, built in the 90s. There he showed us the names 'Tinkel' and 'Pott', one beneath the other, funnily enough.

'Planes were the worst. You had no chance to run.'

'Did you ever shoot and kill an enemy soldier?' we asked.

Not that he knew of; he'd just shot in their direction. They were black dots, mostly.

From the Soldiers' Memorial, over the wall to the harbour below, we went to see whether ships were still arriving. We'd pay a brief visit to the friendly ones, and give a passing glance to the enemy ones. You were not permitted to call an officer 'cap'n', nor a ship a 'tub' or a 'crate'.

Next to Monk's Gate – which had a lion's head with open jaws over the arch, and a bronze bucket, of sorts, on the roof – was our firm. You could see a little part of it on most panorama postcards. It used to be a bar, and it still had a beer cellar with a trapdoor.

My father went into the office and made his telephone calls. (Courtage, tonnage, and dividends.) In the meantime we switched on the copy press.

'You're going to laugh,' said my brother: 'this thing still works. Go ahead, put your thumb under there.'

There was a cobblestone on my father's writing desk that he used as a paperweight. On the wall: Hitler, Hindenburg, and Bismarck, one above the other.

Then we went up Mönchenstraße, in the direction of the Neuer Markt. Cannons lined the street corner, so the buildings weren't damaged by carriages. ('Fritz Reuter used to live here.')

Houses and shacks piled on top of one another. There were fences on the flat, tarred roofs, with stakes for hanging laundry, and high tin chimneys. A sign reading FIRST VACUUM-STEAM-SUGAR-CANDY FACTORY was washed out and peeling on a wall.

In some of the windows on the ground floor there were cactus bowls containing little pagodas and bridges. Now and again, a beautiful stepped gable. But any photographers would have to hunt out these details if they wanted to capture them on film.

We were shown the spot at the Neuer Markt where a fountain used to stand. My father pointed out the small snake at the base of one of the columns at the city hall: its origin and purpose a mystery.

We were in the square for a military concert due to take place by the monument to Friedrich Franz III, under the oak tree, at midday. Fathers were there with little children on their shoulders.

The conductor limped out, then snapped at the audience when they pushed forward. The musicians began with the overture to *The Thieving Magpie*. ('Man, can they blow!')

I watched the trombones, which always seemed to me to be awkwardly designed. The oboe player, a private, had cotton wool in his ears.

Then, a tap of the baton and the soldiers packed their instruments away and took the streetcar back to the barracks.

On the way home we kept a look out for 'characters', like Herbig, who sprinted to Kösterbek on Sundays with a violin in his rucksack. Or Professor Totenhals, who always covered his ears.

Once, a man who was completely bent over had approached us. Why would he be walking like that? we asked.

'Because his sons gave him so much trouble,' my father said.

It already smelled like roast in the stairway, and when you opened the door to our floor you could hear the cutlery clinking.

'Time to eat!'

'Lovely that you made it, I had just about given up hope.'

4

On Sundays we had pudding shaped in a mould to look like grapes on a vine. Even at sixteen, my sister insisted on a serving of only the fruit and not the vine. ('It's all the same, Ulla.')

My mother made sure we gave thanks after dinner. My father said, 'Amin-amahn' and pushed the table away from him.

'God, Karl . . .'

'What?'

He walked, stooped over, to the sideboard; that's where the biscuit box was. He snuck himself a generous helping.

'I don't understand!' said my mother, hadn't he eaten good and plenty?

'Quiet, woman! I have to fill every last nook and cranny in my stomach,' he said, counting each biscuit aloud as he put it in his mouth.

Robert, Ulla and I left in a hurry to make it to the movies on time to watch Laurel and Hardy as electrical appliance salesmen. My brother was always a few steps ahead, while Ulla grabbed me by the neck and turned my head from left to right, depending on where I should be looking.

We moved quickly because we had to stop by our grandfather's house to beg him for the money. He lived in the Steintor suburb, between two villas – Consul Böttcher and Consul Viehbrock – both of which were decorated with an assortment of smiling masks.

DELIVERIES PLEASE USE THE BACK ENTRANCE

A ramp had been placed on the stairs for his wheelchair.

The house was very roomy: spread across two floors, all of the rooms were gigantic. He used to host lots of parties here.

A mahogany display case in the entryway contained porcelain crockery, along with a gold cup that Queen Luise had once drunk from, and little Stierbändiger figurines from Copenhagen. Next to the vitrine was the stool with a catheter. The museum director came from time to time to ask about the little Rostock watercolours that were hung on the wall.

The old man would sit in the bay window and read. A little Steinhäger bottle with warm water on his stomach. ('Good old friend.')

When acquaintances passed by outside, he gave them a friendly wave before murmuring, 'Asshole.'

We greeted him, and he ripped a page of his book while folding it down to mark his place. (*The Last Days of Pompeii*.)

Then he scratched out some folk songs for us on his violin and told East Prussian jokes, his ivory dentures flapping down as he spoke. We were afraid we might not get the jokes, so we laughed too soon.

(When he was young, he knocked over an urn containing someone's ashes: that was why he was crippled now.)

'Grandfather, we have to go now.'

'Well, give me my coin purse . . .'

He teased it open with his weak fingers and fumbled around in it for some coins.

'That enough?' he asked, laying five pennies on the armrest of his chair as though he had never seen them before.

'No, Grandfather.'

'My goodness now,' and he laid out another coin. Sometimes he'd pull out a fish scale he'd put in there on New Year's Eve in the hope that it would bring good fortune. That way his purse would never be empty.

When he'd doled out enough, we grabbed the money and dashed off, jumping down the stairs and flinging open the door. The old man knocked against the window with his cane and shook his fist as we ran off.

'I bet we don't make it.'

We always did, though. A few minutes before 2 p.m. we reached the Ka-Li-Sun, a cinema attached to a dance hall.

SWING DANCING FORBIDDEN, a sign read.

The bustle of children. A gong sounded and the curtain turned green, red, and orange. As the children whistled shrilly, Stan Laurel and Oliver Hardy dumped eggs on to a greengrocer's head. To get back at them he ran their pocket watches through a centrifuge.

It was hard to sit next to Robert. He was always poking me, 'Did you see that?' Afterwards, the film was either 'epochal' or 'glorious'.

One time, we saw the film *Daybreak* with Adele Sandrock, which was a wash-out. We wanted to laugh the whole time but there was nothing to laugh at.

After the movie we went to the café, where our friends from the yacht club would sit around.

JEWS NOT WELCOME!

Heini, wearing a white, shawl-collar sweater, with copper coins in the band of his wristwatch, deliriously energetic; Michael, with his bored, sniffy affectations, whose father, it was said, had a real Rembrandt hung on his wall (though you couldn't make out a thing in it, it was almost completely black); and Bubi, a 'proper lad', as my sister said. They'd all be sailing soon.

'I've made a horrible discovery,' my brother said, and patted both pockets: nothing left to smoke! He smoked double-fermented R6-brand cigarettes.

'Can I have the empty packs?' I asked.

I should have known to keep my mouth shut and to make myself scarce.

*

Wilted snowdrops in the garden out front. Boxwood growing along paths that no one ever used. Rusty iron fences, a pissing dog.

CHAINING YOUR BICYCLE HERE IS FORBIDDEN

If we saw anyone coming, we took a detour to avoid them. Over the lower wall, with the benches that weren't attached. Through the Schröderstraße, along the crumbling wall of a cannery, and past Wernicke the potter's cellar window, with its ovens and green stoneware owl. Every time he passed it, my brother said that one day he would buy the owl and smash it to bits.

Whether out in the woods or snug in your den,

Enjoy Dr Krause's Mineral Water.

The factory was closed and the gate was secured with a chain. In the stairwell, the light clicked on. It only stayed lit for a minute, just long enough to make it up the stairs.

I carefully retrieved the key to our apartment through the milk flap. It then took time to unlock the door, as we had to do it without making a sound. If it clicked, my mother appeared with the pattern from the cushion imprinted on her cheek. And then my father would wake up, wherever he was. ('Snot-nosed brat!')

His boater hung in the wardrobe. Next to it was my mother's hat with a little stuffed bird that was always on the verge of falling off whenever she wore it. Walking sticks stood in the umbrella stand. One, like a strange umbrella, could be snapped open and used as a seat.

I strode through the apartment. During the move, a slipper ended up on top of the grandfather clock. We searched for it for years, in vain, before we eventually found it there.

Decorative pears were glued to the sideboard, where the crystal and a Meißner bowl were kept. The seam on the carpet could be used as a track for Märklin cars.

With a little bit of luck, it was still fairy-tale hour on the Graetz radio. Mostly though it was just Jean Sibelius's *Symphonic Poetry*.

The bookcase to the left of the radio contained Luther and *The History of Rauhes House*. The bookcase next to it housed Wiechert, Hesse, and Ruth Schaumann, but also *Buddenbrooks* and Heinrich Mann's *Professor Unrat* ('Well, I say'). At the very bottom there were art books containing the essential works of the Great Masters. I'd marked them with scraps so I didn't accidentally open them up to pictures of the crucifixion or *Judith Beheading Holofernes*. In the cabinet to the right there were regimental histories: Chamberlain, Stegemann and Lily Braun.

I had no real interest in the sheet music shelf, though the spines were tempting: flutes and violins wreathed with flowers; the piano player's secret script, held together by great arches of ligatures.

On the writing desk was an inlaid portfolio containing a French calendar: various letters tumbled out when you opened it. This sat alongside the Löser & Wolff catalogue, from which my father decided which cigars to order for himself – and which to order for the distributors.

A box containing photos was stored in the desk. Pictures of my grandfather on thick brown photographic paper (*To our beloved parents for their golden wedding anniversary, 1905*), and on thinner paper with deckle edges more recent photos of happy picnics (my mother with a man's haircut, wine bottles on the blanket). The dog stepped in the butter, they had once told us. ('Are you still going to Rostock by horse?')

My father's desk also housed maps of Flanders. He liked to read these on the toilet, in order to 'get the lie of the land', as he put it.

Gently, gently, with manner pious[1]

I already have my first patrol behind me, he had written. *What a sight my uniform was afterwards! I had to walk along an irrigation ditch . . .*

He didn't like it when someone came out of the toilet just before he went in – he hated that the seat was still warm.

*

Coffee was served once we'd finished eating. It was then that Manfred, a quiet friend of mine from school, usually came by. He had nickel-framed glasses, and always ate cheese sandwiches. His skin was thick and full of freckles; he could have jabbed himself with a needle and not felt anything.

'Red-haired, right?' my brother said.

The first time I invited him, he told me that first he had to ask his parents whether he could play with me: they had no idea what kind of people we were.

He had inherited some pewter figurines from an uncle – Aztecs and Spaniards – completed with a first-class paint job. They lay in cigarette packs, one next to the other: Jaguar warriors and broadsword soldiers; storming and fleeing infantry; sunwheel bearers; fallen heroes.

My mother, holding the figurines out, far away from herself, thought the Aztecs had no chins, like birds.

Manfred had borrowed a book from the public library: *The Conquest of Mexico*. A note inside it said *Keep me clean*. It was illustrated.

We pored over intertwined stone deities, and the stepped pyramids; coloured hearts in the gullet of Quetzalcoatl and blood-encrusted priests with obsidian daggers standing before cowering sacrifices. Their worst criminals were bound to a wooden frame and the skin was sliced off their faces to attract birds of prey.

(Huitzilopochtli, a difficult name. I was shocked that no one was amazed when I could finally pronounce it.)

When we were left on our own, we put on plays. One was called *As You Do to Me, I Do to You!*

Manfred was playing Cortés, and lay on the couch. I had to shake off my chains, throw myself at him, cry 'Freedom!' and then bind him like the Aztecs did ('Pull harder!') before shouting, 'As you do to me, I do to you!'

The first time I said it, he couldn't bear it: the derision, the humiliation. But we continued regardless: he was curious to see whether he could take it. I had to hit him on the ankle with a ruler, lightly, over and over, until it turned red. Should I keep going?

'Yes, keep going, keep going.'

Finally, he wanted to be stuffed under the bed. I flung bread at him, and he would snatch at it with his teeth. The thought that I was about to go off somewhere and leave him there alone was awful, he would say. I was to go just as far as the door to see whether he could bear being left like that.

One time I shoved him into the broom closet and shut the door.

I got the Yellow Uncle walking stick out of the wardrobe and swung it a few times quick and hard. The brass dustpan rattled and the mop fell down.

'That was gruesome,' he called out. 'Where did you get that idea?'

*

'Well, Huitzilopochtli,' my sister said during supper. 'You're glowing.'

'Manfred and Walter have been running wild,' my brother said. 'He's the scourge of humanity.'

But he refused to believe that the Aztecs had heads like birds.

'What does *Kohlöppvehna* mean?' my father asked me, before turning to Ulla: 'My child, make like the Mecklenburg buffalo and disappear.'

When we started secondary school, Manfred began picking me up every morning. We were usually still eating breakfast when the bell rang, the table laid with the Bunzlau crockery and the colourful coffee pot bought at the Whitsuntide market. Everyone had their usual place at the table.

'Is Waller there?' Manfred would ask from outside.

'He very well may be,' the maid would answer, and let him in.

While I spread butter on my rolls Manfred, legs slung over the chair, would sit in a nook by the staircase, which Quade, the architect, had set apart from the dining room.

Next to him, six side tables were stacked one on top of the other. A picture of the Baltic dunes at Graal hung above him. My parents met for the first time in Graal. ('He wanted to kiss me the whole time, and I thought it would get me pregnant. What a fool!')

'Have you done the religion homework?' Manfred asked.

> Commend your way and what ails your heart
> To the everlasting care of Him who guides heaven.[1]

The horticultural-show stamps had come out the day before;

they were dark green and purple this year. I probably wasn't going to get any, though. I had also tried to get a book of 'Munich-Riem' stamps, commemorating the horse race at the Riem track in Munich, but they cost 15 marks.

'Munich-Riem? What's that?' my father asked, egg yolk running down his finger.

Rolls buttered thickly and spread with thin currant jelly were my favourite things to eat. I was permitted to dunk them in my coffee. I then had to take my calcium tablets and a spoonful of cod liver oil.

Where had Manfred's old man served, my father wanted to know.

'I see, I see, in the artillery.'

The cavalry would have been better; the navy considerably worse ('They betrayed us back then'). You had to be good at maths in the artillery, and he was always amazed by people who had no idea who they were shooting at. They also wore different helmets, which he liked.

My sister was eating pickles, washing them down with lukewarm water. She put her eraser into her fountain pen case and zipped it shut.

'Now be a dear and focus at school,' my mother said before handing her the blue octavo notebook, where she'd made some corrections.

My father was sitting in front of his calendar again.

1689 – the French lay waste to Heidelberg

'You should finish your sandwich, it would be a crying shame to throw it out,' Robert said. 'Poor people are starving and you're always throwing your sandwiches out: you should be more thankful.'

*

On the way to school we passed a narrow house. On the door it said ANNO 1903. Two Pekingese dogs were always lying in the window. When they saw us they started yapping like mad. Beside the house was a burnt-out synagogue, with a broken star of David on the wrought iron gate.

'That's where the real Jews live,' said Manfred. He had looked the building up in the directory. ('Abraham Glücksmann, synagogue porter'.) Someone had found a severed finger there, according to Manfred.

'The work of Israel,' he said. 'They murdered Christians, dismembered them and chucked them out. There was a cellar crusted with blood in every synagogue: that was how they got into heaven. And in the Jewish stockyard all the animals were tortured. They suffered slowly until they died.'

Robert caught up with us by St Margarine's Secondary School, as he called it. He was carrying a tiny briefcase – a barber's bag, he called it. When we made fun of it he said, 'Fools laugh loudest.'

At the Café Drude he tossed his cigarette behind the telephone booth. The school wasn't far off: he might run into a teacher at any moment.

Our secondary school had been renamed 'School at the Seven Lindens'. ('That's dumb,' said my father.) Now, instead of *sexta, quinta, quarta*, you had first grade, second grade, third grade. Wearing school caps was also now forbidden.[2]

A replica of *Laocoön and His Sons* stood in the hall, flecked with ink. Any jackets left lying around were hung on the two child statues. A Hitler Youth insignia hung on the wall.

'Don't leave that paper lying there like that.'

'Report to the Sports Palace on Wednesday, three o'clock.'

'Take your hand out of your pocket, boy.'

During the entrance exam for secondary school I had written *weil*, 'because', with an *h*. But, in spite of this and a number of other mistakes, I was accepted, of course: I was Körling's son.

On the first day we had been asked what our fathers did for a living. Bank director, head of the district authority, head aeroplane engineer, came the replies.

'Shipping agent and ship owner,' I said.

'Isn't one of those jobs enough?' The retort came from a boy wearing glasses. 'Division head at a building society,' he then said; which didn't sound particularly alluring.

That same day we were presented with two teachers: a short, bald one and a taller, darker one with a head like an owl. I imagined that the little one would be pleasant, and I wanted to avoid ending up with the owl. But sure enough, the bald teacher left with his students, and I ended up with Hannes, the owl. Typical.

We had him for everything, including religion. I was in his favour right off the bat though, because I knew the opposite of 'absolute'. It also worked in my favour that Hannes hadn't taught my brother, who'd had Kniese, the little fat one.

Hannes was always talking about war being glorious and the foxhole being a sacred site. He wore an intricately worked Iron Cross on the back of his hunting jacket. One day, after noticing that it was missing, I asked whether he had lost it.

'Close,' he said, in a way that didn't encourage me to guess again.

Like my father, Hannes was a member of the Society for Rostock Antiquities. It was said he'd soon be getting his honorary doctorate; he'd catalogued thousands of street and district names on notecards.

For the morning's exercise, he tasked us with drawing our city.

> *Rostock, a maritime city: 121,300 inhabitants; industry, trade and university city; on the left bank of the lower navigable segment of the Warnow, fifteen miles above sea level.*

He lived in Borenweg 6, he said; we should note that down, in case something ever came up.

Blutstraße, the name of a road leading to Neuer Markt, came from *blot*, or *bloß*, meaning 'bare'. The streets weren't cobbled, hence bare. We thought it came from *Blut*, though: the blood that once flowed from the heads of those decapitated in the square.

St Mary's, we learned, was twelve graph-paper squares long and ten graph-paper squares wide, not counting the transept.

For St Peter's, the ratio was 4:16. Plus its tower was crooked, 'like so!', Hannes declared, before imitating the hump.

The city hall was easier to draw: I left two squares between each of the seven towers.

Hannes asked whether we had heard that the city walls were going to be renovated: every single brick was going to be individually sand-blasted.

'It's amazing that Hitler's doing this,' he said. We could be proud and happy that we would be there to see it.

As a lover of nature he would also let us draw animals. One lesson he asked us to draw a whale skeleton, but because it was so intricate we could only draw with carbon copy paper, which left smudges in the textbooks, ruining them for ever.

'Whales belong to the mammal class,' he told us: 'they give birth to their young in the ocean.' He also told us that we human beings would soon cause these animals to die out; that we were brutal, ruthless. There were fewer and fewer storks and ravens, too. We were slaughtering them out of existence.

'Although, bison are being released again now. So some animals are on the up and up.'

We wrote essays about the meadow in June. Hannes busied himself at the lectern, writing an article on the same subject while we worked. It appeared that Sunday evening in the *Rostocker Anzeiger*.

'See, I have to do schoolwork too,' he said. It annoyed him when we were done: it disturbed his writing.

During arithmetic he sometimes raised both arms without warning, looking like a priest. When he did so, we had to jump up. He'd give us a problem, then we'd shout the answer and sit down. The last one standing was usually a boy named Blomert.

'Better become a barber, Blomert!' Hannes said.

At the board, Hannes explained that we should start using more sophisticated terms, such as 'equals', because we were grown-up now. To clarify this, he drew a scale and put two 1s on the left side and a 2 on the right. They weighed the same, he said, which I found hard to accept.

The lowest common denominator was important to him. If we didn't get that, he said, we wouldn't be able to grasp anything that followed, all the way to integrals.

Klaus Greif, my neighbour in class, had top marks in organisation and cleanliness. He wrote beautiful, perfectly circular numbers; one in each square. He filled his fountain pen with a pipette, screwed the nib in and out, and then wrote his lovely numbers with it.

Greif loaned me a book of trading cards: *Glorious Chapters of German History*. They showed the triumphant attack at Onganjira on 9 April 1904 – the camel riders with their hat brims high on one side – and Simon Copper on the trail of the Hottentots in the Kalahari Desert.

When the bell rang for break, Greif would seek out a victim. He got him in a headlock and dragged him across the floor.

Manfred asked whether I had seen how he'd dragged Blomert around the corner.

'He'll get his soon enough,' he said.

Manfred had a new pen with a glass nib. He dabbed the spots he made with it with the corner of his blotter.

Struck and Stuhr sat in front of me (it was hard for the teacher to tell them apart); a fat boy called Krahl sat behind. He wore a pocket watch with a nickel chain. On the chain hung tiny knives and saws. His father sold butcher's equipment.

One day, fat Krahl brought gouged-out calf eyes into class in a licorice bag for Hannes to examine ('Very nice, my boy, lay that over here . . .'). During breaks he would sit and melt shoelaces with a magnifying glass.

There was also a boy called Fohmann in the class, who looked like Hitler.

'*Sieg heil!*' he'd cry. Now we had two Hitlers in our midst.

The school's rowing club met in the circle of seven linden trees that gave the school its name.

'Who's rowing over the Warnow today?' they asked. Those who were due to cross the river would then raise their thumbs.

While I was waiting for my turn, I saw my brother surrounded by his friends from the yacht club.

> In the little sky-blue limousine
> Rides happiness, a little blond passenger.[3]

Bubi was there, with his tousled hair, as were Heini in the white shawl-collared sweater and posh Michael, who said he was headed down to Berlin over the weekend.

'Maybe I'll see what's going at the Delphi, maybe I'll meet Marion, could be that she'll show up there. Then maybe I'll return, and get you all out of here.'

'You can leave me on land,' Robert said.

They called me Robert II. They said I had a funny pickle on my neck. 'Or is that your head?'

On the way home we wore our rucksacks on our stomachs and played a game called locomotive, which consisted of seeing who could say 'Toni Leo' the fastest ('Toni Leo, Toni Leo, Toni Leo . . .').

Greif then left with Blomert; he had him in a headlock, as always. Fat Krahl stood up on his bicycle as he rode away – he often referred to it as his moped. Struck and Stuhr took the streetcar; they lived by the Sports Palace.

I threw my sandwich into Dieken the jeweller's garden and made sure I got away: St Margarine's Secondary School would be getting out soon and the students had shaved heads.

Sometimes my brother called me back.

'Here, jerk, take my bag. Tell them I'll be home later.'

He was friendly though, really.

('Leave him alone, the kid's okay.')

*

'Coming!'

As soon as you returned to the apartment someone called out, 'Wash your hands, comb your hair.' You then had to move quickly, because 'If you don't get into your seat, you don't get a bite to eat.'

At the table, I had to give a report of what had happened at school. ('How often does your brother make it in to school? Answer quickly.') We were having pears, beans, and bacon for dinner. The pears stayed warm, it wasn't clear how you were supposed to remove the stem.

'Here, give it to me, Walter, my Peterpump.'

('Did he make it in or didn't he!?')

The hard parts of the bacon got stuck in your teeth.

Dr Otterstedt had asked about inner truth, my brother said, when he finally made it home.

'About inner truth?'

'Yes, about inner truth.'

He'd been badly wounded in the war: he was a Two-Fourteener, he often got terrible pains.

'Impeccable suits, though,' said my brother.

Dr Wolff, meanwhile, was a real sight: he definitely bought his clothing in clearance sales, as they never fitted properly, and he often wore knickerbockers to school ('How does his wife not catch something like that?').

No wonder he couldn't maintain discipline.

We still ate 'fly soup' every week – ragwort with a handful of raisins – a hangover from the days of the financial crisis. ('Sour stewed wort.') My mother ladled it out of a tureen and made sure my father ('Typical!') didn't get the lemon peel.

'How much do the Munich-Riem stamps cost?' he wanted to know. I should find out.

6

Fat Krahl had a big room all to himself, and I visited almost every day. There was an AEG-Mignon typewriter under the window and a bed in the corner. A table was pulled out into the middle of the room, and on it a building-block city, with shops, advertising columns, and a city hall. It stayed out every evening.

I was a shipping agent. I moved three Märklin long-distance trucks with white stripes through the city, before reversing them into the loading yard and setting them next to one another.

Fat Krahl was the banker. He managed the accounts of Greif, who did good business trading in building materials, as well as those of Manfred, the owner of the gas station. He took 6 per cent from every amount on his books. ('How do you figure out the percentage?')

Manfred was no good at these games, though. No one bought his fuel. We were pushing the cars, after all. One day he brought along a pipette: he wanted to use it to squirt water into the cars. He proposed that cars could only drive if they were wet. This idea was rejected.

Fat Krahl was also mayor, judge and 'pocileman'. He lived in the side wing of the city hall. There was an open black Mercedes – a six-seater – in his garage (which we'd borrowed from Struck). In the catalogue it was called the Führer Mercedes.

The city hall had a tower with an alarm clock inside it. The tops of all of the buildings were open, so you could push the Halma pieces around. They sat in their comfortable rubber armchairs, at rubber tables, drank out of rubber cups and ate rubber cakes, which were green with yellow spots. It was Rubber Town.

Frau Krahl came up for coffee occasionally, wheezing as she ascended the stairs, honouring the familial corpulence. She put out bread with schmaltz for us, and everyone got a cup of hot chocolate too. The schmaltz was top notch: there wasn't too much apple in it, and the crackling was crispy and aromatic.

('Are you playing nice up here?')

Herr Krahl, who was choleric, and similarly large, was rarely to be seen. He had a boxy car with curtains in the windows.

'Well, you lazybones,' he always said to me, and once, when I asked him whether I could play with his son: 'Not today, there are already two up there.'

Greif built a museum in the town out of Anker stone blocks, as they were durable and uniform: a row of high columns in front, a rubber frieze on the gable depicting the Battle of Thermopylae. The museum had various sections, hung with trading cards. ('Gothic Painting', among others.) Posters for the Winter Relief of the German People, encouraging donations, were affixed like epitaphs in a hall that led to the inner courtyard, which we dubbed 'the Workers' Hall'. In the inner courtyard, two Lineol soldiers were on display as sculptures.

The Halma people turned out for the dedication of the museum. We assigned the green checkers to the military. The blue ones were seamen from Kiel, and the red ones were volunteer firefighters. The black ones were SS.

Mayor Krahl's alter ego rode in the Führer Mercedes along Main Street, which had been decorated for the occasion, followed by a motorcade of silver racecars. Yellow Halma checkers – the SA – were stretched along the route.

'*Heil!*' we called out in a whisper that sounded loud and distant all at once.

We decided we'd better remake the marketplace, but were also deciding between adding a church or a movie theatre. Fat Krahl owned a magic lantern, which decided it: the city would soon have a cinema. Manfred's gas station, however, had to go.

'It's always me,' he said.

'Well, you are a Jew.'

Manfred reached into the banker's register, so Greif put him in a headlock until further notice. The mayor then threw Manfred's Halma checker into a crate equipped with matchstick bars.

The walls of the gas station were torn down, and the rubber furnishings of the apartment were auctioned off at the marketplace.

('We have no idea how long you've been stealing from us!')

What was to be done with his Halma figure, though? Were we to cut off its head? Throw it out the window? Burn it? Bury it? This matter required an orderly court proceeding. Manfred interjected, shouting that he had to go home now.

'Haha! We're not letting you go!'

'No! You have to let me go! I haven't done my homework yet, and I have to go to the dentist! Plus someone is coming over!'

Greif threw him on the bed.

'Now you'll see what happens!'

But Frau Krahl saved him: 'Walting,' she said to me, 'your father called again, you're supposed to go home.'

'What do you think Klaus Greif was going to do to me?' Manfred asked on the way home. 'Tie me up? Punch me in the arm?' (There was a spot on the upper arm that, when you hit it, your whole arm went numb for a long time.) 'Or what? Whip me, maybe?'

Had I ever heard of foot-whipping? he asked me. I hadn't, so Manfred went on to describe how you were hung upside down, with your feet tied up, and beaten with a stick.

'I can't imagine it to be that painful,' he declared. 'I could take being strangled, too.'

But having his arm held in boiling water and then 'de-gloving' was too far. It was insane!

'Do the veins come off too, or do they lie there on your flesh?'

In *Between Red and White*, Erich Dwinger described how they smashed prisoners' balls between two bricks.

My late arrival was accepted with benevolence, since I was talking about money transfers and cheques. My father only wanted to know if anyone had gone bankrupt, 'like Herr Lange'.

'You know him, don't you? He's the one who has to make a miserable living tuning pianos now. The poor man. Or Kruse, the estate agent, once a fierce competitor. The economy is ruled by supply and demand; the weak are crushed. And that's that!'

'Marvellous, that you had such a nice time playing,' my mother said. 'Fabulous.'

'Keep them close,' said my brother. He didn't have such good friends when he was my age.

7

No homework was assigned for Wednesday and Sunday evenings, as we had service with the Hitler Youth those nights. When the bulletin said 'Bring your athletic gear,' it meant there would be boxing.

There were extra-thick gloves for Youth members, so that it didn't hurt quite so much. But it still hurt enough.

The sessions we spent marching were more pleasant. On the Reiferbahn, under the chestnut trees with their stiff buds, we learned the difference between commands and preparatory commands. We learned that you were supposed to turn on your left heel and that your hands had to be at your sides, thumbs cocked, when at attention.

Although the by-laws for the Hitler Youth said that order trainings were not to last more than fifteen minutes, we were often dragged around for the whole afternoon. The nearby Finance Office had to close its windows because of the noise, and old women got up and sat somewhere else. But Bartels, the senior teacher, stayed and watched.

'What are you doing with your hand?' thundered Eckhoff, my leader, before putting it in the right place. (Bartels nodded.)

'You're a pissant, have you got that through your head?'

At home, my sister took my picture. The sun was shining in my eyes, so I had to squint. 'There we go!' she cried. I was to look nice and cheerful when I turned towards the camera, my hands at the seams of my trousers.

One evening Ute tried my gear on. ('Just don't let anyone see!') I fastened the belt for her, even though the trousers sat rather tight. She marched back and forth a few times and did a 'Heil Hitler!' in front of the mirror. She thought the cap was swell, and asked whether we fought a lot in the Youth.

Then we lay down under the table. It was nice and warm, and cosy.

*

One weekend we took a trip to Doberan.

'By golly!' my father shouted. 'You're "on the move"? The blue dragoons, they ride!'

My brother called me a real go-getter, while my mother said that if anything came up I was to go to Aunt Luise, a good-hearted woman, who lived in Doberan.

'Be careful, my little Peterpump.'

The service command had said: 'Report to Central Station at two o'clock.' We were to gather under the big clock.

Schuhband, a little blond scout, marched diagonally across the square, as though he had to keep lockstep. He even did a change step.

Everyone had kit bags, except for me. Instead I had a shapeless hiking rucksack from my parents' honeymoon trip to Tegernsee in 1920.

For a blanket my mother had given me the tartan throw with the fringe that usually lay on the couch in the guest room. Since it couldn't be tied over the rucksack, I held it under my arm.

The command had said that writing implements were to be brought along, and I had been given a carpenter's pencil, along with a notebook that had gilt edging and smelled like eau de cologne from my mother's handbag.

Above the granite swastika installed over the main entrance to the station were the Olympic rings, somewhat faded but still visible. We remembered how Jesse Owens had run a 10.2 and that First Lieutenant Handrick had got a gold medal even though he broke his collarbone.

('I call upon the youth of the world!')

Eckhoff, our leader, said he had sharpened his penknife. A reporting pouch with six sharpened pencils hung on his belt. He warned us that we should take care during the field games, and not press down on the ribcage of any prone party. This had happened before, apparently.

'Is that clear?'

While we were waiting for Scout Habersaath, who was late ('what a moron'), my mother and Ulla came cycling up Bismarckstrasse. They jumped off their bikes, their dresses flying, so they could say goodbye to me.

They mingled with the scouts, happy looks on their faces, and Ulla laid her hand on my shoulder and said that I was already a big lad.

'Who's the leader?' my mother asked. 'Him over there with the sunburnt face? *That's* Eckhoff the teacher's son? Well, how do you like that . . .'

In the meantime Habersaath had arrived, wheezing: we could get moving.

'You shouldn't worry about the rucksack,' said Eckhoff. He told me I could bring up the rear, then people would think I was the leader.

*

In Doberan, we slept in a barn. Someone had brought in straw for us. The boy next to me, the short and blond Schuhband, whistled happily to himself. He made sparks in the yard with his shoes, whose soles were cobbled with hexagonal hobnails.

'The Holy Ghost will be coming tonight,' he said, 'that much is clear.'

He was referring to the practice of someone being pinned down and smeared with shoe cream, or beaten and held under a water pump.[1]

Eckhoff led us over to the cathedral, with its white wooden swan that sat atop a column overlooking a meadow. Supposedly, Eckhoff told us, the swan had shouted, 'Doberan! Doberan!' and that was where the name of the town came from.

'There's always a grain of truth to these old sayings,' he said.

He told us that during the last century the cloister wall had been used as a quarry, and added that the Führer would never permit something like that to happen now.

'Everyone listen up! When we go inside, be aware that this cathedral is a product of German history. Art, *Kunst*, comes from *künden*, to proclaim. Architecture proclaims the German spirit. We should have developed our own style back then, instead of always looking to Italy.'

The door was open, and he marched us in one by one, like bottles in the factory. We were to clean our shoes off quickly in the doorway.

'Hold your foot up, show me your soles. Whoever doesn't do what he's told stays outside.'

Inside, an organist was practising.

The sexton asked whether we could see how the pillars were built to look like they were flowing down from above: 'No one knows how they were able to do that back then.'

The Cistercians deliberately avoided towers, as they don't serve any purpose.

'Oh, but they do,' said Eckhoff, and blinked at him. 'Oh, but they do.'

The sounds of the organ suddenly broke off.

'What a joke!' the organist shouted loudly: he'd tripped several times on the same passage. 'A joke!'

Another feature of the church was the gravestones.

> Here lies Herr von Sallern,
> My God, how he hollered,
> How he knocked the farmers around
> So they stuck him here in the ground.

They had a sense of humour back then, obviously.

There was a social event in the evening, in a gym that smelled like cold sweat and Lysol disinfectant. The idea was to get to know one another.

We sang:

> Wild geese rush through the night

Honking loudly towards the north . . .²

Then Eckhoff stepped forward and read poems; his thumbs on his belt, gesturing tersely with his fist.

> 'The Führer speaks' by Richard Euringer
> That which scatters, that is chaff.
> What is left stays true
> And what stays true
> Can be counted on, like two and two.
> The chaff is gone, the wheat remains,
> And with it I will sow Germany anew.³

Next, he read from Erhard Wittek's *Breakthrough '18*:
    '. . . The two machine guns stopped the right wing of the first wave with two swings back and forth of the barrel, and the black men screamed, writhing on the earth. The barrel lifted a few notches higher for the second wave, and, before the Negroes even understood what had happened, the entire second wing had slumped down.'

Finally Eckhoff took another book, quickly looked inside, laid it aside, nodded and spoke in a singing tone of voice:

> Over all the hilltops
> Is quiet now,
> You hear
> In all the boughs
> Hardly a breath;
> The birds are asleep in the trees:
> Wait, soon, like these
> You too shall rest.⁴

'And now we can have fun!' Eckhoff cried. (Was that a joke?) 'What does half a potato look like most? The other half!'

> Hahaha,
>> hahaha,
>>> hahaha!
> The echo sounds our jubilation back to us.
> Let us be happy and laugh,
> Because happiness does not always last for ever.[5]

One boy was asked to go outside, where he was surprised by a friend who blew flour in his face.

Others performed a short skit titled *Murder and Robbery*. In the first scene, they were beating each other up. In the second scene, they were beating each other up. So, in summary, they were beating each other up.

In the meantime, someone had started a fire outside. We huddled around in a circle to recite:

> May envy and cowardice,
> Jealousy and pride
> Burn up in
> The fire of these flames.
> Night be defeated!
> The sun will triumph!
> They forge us into bronze
> And make us invincible.
> The senses are purified into a solstice of the heart.
> Unite in the flame – may you all make ready![6]

The bells of the cathedral had started to ring, and bats flitted across the night sky. The hosts came out of the house, and with that the evening was over.

'That's how it's done,' said Eckhoff: 'serious – cheerful – serious.'

*

It was a long while before everything settled down that evening.

A dead mouse was thrown around for a while ('Quit it, you pig!'). The plaid blanket was hard as cardboard. It was cold and the straw prickled. Underneath, the threshing floor pressed up into us.

I thought, terrified, about the next morning. I was sure we would have to wash with our shirts off.

Schuhband was crinkling a candy wrapper. He tickled my nose with it and gave me a Chinese burn before sitting on my stomach. Finally I was warm.

At that moment Eckhoff came in and screamed:

'Quiet! If I hear another sound, I'm really going to crack down.'

He was disappointed that he couldn't rely on us. Tomorrow he was going to wipe the floor with us, we could count on that. He'd tear our arses open, and grind us down until our butts burned. We all knew he'd wanted to go into the city; that's why he was so angry.

I woke up in the middle of the night, with the full moon shining into the barn. I was lying in the passageway. The tartan blanket was gone, no straw was underneath me. It was a long time before I found my place again.

The next morning, boards were laid on the top of trestles and we were served rolls alongside four-fruit marmalade.

At home, Father would be eating his egg; the yolk would be running down his finger.

Someone had kept the mouse from the night before, and put it on Habersaath's roll, the tail hanging down over the edge. Eckhoff said he was glad we knew how to have fun. ('A proper scout is always cheerful.')

We fell in after breakfast.

'Politeness doesn't permit me to discuss what happened last night,' said Eckhoff. 'But let's draw a line under it. A clean slate.'

Today we were going to play field games, so he could see what kind of men we were.

'*You* take the flag, and *you* try to steal it.'

'We're going to wipe the floor with you,' the boys from the other team shouted, before marching into the woods, shaking their fists, chanting:

> We love the storms, the churning waves
> Faces raw from the ice-cold wind.[7]

Nickel, the leader of the Youth Troop, son of a farmer, volunteered to be the lookout. I was the messenger.

'Do you have any idea how a report is supposed to be written out?' Eckhoff asked me. 'No? You moron! Who, what, where, when and why. What's he doing over there? Why is he doing it? Got it?'

Nickel pulled his trousers down, shat, quickly wiped and pulled his trousers back up.

'Okay, now we can go.'

The two of us took off together.

I hid the notebook that smelled like eau de cologne and the farmer's pencil. (Who-what-where-when-why.) I checked my bag: bill of health, identification, first aid kit, songbook; all there.

At first we went down the path the others had taken. We heard noise in the distance.

'This is lovely, isn't it?' said Nickel. 'The beautiful blue sky and the clouds floating. It's a shame there aren't wild ox running around here any more. But I'm sure they'll be back before long.'

There was creeping bugleweed everywhere, and plenty of birds too.

Nickel pulled out his travel knife, and wondered aloud whether you could fell a tree with it.

'What do you think?' he asked me; could he do it?

'Maybe,' I said, 'but watch where it falls.'

We carved a ship out of bark, pointed in front, straight at the back. We bored a hole in the middle and stuck a branch into it as a mast. We built a harbour out of moss and stones, and used a fir cone as a lighthouse.

'Shame there's no stream here.'

Hours went by. But then we heard shouting far away: the flag had been captured, without our efforts.

'We better get going!'

The flag was worth more than our lives.

We soon reached a tangle of Youth members. I tried to crawl underneath the groaning, swaying heap. Who could possibly still be breathing under there?

Eckhoff bent over, the trill whistle in his hand: he wanted to know too, it seemed.

It was no use though, I couldn't see. Then I saw Schuhband climb down from a tree. I ran over to him, and the two of us hatched a plan, despite him being on the other team.

We gripped each other and wobbled a little. The others were supposed to think we were in a violent struggle: it was a distraction, a means of freeing whoever was trapped.

Suddenly I got a metal bucket to the head. Who knew where it came from. Blood was dripping everywhere.

'Oh my God, lean over to the side!' Eckhoff shouted.

(Head wounds always bleed a lot . . .)

Eckhoff with the narrow brown face and the evenly distributed freckles.

'Take your belt off,' he whispered to me. (Did I have it on?) His green leader's lanyard hung down. Long, sabre-like thighs that smelled like earth. He put a bandage on the wound; he wound it round so that it looked like a hat.

'Can you stand up?'

I could. He clapped me on the back.

'*Now* we have a serious injury.'

I was a real man. I could be relied upon. Eckhoff had even cried a little.

*

'Oh God, what did you do?' my mother cried. 'This is how they return your child?'

I was allowed to lie down in bed immediately. I was brought crispbread with butter and blackcurrant jelly.

Frau Eckhoff called: her son had told her I was injured.

'Was it bad?' she asked. 'Is he in pain? He might have tetanus . . . Surely it's better to get immunised right away?'

The Hitler Youth had health insurance, she knew that for certain: the Leipzig Union Barmenia.

'Should I try and give them a ring?'

My father thought I seemed pretty battered: 'How was this even possible?'

Robert teased, saying I looked like the Nizam of Hyderabad.

It had been a long time since I'd felt so well.

We were eating mutton with cabbage for lunch.

'You can invite your friends over as often as you like,' my mother told Robert. ('One has to know what one's children are up to, after all.')

'But not Schneefoot,' said my father. 'I don't want to see him in my house. He's a snot-nosed brat.'

Schneefoot had once shoved my sister over in a cornfield and tried to kiss her.

'He's got such a funny walk,' said my mother, 'you can see right away something's not right with him. He doesn't even look you in the eyes.'

'He's lousy,' said my father, chewing, 'and always looks so shabby.'

The meat got stuck in your gums when it got cold.

The bell rang.

'Is Waller there?'

'He should be.'

Fly soup again. Hopefully my father wouldn't end up with the lemon rind.

'Well, Munich-Riem,' he said to Manfred, who was wearing his imitation lederhosen. He was, as ever, sitting next to the six nested tables, on which stood a bottle of Steinhäger with a drip stopper shaped like a harvest wreath.

'Have you done your schoolwork? Reading, writing, arithmetic? You should always be working; you must always be diligent.' My father pointed at me with the spoon: 'And don't you try and tell me which lessons are important and which ones aren't.'

He was going to have to do something about his stress levels soon.

My brother pinned pictures of Tommy Dorsey, Harry Roy, and other jazz greats on the walls of our room. He got them from record catalogues. To make room for them, he took down the picture of some chickens in a farmyard from above our bed.

'Why are you doing that?' my mother asked.

'I'll tell you why,' my brother answered: 'for the simple reason that we've looked at it for long enough.'

He wore headphones when he was listening to the radio. He was the only person who could hear anything when he turned it on. He played 'hot' jazz to himself. But it always happened that someone would come in and crank the volume up, thinking, God, it's so quiet. It never failed to get him out of his seat. He would frantically yank off his headphones, which were blaring an extremely loud foxtrot.

The boys would come over at around three. Bubi always ran through all the rooms, tinkling a few notes on the grand piano, tapping the barometer, or checking the flowerpots to ensure they had enough water.

'Is your sister here?' he asked.

'She's at Christa's.'

'Shame.'

The sturdy Heini, meanwhile, could burp the whole scale. When he wanted to fart (which he'd always do as loudly as possible), he pressed himself up in his chair and said, '*Nuntio.*'

There was a rumour going around that Michael only listened to classical music. (He thought Liszt wasn't so bad, and quite liked *The Love Dreams.*) He hated that they only wanted to play fast records.

'Fast – slow – fast: that's how it's done!' he'd cry, before explaining that that was how symphonies and sonatas were made.

Michael came into the hallway where I was playing with Manfred: he wanted to see the cars, he wasn't interested in the Aztecs. He told me that if he ever happened to have an iron girder, he'd lend it to me. They made good race tracks, he said.

'Do you have cars too?' he asked Manfred, before suggesting that we buy Hans Stuck's car, from Catalogue No. 2. He agreed with us that the red Alfa Romeo looked silly.

'What do you expect? Italians.'

He looked elegant in his rust-brown double-breasted suit with the fine pinstripes. He'd bought new sunglasses in Berlin – Zeiss Umbral – and a special lighter in Gedser. It supposedly had a platinum catalyser, which you couldn't buy anywhere any more because it would put the match factories out of business. The plans were lying in a safe somewhere, he said.

He had driven over to Gedser to have a coffee, he continued. Or rather 'Gesser', as the Danes called it.

'You wouldn't believe how rugged the coast was there,' he said. There were no sand beaches; they couldn't even go swimming.

In the shade of an old apple tree

Where the love in your eyes I could see[1]

Then he took his leave: a solo on the gramophone was coming up, he couldn't miss this one.

Robert had bought himself the gramophone with his pocket money, it was the kind you wound up. His first record was 'In Goosestep'. The saleswoman had talked him into it.

One time Heini had reached over the counter and slapped her. 'And that was the right thing to do,' the others said.

German dance music was a lot of fluff, Robert said, blue in the face. Kurt Hohenberger was all right – he liked to listen to 'Amorcito mio' on the wireless – but Peter Kreuder, or even old Igelhoff . . . 'Good grief!'

But why? The Germans did have good soloists, it was just that the arrangements were a whole lot of nothing. The French, meanwhile, were all shit. Maybe somewhere in northern France there was a band no one knew about that was half decent, in Boulogne or Le Havre perhaps, in a smoky waterfront bar, with hardly anyone listening, cigarettes in their mouths, heads slumped.

'It's possible.'

The Italians were too wimpy. They came up short in both skill and composition. It was probably on account of the heat: they were weak.

The British and the Americans were another kettle of fish. There were records from the Andrews Sisters – 'You're Fine by Me!' – and Louis Armstrong. From Jack Hilton and Nat Gonella. Certain drum passages were played again and again, and the records were worn out in those sections. They did the *Schuhplattler*, and stamped so hard with their feet that the lamps shook. They screamed, groaned, waved their arms, hit imaginary cymbals – *tz-d-d, tz-d-d, tz-d-'* – and leapt around until the Woldemanns banged against the ceiling.

*

The daughters of Herr Mahnke, the shipyard director, also belonged to the sailing club. ('They're very proper people.') They didn't understand the first thing about jazz, but the boys forgave them, because they had a yacht that they could use.

The *Lucia Warden* was sixty square metres, and had a dinghy as well as a spirit flame for roasting potatoes.

The older daughter was named Sylvia and always wore grey flared trousers. The younger daughter, Sybille, had black hair. She loved having her photograph taken and would pose, shaking out her hair, staring off into the distance while standing at the mast, one leg jutting forward. Both rolled up their white sleeves high and laughed at all of them: at Bubi, who pushed his hat back and did the *Schuhplattler*; at Heini, who had slicked his hair; and at Robert with his barber's bag, who, if they weren't completely mistaken, had once again failed maths.

Bubi climbed down into the cabin.

'Are these new curtains?' he asked as he stuck his finger through the cabin door's brass ring. 'It's so tidy.' There was a photo of Laboe over the berths.

Michael hoisted the sails. 'Off we go.'

On the beach in Warnemünde, the girls wore two-pieces. The boys, meanwhile, wore triangular trunks through which you could see the cracks of their asses.

The sand was hot, and the water was nineteen degrees. Bubi was spreading suncream on the girls, who were already tanning without it.

'Just a little bit more here, please, and really rub it in.'

Little blond hairs on brown skin.

'A little massage, perhaps?'

'No, thanks.'

The beach chair was tilted back. It had BEUTEL 96 printed on it, and a small canopy to shade your face. Someone had balanced a white seashell on Sylvia's stomach. Heini gave Sybille a cigarette.

PATRONS WHO STAIN BEACH CHAIRS WITH OIL AND GREASE
WILL BE HELD RESPONSIBLE FOR ALL DAMAGES

While the girls sizzled in the beach chair, the guys played music on two gramophones: while one was running, they dug up a record for the other one.

'Always with this nigger jazz,' the people nearby complained. We'd kick over their stuff in the evening, just when they'd gone topless.

Mister Paganini, please play my rhapsody
And if you sing it,
You simply have to swing it . . .[2]

The boys discussed how Art Tatum was blind and Chick Webb was crippled; how Artie Shaw could switch to playing classical for a whole night; and how Teddy Stauffer conducted (one hand in his pocket, laid back). They tried to remember what Count Basie's drummer was named.

('Heini, can you pass me another cigarette?')

Manfred and I sat at a distance and watched. High in the sky a double-decker plane turned one loop after another, and further still, the navy had rifle practice.

'How long do they plan to sunbathe?' asked Heini.

A can of seltzer sprayed with a hiss, and then a ball of seaweed was thrown into the beach chair. The chair was tipped over and Sylvia was carried by her hands and feet to the shore before being tossed ('Forward – back!') into the water.

Before she'd had a chance to shake out her hair, Heini lifted Sybille up on his shoulders, stamping and whining, and climbed up on to the embankment. Off they went, splashing back and forth in the shallows, with children and grandmothers stepping aside, before venturing further in, up to their stomachs. There they fell over and disappeared under the water for a while.

(Michael took photos the whole time, including one that we went on to call 'Heini in Action'.)

Further out, you could just make out Sylvia and Bubi. Only their heads visible. They had swum out to a sandbank.

Afterwards, everyone came back to our beach base. Sylvia combed her hair; she held the clips in her mouth. The new shirt that Michael had sent away for from Munich, they filled with wet sand, and set a volleyball for a head on top.

'Have you got a chair for him?'

Heini put on a wet bra and draped himself in a red towel.

'Got that rhythm, boys!'

In the barber's bag was pudding that was spooned out for everyone. When it was gone, Robert still had some bread to share.

'Great, magnificent,' he declared.

'The next assignment will go better,' Heini said to Robert,

consoling him on his result in maths. 'Herr Schinner always lets up.'

'I can't count on that,' Robert said. He had to see how it turned out, maybe he'd come up with something.

They put records on again, and the *Schuhplattler* recommenced: arms waving, cymbals striking, *tz-d-d, tz-d-d, tz-d-d*. You could see beach waiters, in uniform, carrying vendor's trays, all along the snow-white promenade.

> Apples, pears and bananas,
> Taste good before and after a swim . . .[3]

And the biplane made another loop.

Manfred and I took the train back. We sat on the left in the compartment, as you could see Heinkel's aircraft factory from that side.

A thin woman with curly hair sat opposite us. She didn't pay the least attention to anything outside. She kept rummaging around in her oilcloth bag. Had she forgotten something?

Then a 100-11 landed, growing bigger and bigger as we got closer to it. Manfred told me that they had another model that had floats, 100-14s, which could 'splash down', as they said. What did the 100-12 and 100-13 look like, that's what he wanted to know.

The enamel sign under the emergency brake had been amended. It now read: JEDER MIß_AUCH WIRD __ STRAFT.[*]

---

[*] The full text should read: '*Jeder Mißbrauch wird gestrafft*', 'Any misuse will be punished.'

Before supper, my father wandered around the apartment with his watch in his hand.

'You still don't see the boys?' he telephoned.

'No, Herr Kempowski, they still haven't rounded the corner.'

'A damned disgrace,' he said and hung up the receiver. He was sure they were sitting by the telephone and having a laugh. His skin was itching again; he couldn't take it.

'They'll be here soon enough,' said my mother. She was sitting on the balcony, enjoying the summer evening. 'Children, how lovely it is, no? How lovely. Boy, look how brown you are . . .'

Swallows flitted by, and Dr Krause checked to make sure the door was locked for the last time. The bells of the Catholic church rang loudly.

'It really is kind of terrific, isn't it?'

Ulla was sitting in the lounger, wearing a checked pinafore dress.

On the bright beaches of the Saale[4]

What a shame, she would have loved to come along to Warnemünde.

'It was just as well,' said my mother.

But Ulla wanted to know whether Bubi had come along, and then made a sad face.

Finally, as the stairwell light clicked on, my brother climbed the stairs, snuffling.

'It's about time! The whole evening is down the drain!'

The family was waiting while their son deigned to go sailing.

The tea was poured, the balcony door was closed. Ulla lifted her dress so it didn't crinkle and sat down. Sandwiches with tomatoes, along with sausages, served in glass bowls on a long nickel tablet, with radishes and parsley as garnish: there was *Mettwurst* and

Lebenswurst, Rügenwalder and boiled ham, as well as wheat-rye bread, which was pitch black in colour. It was from Lampe, the baker, and was both fine and rough, with a particularly thick crust.

'Else, please bring the carafe with the rum . . .'

'Was Schneefoot there?' asked my father, scratching himself.

'Of course not!' said my brother.

Robert's response seemed a little defensive. My father stabbed the butter rose on his knife and spread it on his bread.

'How was your schoolwork? Have you done it? We haven't heard a peep from you.'

'You think I haven't done it?' my brother said, and looked at him straight on. He shouldn't get so fresh, I thought, or he'd get a clip or two on the ear. And look at him! That hair! He looked completely shabby.

'You look a lot like Heini,' said Ulla, 'or a pimp. That's more like it, actually: you look like a pimp.'

My mother agreed: 'You have a huge mane of hair . . . If only you knew how ridiculous you look.' Apparently, Frau District Court Counsellor Warkentin had recently asked whether he got his hair curled.

And all the while my brother kept eating, unbothered: 'What does the proud oak care about the bleating of the stall animals?'

That did it. My father tore the napkin out of his collar and barked: 'Snot-nosed brat!' He stormed into the next room, but cooler heads prevailed and he quickly came back.

My mother implored my father to give him a clip on the ear. ('It would definitely do him good!') The canary hopped on its swing and began to trill.

'Things will be different now, there'll be a new regime around here,' my father thundered. 'And *you*' (meaning me): 'don't wobble like that in your chair! We've told you a thousand times.'

'It's just like Gustav Robert Högfeldt,' my brother said, cutting the fat off his ham. '*Family Circus*, do you know that picture? With the father screaming his head off at the children?'

My father sat down and stuffed the napkin into his collar. 'By golly,' he said, with a wry expression, 'I would never have been permitted to do something like that by *my* father. He ran a much tighter ship.'

Once, when he was beating him with a cane, his father had accidently broken his lamp, causing a rain of glass. He had cried, 'God damn it!' and then laughed, of course.

'Yes,' said my mother. Her mother had beaten her with a cane until it had worn down to a stump, because she hadn't wanted to say grace at the table.

'You wanted to do the same thing to me with the Yellow Uncle,' said Ulla; 'I couldn't get away from you.' It still hurt whenever she thought about it.

9

Before our big holiday, my father had declared that he was completely exhausted; he had to get away.

'Me too,' said my brother.

'The best thing would be to travel to the Harz,' my father said. According to him, we could get affordable accommodation, as the Reich Association of German Officers kept a guesthouse there: money was no object. There were all kinds of things to see, too. The Selketal River, for one, which was supposed to be wonderful.

My mother had never been away, not once. She'd only ever been to the lake. ('It's enough to drive you to despair . . .') Hertha, for example, had been to England, and Richard had visited Hong Kong. But she only ever went to the lake. It was preposterous that, as a Hamburger, she had never once set foot on Helgoland, despite it being so close. ('How was it even possible!')

My father pulled out the portfolio containing all of his maps from 1914–18, along with his binoculars. He also had a horn-rimmed pince-nez made for him, through which he looked straight down from above. The country air would be good for his skin. My mother got a hiking bag, as well as shoes made of snakeskin.

Ulla was allowed to cut off her braids, a long-cherished wish.

They were wrapped in silk paper, as insurance in case she were to lose her hair later.

'Was there edelweiss in the Harz?' she asked. She really wanted to do some climbing.

'What? You're going on holiday?' my grandfather said. 'I can't believe it. I never went on holiday.' He did, however, go to Oeynhausen every year.

The train was full as we departed. 'This might get hairy,' said my father: 'we're definitely not going to get a seat.'

People were standing in third class, and there were no free seats in second. We had to bite the bullet and transfer to first. (Was this allowed? Hopefully no one would give us any trouble!) Amid much cursing, we manoeuvred the trunks down the aisle. The largest – the big blue one – was very heavy.

'Karl, this is a sin.'

In the first class carriage, a fat man was laid out on the upholstery; he was reading an English detective novel, *The Pools of Silence*. We started to climb over to him, and he casually took his legs down.

'Oh God,' my mother whispered, 'look at this fat Jewish spy . . .'

'Don't touch the ashtray! Come on, we're going to go wash our hands.' Whenever Aunt Silbi travelled to Schreiberhau she took a laxative the day before she left, and then something to constipate her on the morning of her travels: anything to avoid having to use the toilet on the train.

How fast were we going? I wondered.

'Always to the lake,' my mother muttered. Perhaps best of all, she still couldn't swim.

'But didn't you go to Tegernsee with Father?' I asked.

'Yes, for our honeymoon, in 1920, but it was a total washout . . .'

'Why aren't you asleep?' her lovely spouse had said back then, late one night. 'You have to close your eyes. I can't get to sleep knowing you're there, staring.'

But before long he'd returned to snoring. There wasn't a healthier man than Dad. ('He's never sick, and he sleeps like the dead.')

A flower procession that took place once every ten years happened while they were in Munich. My mother wanted to go to the galleries too. But, instead of exploring, my father had insisted on staying put – so he could rest.

'When are we going to be here again?' my mother had pleaded.

The honeymoon was a disappointment.

The chaplain is a moron had been written on our compartment door. My parents weren't amused by it. It was a distinctly Bavarian humour; they were a funny people. I found it funny to think that they too were Germans now . . .

My sister was walking through the train. ('Don't touch the doors! Every year someone falls out.') My brother, meanwhile, stood in the aisle and stared out of the open window keeping watch for the mountains, his quiff fluttering back and forth.

'Don't lean so far out!' my father shouted.

Moments later my mother called for us: 'Children! Look, there they are!'

'For God's sake!' Robert had been standing on the wrong side of the carriage.

'Well, when we get there, you can see everything at your own pace,' said my mother.

The spy didn't move; he just lay there, breathing heavily, deep in his novel. The mountains evidently didn't interest him.

In Sophienbad, a river tumbled down into the crags below. ('Fine and dandy!') But no one had come to receive us. To our left and right, attendants were taking the black, brass-studded trunks of the few guests from the other carriages and loading them on to carts.

'So we have to look after ourselves? Unheard of!'

Had we registered correctly? Did the train arrive too early? One theory was that the train was full of generals. Father was only a lieutenant in the reserves, so perhaps we didn't make the cut (even if he had been awarded both Iron Crosses, the Mecklenburg Service Cross, the Hamburg Hanseatic Cross, and so on).

'And it's definitely going to rain tomorrow,' my father noted.

'Nothing we can do about that,' said my mother.

Our 'home', as my father called it, was a small clapboard house, in the usual architectural style. It had a large, completely overgrown garden, which was enclosed by a wooden lattice fence. My brother climbed up the slope right away. But there was nothing to see: there were trees everywhere.

'You'll see,' my mother said, 'we'll work out which are the right places to visit, and it'll be wonderful.' It was always like that in the beginning: you took a lot of paths that went nowhere before stumbling upon the best route.

'We'll ask around, and then only go where it's beautiful.'

My parents took a bedroom full of mismatched furniture; my siblings a second room that also spoke to a life 'of slender means'. I was to take the couch at the end of my parents' bed. I'd be sleeping by their feet.

'You'll see,' said my mother, 'I'm sure you'll sleep well here. The sofas are usually very comfortable.'

On the front of the house, above the window, a sign read WALDFRIEDEN GUESTHOUSE. Inside, the walls were painted white; the wooden furniture varnished.

My father had set his shaving kit on the washstand. He carried Kaiser borax powder to soften the water, along with Sparta cream. Both would be good for his skin. He switched on various lamps and let the taps run.

'Ring-ring! Both engines, full steam ahead!' he cried.

'I'm going out,' said my sister.

For meals we had our own table, tucked away in an alcove of the dark dining room. Various elderly people sat at the long table and all the way at the head was the owner of the guesthouse, Frau von Schmidt. Her husband had been killed at Langemarck – in the prime of his youth, as they said. She was the one who'd failed to give us an appropriate reception, despite my father having fought alongside her husband against the French. ('It's infuriating. I just can't understand it!')

Two old women, dressed all in black, with banded collars and doilies on their heads, were both addressed as 'Your Excellency'. ('The Excellencies'.) They wore shoes that slapped against the wooden floor.

Further along the main table was a man of around fifty, a colonel, with wide scars, from a sabre, on his steeply rising bald head. His eyes shone with untold experiences from the war. When he was speaking of his time in northern France, he didn't say 'Arras', like my father, but always 'Arra'.

My father held the door for him: 'If it pleases the colonel?'

'Thank you, comrade sir.'

None of us had ever had fish casserole, and were pleasantly surprised that it tasted pretty good. For dessert we had warm chocolate pudding. My father ate until he was full.

'*All Inclusive*: do you know that movie? With Pat and Patachon? They had to pay for everything after all, and were left without a penny in their pockets. Oh, how we laughed.'

Finally butter came round, laid out in the shape of a clover leaf, a rose or a fish. Getting hold of more was no easy matter though, and the sausage plate only went round once. ('Behave yourself, boy.') At this point, political economy was discussed.

At another table, in the sunlight, a lieutenant sat with his wife and two daughters. He was calm, his wife quiet, the daughters silent.

'Excellent,' my mother said when she noticed them, 'you'll have a lovely time playing together.'

The lieutenant, it transpired, was on active duty and came from Königsberg. The red braid on his uniform, my father noted, meant he was artillery. (Cavalry would have been better, navy considerably worse.)

'Don't stare like that.'

Instead of his order insignia he wore a silver riding badge.

My father doubled over in greeting, a gesture that the man returned accordingly. After eating they stood at the window together, cutting their cigars.

'You're from Königsberg?' my father confirmed, before asking whether he knew a fruit merchant there named Kempowski ('kay-ay-em, pee-o-double-yew, ess-kay-eye?'), Arthur Kempowski, his cousin, who lived right in the city centre.

'No,' said the lieutenant, pronouncing the word roundly, and spitting out some tobacco, 'not that I know of.'

I ran with the girls into the garden. Lily, a year older than me, taught me a game where you pressed all ten of your fingers against someone else's at once. She had clear blue eyes and long thin plaits, which she would occasionally toss back behind her. Elke, the younger of the sisters, looked exactly like Lily, and they both wore blue dresses with colourful little flowers. Elke hopped, whereas Lily walked more seriously, carefully.

We drew squares in the sand and played hopscotch, then we moved on to hide-and-seek, at which point it was agreed that no one would look too hard, because the two of them weren't allowed to get their clothes dirty.

'Now, a robber comes and attacks us,' I said.

'Our parents wouldn't like us playing that,' the girls answered.

I had been given two blue polo shirts and a sleeveless pullover for the trip, along with some light flannel trousers. I was finally free of my Hamburg suit.

'You look awful,' said Robert, 'like a horrible little animal.' He brought over my mother's mirror, made of real tortoiseshell, and held it in front of me. I thought I looked a lot better in my new clothes.

In the mornings, freshly washed hair bows lay over the balcony railing, drying. The ramshackle outdoor space where the loungers were was always quiet; there was never a grown-up to be found. Roofing paper and mouldy wood had been left lying around, and the whole area was surrounded by wild jasmine. There, the girls treated me to smushed knackwursts in bowls made of bark. 'Roast', they called it.

Sometimes I was 'ill' and then I had to lie down and have my temperature taken with a twig.

'Should you maybe try to resuscitate me?' I asked.

But they didn't go for it.

The train ride from Königsberg to the Harz had taken an entire day, they told me. ('Just think about that!') The corridor of the train had been locked, and the curtains drawn. They had been passing through ancient German land, and they weren't permitted to look out of the window: they'd been told there was a death penalty for anyone who tried.

'He doesn't know Arthur, apparently. What an idiot. He's a real arsehole,' my father declared at supper that evening.

'And how can you call your child Elke?' my mother chimed in, shaking her head.

'The fruit stand is right on the Domplatz. If he's from Königsberg, he *must* know him.'

'Don't take it the wrong way, but the wife is quite common. She puts her elbows on the table. And don't get me started on those curls! They seem to be of very simple stock.'

My sister clung to a girl called Elisabeth von Globig, who had come with her mother from Berlin. She had a double chin and a club foot, which my brother noticed right away.

'A *nice* girl,' my father stressed.

'Yes,' said Frau von Globig.

'. . . and so modest.'

'Yes,' said Frau von Globig. 'You have no idea how clingy she is, though. She tells me everything.'

Now and then the two of them sat at the piano in the recreation room, Elisabeth playing a Kuhlau sonata, my sister doing the clog dance from *Zar und Zimmermann*. ('Now let *me* play. Do you know this?')

While they played, the colonel went back and forth by the open window, gnashing his teeth.

'Pericles with his helmet,' as my brother said.

When the weather was good we would all march up and down the Bahnhofstrasse. On one occasion though, we went to the casino, where we found a trio – cello, violin and piano – playing 'In the Persian Market'.

'Bad violin players get ambitious and try to play difficult pieces,' my brother said. 'And this one really is much too screechy.'

The pianist looked nervous, smoking a cigarette. But Robert deemed him a good sort. ('He definitely plays jazz at home.')

Soon we made out a dark, southern type, whose hairy legs stuck out of his too-long lederhosen. He was wearing sunglasses over his heavy-lashed eyes and had a badge from the German League for Physical Exercise on his lapel.

'Light in the loafers,' my brother said.

'Esau', the girls called him.

He mostly hung around in front of the gift shop, where they sold toys and medallions and herb liqueurs. When we were looking for postcards, he put his arm around Ulla.

'Take these postcards instead.'

Soon after, we met him again at the indoor pool. ('Do be careful, every year someone drowns.') The hotel management had thrown a large wooden cross into the water, which we swam over to and began to climb on to, screaming and splashing.

Meanwhile Elisabeth, the friend with the double chin, didn't come into the pool. She stayed out of sight, wanting to be alone with Esau.

After our swim Esau lay in the grass, reading, a white terrycloth towel around his neck like a scarf. The girls tossed a ball back and forth over him: Elisabeth awkward and wobbly, Ulla tanned and quick. But he wanted to sunbathe, damn it! They could at least light a cigarette for him – that would be nice.

Finally, my sister poured cold water on to his stomach with her bathing cap. That got him up. Ulla jumped up and ran away, the frills of her trousers rustling against one another. She ran quickly, too; he had trouble keeping up with his short legs. She jumped over a ditch filled with old buckets, and into the bush. That was the end of the chase.

Elisabeth looked at her thin gold watch. 'I think we have to go home now.'

*

One lovely day, we went on another excursion that had been planned well in advance.

Treat yourself, smoke Welp Cigars!

My father packed a load of black cigars. He also took his binoculars with him – they had stood him in good stead in Flanders – and the folder with the maps. His skin was doing fine ('pretty Goodmannsdörfer'): no oozing spots, no itching at all.

The colonel and Frau von Globig joined the trip, with the lieutenant's permission: she wore a wide-brimmed hat; he was entirely in grey.

At the last moment Ulla suggested that she should stay home, so she could keep Elisabeth company.

'Completely out of the question,' was the answer. Our family wanted to go on the trip all together. Otherwise, before long, we'd hardly see one another any more. We might as well have stayed at home. ('Why must everything always be so difficult!')

We got into a three-axle bus; it had a long radiator, and a ladder on the back so that you could get up on the roof. My father asked as he got on the bus whether the driver had served.

'*Yes, sir!* Orderly at Ypern, 238.'

'Well how about that! Did you hear that, Herr Colonel?'

'Amazing!'

'In God's name, let's go!' the colonel implored, falling into his seat with a groan.

The trip was planned so that we could go on foot for a while. We found our way using trees marked with white or red crosses. ('Children, this is how things ought to be.') There were even railings and steps for places where it was hard to cross.

'It's just so beautiful,' said my mother. Then, a little while later: 'Look children, a doe!'

Her Salamander shoes were wonderfully comfortable, she said. 'Why can't it be this way all the time?'

My father had shouldered his walking stick and was whistling Lummert's parade march. The pince-nez was still in great shape – there were no pressure marks behind the ear.

With measured steps the colonel made his way over to my sister. 'How's school going?' he asked.

'It's going,' my sister answered, and tried to get away.

The colonel had attached his hat to his jacket with a clothes-peg and was farting gently and rhythmically to himself. Robert, who had put his handkerchief on his head, all four corners knotted, imitated him.

'Knock it off,' said my mother, 'knock it off right now.'

As we looked out, a number of pylons rose from the vast swathes of countryside.

'This is the new age,' said Frau von Globig, teetering in front of me on her thin legs. 'Is that the church I see down there?'

The two towers, of the church and Wernigerode Castle, were pointing up to God like the two fingers on the hand you swear with – admonition and obligation all at once.

> Build, young master,
> Build bright and wide,
> But don't forget the crypts . . .[1]

We entered through a side door into the darkness of the church, and a smell like Lysol. I commented on how the columns were built to look like they were flowing down from above.

'What did the boy say?' asked my mother. Frau von Globig threw her a look, but I wasn't sure what she meant by it.

'Think of the German kaiser,' said my father. 'Are there ravens flying around the tower, like in Rückert's "Barbarossa"? And to think the crown is finally coming back to Nuremberg, after such a long journey . . .'

'That's exactly where it belongs,' the colonel said sharply, as if anyone had said anything different.

Two men were speaking on the organ platform.

'I think that's Prince Wernigerode,' said my mother, 'all of you be quiet now . . .'

At that moment they also fell silent, and looked down at us.

In the castle museum we were received by the castellan, dressed in the uniform of a medieval *Landsknecht*. He set his halberd aside and showed us a set of old seals kept in a glass cabinet.

'Well, that's something at least,' my father said.

To end the trip, we took a number of photos against the castle's door. ('Please take another step back, so you're all in the photograph.') Lizards were sunning themselves on the warm stones. My mother's dress and pelerine fluttering in the gentle breeze, three buttons with knife pleats like suns on her chest.

To be on the safe side, everything was photographed twice. My brother used my parents' Ikarette. They'd also had it with them in Tegernsee, but you couldn't close it properly any more: a rubber band had been jerry-rigged to hold its insides together. Ulla's camera, on the other hand, worked with no problem at all.

'Keep it simple,' said my father.

'Yes,' said the colonel, 'fabulous, how Hitler understood that.'

*

Whenever it rained – and it rained often – I sat with Lily and Elke in the lounge and let my legs dangle off the edge of my seat. Black snails inched along the path, water poured out of the broken gutters, and yellow bubbles swam in the puddles.

My father stood under the door with a cigar and said, 'Typical.'

He couldn't believe how much water was coming down. 'I have no idea how many tonnes it would come to if you counted it all up . . . Where's it all coming from?'

The rain drove my mother to despair. 'It's bound to stop soon. It can't rain for ever, can it?'

That's how it usually went, Mother said, and before you knew it the sun would come out again. And how lovely that we went in July and not in August; it meant we still had some sunny days at home to look forward to.

'How are my flowers doing on the balcony, I wonder?' she asked of no one.

My brother sat on the landing and played with his yo-yo. 'You really should walk around a little,' said my father. 'Other boys your age are out there living their lives.'

'Walk around in the rain?' my brother questioned: how exactly did he imagine Robert was supposed to do that? Using an umbrella would be extremely dicey.

When it got too damp in the lounge Lily, Elke and I ran into the dining hall and played Sorry.

'We should make it so no one can knock anyone else out of the game,' said Lily: that way no one would get angry, and the game would go faster.

'Didn't Robert want to play too?' she asked.

He probably thought we were being silly playing a board game . . . 'What nonsense,' he'd say.

He tried to get the Beromüsterstation on the radio in the recreation room: they played dance music.

'Turn that nigger jazz off,' said the colonel, who was there to retrieve Lieselotte's letters on the Palatinate: a book that grew more remarkable each time you read it. 'Put the news on instead,' he suggested. 'Are the Polish provoking us again?'

The next day the grand piano on which Robert played 'Harlem' with one finger was locked.

The Königsbergers left three days early, and so I said goodbye to Lily and Elke. They were going to travel a whole day through ancient German country again, and they wouldn't be allowed to open the windows. ('Hopefully we'll make it!')

'Oh,' said my mother, 'the situation with Poland doesn't sound good. How could this be happening . . .' (Our ship the *Consul* was, thank God, in Greifswald.)

'I think we're also going to head home,' said my father. He was exhausted.

'Agreed,' said my brother, who was also shot.

The guestbook was retrieved. An artistically-minded guest had, in the absence of paint, rendered a landscape using coffee grounds.

Esau gave my sister a hollowed-out cork with three tiny dice inside: 'Think of me whenever you throw three ones.'

He had cleared out the vending machines for himself; there was no chocolate left to buy in the shops.

My mother bought a case of Pfeilring soap. ('It's scarce wherever you go.') Ulla added the Sophienbad crest to the coats of arms on her bracelet, which was already quite heavy.

'Will you write to me?' asked Elisabeth. 'Don't forget, or you're in trouble!'

'Let's go, children! Come on! It's time.'

Frau von Schmidt shut all the windows.

10

I met Ute in the stairway, where sandbags and buckets of water had been distributed as a precaution against air raids. She didn't want to learn the finger game.

The war was going to last just fourteen days, they said. England, that little pee-pee land; we'd finish them off quick. She'd been in Bad Reichenhall when they heard the news.

'On the railroad?'

'Railroad? It's called a "train".'

It seemed that I was the idiot.

'Be quiet out here,' said Frau Woldemann, 'or I'll bang your heads together.'

Ute's family wanted to go to Berlin for a few months, until everything calmed down, as they'd be out of range. Though maybe one day they would move there permanently. The sound of crates being hammered together was audible through the open landing door. I watched them packing away silverware and clothing.

'Well, you scamp,' said Herr Woldemann, who was supervising the packing. 'Tell your father hello.' He had a bottle of wine in his hand, from which he took a gulp.

Ute said she was quite happy. Her cousin lived in Dahlem, and he wasn't a dumbski like me.

'What does the Wehrmacht report say?' asked my father. He had hung a red sign in front of the loudspeaker:

PLEASE REMEMBER THAT LISTENING TO FOREIGN STATIONS IS PUNISHABLE BY LAW

'Not bad,' said my brother. For the first time, the Waffen-SS units had become involved in the fighting. 'What do you think? The way they go at it, there's not a blade of grass going to be left growing, just slime and muck.'

'Absolutely,' said my father, 'they'll make short work of it. Old Hitler has a good head on his shoulders.' It would all be over quickly.

On the German radio a report from a Catholic priest: a Pole had 'struck him in the reproductive organs'.

'Human beings can't live in peace,' said my mother. The people at the top should get into a boxing ring and hash it out between themselves: that was what *she'd* like to see.

Every evening she pinned brown paper on to every window, cursing the blackout the whole time: 'What a drag, what a slog.'

Someone outside would then shout, 'Lights out!'

(Our ship, the *Consul*, was thank God in Lübeck.)

And the business with the ration cards was starting up again, 'It's enough to drive you to despair,' my mother said. During the last war they'd always had to eat turnips and dehydrated vegetables. Oh, she remembered all too well.

'No,' said Dr Krause, everything had been organised better this time. 'Hitler has set aside enormous stores, otherwise he wouldn't have started the war. The man isn't crazy, after all.'

My mother bought one small glass bowl for all of us. With it we picked up the weekly butter ration of a quarter-pound each. I got a double serving on my children's card.

The rations were the absolute minimum you could survive on, a professor said; eating any less was hazardous to your health. That was why everyone had to get their portion no matter what.

(I divided my half-pound exactly, a finger-sized piece for every day. Anything left over at the end of the week was always a bit rancid.)

'The Polish Corridor was stupid; everyone should have known another war was coming.'

'There's no way it could have gone well.'

'They must have known.'

'Clearly.'

'It was stupid, always having to get to and fro by ship. Where did you ever hear of having a patch of your country somewhere else? We could have lost the Klaipeda region and no one would have made a peep, but not Danzig and all that.'

The stop sign at the junction was changed from the English (STOP) to the German (HALT).

Fraulein Reber, a volunteer, brought the ration cards from building to building.

'I'm bringing you something to eat,' she said to old people, who examined both sides of the paper and held it up against the light. Her brother Otto – whose name read the same both backward and forward – had already flown a few missions.

'That's just a fraction of what she's got,' said my mother. 'You've always got to keep an eye on her.'

Since everything was going to be scarce, I liquidated my savings book and used it to buy a bicycle and some silver spoons. All of this impressed my father ('you clever rascal') and my brother, who got himself a silver cigarette case, and had his initials engraved on it, before immediately losing it.

In school they told us we should be proud to be living through these times. We were supposed to study twice as hard now; whoever didn't work was a saboteur: that was the same as being a traitor to your country.

The maps of Poland in the library, physical or political, were permanently lent out, so Hannes made do with rough sketches on the board. He held the chalk diagonally and with big motions drew fat columns, from the north and from the south: those were German troops, that was how we should picture it. And then from behind, the Russians (red column), and up above, the air forces. He pounded with his fist.

'Everything today is different from how it was before: in the World War you barely got your head out of the muck.'

'What will this war be called when it's over?' someone asked.

Civilian gas masks were handed out in the school basement. 'Fabulously organised!'

'Do children also have to have one?'

Herr Krahl stood in the building doorway, looking down the street, the Service Cross from 14–18 on his lapel.

'Well, lazybones?' he said each morning. 'They're all awake upstairs, go on up.'

His box-shaped car had been requisitioned for use in the war. He had been asked whether he would want the same car back, or money, once the war was over.

Now, we played with linoleum soldiers in the drying-loft. It had been covered with garden peat: the brown soil of Poland, earth that had been cleared for foxholes and trenches, for the lines of advance.

Fat Krahl had lots of linoleum soldiers – kneeling, lying and standing.

Klaus Greif brought along a medic's tent and a pack of wounded soldiers on stretchers – the bandages on their heads full of blood – and nurses with buckets, as well as a box of charging soldiers. They were led by a galloping lieutenant. (How were the soldiers supposed to keep up with him? we wondered.) He had a soldier with a flamethrower, which had already fallen apart, unfortunately: you could see rusty wire under the yellow-red flames. And Manfred had a foxhole with a gas alarm gong. It came with a special mask-wearing soldier. There were little bushes of brightly painted wood shavings on it.

Unfortunately, the Fohmann toy shop had no Polish soldiers. We were always asking for them. There was already a captured Polish tank on the marketplace, but there were no Polish soldiers. Fohmann said he was sorry.

As replacement enemies we took French soldiers – in their blue *poilu* uniform – and British soldiers with Brodie helmets, for 30 pfennigs each. The British seemed especially silly to us. How could you win a war with Brodie helmets like that?

We stood Blomberg, the commander-in-chief, at a little card table, in front of the foxhole, next to the steadfast soldiers in gas masks. A soldier marching for inspection was at his side and a battery-powered campfire right next to him: 'That way he can warm his fingers'. Also by him were some soldiers playing the concertina.

Sometimes we let our three tanks climb the garden peat

simultaneously. We all had the same model. We wished we had twenty of them, or forty: they'd steamroll over everything.

Frau Krahl brought us some sandwiches with schmaltz.

'Are you shooting again?' she asked.

*

At supper my father was surly, clinking his tea glass; his gold spectacles shining. (He'd got rid of the pince-nez, it had left pressure marks on his nose.)

'Where have you been? You have to be on time, to the minute!'

Someone was always telephoning for me: 'From now on you'll have to sing a different tune. You can't just do as you please!'

He half listened to my reports.

'Yes, yes, very good . . . Don't wobble like that with your chair.'

They hadn't taken him. When the day came, my father had opened the blue envelope, which had been lying in the writing desk for years, swung himself on to his bicycle and ridden to the recruiting district headquarters. It was his country, right or wrong, and he longed to serve. But they hadn't taken him.

'Dad will never get over it,' said my mother. He had worn his steel helmet and participated in all the drills during the Weimar Republic – the System Era – and the whole of the World War: Ypres, Somme, Kemmel. ('What, you want to be heroes?' his old captain used to say.) He was always on the front line, and all without being wounded, not a scratch. (Except his skin condition.)

'Well, who knows, it might be for the best.'

Car doors slammed in front of the house: the Woldemanns were driving to the train station.

'Don't you want to run down and say goodbye?' asked my mother.

I jumped down the stairs that Quade had built.

('Careful, you scamp,' said the wood handler. He was holding a fine pigskin trunk in his hand, which he gave to his wife.

'And the pumps, do you have the pumps?' she asked.)

I got there in time to see Ute flipping me the bird through the rear window.

I pulled myself up the banister hand over hand, like a funicular, and listened at the door. I smelled the keyhole: the furniture was still there, the gramophone, the crudely broken-down coffee table, and the little picture of the poultry farm too, the one with the thick frame. There were also idyllic pictures of the German homeland in the pharmacist's vitrine: the Stone Gate in winter, covered in snow. Maybe they were coming back soon.

'Sweet,' said my mother, 'look how sad he is. It was a lovely time, my boy.'

'Yes,' said my brother, 'you'll remember it for a long time.'

11

On 2 October, at around seven in the morning, the telephone rang: my grandfather was dead.

'Röbbing', as my father had always called him.

'The swine', as Aunt Silbi had always called him. Obviously, his difficulties walking had nothing to do with the fact that he'd knocked over an urn.

My mother opened our curtains, pulled up the blackout roller, and then announced that he'd died: 'The good old man. Get dressed quick.'

'Remarkable,' my father said, 'two-ten, the same as his regiment number.'

> Greetings to you,
> He whispered softly . . .[1]

He put Kaiser borax in his shaving water, ran to the medicine cabinet doubled over as though he couldn't stand straight, and got a pack of razor blades.

We'd finally be able to sell the standing desk. We could finally get an adding machine. ('I won't have it,' he'd always said, 'nothing but a bunch of worthless junk.')

We went to Seitz's – the funeral parlour – of course. The funeral director came at noon, in a black suit, with rimless octagonal glasses; the corners of his collar turned down. You couldn't do something like this without Seitz. There was a grand piano in the corner of the room. Next to it there was a bookshelf, with tiny ivory mice in front of the works of Lafcadio Hearn. There was a round table too, with a lace cover.

'How do we retrieve the body?' my grandfather had said when his wife died in Bad Oeynhausen.

The lovely house on Stephanstraße – yes, if only we'd known. But – move again now?

'We're talking only the best for your father, of course,' said Herr Seitz, 'the best of the best.' From his black portfolio he pulled out a black photo album with various obituaries and set it on the round table.

'This is wonderfully organised,' said my father, truly impeccable: Tadellöser & Wolff.' All we had to do was pick one out. ('Go get the port!')

'A wake is out of the question.' We had to get him in the ground quickly, 'otherwise they'll all come running'.

The cremation would take place in secret – that way we would avoid running into Aunt Silbi – but we agreed on the best of the best.

Seitz finished his glass, clapped the portfolio shut and said, 'Herr Kempowski, you'll see, everything will be good. For now, my sincerest thanks,' and took his leave.

We'd only been at his house two days ago. Now he was lying there all alone.

Wally, the housemaid, had opened the door for us. (The Rostock watercolours hung on the wall.) Sometimes he used to imitate Humperdinck's death mask, leaned back with eyes closed, mouth open. That's what he looked like now.

My mother had opened the windows and set out grapes for the old man. The good old man. His nightshirt much too big for him. And his skinny arms!

Dusty Christmas presents sat on the bedside table, along with a cardboard train station cut out and glued together by children, with running people, all perfectly upright, a man selling plums. There was also a picture Robert had painted, *Planes over Rostock*, and a thick gold clock in an ornate lead casing. (We'd have to keep our eye on that now.)

'Is Körling still there?' he had asked. 'Körling, is he still there?'

He'd wanted to give me 'fitty cens', as the old custom said. But his wallet was empty, he rummaged around in it with his weak fingers but to no avail. He held it out to us.

'Here, take a look, empty! Can you believe it? Not even fitty cens . . .'

There was once a time when two grand pianos had stood in that house, and the singers from the Stadttheater had a singing competition. He'd once had six servants, and was the third person in Rostock to own a car. But his bladder had given him trouble his whole life.

> Once a year a dove
> Comes down from heaven . . .[2]

'Did it hurt when he put his catheter in?' my mother asked.

'Oh, come on . . .'

And how was his worn-out back doing?

('It's out again.')

Then some men had arrived. They wanted to weld off the garden gate, take it as scrap iron, for the war. (They'd ripped up the gates in front of the Catholic church too, with tractors, in the middle of the night.)

'What the hell!' my grandfather cried, sitting up. But they'd already been at it for a while.

Juniper, medlar and white cedar were in the old cemetery, which was laid out like an accounting book: each grave beside the next, listing the names of the dead. In the new cemetery the graves lay tucked away in enclosures, like parks. It felt like we were in the City Zoo, but there were no donkey noises and no sign of any parrots.

BICYCLE-RIDING, SINGING AND LOUD NOISE-MAKING
ARE PUNISHABLE BY LAW

The crematorium was located in the centre; you reached it by walking up the wide steps of a brick building from the 20s, where you noticed the high chimney that had been incorporated into the architecture. The chimney wasn't smoking: they hadn't started yet.

Father was afraid that Aunt Silbi would come. But there was no need to worry, she didn't show. Frau District Court Counsellor Warkentin was there, though.

'Funny,' she whispered, 'all the old ones are dying off now.'

The mother of her best friend, Herr Papst from the Loignystraße, had passed away recently, and now my grandfather.

There was something cinema-like about the hall. At the front of the auditorium, the coffin was covered with many wreaths: half the city knew him, old Herr Kempowski. The 100-mark wreath from Consul Discher ('By golly') was all the way in the front.

The pastor raised his arms and said: 'A light in the darkness. Such a man is rare.'

He had never been too big on going to church, though. He hadn't even attended his own wife's burial. My father had a photograph taken of the grave to show him how uncared-for it was, but the old man hadn't wanted to look at the photo, not once.

Speaking to a waiter, he'd once declaimed:

> Jesus is my life,
> And death my reward.
> He won't give me anything more
> And has put me out of mind.[3]

Then it was time, and the coffin rode away calmly, steadily, without shaking or trembling.

> How quietly all
> The dead are resting . . .[4]

('The Lodge song', as my mother called it.) The women's eyes welled up with tears and the men's voices trembled. The musician up above at the harmonium gave it his all. A light in the darkness.

(The fire turned blue from the heat in the furnace, my mother told us. The corpse reared up one last time and then crumbled.)

'You play such beautiful piano,' my mother said to my father on the tram, 'but you can't even sing a simple chorale! You get everything completely mixed up. You really should be ashamed.'

After military funerals they played the most cheerful marches, my father told us. They start with funeral marches, but then once the dead man has been buried everyone must sing and be merry.

*

A lot of French was spoken in the days that followed. There was talk of mortgages and debts and of a dispatch box that had been found full of statements of account; some of them hadn't even been opened. ('Do you have anything to say?') It seemed the old man had lost track of his affairs. He had bought red wine by the crate, and treated everyone, but had never settled up. ('Kempowski, truly, you're a good guy.')

'And they're such nice, polite letters of demand,' said my mother, 'but he just ignored them . . .'

Aunt Silbi didn't show up when the will was read, even though my grandfather had taken care of her generously. She got the birchwood furniture, the cabinet with the cups, and the rare landscape of the old Rostock University, which the museum director enquired about now and again.

'You've got to be on the lookout,' my mother said: Aunt Silbi was a thief. She'd make off with something else, she was more than capable.

'Let her,' said my father. 'I don't want anything.'

He had a retailer come, who drove off with a 'shitload' of his belongings.

> Nothing is the same
> After war and blood is spilled,
> Let us by the grace of heaven
> Delight in the joy of peace[5]

But my father did keep a tobacco tin – it was a real Iserlohn[6] –

and the golden clock, of course, which he took out of the lead frame. We also kept the leather armchair, a small silver-plated bowl and ('Hang on a second') the icebox ('Where is it, the icebox?') with a drawer for chipped ice: we could put that out in the corridor, in the summer, for the butter.

And my mother got pudding bowls shaped like fish, a leather armchair, and the winter coat, which was brand new and could be made into something for Robert.

We inherited the house and the business. The house had been built around the turn of the century. Back then it had cost 45,000 gold marks, but we more or less had to buy it again, that's how mortgaged it was.

'This inheritance is a real poisoned chalice,' my brother said.

'Very true!' my father cried. We'd have to tighten our belts. The tobacco tin would sit next to the telephone, so we could collect pennies in it.

'It's so good that you're not on the battlefield,' my mother said. 'I don't know what I would do otherwise.'

She got an account book, laid it on the grand piano, and entered the debts. My father watched at a distance.

'Eleven per cent interest! How is that possible? It's daylight robbery!'

When everything was going well for the old man, everyone had got drunk with him. But when things started going downhill for him, no one was there.

'A bunch of white Jews. Eleven per cent!'

Friends whose debts were called in got into a huff, stopped saying hello to us. But my mother was firm, we had to pay off the debt.

'Oh God, I can still see them playing the piano; up the scale, down the scale – schnapps. Up the scale, down the scale – schnapps . . .'

'What would you think if I left the firm now?' my father asked, and worked his pencil under his wedding ring. 'What would you all say to that? I could become a tax officer, like Kröhl . . .'

(Our ship the *Consul* was in Kiel at the moment.)

But he couldn't do it, of course: the firm was 140 years old, after all; tradition compelled him.

'You can't just throw everything out the window like that and run,' said my mother. 'Slow and steady wins the race.'

The house had to be rented out. We found a charming vet, Löwes, from the slaughterhouse, who had married young. The whole mortgage could be paid off with the rent.

'How nicely we could have lived there,' my mother lamented, and sketched in her account book. 'Instead here we are, sitting on the second floor.'

'We've got a 2,500-tonne ship and we're living on the second floor,' my father said.

'Forget it,' said my mother. 'The wheel is turning. At least we're healthy.'

The place had to be cleaned before we let the tenants in. The floor – first class parquet – was crusted with filth: a real shame. My parents told Wally to leave the house immediately. ('To let the old man die in filth . . . Lazy as a sack of beans.') They asked after the ration cards, too. But she didn't know where they were. She warned my mother not to lose her temper, or she'd go to the Party.

Aunt Mieke wanted to know why my mother hadn't looked after him: 'You could easily have done so,' she alleged.

'That's rich!' my mother shouted. 'You run around doing everything for everyone, you work your fingers to the bone, and *still* you get complaints!

'The old man had stopped letting anyone in. He didn't trust anyone. Yelled at me, he did! And threatened me with his walking stick. A very stubborn old man.'

'If I were you, I would still have looked in,' said Aunt Mieke.

We found all sorts of things in the many empty rooms: dictionaries for a number of languages; a catheter; a pencil holder shaped like antlers. In the coal cellar there was an old gramophone with a tin horn, and in the attic we found hundreds of Punch notebooks and piles of unplaned cherrywood boards.

'He probably accepted these as payment for something,' my mother posited.

Ulla and Robert raced wheelchairs in the garden, doing laps of the pear tree. My brother had his old pince-nez on his nose.

'Would you do me a favour and stop that,' said my mother, the old man was barely under the ground.

The next day, my mother said that her head ached; that she felt woozy. She thanked the good, great, gracious Lord that it was all behind us.

'What a mess that was.'

'My muscles don't ache at all, though,' my brother chimed in, while hammering a nail into our bedroom wall, next to a picture of Teddy Stauffer. He hung his violin on it.

He had three days off school, during which he was on siren duty for the maintenance council. He was hoping there would be an alarm so he'd get a chance to press the button.

12

On the first day of the Christmas holiday, I got scarlet fever. We'd never eaten goose in peacetime but, with the outbreak of war, some friends from the country had sent us two right away. But because of the illness, I didn't touch the goose leg on my plate. All I could do was pick at it. My mother thought it was strange behaviour from me.

'Take a look at this!' my father shouted. 'The whole holiday down the drain. Things will have to change. You can't just do as you please, you'll have to eat whatever's on the table.'

My brother agreed: he felt I couldn't just let the food go to waste; that I should at least try a little.

'It doesn't taste bad at all,' he said.

'He's got a fever,' my mother interjected, and put me to bed.

Dr Kleesaat visited with his medical bag. Outside in the hall my mother told him that her little Peterpump was sick. When he entered the room he pulled back the covers, looked at my chest and started to spell out his diagnosis: 'S-c-a . . .'

'Oh, for goodness' sake!' my father cut in, 'just say "scarlet fever". We're not children, after all.'

The doctor's hesitancy came from working with labourers; they wanted to be treated that way, like children. You could even whack them on the behind.

My body's defences were fighting off the bacteria like soldiers, Dr Kleesaat said before he left. He put his stethoscope in his pocket and picked up his bag. My mother asked whether binding my chest with a Priesnitz wrap might help, but Dr Kleesaat dismissed the suggestion.

'It never turns out well when you meddle with the natural defences. The only thing that will help is rest, rest, and more rest.'

We were looking at six weeks. The doctor said he would check in again soon.

'I could never be a doctor,' my mother said after he'd left. 'Looking into other people's mouths and God knows what else . . . Not for me. But then again, someone has to do it.'

I was quartered in my sister's attic bedroom while I recovered, which Ulla didn't like very much.

I wasn't able to get up the stairs by myself though, so they had to carry me. They left me with one of my father's walking sticks, the one with the medallion from the Harz: I was to knock on the floor with it if I needed anything.

*

As was tradition, my mother had baked a vast amount of *Pfeffernusse* cookies just before the holiday began, enough to fill our wash basket. She kept them in tins, from which we were allowed to help ourselves.

My sister wrote a sign – STOP, THIEF! – and put it on the lid.

Ulla constructed a writing case out of Lamps paper as a gift for

Aunt Silbi – 'she is our relative, after all' – and Robert had painted a tin box with camouflage colours for Uncle Richard, who was serving as a lieutenant colonel in the Führer's headquarters.

'He can put his cigarettes in there,' Robert mused, 'or use it to store spare buttons.'

The 24th was a Sunday. Everything was crazy that year, because of the war. After the service, my mother read from the Book of Luke at the round table with the lace cover, wiping droplets from her nose as she did so: her father always used to read it to her ('. . . that all the world be taxed').

Then it was time for the endless singing: how boring that always was! Through it all, the blackout shades were kept flush against the windows with clothes-pegs, so that we wouldn't get shouted at from outside. ('Lights out!')

'We should think of all the soldiers,' my mother said, playing with her topaz, which hung on a thin chain, 'of all the soldiers out there on the battlefield who aren't as nice and warm as we are.'

She held a fir branch in the crackling flames and my father began to tinkle the ivories. Before long he was swaying backward and forward, singing all seven verses of 'The Christmas Tree is the Loveliest Tree' in falsetto.[1]

While he played I looked into the back of the grand piano, noting how the hammers of the soft pedal lifted. You could never guess in advance which would rise next.

('The *Berta vom Busch* could have been freighted for a good price and our ship the *Consul* is on its way to Wilhelmshaven,' my father said.)

The lights that my mother lit behind the curtain reflected in the glass doors of the book cabinets.

'Did you put water out?' she asked.

There were presents laid on each of the six side tables.

'Just look at the tree! Isn't it wonderful?' my sister asked the room.

My father confirmed that water had been put out.

'Last year our tree was bulky, but the year before last it was just a stalk.'

My brother received a globe, a Wild Game and Hound calendar – containing pictures of drovers who'd been shot at on a hunt – a tie pin and a pack of gramophone needles. The lines on the globe had been glued on sloppily, and the borders of Libya and Egypt didn't quite meet.

'Can you see,' said my brother, 'there are five hands of water on the earth and four hands of land.'

Germany was pretty damn tiny.

I got the *Through the Wide World* yearbook, which had brain teasers on the last page:

> Gaius Julius Caesar preferred to eat oysters
> And lampreys to cabbage and cow's cheese.

I also unwrapped a cuckoo clock that you built yourself, and a pin-up calendar that included the Austrian *Jänner* for the first month, not the German *Januar*.

My father smoked a good cigar and leafed through a book with pictures of ships in it. The bibliography began on page 210, much earlier than my father had anticipated. It wasn't a good sign of the quality of the book. He would have at least hoped to see a four-mast bark in there.

'Mother, what did you get?'

'Your love is all the gift I need,' she said, once again. 'Your father is no good at giving presents.' He'd never gotten her anything.

'You already have everything,' he always said.

He asked us to look at him from the side.

'Don't you think that, at some point, a little Jew has passed through the family?' he asked. 'This nose!'

My sister startled us by screaming all of a sudden, 'Secret Santa!' and throwing a packet across the room, ruining the good mood.

'Good grief,' said my brother, who was occupying himself with the cuckoo clock. He shook his head.

The Secret Santa was addressed to my mother. In the huge packet there was a small piece of paper with a message instructing her to go into the basement. There, on the meat safe, something fine was waiting for her.

'You sweet child,' said my mother, 'this really is unnecessary.'

My father breathed in sharply through his nose. A trick like this wasn't to his liking.

My mother returned with a small package: metal clips for holding cabbage rolls together. It was exactly what she wanted, she said.

'They're charming!'

'Well then, we can all sit down again now,' said my father.

Later, we went on to the balcony and looked out into the night. The blackout had its good side: Ursa Major – the Great Bear – was up above us, and the Siebengestern, the Seven Sisters, were behind us. There was also Ursa Minor, but I didn't know where to look for it.

The searchlights were a waste of space. As were the people working the sound detectors, who just sat at the machines twiddling the knobs. They ought to be thrown on the junk heap.

'Be quiet for a second, we might be able to hear the Krause family singing!' Robert whispered.

'If only it would snow now,' said my mother, before gently singing:

> I'm dreaming of a white Christmas
> Just like the ones I used to know . . .[2]

'Last year we were at your grandfather's, the good old man. We had to drink everything out of his red wine glasses.'

Where is he now? I wondered.

'Children, time to come inside or you'll catch your death,' my mother said.

'Yes,' said my father, 'blessed is he who has a home right now.'

*

As the days of high fever passed, I got quite comfortable in the attic. My sister's room had floral curtains, with table covers and a lampshade made from the same material. Her toy chest doubled as a night stand. She had a bookshelf in the corner of the room, which contained *Schnipp Fidelius Adelzahn* and *The Father* by Jochen Klepper. On her wall she had a reproduction of Hans Thoma's *Children Dancing a Roundelay*: dancing children from the country, their limbs wonderfully outstretched.

A thin wallpaper border, set in the middle of the wall, ran along the entire length of the bed, and above the head of the bed was a marble confirmation cross. Occasionally it fell down when I made the bed.

A little stuffed terrier made of varnished cambric sat on the bedside table, along with a little bell, and the cork containing the three tiny dice: a keepsake from Esau.

('Think of me whenever you throw three ones.')

My mother's constant cleaning annoyed me, though. Once a day she would come into the room and set to work. She even washed under the bed with Lysol.

'Do me a favour and stay in bed,' said my mother. 'Otherwise you'll have a relapse, and then you'll have to stay in bed for six more weeks.'

Relapses, she said, were usually worse than the actual sickness. You could go blind and deaf. Struck – or was it Stuhr? – also had scarlet fever, and Fat Krahl was a germ carrier.

In the afternoons she read aloud to me. It was a story about a group of good girls who set up a raffle, for orphans, but she never got to the end of it. She started crying every time. I could never tell whether she was crying because of the story, or because I was sick. She just sat on my bed sobbing.

('Doesn't she look like a countess?')

If she was in a more cheerful mood, she showed me how she could wiggle each of her fingers individually. I attempted this too, without success.

She always told me that she wasn't afraid of needles.

'Nothing's going to happen to me, I know that.'

Although a sickness at her age could mean big trouble and have serious consequences.

My father looked in on me in the afternoon when he came home from work. He stood by the door, which he opened with his elbows to avoid getting germs on his hands.

'Well, how's it going? Tell me, quick!'

He threw me a few chapbooks, which fluttered into the room like birds. Someone had told him I needed something to read. *Thrilling Stories*, they were called: thirty-two pages for 60 pfennigs.

I pulled them over to me with the walking stick. I got numbers 32, 15 and 7 in the series first; once I'd finished them, I slid them back for my father to collect.

One of the books was called *The Drumbeat of Death Before Ypres*. I remembered how the whole business with my father's skin stemmed from Flanders. He had told me how he danced with one of those 'cute little Belgian girls', after all. A story that my mother didn't like to hear. He also told me about the little rice cakes they had in Ghent, and how they'd requisitioned a piano, against the wishes of the populace. How they had begged and pleaded for it to be returned, but no, 'war is war'.

Another book was called *In a Sailboat to India* by Hans Zitt. He recounted how, in the middle of the Indian Ocean, a strong voice shouted, 'Get out!' He fell out of the sailboat and saw a wall of water as high as a house rolling towards him.

I needed books like that to see me through the hours of isolation. The bookstore kept an eye out for additional volumes for us, and told us that the first copies of the *War Book for German Youth* were coming out in January.

That should see me through, I thought.

Alongside my reading, I raised an army from my Halma pieces. The king was the one with gnarled wood on his belly – because he looked as though he were predestined to lead – and every company got a standard bearer: I drilled a hole in their head for the flagpole.

My mother ran around the entire city to ensure that my army grew. Sometimes I needed a few green Halma for the infantry, or some more black ones for the Waffen-SS. She drove all the way to Reutershagen on one occasion, as there was supposed to be another toy shop over there.

'What do you want with all these Halma pieces?' she was asked.

And before long, all of the shops were sold out. She only managed to get four from Heinemann, the paper merchant on our street. I was especially thrilled about those four, though, because they had grooves under their heads: they were enemy agents. For their misdeeds, these Halma men were sentenced to death. They had long conversations on the telephone with their wives before being drowned in the chamber pot.

'Those poor men,' my mother said, fishing them out again.

*

It was cold outside. The outdoor thermometer read minus sixteen degrees. The snow lay like a wall on both sides of the street, and sleighs with bells rode past. I counted them; they were ridden by nearby landowners or farmers, with big hats, and fur collars on their heavy jackets. Steam blew out of the horses' nostrils.

Frau District Court Counsellor Warkentin went out too. She tapped the ground ahead of her with a walking stick.

'She looks like she's walking on eggshells,' my father quipped.

Heinemann the paper merchant waved to her: 'Wow, what a mass of snow. I hope it all works out okay for your boys on the front . . .'

We hadn't had a winter like this in for ever, it was said.

'It was 1929, when you were born, that it was last this cold,' my mother said. 'Young girls were being sent to the clinics one after the other for issues with their wombs. The ones with thin underwear.

'The plumbing was all frozen, too. Your hands were always blue from frost. You could have walked to Denmark. Think about that.'

Icicles a metre long and as thick as your arm hung down from the glass roof of our balcony. If you got one of those to the head, it wouldn't be pretty . . . Ulla took photos with her box.

'You look like a walking corpse,' my brother said, when I came down from the attic for the first time. 'This must be a happy day for you?'

I was a jerk, a squirt, an old villain, he said.

In February, it was hard to find any heat. There was enough coal, but no wagons to distribute it. The schools were closed because of it too, and so I didn't have to go in at all.

My father called the mayor ('Kempowski here') to emphasise the fact that his wife had to get coal from the harbour by the hundredweight while, in the House of Estates, they were throwing the windows open.

'You have to admit that it's a mess, no?'

Despite the unpleasantness, Wally still came: we couldn't find a replacement.

Maybe it was a good thing. Who knew what else was coming? And who wanted a stranger in the apartment all the time?

13

In 1941 I pinned the recipients of the Knight's Cross over my bed. Mölders, Kretschmar and Günther Prien. ('You'll wreck the wallpaper, boy.') I cut Günther Prien, the victor at Scapa Flow, out of the *Berlin Illustrated*: he was larger than life, posing with a white telephone. I painted one of the corners with india ink, to mark his passing.

I wrote letters of support: *To an unknown soldier*. I never got an answer. Manfred also wrote to unknown soldiers, but he got a grenade fragment in the mail and a bag of buckwheat.

Manfred had inherited a collection of rifle rounds from his father: French and Polish, copper and brass. The French had even used dumdum rounds in the World War. An extra mechanism in the rifle so that the point of the bullet broke apart. They tore through the flesh in fist-sized holes. But dealing people as much harm as you could wasn't the whole point: you didn't necessarily want to kill them, they just had to be taken out of commission.

It was a gut shot that frightened Manfred the most: your green intestines hanging out, and the ground coming up at you. Because of this, soldiers weren't supposed to eat anything before an attack. Otherwise, if you were wounded the digested food got into the stomach cavity – pea soup or potato salad – and everything festered. If it were up to him, he'd rather get shot in the thigh. But only a flesh wound, of course. There was also concussion, or typhus – either of those would be better.

And no hand-to-hand combat! During an attack he'd pretend he had sprained his foot. Then later, when the whole thing was over, he'd stand up again.

Had we ever written a chain letter? Manfred wanted to know. They instructed you to make six copies of every letter, or else you got bad luck. If even a few people did that, the post office would be flooded. That's why it was strictly forbidden.

An astrologer who made only accurate predictions prophesied that the war would end in July.

> The conflict began in September,
> A year is quite long.
> Buy a new dress in April
> And by July it's all done.

The 'new dress' in question was the Africa Corps.

In Hamburg they'd imported an English steamer carrying a load of fat. The whole city could live off it for a month, a year even. And that was just one steamer, if you thought about it! But – Germany triumphs and triumphs; Germany triumphs to death. That was what Churchill said, at least according to the *Revaler Zeitung*.

Manfred and I were among the lucky few who got to take bike excursions with Hannes. We'd go out on Sunday mornings at five-thirty. He called us his 'natural history club'. We took Schmeil's plant directory with us and *What's That Blossoming?* from Kosmos.

'Did you pump the tyres up properly?'

The country road to Bad Doberan was the loveliest in all of Germany, Hitler was supposed to have once said.

'The trees are just magnificent. Like a cathedral.'

At the Convent Lake, we beat our way into the bushes. The air was full of birdsong. Hannes explained which song belonged to which bird. We just couldn't tell which song he was referring to at any given moment. The chaffinch was easy to identify though, that was the one that was always crying, 'I'm the Herr Forest Secretary.'

He even knew about the farmhouses. He showed us a rare gatehouse and cursed when one of the barns had been covered with corrugated iron again.

On the old houses the window hinges weren't attached to the frame, but rather to the mullion and transom, that was how you could recognise them.

Hannes showed us an old bible in a vicarage, and pointed out the various tools in a forge situated on a road lined with birches. The woman who worked there gave us milk and a piece of bread she had baked herself. We drank the milk and waited for Hannes while he left with her. He finally came back, carrying a metal bucket of honey, which he clipped to his bicycle rack.

Had we made the most of the time while we'd been waiting? Had we identified all the plants on the ridge? No? – He didn't understand us. How could we lumber around nature so blindly?

We saw storks once. The whole sky was full of them, circling.

'O do not disturb nature's celebration,' said Hannes. Any attempt to count them would have been in vain. And why would we even bother? Instead we lay down in the grass and looked up at the sky until our eyes swam.

In the museum there stood a stuffed stork with an arrow in its neck. A Negro arrow. Yes, there were bad people down in Africa.

*

Later that year a report came that Peule – a teacher from my school – had fallen in Yugoslavia, on the field of honour. He'd always worn such baggy suits.

'Kempowski stays after class for another hour.'

'. . . But Herr Doctor!'

'Kempowski stays after class for another *two* hours.'

'. . . But Herr Doctor!'

'Kempowski stays after class for another *three* hours.'

And now he was dead.

Hannes gave the memorial speech in the gym, among the dangling ropes. (We were never allowed to use the rings.)

'Peule was a wonderful human being, a diligent student of Latin, a humanist from the crown of his skull to the soles of his feet. And here' – he paused, searching between the bars, ladders, and poles for an appropriate place – 'a bronze plaque will one day stand in his memory.'

Then Hannes spoke of the godly life in war, raising both of his arms emphatically, as he always did when counting out a sum in his head. We knew what to do. We'd been drilled after all, hadn't we? At once, all of the students jumped up. The teachers however were none the wiser, and simply looked around confused, stretching themselves tall. Had the district leader shown up?

Hannes protested, but to no avail.

'Stop it, stop it!'

Everyone stood still. In front of me Eckhoff stood especially straight: he stood for Germany.

The time is hard and will get even harder.
The warrior needs steel-hard comrades in his struggle.[1]

Finally, the dishevelled headteacher gave us the pitch for the national anthem. It was much too low, as it soon turned out.

From the Maas to the Memel,
From the Etsch to the Belt![2]

We saluted throughout the anthem, despite our arms growing heavier and heavier. We ended up leaning our arms on the person in front of us for support.

We were told to wait behind afterwards, while Hannes gathered up his papers. The principal climbed up to the podium to inform us that the wearing of caps in school was forbidden. But we knew that already. He reached into his breast pocket, where, as we all knew, he'd hidden a flask of schnapps. But he left it there.

Then, another announcement – 'Shut your mouth, there in the back, yes I mean you!' – he had already let it be known among the faculty, he'd already ordered it to be said, during dictation, during transcription, that 'improvements' would now be called 'corrections'.

That was bad German.

The BBC had even mentioned the thing with the caps in school, my brother later said.

'All of a sudden I'm thinking, I can't be hearing this right.'

We still had biology with Hannes before the end of the day, unfortunately. He was telling us about the primordial cell: life must have started somewhere, after all.

Because I could wiggle my ears, I was presented to the class as a kind of Neanderthal. I had developed out of the ooze.

Schulze, the music teacher, had one leg longer than the other. He would stand on the pedestal and bang out the beat against its side with the longer one, the one that hung down.

He cursed terribly through a song: 'Great Moors' or something like that.

> Let the youth, the youth
> Run along their path . . .[3]

Our music classes were soon cut.

Our class teacher that year was Dr Finck, a little man with sharp glasses, or 'Liesing,' as they called him, from *liesing* or 'very quiet' in German, since he spoke so quietly.

'He looks like he swallowed a globe,' my mother commented.

You couldn't put anything over on him: one of the students had to write *Liesing* a thousand times because he'd shouted out, 'Liesing's coming!'

If you didn't know the answer to a question he'd pinch the skin of your upper arm. 'Vitamin P', he called it. Blomert even got a few lashings from his stick for saying vandals instead of the German *Wandaler*.

Most of the students avoided the need to wear a tie, instead opting for a sleeveless sweater, a *Schwubber*. (We were no longer permitted to call them 'pull-unders', as we once had.)

One day, Liesing flicked my tie out of my jacket.

'Hey, look at this fancy prig: he comes to school with his tie on. Though it seems he has something against barbers . . . Or is it that your father can stretch to buy you a tie, but is too poor to afford a haircut? Should I lend you the money?'

He picked up my comb with two fingers and threw it out the window.

I inherited my brother's history book.

'A thoroughly worked-through copy', as he called it. He'd underlined the word 'Nordic' on every page. In the back he'd sketched pictures of giant graves and the Oseberg ship. The King's Tomb of Seddin also featured. The class was interested in knights and castles too, and asked endless questions about the *Dansker* – that is, the toilet.

Liesing had been to England in the 20s. He told us about it now and then.

'You can't open or close any windows there; there's only windowpanes – so-called English windows – and they swell.

'And they use the standard system of measurements!

'And they think they're going to win the war!'

Not long after independence, there had been a debate in the American Congress on whether American English or German would be introduced as the nation's administrative language. The vote had come out a tie. But one pastor – and a German at that – broke the deadlock. We had this man to thank for the whole mess. If only the American farmer boys, fresh off the boat, hadn't shown up . . .

> The German has laboured over all the world,
> Laboured and toiled, and lost it all anyhow,
> Because he is the lowest of the low, a credulous fool . . .[4]

Klaus Greif raised his hand. He had read a story in which a German captain was accosted by a Jewish American. This guy stepped too close to him, so the captain laid him out with a single blow.

'A threat is as good as an action,' Liesing said strictly.

In geography, Liesing put particular emphasis on the term 'watershed'. He didn't seem to care about anything, but we had to know what a watershed was. To demonstrate, he used the class book and broke its spine.

He illustrated folds in the earth's crust with a handkerchief. He held the edges of the fabric and slowly pushed the corners together.

'This is how the Alps came to be.'

'I can recite the whole thing with the book closed,' Liesing liked to say.

> Marienburg's red reef rides defiantly in the east,
> From St Thomas's organ Bach sends fugue after fugue
> into the ship . . . [5]

We were supposed to learn the whole poem, all the cities, all the landmarks. Then we'd know all of Germany by heart.

'How is it,' my brother had asked Liesing once, 'that the waves beat on the beach in Warnemünde and also in Denmark? Surely the water has to change direction somewhere . . .?'

'The Kempowskis are interested in everything out of the ordinary,' he replied, 'but they know nothing about the matter at hand.'

During the Norwegian campaign we had to learn all of the fjords. Then there was always a map of Africa hanging on the easel, and we'd hear of the passage from Marsa Matruh to El-Alamein. (In the newsreel, we watched soldiers fry eggs on their tank: that's how hot the iron got.)

Our homework: What does all of this have to do with India?

In German he assigned the essay topic 'The *Thingstätte*': we were supposed to describe one as vividly as possible. They were built a few years before as open-air theatres, but they were mostly used to house troop deployments during layovers.

'Are we imagining it as empty or full?' asked Struck or Stuhr.

Fat Krahl wrote that they were about four and a half omnibuses wide.

We were supposed to avoid using foreign words. Borrowed words, too, if possible. But using *Löschhorn* instead of nose, because *Nase* was supposedly English, was silly, and finding a substitute for *Interesse* – 'interest' – was tough.

> German language, when I hear you,
> Mother! Life! Then faith follows.
> You, o blissful land,
> Are mine as something profound.[6]

What was the difference between seeing, *sehen*, and watching, *schauen*? Which did we think was the more significant act?

One dictation began with the words

> It astonishes me and almost makes me
> Sorry, that you weren't
> More careful in your
> Dangerous undertaking . . .[7]

That had about as many tricky spellings as a sentence could have.

But what kind of dangerous undertaking it was, was never said.

When the *Bismarck* sank, Liesing tripped up while trying to write about it on the blackboard: was 'Bismarck' spelled with a *ck* or with just a *k*?

'After *l*, *n*, *r*,' I'd say, 'never write *tz*, and never *ck*': it was a rule that was made to be broken, one that could trip up even the cleverest person; that's how rich the German language was.

Stüwe, my classmate, knew everything there was to know about Bismarck, down to the last detail. He was born on 1 April and got his middle name Bismarck from his father, he told us.

By his own admission Liesing kept a card file where he wrote down information about his students. He wanted to see how their lives turned out later.

'You've turned out to be a very respectable man,' he once said to my father.

Liesing had also adopted three children, my brother told me:

'Very honourable.'

'But strange,' said my mother, 'they were all good-for-nothings. That's how it is with most adopted children . . .'

No one had any idea where they came from.

'Probably adopted from well-off families,' was what everyone said, 'but they always turned out to be completely anti-social.'

'No, I would never do it,' said my mother.

*

The show times at the movies (*Ride for Germany*) had to be changed because of the long newsreels. War stories from all over the world. To save money, two cinemas got just one newsreel between them. The projectionist from one cinema rode it over to the other by bicycle.

There were first-hand accounts in the newspaper:

The first major attack against Coventry was quite the affair. The aircraft mechanic looked up out of the chancellery at the unbelievable wall of flame. Poor Tommy, you're in for another rough night.

Ulla's dance instructor was already a lieutenant. Lieutenant Maurer.

'Now that I've got something here,' he said, pointing to the officer's cord of his cap, 'I have to get something *here*,' gesturing towards the empty medal mounts.

The leader of the flight mission said: 'Well, men. Now it's time for us to do our bit, eh?'

The crew's assigned target was a factory in the south of the city. It wasn't hard to fly up and drop another row of bombs on them.

Uncle Richard became a colonel. It was said that another of my uncles was going to be an *Ober* soon.

'What's an "*Ober*"?' my father asked.

An *Oberzahlmeister* was master purser – an officer rank.

'You don't see something like that every day,' he said. He flew a wide pass to show the men the destruction of a city.

> The flak defence of Coventry was pitiful.
> The British defence was laughable.
> How quietly all
> The dead are resting.

That summer, Father got leave from work. He still hadn't been drafted though. His military cap was now hung in the wardrobe instead of his boater. ('Impeccable thing, that.')

He had his first mission under his belt: a munitions transport to Brussels. He had shown up for training in his leather gaiters and riding trousers from the World War.

'Father looks like a figure out of a shooting gallery,' my brother commented.

'But Herr Comrade,' the major had said, 'you can't walk around looking like that.'

He was furious when he came back from France. There was so much being plundered. No, there wouldn't have been anything like that in the World War. He was defeated. A boy in his battalion had wanted to give him golden spoons that he'd stolen from a castle.

My mother got grey fabric, with a fishscale pattern. She paid for it fair and square.

'It's just typical,' said my mother: he hadn't thought of the boys, or of Ulla; they needed something to wear too. 'Every maid is running around in a fur coat now.'

My father had let us down; he was so caught up with propriety. And he hadn't brought back a single bar of chocolate either. He had, however, returned with a case of Petit Beurre.

'They do taste great,' my brother said, snatching up one biscuit after another.

A large number of troop transports were heading towards East Prussia. Freighters full of soldiers were massing in the harbour.

'They're ten-thousand-tonners,' said my father. 'They wouldn't have got into the harbour if they were any heavier. But the soldiers were light, so it's just deep enough.'

Things were looking bad in the east, too. Something was brewing.

In March the *Consul* hit a mine and sank off the coast from Wilhelmshaven. The captain had been able to shout, 'Abandon ship!' just before a tear seven metres long opened up underwater. A machinist hadn't made it out; divers found him clinging to the stairs. The insurance company was negotiating with the Reich now regarding a payout.

'Maybe we'll get a modern ship,' said my father. 'One with all the bells and whistles.'

A map of Europe hung over the sofa in our living room. Colourful drawing pins marked how big Germany was growing. They were bound with red cotton thread from the sewing table.

'Verdun has fallen,' the news announcer said laconically, as though it were nothing special.

'By golly,' my father shouted, 'that's great!'

One day, he noted, we'd have to buy a picture of the Führer. Maybe the one where he's wearing a coat and looking over his shoulder.

'He looks very wise in that one.'

'The French are a people without culture,' said my brother. 'They have no famous musicians whatsoever.'

'They do,' said my father, 'César Franck made good music.' And they'd written good books too: Émile Zola, for one. 'You'll have to read some one day. *J'accuse* is all about the misdeeds in the army and the judiciary. It must be very corrupt there.'

Ulla was supposed to report for work duty soon. At her prom she would be singing 'Fritze Bollmann' as a minstrel, her flat cap askew on her head.

'I'm looking forward to that,' said Robert, 'you're going to get a maiden dress with a brooch.'

The pear tree in our garden blossomed, and behind it, as ever, stood St Jacob's with its green tower. The landlord, Dr Krause, walked across the yard breathing deeply. The air was thick with pollen.

Otto Reber – whose name was a palindrome – had fallen in Greece. But Fraulein Reber wasn't sad about it at all; she was happy, celebratory.

At the table we wanted to know whether there'd be another leftovers day, like those the Pfundig family always had in the comic strips. Would we be having a Pfundig potluck? No, but there was noodle casserole with potatoes; a meal that my father loved.

He demanded to see my school report. ('Show me, quick.') His skin was dry: no oozing spots at all.

'Do you get called on? Do you have the right answers? You must always work hard, and you must always raise your hand!'

By golly, the food was hot. ('Cooked on fire!') The potatoes especially: they held heat.

My brother hadn't done his maths homework for a long time. It was the Polish in him coming out.

'You're not hiding anything from us, are you, boy?'

'Starting tomorrow morning I'll show you every single assignment I'm given when we sit down for dinner,' my brother promised.

'It's no wonder you're able to give them the runaround,' my mother chimed. 'All the teachers are so old! They were looking forward to their pensions and now they have to work again.'

'It's truly sad that Peule Wulff died,' my mother said. 'How did he even make it into the military? He was always so impractical . . . It's a good thing you're older, Karl, you're definitely not getting sent to the front.'

She would never comprehend why he'd even enlisted. They probably wouldn't take Robert either, she reasoned, what with his thick glasses: if he had to boot up and enter the fray he wouldn't be able to see a thing. And I, thank God, was too young: the little Peterpump. 'He'll be staying with Mummy when all the others go away.'

'What do you want to be when you're eventually called up?' my father asked.

'Flak,' I said.

'Why flak?'

'They're always at the back.'

That wasn't very brave, now, was it?

14

Often, of an evening, I would idly play the piano. Sometimes my mother would whistle along with the melody, and when I didn't know how the rest of the piece went, she held the note and felt for the next few, as if to show me the way.

Frau Kröhl – who belonged to the Rosary Society – stood by the radiator in the dining room and listened.

'What a light touch he has.'

Occasionally I would make use of the transposing lever to shift into a minor key.

'Can't you play something a little higher up on the keyboard?' my brother asked, pointing out all the keys that I hadn't touched. 'What about "Harlem on a Saturday Night"? Now that's a snappy piece. And the left hand goes like, *bum-da, bum-da, bum-da*. Do you want to hear the record? It's got "Fate" on the other side too . . .'

'What a lovely head Walter has,' said my father, 'look at it: he's got lots stored away in there.'

He told us about Frau Lübbers, his piano teacher. He'd never got anywhere with her, naturally. She'd only given him stale cookies, which he threw out of the window right away.

> You've got no clue,
> You little doe, you[1]

He'd started again when he turned thirty. But properly this time, learning to play off the sheet with Löffelholz, the leader of the orchestra (*Dances of the League of David*).

'Oh, I remember how Frau Speer tried and tried with your father,' my mother laughed. '"Please stop, Herr Kempowski, I can't bear it!" She was a really nice woman.'

I had piano lessons every Thursday. I brushed my hair with water beforehand and went off to the conservatoire with Schumann's *Childhood Scenes* under my arm.

Each time, I went by Samuel the factory owner's green villa. Once, in November 1938, he'd left records strewn across the lawn, and his curtains were blowing out of the shattered windows.

My lessons took place in the conservatoire in Schillerplatz, a triangular park with a fountain in the middle, which wasn't usually running.

On the building's white gable there was a stone jug with stone grapes. Whether the building would remain a conservatoire or one day become a high school was much discussed at the time.

I was afraid before every lesson. I didn't practise systematically and the Schnabel woman ('the best we have to offer you!') wasn't very much fun.

The entrance to the conservatoire – a wide portal – was always nailed shut, and so I had to go round the back. (PLEASE CLEAN YOUR FOOTWEAR CAREFULLY!) The voice of a singer who was constantly correcting himself would drift up from the basement:

> An evening wind whispers in the ge-entle a-arbour

In the hall, a fireplace with cardboard boxes full of old forms. Hung above them, Beethoven under glass; a print in a gold frame.

The silver bells of May tinkle in the grass . . .[2]

There was the plinking of piano keys on the second floor, doors slamming. Girls appeared, carrying violins. One of them was Gina Quade: she was the daughter of the architect who had designed the building we lived in. She wore a dark blue pleated dress and a so-called Mozart braid.

A pale seminarian usually had his lesson before mine. He wore tennis shoes. His mother was a chorus singer in the theatre. He probably longed to make something of himself some day.

The Schnabel woman's lower body stuck out, such that she looked like a triangle. Through the doorway, I would see her waddling around the room. Her grey hair was sealed to the back of her head in a vast number of plaits.

I went up to her warmly, as though I were happy to see her again. She stuck out her hand to me briefly and said, 'Don't keep me waiting like that.' It was two minutes past. She then set the stool a few notches higher ('Wait a second') and looked at the barometer.

'Now, I'm curious to see whether you've practised,' she said.

She'd set etudes; short sequences that ran over the whole keyboard, sometimes with the left hand, sometimes with the right. Then in parallel with both hands. They were to be carried out with fluid hand movements.

'Gentle! Soft!' she shouted between each one. 'Raise! Lower! And – rest.'

I had to learn to separate my hands, was what that meant. It was difficult. I checked the clock: seven minutes had gone by. (That's half of the first third of the lesson.)

When I played a false note, which didn't take long, the Schnabel woman investigated my nails. I had to stand at the window while she inspected them.

'Give them here. What funny hands . . . The nailbed comes out so far . . . I've never seen anything like it.'

She pointed out that the fourth finger is the weakest, as that's where the tendons cross.

'Yes, my mother has said that,' I replied. 'She can move all of her fingers individually, one at a time.'

'Now's not the time for idle chat.'

Once we'd finished playing through the etudes she would get the assignment book out of her bag and open it up. (Fifteen minutes gone, that's the first third.) It was now time for the pieces, beginning with Schumann's 'The Poet Speaks'.

'Hurry up a bit,' she said: she was dying to see whether I'd practised, she'd be really quite amazed if I had . . . These opening phrases were to be carried out with the wrist, the staccato from the elbow; they were feminine and masculine phrases, respectively.

'*Da – dia – dam!* And – two.'

(Seventeen minutes gone.)

'Can't you hear that?'

Yes, I could hear it.

Now, the cadenza. Father would play this passage so beautifully in the evenings, when I was lying in bed reading (*Paul from the Serpentini Circus*).

'Don't guess what you're doing; *know* what you're doing!'

I wasn't supposed to say 'Lord God'.

'Leave God out if it,' Fraulein Schnabel would say, 'he can't help you now.' Instead I was supposed to say 'Lord Walter'.

'Keep going!'

Try as I might, though, it wasn't coming together. Was I sitting too far to the left? Were the keys unusually wide? Perhaps it was because my trousers were too tight?

'You're not paying attention to your fingering, are you?' Frau Schnabel had already sunk back, her head shaking. 'Well?'

I remained mute; it was almost exhilarating. But while I was trying to figure out where I even was in the score, she suddenly snapped, throwing her pencil against the keys (*pling!*), screaming: 'You didn't practise again, did you?'

The lacquer on the keys was chipped from all the times she'd done this. Her veins were throbbing.

'I swear you think I'm a clown. Now listen up and listen good! You sit there like a piece of quartz. You haven't practised at all!'

And she took my fingers like cigars and pressed hard on the keys. 'Like that, and that, and that! That's how it's done.

'Have you lost it completely? Like that, that, and that – *da dia-dam*. Is it really so hard?'

Her gestures became wilder and wilder, and finally my tears began to fall on to the keys. (Twenty-five minutes, that was half the lesson.)

Seeing this, she sprang up, nudged the plain bronze cross atop the piano back into place, set the chairs right and wound up the metronome, while I sat there sniffling.

'We'll have to start right from the beginning,' she said. 'I suppose I'll have to teach you like I would a little child.' (That exhilaration again.) 'Maybe we should swap to playing a birthday march, or some simple jazz?'

She snapped the red point of her pencil while writing *Practice!* in my notebook. She added several thick lines beneath it, and the paper bunched up beneath the force of the strokes. (Twenty-six minutes gone.)

She thundered out a new piece to distract me ('Snap out of it!') and as she played she screamed at me: 'Reprise! Interlude! Cadence!'

'Look: for people who practise a lot, their thumb muscle bulges out.' She let it swell out, like a pink block of metal. She even let me touch it. It felt like cold chicken meat.

'Maybe we should have a go at a Tschopang, that would certainly be fun for you.' (Forty minutes.) Tschopang was a Pole, but had lived in France.

Instead she searched my eyes. Noticing how red they were, she said: 'Well I'll be . . . It's fine. Pack up.'

She waddled to the padded door, where a photo of Edwin Fischer was hanging. '*That's* a pianist . . . Now, pull yourself together a little.'

A girl called Heidi Kleßman stood outside.

A flower from the ashes of my heart.[3]

She wore her blond hair in a topknot. Her left canine stood at something of an angle, and a little chip had splintered off it. We danced around one another as I left the room. Left-right, left-right . . .

'Well, which way am I supposed to go?' she asked. Eventually she pulled the squeaking door shut behind herself.

As I left I saw her bicycle by the fence. It had big tyres and a strange seat; it wasn't like a boys' saddle, the front tipped upward.

*

The annual recital took place in July, just before the holidays. All the parents sat in the hall. Crates containing organ pipes that had yet to be unpacked were moved into the basement beforehand.

My mother sat – grey cotton-wool balls in the taut net of her hat – continuously waving to me.

('Tchaikovsky's head was always too heavy for him. That's what it said in the book *Beloved Friend* . . . And Beethoven's Fifth is the one that keeps climbing higher and higher. Little by little, I'm learning about all of it. It'll be very lovely to sit through the recital, none the less.')

Next to her sat Frau District Court Counsellor Warkentin.

'Ade-la-i-hide-!' her son sang.

The Schnabel woman had selected a piece for me that was intended for first-year students. It came together well. Afterwards she said I'd come at the thing so fast that she'd thought I wasn't going to make it through.

After me, the vigorous Eckhoff played the violin, with his curly hair and trousers that were far too short. ('You can practically see his thingaling . . .') He let the bow skip, like the gypsies did. He expressed his gratitude for the applause by giving the German salute.

Heidi Kleßman played a piece called 'Kasperle'. It went *rummel-dummel-dumm!* and *rimmel-dimmel-dimm!* Red pom-poms hung from her dark blue dress. They were set into the most intense motion by her movement at the keys.

Gina Quade was supposed to close out the performance with a piece by Brahms. But she failed within several bars.

Professor Maßlow stood up, breathing heavily. He was the director, and had two grand pianos in his apartment. He ran his hand over Gina's Mozart braid before leading her, crying, into a back room.

'Thank the good, great, glorious Lord that's behind you,' said my mother at the supper table.

'Yes, a happy day,' my brother said, before asking: 'Did anyone play the "Rage Over a Lost Penny"? And was the applause frenetic? It never fails to get the crowd going . . .'

My father opened his wallet. Then, changing his mind, he took some crumpled banknotes from the cookie jar, and gathered together some change from the leather sheaf, before handing it all to me. Then, he snatched up a radish rose and bit into it with a crack. 'Who's the *Lebenswurst* from?' he asked.

'From MM.'

'Then it'll be good.'

MM was Max Müller.

'What a wonderful head he has . . . Maybe sometime we could play four-handed,' my father suggested. There were whole symphonies we could play, Bruckner and Tchaikovsky.

'Shall I buy some sheet music for us? It needn't be anything too fast, as long as it conveys emotion.'

'There's nothing Polish in me,' said my mother. Frau District Court Counsellor Warkentin had said that of her, not realising that our family's ties to Poland were from my father.

'What a nice son you have,' she'd said too. 'He sure is loved.'

My father stuck his napkin in his pocket. It looked like his shirt had come untucked. (I remembered how someone had walked up to the podium looking like that once at a recital.)

Who falls from the horse when it farts?

That's the Kaiser's cadet.[4]

My father slapped the table (*bang!*), and leapt into the story of how his father had once practised scales (up the scale, down the scale, schnapps!, up the scale, down the scale, schnapps!) before (*bang!*), a story of the Salvation Army, where a man with a kettle drum sneaked up behind a singer (*bang!*), and what a face Kröhl had made at the electric piano.

'Children, I can't any more!' cried my mother, her handkerchief in front of her mouth. 'Oh, how funny it is! Oh, how hilarious!'

And Ulla gasped: 'Oh! I'm going to wet myself!'

'Do you remember the first SA men marching by below? I can see it like it was happening today,' said my mother.

They always sang:

'To Adolf Hit –

And then for a long while nothing came and then it went on:

– ler we have sworn'[5]

'I thought they were binmen at first! I said, "Karl, what kind of garbage men are these?" – No, how is it even possible?'

15

Because I played the piano, I was placed in the Hitler Youth Musical Troop. This entailed reporting for duty with a violin, and ready to sing. There would supposedly soon be a painting troop too. Apparently the Painting Scouts had an armband that depicted a brush and palette. A lyre had been requested for us, but no one knew whether we were going to get it: the triangle for our region and the victory rune would appear on our left arm; on our right, a silver lyre on a red swastika. The higher ranks would probably get a golden lyre, we thought.

> Holy Fatherland
> In danger,
> A show of weapons flashes
> In every hand . . .[1]

One of our number could play marches such as 'Greetings to Kiel' on the piano. I couldn't keep up, stuck as I was with my Schumann.

Löffelholz, the son of the concert master who had taught my father to play the piano, was the troop leader there. He had a head like a box of cigars, and he conducted with his fist.

I'd been told to pass on a hello to his father, and to ask how he was doing.

'He can't complain,' Löffelholz said. 'Tell your father hello. How's he doing?'

And how were things with my mother, someone else asked. I was supposed to tell her hello as well. Because Löffelholz spoke with an accent, no one had any idea what he was on about.

We had service together with the girls.

> Out of the walls of the grey city . . .[2]

The fat female troop leader was out in front with a flute whenever they approached. While we sat and sang on the left side of the church, they sang on the right side. In between us was no man's land. In front of the 'maidens' we were supposed to take a little pause and give them a 'mischievous' look.

Their dresses had to be buttoned up, and belts were not permitted. Gina Quade wore a simple, dark blue pleated dress – her parents probably hadn't wanted to pay extra. She wore glasses when we played a quartet. She kept squinting over at Eckhoff, who also found himself here, on account of his violin-playing. He had an aristocratic profile, what with his short curly hair: it really was something to admire.

We would speculate that maybe one day they would send us to entertain the troops in a military hospital, or on the radio.

In the summer we danced in a forest meadow, amid yarrow, butterbur, and probably creeping bugleweed too.

> If there's a pot with beans,
> And there's a pot with brie,

Then I'll leave the brie and beans alone
And dance with my Marie[3]

'It's a shame *Midsummer Night's Dream* can't be played any more,' my father always said; it was by Mendelssohn after all. 'Such wonderful music, though. Fine and dandy, indeed.'

'Yes, quite enchanting, simply lovely. There was always such applause from the orchestra pit, no?' my mother contributed.

When you danced, you had to make as though you were either falling forward or backward, as though you couldn't hold yourself up straight. We were to place our hands on our hips. Löffelholz demonstrated.

'It's funny, you'll see, it'll be very funny.' And the fat female troop leader demonstrated too, and also found it funny.

Once we'd mastered that we would finally dance a ribbon dance. We would need a stick and long, colourful ribbons that crossed over one another – like life itself, which also ran along tangled paths – and a dance floor, of course; we'd also need that. You couldn't stamp your feet defiantly here.

To get out of dancing, I claimed that my great aunt had died, and withdrew into the shade of the trees. When I said 'great-aunt' I was thinking of Aunt Silbi. If only we could have played a scouting game, maybe one against the girls.

Klaus Bismarck Stüwe said he'd fractured his foot and sat next to me. He showed me the Warnemünde pine, so tall you could supposedly see all the way to the sea from the top. Presumably you could also see the Warnemünde pine tree from the sea. But only when the weather was clear.

Down below, Gina Quade hooked Eckhoff and leapt into the

circle. His green führer's braid dangled, and now and then Gina's pleated dress offered a glance at her well-formed calves and her little brown socks.

Löffelholz shouted: 'Easy! Softly! And – stop.'

While the dancers, wheezing, took a break – Gina tumbled into her circle of girlfriends – the corpulent female führer trudged up to us.

'Fatty-fat-fat,' Klaus Bismarck Stüwe whispered. 'How she must be sweating.'

She stood before us and made as though to throw us out. She was fed up with our shenanigans; we were real drags. 'Don't you at least want to clap along to the rhythm? Or does the news of your aunt mean you can't do that either?'

*

In winter we headed out with our collection boxes. We sold colourful wooden figurines for 20 pfennigs each. The suggestion that each scout should always be accompanied by a young girl was rejected.

Klaus Bismarck Stüwe danced for joy when I told him we were partners. We were supposed to start at the Rostock Bank and go all the way up to Ratschow Linenmakers.

'Well, let me see,' said a passer-by, adding coins to our collection box. 'Wow, it's pretty heavy already.'

We met old ladies dressed all in black, soldiers, a lady conductor. I was to keep an eye on my teeth, she said, give them a good brushing every morning and every evening – after every mealtime if I could: they were still so nice and healthy.

Other people pointed to their coat without a word, highlighting that they already had something hanging there.

One man was dead set on the Moor, as he didn't have any yet.

'You can have a knight, we're out of Moors,' we offered. But he already had a knight.

'I don't have any small notes or change' was a good excuse.

'We take large notes too,' Stüwe would say.

But there was trouble when he stood in the way of an old man with a pince-nez. Holding the box under his nose, Stüwe said, 'You *have* to give us something . . .'

Then a crash, as the man struck him aside, clearing a path with his umbrella.

'That is quite enough! What do you mean, *have to*!'

'That was probably Krasemann,' my mother said when I returned home, 'that's so typical of him, he always gets worked up. He used to be a Social Democrat; he's just bitter.'

My mother stitched me a kind of flag out of blackout material, on which I could pin the badges I'd received over time. I had butterflies made of porcelain; beetles preserved in glass; runes pressed in leather.

'It's coming together into something quite pretty . . .'

'But not all of these badges belong to you,' Robert said, pulling out his watch. 'Some of them belong to me too. You're getting to be quite a criminal . . .'

On Christmas Day, the Musical Troop performed a cantata in the Stadttheater.

We're looking for a homey home . . .

This had been inflicted on us by a violinist in the City Orchestra. Egon Warkentin sang the solo; he was a soldier now. Over his Iron Cross he wore the Service Medal of the Hitler Youth.

We're looking for a homey home
And forgot what street it's on . . .[4]

I was supposed to play Tom Thumb.

The troop leader gave a speech in which he called December by its pagan name *Wintermond* – Winter Moon – and cursed Jesus. 'Child of light,' it was supposed to go, 'Baldur the Primordial Light is there.'[5]

He wore breeches and leather boots with a substantial heel, to imply that he occasionally went out riding. We looked up into the girders under the roof and touched the cyclorama as he spoke.

As the speech wore on, some people began to feel unwell. They were given permission to rest behind the stage, and a regular relief duty was organised. ('Now you go, and now you,' so everyone had a turn.) There was a lot of clutter – and dirt – behind there.

'What's that chair for?' someone whispered.

'It's the chair for the curtain puller,' came the reply.

Finally the speech was done. The *Kreisleiter* shuffled his papers together and strode off to the side.

Löffelholz said: 'Keep standing for just a moment!'

The *Kreisleiter* would want to express his gratitude to us. He had the feeling that this was the best yuletide in years. But the *Kreisleiter* didn't come, he was in a rush.

'You all did your part very well,' said my mother. 'Your troop leader – just wonderful.'

She loved clapping, even though it wasn't permitted at a celebration. But what the district leader had said was truly outrageous.

'How is it possible? Saying "Child of Light" and all that pagan nonsense. I could never say that myself, otherwise I'd be in a hell of a lot of trouble. Do you hear me?'

16

'You're supposed to take your uniform off,' my brother said when I arrived home. I now had a grey knickerbocker suit; my mother had saved up enough ration points to buy it. I'd much rather be wearing the suit than my uniform.

I looked in the mirror on the dressing table. Yes, it looked fine. All I had to worry about now was the fact that my head was shaped like a cucumber.

'And make sure to wash properly, you're getting mouldy,' my brother shouted through.

He held the burning cigarette clumsily, so his fingers turned properly brown. They were North State, four in a pack.

Yesterday he'd sat up half the night writing an essay for class. ('English and Japanese Formations of Empire, a Comparison'.) I ought to see his fingers. The same would happen to me. I could count on it.

Once, he was carefully cutting his nails. 'Why're you doing that?' I asked.

'For the simple reason that I want to learn to play the piano,' he said. 'Or do you think you have a monopoly?'

But nothing came of his piano-playing: he was scared of the Schnabel woman.

Whenever his friends came over I pulled up a seat to join them. Sylvia and Sybille, both long-legged, wearing grey trousers that were rolled up slightly.

Sylvia told me that I shouldn't hold out my hand to her so limply: 'You've got to squeeze.'

They asked whether I was a troop leader yet and whether I was getting into fights. Sybille, with her black hair, barely looked at me.

'Blast, I can't come to Krefeld now, what with the air raids. I'd been *so* looking forward to it,' she said.

I ought to stand up right away and let *her* sit down, Robert said.

Heini asked whether we had any orangeade for her.

'Can't you rustle something up?'

Bubi strode uneasily through the room. He found it a real drag when Ulla was at her work detail, so he started idly throwing pebbles into the courtyard from the balcony.

He came back into the room wearing a napkin ring as a monocle. Did we know who started the war? He mimed the moustache: Hitler. And now Wagner was being played again, while Bubi reeled off the parts of the cycle: *The Valkyrie*, *Twilight of the Gods*, *Siegfried*. He always forgot the fourth one.

'Oh yes, *Rheingold*.'

'It's grim in Berlin; Marion is depressed,' Michael said, dressed in his russet double-breasted suit and speaking with his usual lisp. He had received a draft notice.

'The army, at least that way you get to see something. France will be a lot of fun – the Eiffel Tower, Montmartre – or Denmark; there ought to be something going on there.'

Anywhere but Russia – that was the main thing.

My father was in Pomerania at this time, and Ulla was detailed as a maid. After the whole incident with my sister, when he'd tried to kiss her, it was only occasionally that Schneefoot got up the courage to come to our apartment.

'You have to be able to forgive and forget,' my mother said to me.

Schneefoot's father had brought back a tiny radio for him from Holland in a case with a travel seal – a Philips – along with records that allegedly couldn't be broken.

'But surely you still have to be careful with them?' my brother asked, before letting them roll over the carpet.

'Well, that's glorious,' he said, seeing that they were undamaged. He was green with envy.

Robert kept French magazines in his bedside cabinet. I wasn't allowed to see them. A tanned woman stood at the kitchen table, topless, examining a dead fish; an ugly man with a flintlock musket, hunting duck; a woman emerging from behind some swampy birch trees, grinning.

Later in the magazine, this woman and the ugly hunter were both in a cabin. In the first picture in the series, she's lying down while he looks through the window. Picture 2: he sits at the edge of the bed. Picture 3: he's on the bed, with his shirt open. It continued, as text, in French.

Heini sat at the radio, switching between two stations, asking us which piece of music was better. The group talked about how Art Tatum was blind and how Chick Webb was crippled; how Artie

Shaw could manage to play classical as well as jazz, and how Teddy Stauffer could conduct.

In the shade of an old apple tree . . .

They would call their friends and hold the receiver in front of the loudspeaker.

. . . where the love in your eyes I could see . . .[1]

They would try to write down the lyrics as the songs played.

They found good records in Löhrer-Wessel's second-hand shop. If you wanted to buy a new record, you had to give up two old ones. Through this they made some terrific discoveries: 'Black Beauty', a piano solo from Duke Ellington, fished out of the second-hand section; they gave Beethoven's quartets in exchange.

'Beethoven is shit.'

'Don't say that. . . ' said the shopkeeper.

Robert had another record up his sleeve that evening.

'It's cracked, completely bust.' He was going to play it for the last time. 'Everyone up; no more sitting around.'

Everyone listened, smitten, all except for Sybille. She crossed one leg over the other and leafed through the *Berliner* while it played. She hadn't had anything to smoke for hours, but no one cared about that, did they?

On one of those evenings the record needles ran out, so they tried using cactus spines instead.

Lieutenant Maurer, Ulla's dance instructor, wanted to join them. He wore his watch on the underside of his wrist, and had fifty-six hand-grenade fragments in his body.

('Sunk in the muck, I grabbed a rope with my teeth, and a tank pulled me out. Honest, you don't have to believe me.' Things didn't always go elegantly in war. Why, for example, would you open a door when you could just drive into it with an assault gun?)

He had a 'hot' record or two, could he join the club? They agreed on a trial period. He wasn't allowed to wear a silver chain, only a gold one.

Once, hoping to fit in, I attached a little chain to my jacket. 'Are you out of your mind?' Heini asked, and tore it off.

My mother comforted me. She wiped tears from my eyes with her handkerchief, which smelled like eau de cologne, and said she'd go with me to Ehler, the jeweller, and have a little silver saxophone made. I could wear it as a badge.

'That will be nice, no? My Peterpump.'

The club's membership grew thanks to the addition of several Danes who worked at the harbour: Sörensen, Jenssen and Berg.

Sörensen worked for our company. He'd come to Germany voluntarily.

'As a shipping agent you *have* to go to foreign countries,' he told us. Though if the war hadn't broken out, he would have gone to England, of course.

Everyone was glad to see the Danes.

'Maybe we can toss a Dutchman in,' said Robert. 'They're all right too.'

Poles and Czechs wouldn't work, though; you weren't allowed to be around them: they were Slavs, after all.

Sylvia was warned not to go to the movies with Berg. It was likely that the Nazis would cut her hair off if they found them. This had supposedly happened to Frauke Meier.

'It was because she was going out with a Romanian,' said Sylvia.

('But aren't the Romanians allies?')

'Besides, I don't want to go to the cinema with him, he's too pimply for me.'

The Danes didn't want to wear the gold chain. They wore the crest of King Christian instead. It was normal to wear a badge in Germany, but they didn't have them in Denmark.

They brought records from Copenhagen: Svend Asmussen and Leo Matthießen.

> Anita, you're lovely
> like blue skies above me . . .[2]

Sometimes they arrived with real coffee – from beans – which made my mother happy.

Robert ran around with Danish newspapers.

'At least they have something in them,' he said.

In the *Berlingske Tidende* there were jokes, pictures and even lists of married couples on the last pages. Where could you even find something like that in Germany? Everything was so beastly serious here.

He didn't bother with the *Foedre Lande* though: if you wanted a Nazi paper, you might as well buy yourself a copy of the *Völkischer Beobachter*.

In the afternoons we'd listen to Radio Musik from Restaurant Vivex. You'd hear the live audience, just a handful of guests, applauding lamely. Sörensen said that next time he went on vacation he would go there, walk by the microphone and quietly call out Robert's name.

The Danes came almost every day.

'Where else are they supposed to go?' my mother asked. 'I think they're very nice.' All with the exception of Jenssen, whom she confessed to finding a little creepy: 'He's not on the level; he's definitely a spy. He's always looking at you in that weird way of his.'

Sörensen brought along a letter, which he read aloud from. It was from a friend in the Ruhrgebiet, another Dane.

'We clap our hands as the bombs fall and mothers throw themselves over their babies,' he'd written.

That spoiled the mood a little.

There were other hassles too.

'Bring your whole family,' my mother said again and again. 'It makes me happy when you all have this lovely music on.' She even sang along to their music as she did the dishes.

> To be or not to be,
> That's the question, but not for me . . .[3]

But she wasn't always jolly. She once heard one of the Danish boys declaim that 'God is shit' during one of our sessions at the apartment: 'How else could He let the war happen?'

It got to her. She was a member of the Confessing Church though, and in her hour of need she zipped over there, her pelerine dress flapping. Not to Pastor Nagel, as he was good for nothing, but to Professor Knesel.

She never knew what she was supposed to say to the boys, she complained, so Knesel came and discussed it with them.

'You have to look at it a different way,' he said. 'God is not *schiet*, as you have claimed, with youthful exuberance. And in any case the effect of this expression in Low German is in no way an offensive one. This war – though a painful process – is washing clean all that was bad. I know it.'

He told them to come along to his consultation hours whenever they felt themselves at such a loss.

'We just have to make it through.'

When Knesel was gone Heini said, 'That's a smart guy. He almost won me over.'

'If, like the Germans, you don't fear God,' Sörensen said, 'you can see where it leads . . .'

17

In April 1942 the Woldemanns came back from Berlin. They found nothing changed at their apartment. Herr Woldemann stroked his shiny, brushed black hair and scratched his middle finger along his sharp parting, the little finger with the signet ring sticking all the way out.

'Well, how are you, you scamp? I hear your father's not here any more?'

He reassured us that things in Berlin weren't bad at all; we'd see what would happen.

The same couldn't be said of the Woldemanns' marriage. At night you could hear loud cursing and the slamming of doors.

> Everyone was happy, everyone proud,
> When he had her,
> Fräulein Gerda.[1]

Frau Woldemann laughed brightly while her husband yelled.

'Their marriage seems to be coming apart,' my mother noted. 'They can't stand each other . . .'

Ute had changed, too. She wore a dress with diagonal checks that made her behind bulge out. Her hair, which she usually had in a pageboy cut, now hung over her ears. She wanted to get her hair washed and curled – either in or out, she hadn't decided yet, it could go either way.

I tried to lie down on the carpet at her feet one more time: it was always so warm and cosy there.

'Should we play hide-and-seek in the dark?' I asked.

'But it's still light . . .'

'We could pull down the blinds—'

'It'll still come through.'

(The coffee table on which the legs were only crudely fastened; the armchairs' belts, reminiscent of those worn by the movers.) She stepped over me and walked towards the black gramophone.

> Oh, forgive me, madame,
> Gottfried Schulz is my name,
> And I love you . . .
> For certain I love you . . .[2]

'What do you think?'

'A lot of fluff,' I said, 'you should play a proper "hot" one, something from Duke Ellington or Jimmy Dorsey, instead.'

We looked through the records together until we found something that might suit. (She used to smell like mandarins.)

> Banjo, muted trumpet,
> Tuning! The tango begins,
> No one dances like Grete,
> The little golden blonde child's so sweet.[3]

We sat on the sofa. A seascape hung over the bookshelf. I'd never noticed it before. The rough, green waves looked deceptively real. They were hand painted.

I pulled out my pocket knife, which to my annoyance only had a little blade, and said I wanted to murder her now.

'You should stop that nonsense,' she said.

'No, no, I mean it. Seriously,' I whispered in a disguised voice, setting the knife on her knee. She had a little scar there, I knew it perfectly.

She grabbed my wrist and tried to turn it away. With a soft hissing sound, her full lips pulled back to reveal her large teeth.

> Otto is usually too ironic,
> Otto is usually a rogue,
> But here he's getting platonic
> Whisp'ring to her as they tango.

'It's certain,' I said, 'I'm going to murder you now.'

We wrestled a bit, and suddenly she collapsed under the table. Her dress slid up and her light green panties were visible; frayed patches on her stockings.

> Oh Fraulein Grete, when I dance with you,
> Oh, Fraulein Grete, I belong to you![4]

She lay there under the table, stretching, drawing herself out, and looked at me almost submissively. I nudged her a little with my slipper.

'One of us is going to have to put a new record on.'

Then her parents came home. Herr Woldemann threw the *Rostocker Anzeiger* on the table and grabbed an open wine bottle.

> *Exeter Bombing Has Great Impact!*

'Time for you to go back upstairs. Don't stay too long, or you'll get a box on the ears.'

Ute accompanied me to the door. The cursing had already

started up. The wife laughed brightly while he yelled.

'He's about to cry,' Ute said.

There were more air raid sirens nowadays. British planes – Vickers Wellingtons – flew over the city at a great height. At the garden fence we found pamphlets containing photos of dead German soldiers in Russia.

The Party ran a rebuttal in the *Adler*:

> The enemy tries to wear us down
> with propaganda pamphlets in balloons.
> He didn't get a chance to speak –
> now the leaflets have been hidden away!

'Children, hand that over,' my mother said when we found the pamphlets. 'Best not to look inside. What's in there?' She told us that if we ever came across fountain pens or candy we shouldn't pick them up. 'They have explosives in them, and blow up when you touch them. A girl's right hand was blown off in Lütten Klein.'

We jumped under our beds as soon as the sirens started howling. We put on our sweater vests and filled up the water pitchers. We raised the blinds and tilted the windows, so they wouldn't shatter if a bomb hit the glass – though no one believed this would actually work.

Robert was a messenger. He had a shapeless air-defence helmet which he would put on before cycling to the precinct. My mother meanwhile was the air warden for three buildings, and she had to knock on all the doors, ensuring everyone was awake. The married couple next door never wanted to come down.

'You knock, you ring!' said my mother, 'and they don't move a muscle. What idiots. "Let them knock," they say, "till they're blue in the face!" It's enough to drive you to despair!'

Yet she was still responsible for them.

The residents gathered in the cellar in dribs and drabs, including Matthes from next door, who arrived with his wife. She was Jewish, so she wasn't really permitted to be there. Matthes wore his briefcase around his body on a leather belt. It was full of papers. He was a secondary school teacher and lived off his tutoring.

One time, his wife had wanted to throw herself off the building. She had tried to jump from one of the little iron balconies, where the scallions grew in crates.

It smelled like potatoes and empty wine bottles in the cellar. 'You sit around like a doll! Like someone just left you behind and never came back to get you.'

There was a pickaxe in the corner, along with communal gas masks, jam, a sack of sand, hypodermic needles and a wooden shield. There was also a Primus stove and cans of Sterno, just in case.

You needed the wooden shield to get close to the burning firebombs. With the shield protecting you, you held the sack of sand over the flames, the bottom of the sack would burn through and the sand poured out, smothering the fire. We had a poster that showed the whole process.

The cellar belonged to the Woldemanns. They would just lie down on the air raid beds and sleep. I tried to read, *Land of Fire and Water* on one occasion, but I was forbidden. ('You want to ruin your eyes with all that violence?')

Now and again Herr Mattes read aloud from *Pole Poppenspäler* or *De Reis na Belligen*. But Herr Woldemann didn't like that; he said he couldn't sleep.

The flak, as the grown-ups called it, bellowed. As the attack continued, they hazarded guesses about how much all the shooting cost.

'An eight-eight-grenade is two hundred and fifty marks,' one of them noted. 'And all they do is draw the Tommies' attention . . .'

From time to time they discussed the cellar's safety. The laundry room with the drainage pipe was above the air raid shelter, they noted. They knew it was a death trap: if a pipe were to burst, it was goodnight. But even though our building was pretty much entirely made of plaster, it had at least two exits.

Occasionally we would go outside to look at the stars. There we would see the triangles and trapezoids of the searchlights – 'like ghost fingers' – and the tracer bullets too: a 'grandiose firework'.

'The neon signs were beautiful in peacetime,' the adults would reminisce.

If things started getting out of hand, we had to go back down.

To distract herself, my mother grated purple carrots ('Eat, it calms you down') while we threw rubber rings at a bottle. It worked especially well with Herr Woldemann's oversized champagne bottles.

If the all-clear came after midnight we got two hours off school, which was nice, sometimes even desirable.

*

At the end of April I had to write a Latin essay. I prayed to Santa Claude, my private goddess, for an air raid siren. And I got it!

Schwubber on, water filled, blinds up, windows open, run down. It happened so quickly, since they were already shooting. I took the stairs three at a time. This time, however, they were shooting harder than usual.

I darted back upstairs quickly ('Boy, stay here!') to get the crate of records.

> In the shade of an old apple tree . . .[5]

I almost turned on the light.

'Where's the chest with the silver?' screamed Woldemann.

They brought it down every time the sirens blared, and yet this time – when push came to shove – they'd left it upstairs.

'You should have remembered,' his wife replied firmly.

Strange bangs were mixed in with the bellowing. A blue light flickered.

'Well?' my mother said, and straightened the candles.

Bombs were falling on us.

At one point a soldier tramped down the stairs in his boots. He looked around without saying a word. Then he went back up and stood in the building doorway. The cellar probably wasn't safe enough for him.

The earth quaked like it was being stamped upon. The bombs were falling in the far-off parts of the city at first, but before long they started drawing closer. The walls trembled; we cowered. The sound of another broken window. (Not one of ours, hopefully.) A shower of grenade shards on the plaster.

Suddenly, a series of bombs. The first one far away, the second one closer, the third closer still, and then, with a roar, the fourth.

The vitrine of Dr Krause's Mineral Water splintered apart, and the shards fell on the basement window, shattering it.

> Whether out in the woods or snug in your den,
> Enjoy Dr Krause's Mineral Water.

The basement rattled and shook, and the light went out. The janitor's wife in her housedress started to scream. She needed to calm down, my mother screamed back, otherwise she'd have to reprimand her. ('It's like they've lost their marbles, the whole lot of them!') All the children screamed too, of course. ('Good thing Ulla isn't here.')

The next series of bombs were already on their way.

I sat behind my potato crate and Ute crawled, whimpering, under her blanket.

'Please, please, dear God – help us.'

My mother rushed through the building to see if it was on fire. The soldier tried to block her, saying it wasn't allowed.

'There's nothing to forbid,' she shouted, 'nothing's going to happen to me,' and dashed off.

A little later a small cluster of people arrived, groping their way into our cellar. It was the Heinemanns from across the street, their hair and eyes full of dust; they could hardly speak. ('Water, water.') They had lost everything; had barely made it out.

'Save my wife!' said the husband. 'Save my wife!'

The woman shook him and said, 'I'm with you.'

But he didn't understand what she was saying. 'Save my wife,' he repeated, again and again.

'We're leaving tomorrow,' Woldemann cried. 'We're not staying here another day.'

Then everyone had to quieten down, because new bombs were falling.

My mother laid Heinemann out on a straw sack and gave him cognac to drink. It was the last bottle of cognac we had, from Brussels, saved for special occasions. Then she ran out with a fire beater to the roof, which was tarred, to put out sparks. But she returned quickly; the British were flying low and shooting at the buildings.

'It was probably a Spitfire,' said the solider.

'No idea,' said my mother, 'in any case, it's unheard of . . .'

Robert appeared and stood in the doorway. We asked him whether it would be over soon, and he told us that they were coming in waves, but they'd probably retreat soon: they couldn't bomb us for ever, after all. Everything was muck and mire. My mother retrieved the cognac and gave him a sip.

'I have to leave again,' he said, 'I just wanted to make sure everything was all right.'

Then he was gone.

'Be careful, do you hear?' my mother cried after him.

The all-clear came in the morning, with a hand siren in the back of an open-top jeep, and we went back upstairs. ('Thank the good, great, gracious Lord.')

That the windows opened inward was now an advantage. It was only where they opened outward that there were shards. Everything out back was fine too. But the living room light had been shaken so hard that the little screen, held by claws, had fallen out and shattered.

There was the sound of brickwork crumbling, balconies collapsing, and men's shouts in the distance.

'I thank God on my knees,' my mother said, 'that the windows were open. And that we'd pulled the curtains closed. Otherwise everything would have gone straight into the dreck. What a blessing.'

Then she turned to me and said: 'Do me a favour, go to bed.'

'I'm not tired,' I said.

'That'll come later,' she reassured me, throwing some of the shards out.

Behind our building, the factory was burning. Its interior was lit up dark red. I really couldn't sleep. I pulled a chair up to the window and looked into the glow.

People were running around in the yard. French prisoners of war were retrieving crates of cigarettes from the burning storerooms. Two workers in rubber aprons were smashing mineral water bottles and pouring them out on to the fire.

A woman in an evening dress stood beside them, watching them work. She must have been thinking: I should make sure I'm wearing my best.

'Paneless windows stare out, haunted,' murmured Dr Krause, pointing to what was still standing of his factory's façade, behind which the flames were blazing. He wore a striped pyjama top over his breeches.

'What are you standing around here for?' he shouted at a man who had a cat on his arm and was petting it. 'Better pack up. Is the wagon outside?'

He took a can from the smoking-table beside him and gave each of the Frenchmen rushing past him a cigarette.

'You are brave, very brave,' he said, in French.

'*Ja, planes nix gutt, oh, oh la guerre, la guerre,*' they replied.

Then I saw Gina Quade. She was wearing tracksuit trousers under her dress, and had a handkerchief tied round her head. Her bald father was talking to Dr Krause, who was drawing the building with big gestures in the air, showing how it would be rebuilt.

Gina wiped her nose with a tiny crocheted handkerchief.

'Give me your hand, my child.'

She hadn't even said hello to Dr Krause. She put away the handkerchief and curtsied.

'Oh, you're a big girl now.'

'Did you bring out the carbonic acid? For God's sake, get rid of it. The whole place is going to go up!' shouted Krause, taking a few steps back.

Two black-clad nuns pushed their way through with bedding under their arms. They asked whether Dr Krause wanted to sleep in the Ursulines Hospital next door that evening. He could always count on them.

Then the roof collapsed, sparks spraying up.

'Oh God, children, hopefully it won't spread over to us . . .' my mother cried.

The bad news kept coming. Warkentin's had burned down. Yet Kröhl's place, which was in the immediate vicinity of the gasometer, had somehow remained unharmed.

I was particularly interested to know which churches and which cinemas had burned down. If either the Palast-Theater or the Schauburg had been hit, it would be a real tragedy.

St Mary's, it seemed, had been rescued by the sexton. He'd had to carry every single bucket of water up 282 steps. In the end he'd collapsed from exhaustion at exactly the moment that the military arrived.

'The church? They should have let that old shack burn down,' the district leader said.

Shameless. Oh, the population was up in arms.

The day before, the sexton of St Nicholas's had had the valuable figure of Christ, which usually stood outside in a shed, brought inside the church, so that 'our Lord Jesus's feet don't freeze'. That too had been destroyed.

The bells had started ringing when the tower fell over: it had been terrifying.

St Peter's and St Jacob's were also destroyed.

'The whole cityscape gone.'

How lovely it had been, seeing it over the garden in bloom; the green tower. Now everything had gone down the drain. Typical.

How Hannes must be suffering. And the Club for Rostock Antiquities, for that matter.

I went downstairs. A large pile of shit was lying in the building's doorway, left by the soldier.

Apple juice was given out in the factory. It would have gone bad otherwise. Samuel, with his yellow star, got a bucketful.

'Now he really looks like a Jew,' said my mother. 'The poor man.'

A few buildings were burning on Paulstraße, so no one was permitted to go there. Another building next door to us was burning down quietly, yet no one seemed to care.

I joined in the bucket relay, and left when no water came. The building that had 1903 inscribed on it had been flattened by a single bomb. Where might the Pekingeses have gone? It was said there were still charred bodies in the cellar that would have to be dug out.

Twisted-up iron girders were lying on Michael's father's property – the Rembrandt was certainly gone – and there were sofas and tables in the middle of the street. Household items had been gathered together on Reiferbahn, one street over from ours. I saw a woman carry a tank containing a goldfish up the road, and place it alongside some old newspapers.

I went over to the Schnabel woman, whose apartment looked completely wrecked – she was sweeping plaster off her Bechstein piano – and asked if I could help her with anything. 'Yes,' she said, 'get some quark cheese from the grocer.'

Robert came along with me.

In front of the concert hall was a shop that sold fresh red herring. We always had a hankering for them. They were so fat and tender, they practically melted on our tongues.

'Well, my boy, are you tired, wiped out?' my mother asked when we returned.

Of course. Robert knew someone who had just gone to sleep when the whole thing was over. He'd had to walk through the streets for hours confirming damage: 'cracks in the masonry', 'roof torn off', 'doors and windows blown out', 'totally levelled'.

He was also called on to identify bodies in the seminary on Ferdinandstraße. There he was confronted with what looked like two black pieces of coal: they were corpses.

In the Old Town, people had crawled through the cellars of as many as ten buildings with their luggage, passing between them through cracks in the walls. They'd finally emerge into the light wherever they could find an exit.

The whole of the River Warnow, meanwhile, was swimming with dead fish. A firebomb must have fallen in.

How high was the death toll? No one knew, and figuring it out wouldn't be easy.

An Englishman who had been shot down had been dragged to the police precinct, his eyebrows half singed.

'Where did you take off from?' the officer kept asking him.

He was denied permission to smoke. Eventually a lieutenant and six men in formation took him away.

In the meantime, the drizzle that had set in was something of a relief. Though Robert pointed out that it was far from ideal for the furniture still out on the street. There would now be water damage to contend with, in addition to the fire damage.

Amid the destruction, however, food was in abundance. There was as much of it around as there was sand at the seaside, Robert felt. He had eaten well, and was full. If he'd been able to round it off with a schnapps, everything would have been perfect.

'You'll get one, my boy, you'll get one,' my mother shouted, and ran into the cellar.

But the cognac wasn't there any more. What's more, it was nowhere to be found. Someone had taken it on the sly, from right under our noses! It had been stolen. No wonder, it was quite desirable after all, but who would have taken it?

We tried asking at the Woldemanns', but they'd already run for the hills. No one thought Matthes or the Heinemanns could have done it.

'We really shouldn't wait around,' Herr Matthes bleated. 'Leaflets have been found: they're coming again!'

Robert thought it safe to disregard this warning. Plus, the Nazis were getting together all the flak they could find now.

*

Manfred had binoculars around his neck. He showed me the freshest flak fragments – they were twenty centimetres long, yellow on the outside. He'd also found a large bomb shard.

'What, you don't have any bomb fragments?' No, I didn't have any.

He debated whether we should go to a locksmith and have the shard sawed in half; that way, each of us could have a fragment. I could trade him a piece of firebomb for it. I had three of them, after all. If you scraped something against one of them, it burned.

Manfred had heard the most terrifying stories about the bomb fragments. A woman's head had been blown apart by one. It had flown in through a window, smashed through her skull, and then flown out again through another. She'd been sitting there, minding her own business. At her neighbours', the bomb fragment fell on to an armchair where someone had been sitting. They'd just gotten up.

For his part, he would rather his building got a direct hit from a firebomb. That way you weren't buried under the rubble: 'If it's burning upstairs, you just run out downstairs. You get the hang of it soon enough.' But being buried alive? No thank you.

A police officer who'd been digging had come across what he thought was a doormat, Manfred told me. It soon turned out to be a dead woman's hair.

'Think about it: you'd still be alive, maybe even for a whole day, while buried, and everyone would be walking right by you. You'd be knocking with your last bit of strength, and outside someone might prick up their ears: "Did you hear something?" And just at that moment you stop knocking, because you're exhausted. But when you knock again the people outside have moved on.'

The worst fate was to be hit by an exploding bomb and then a firebomb. Then you were buried and had to watch the fire as it slowly crept closer and closer. A foot or a leg doesn't just catch fire; first it starts bubbling and then slowly scorches.

I told him there were people buried at our place, and asked whether he wanted to see them.

Herr Heinemann kept rolling his eyes: his wife's hand was still hurting her. She'd been frantically clutching a box of matches since the bombs fell, without realising quite what they were, nor why she was holding them.

'I think we should leave, for a while at least,' my mother said.

She packed only the necessities: underwear, papers and the Pfeilring soap, which had been lying around since the war started. Her head was woozy. It had been a bit too much. But the wheel was ever-turning, she reassured us: things would improve; they couldn't stay like this.

I packed my firebombs and my best flak fragments in my knapsack, as well as my stamp collection.

> Commemorative Stamps for Heroes' Day
> 12 + 38 pfg blue-black
> Head of a dead warrior

Manfred's stamps were stored at the Regional Agricultural Centre. His safe had remained undamaged, they said.

18

Ahead of our departure we moved suitcases full of belongings into the basement to protect them: my grandfather's Africa trunk, the blue one made of cardboard, and the heavy one with the papers. We moved my brother's trunk of records – including Ella Fitzgerald and the Mills Brothers – and I brought my soldiers down, both the attacking ones and the fallen. We also moved a picture of Hermann Göring with his arm upstretched.

'In the event that the building is hit directly,' my mother said, 'we can forget whatever's in the dresser. But it would be nice to save the books, maybe. The Hesse and Wiechert and the regimental histories.'

But no one had any idea whether an attack was coming. They had to stop at some point. Everyone was afraid now, but we knew we'd laugh about it afterwards.

We shook some feed on to the dining room table for Hansi, the canary, and let him fly around. More or less immediately he perched on the curtain rail.

'He'll probably hold out there for a while. But leave the cage open, in case he wants to wash.'

'What if the windows break?'

'Then he's gone either way.'

I took a last look around the room. The sideboard with the crystal and the Meißner bowl; the autumn painting, in which I always thought something didn't look quite right; the open cabinet with *Poisonous Fish and Fish Poisons* and the countless issues of *Kosmos Bändchen*.

A record was playing:

> When I have nothing to eat,
> No shoes for my little feet . . .[1]

'I'll hold the fort,' said Robert. 'Maybe I'll get Bubi and Heini to join me.' No one had seen hide nor hair of Michael. Apparently he'd opened the door to his house and, seeing that everything in there had been incinerated, closed it again and left. That was what Robert had heard.

Michael's father was in Berlin right now and his mother in Bad Kissingen.

'How he must have cursed about the Rembrandt.'

Oil paintings bubbled first, then they crackled. Especially old stuff like that. Now it was gone for ever. (But then again, maybe it hadn't even been a Rembrandt.)

Robert walked us to the station. He transported our suitcases on his bicycle: one on the luggage rack, one on the handlebars.

'The station will be packed, but I'll ensure the ship gets to port, swear to God.'

We all laughed. He had never had to stand, he bragged. Never in his life. He was sure that we'd each get a seat, as sure as two and two were four. Only poor saps had to stand.

There was a red poster on the Bismarck Pharmacy:

STATE OF EMERGENCY.

LOOTERS WILL BE SHOT.

'"State of emergency", how stupid,' my mother said. 'We used to call it a state of siege . . . They have to remodel everything. They never leave anything the way it used to be.'

The Olympic rings were visible over the station's swastika, reminding me of the women relay team's misfortune.

A train to Berlin was coming in as we arrived. We squeezed through the turnstiles and a man passed by, waving a pistol: 'I'm with the Gestapo, let me through right away!'

'Get right to the back!' shouted my brother.

But when we got there, the luggage car stopped in front of us. ('Good grief.') So we jostled our way back to the front of the train, and clambered aboard.

There were steel helmets and gas masks stored in the luggage netting. The train was filled with soldiers from Denmark, as well as holidaymakers. Robert stood on the platform below.

'My poor boy . . . take some sour cherries, they're in the stone jar, lower left, in the cellar. And call your father if anything comes up . . .'

Window up.

'Everything's gone,' I heard a woman murmur.

The soldiers were silent.

*

Stettiner Station, Berlin. We refugees were led, in a row, into a freight shed. ('Wait a moment! All right, now the next ones.') We sat on crates or luggage racks, next to some travel baskets made of wicker.

'If you want to be resettled, you'll stay in here until we come to get you,' a man said, and shut the door.

'It feels like they've set us down and won't pick us up again,' said my mother. 'We're not little children . . .'

'Everything's lost,' said the woman. She pulled her trunk closer to her.

It was night when we were picked up. A Red Cross sister slid the door open.

'So,' she said cheerfully, 'come along all of you.'

We carried our luggage through the silent streets. There wasn't a soul in sight, just countless balconies stretching along the building walls in the moonlight. (Where might Ursa Minor be hiding?)

The Red Cross sister was at the head of the procession, a canteen attached to her belt. I was still carrying my firebombs in my knapsack. My mother, carrying all of the luggage, had the heavier load.

'It's enough to drive you to despair,' she said. 'If only we'd stayed home.'

'I can't do anything about that,' said the sister as she waited for two old people to catch up with us.

'The sisters really are so lazy, they could at least try and lend a hand,' my mother said. But they preferred not to lend a hand to anyone, or someone might say they were picking favourites.

An upset man asked whether an omnibus might not have been chartered for us; all of this walking was unheard of.

'What's your name?' he was asked. He fell silent after that.

We came into a large, gasometer-like bunker. The exterior was concealed by red bricks; inside it was whitewashed.

'It's absolutely bombproof,' said the sister. 'Nothing's going to happen to you here. When the air raid siren sounds, just ignore it.'

There was a generator in the middle of the building, which guaranteed electricity, and a quiet buzzing in all the cabins. I did a circuit of the bunker. ('Do me a favour, don't run so far away!')

There were five beds in our cabin. I sat on one and let my legs dangle off the edge. The sister wanted to know whether we needed money.

'Do we have to pay it back?' we asked.

We were brought a plate with sandwiches, and everyone received an orange.

'Eat till you burst,' said my mother. She herself couldn't eat: the whole ordeal had ruined her appetite.

'Everything's gone,' said the woman. 'Where am I supposed to go?'

'I think she's got a screw loose,' whispered my mother. 'The poor woman.'

The next morning I went out into the street.

'This is the Church of Thanksgiving, my child,' someone said, 'from 1871.'

*

When we were relocated to Gartz, the reception was completely different. Father was waiting under the station clock, with a boy named Kirmes, a wide belt with a service revolver around his waist. Kirmes had a pained expression, he stood a half step behind my father.

'See there! See there, Timotheus. The cranes of Ibycus! There you all are!' my father shouted. He pulled first my mother and then me against his sturdy, round, uniformed chest. He smacked a kiss on my forehead, leaving behind a wet spot that I didn't dare wipe off.

Then he looked around to see whether there were other auxiliaries in the area who could help us.

'You're probably all completely shattered, eh? I imagine you've been through all kinds of things . . .?'

The boy stood there all the while, hollow-eyed and pale.

'Forward, march!'

Father was now a first lieutenant. As the local commandant, he had to allocate prisoners of war to the surrounding estates. But he was getting almost all Russians at the moment. French prisoners were in short supply, and you could forget Englishmen.

'The men from the prisoner of war camp in Stettin were scoundrels, prone to all kinds of chicanery. And oh, how the farmers swore.' In the end he couldn't do anything about it and just had to keep hearing them complain: they'd lynch him if he came to them with these shitty Russians.

'But what a bunch they are! The bottom of the barrel. The Yugoslavs are a different kettle of fish, mind, with their glorious moustaches . . .'

But this was all by the by. We needed to relax, and come to our senses. He'd already received his orders, and that was that! Gartz was a nice little city, we'd see. There was no butter rationing—

Here he stopped mid-sentence, and told my mother to remain strong: last night the enemy had returned to Rostock.

'But don't worry, nothing's happened to our place. Everything is in order. Robert has already telegraphed.'

The business was intact too. My mother looked around for a moment, and said, 'Well then, onward!'

Gartz was lovely, wonderful. These were golden times. Things were only getting nicer again. She had her hands in the pockets of her checked smock and held it together in front of her, as it kept flapping open.

But we all felt that there would soon be nothing left standing in Rostock, that there would soon be nothing but rubble.

We returned to the cognac.

'By the way, the cognac's gone. We shared out about half of it in the cellar, and the rest just disappeared.'

'The good cognac?' my father asked, letting out a deep sigh.

'Yes, I poured it as the bombs were falling.'

'Oh, I just can't imagine what you had to bear. Up and down those stairs, again and again, with the building on fire . . .' my father said. 'And the rest just disappeared without trace?'

'Yes.'

'Stolen, then. Drunk! Disgusting. We might as well have thrown it out the window.'

We stumbled over the cobblestones in the marketplace. I walked now in front, now behind my parents.

'Child, stop running around our feet.'

My father's coat opened at the back, his gleaming jackboots were shining. Kirmes carried the trunks for us. There were spies at the windows on the ground floor of the buildings surrounding the marketplace, Father said. I noticed chamomile growing between the cobblestones.

'In the church over there,' my father said, pointing, 'is where you'll find Pastor Vordran; he's a very reasonable man.' We would talk everything through with him. He'd tell us how things would be from now on.

We were pleased to hear this, feeling that something had to

change. Things couldn't continue as they had been, after all.

We checked in to the Black Eagle Hotel, switched on the lights and turned on the taps: all amenities, full steam ahead! Our beds were huge, though the ceiling was sagging. Outside we could see a tarred roof, a coach house and the barred windows of a warehouse. They were washing canisters in the yard.

My father moved in with us. Kirmes brought the trunks over. ('This is how we're living, this is how we're living, this is how we're living every day . . .') For now, money was no object. Who knew how long this would last, though?

'What do you mean?' my mother asked. 'Are you going to leave?'

'Not if I have my way. But I might be redeployed, no?'

My mother piled the laundry in the wardrobe. She was already looking forward to supper, even if she wasn't able to eat properly yet.

A table had been reserved for us in the dim guest parlour right next to the toilet. We were seated near a cattle dealer dressed in a grey work coat. The gnarled stick with which he beat the cows into his wagon was leaning against the wall, next to a wardrobe. My father's belt and revolver hung by the stick, along with my mother's hat.

The owner of the establishment seemed to be grinning, but that was because of his jaws. He was called Denker – Thinker – of all things. He dried his hands before coming over to us.

'What will it be, Frau First Lieutenant? A small light beer?'

I was to show him the firebombs.

'Where did you get those?' he wanted to know.

I got a malt beer. The firebombs were passed from table to table.

'So this is a firebomb, eh? There's no chance it will flame up, is there?' asked the cattle dealer. Once he got the all-clear, he took his cigar out of his mouth so as to inspect it.

'You'll find more than thirty of them on every street,' my father said, addressing the room. 'Sometimes they're just tossed out of the window with a shovel.'

> You've got no clue,
> You little doe, you[2]

'And after the bombs, you get a rain of flak shards at no extra charge . . . Bring them down, my boy.'

'Should I also bring my stamps?' I asked.

'You lovely boy . . .'

('Isn't he sweet?')

I had numbered the flak shards and wrapped them in cotton.

'Very lovely,' my father said. 'But if you were to get one in the head . . . that's the last we'd hear from you.'

He held one up to his forehead.

'They scratch if you just press them to your skin,' I said.

My mother had run upstairs a hundred times when we were back in Rostock, worried that the building was burning. Thinking back on it, she couldn't believe that she'd survived the bombs and the flak and the Tommies shooting at her. Her, a defenceless woman. Sat in the parlour, she ran her hands up her bare arms. She felt rather unwell.

'Not for one moment did I think that something would happen to me. Not for one single moment.'

She spoke with an unshakable certainty. Her voice was quite calm, completely steady. ('Cheers to that!')

'But the men just sat there, in the cellar, having a great time. It never occurred to any of them to join me. They have no love for their fatherland. It's disgusting.'

'Oh, I would have smashed their heads together,' my father said. 'And then they stole the good cognac . . . The best thing to do is to pay no attention to anyone else, let everyone go their merry way. Only think of yourself.'

(Then the whole story was recounted again, for the benefit of a pharmacist who had joined the table.)

A few of them began playing skat. My mother moved away a little, not wanting to join in.

'In the First War they still had fighter plane columns,' said my father. 'You wouldn't get anywhere with those today. And that's that!'

He saw a dogfight once during the Great War, in which they were throwing hand grenades at one another. That had been vigorous exercise. Whenever they could, the pilots waved down to them when the other man died. ('Who's out?')

It was anyone's guess how things had reached the stage of laying waste to a whole city, they said, and I thought of St Peter's and St Jacob's, both gone. It was completely incomprehensible. The technology was so much more advanced now: flak, barrage balloons, fighter planes.

> And now comes the goldfinch,
> And then comes another creature,
> And then comes the farmer.[3]

The game of skat continued.

'You have to go to bed, boy, say goodnight,' my father said. 'What kids today don't get up to . . . We grew up with much more discipline. We were always safe and sound, free of all worry.'

*

The next morning I climbed into my mother's bed. Her head was buried between the corners of the cushions, like Wilhelm Busch.

'Oh, you lovely darling. And to think I'd thought I might sleep a little more . . . This is so wonderful,' she said, half awake, half asleep.

'Stick your nose in the pillow,' her father had always said to her, when she was a child. She never knew how she was supposed to go about that – she always tried though, regardless.

My father felt blindly for his watch.

'How late is it? Eight already? Oh well, five more minutes . . .'

It had got late, yesterday evening. The pharmacist had taken a hiding.

'Black as a Moor's arse.'

'God, Karl.'

'Shame Robert isn't here,' my mother said, 'what a good boy he is. Little . . . But he's all right. He's quick. Nothing will happen to him . . .

'Oh, and to have Ulla here too. To be all together again, like before. How lovely that was, drinking coffee at the table in the morning . . .'

We hoped nothing had happened during the night. We'd have to check. Why was it always Rostock of all places?

'Is Rosinat's place gone too?' my father asked.

'Yes, but not just the shop; the whole street is gone,' my mother replied.

'Where am I supposed to get my cigars then? How annoying. And Stephanstraße?'

'Still standing.'

'We could have moved there back in '39. If only we'd known in advance. It wouldn't have been so bad, having those big rooms. Oh well, it's all the same really.'

My father's officer's salary went straight to the Deutsche Bank to repay the debts on the house.

'Fabulous,' Herr Kerner from the bank had said, 'it's really fabulous the way you have it worked out.'

A flycatcher hung down from the lamp. A book lay on the nightstand – *The World 100 Years Ago*, published by Reclam; a stagecoach on its cover. There was also a second volume: *The Streets of the Reich*. It charted how our culture had developed; most of it happened in Saxony and Thuringia.

'Remarkable. They're sly foxes there . . .' my father said. And he should know: he had some men from those regions in his company. He had some Hessians, too. They said *Gockel* and *Hinkel* instead of cockerel and hen. What nonsense.

My mother had *The Silver Thistle* by Ruth Schaumann on her nightstand. Apparently the author was completely mute. Or was she blind? (But then how could she write something so beautiful . . .?)

'Felix Timmermans is also pretty good,' said my father. He'd read *Pallieter*, and recalled how the eponymous character peed his name in the snow.

'If I make it to Holland in this war, I'd want to visit old Timmermans and tell him how much I enjoyed the book.'

Just then the young boy arrived with my father's boots.

'Good morning, Herr Lieutenant Colonel.'

We nodded our heads.

'Kirmes,' my father said, 'dust is the enemy of leather.'

'Certainly, Herr Lieutenant Colonel.'

'Polish the front first, then the rear.'

When Kirmes had left the room my mother said: 'God, Karl, you really can't humiliate him like that, he's a grown man after all.'

'What do you mean? I was right, though, wasn't I?'

'Right. Up and at 'em.'

He got out of the bed, pulled his breeches and slippers on and began shaving, his braces hanging down behind him. He ran the blade carefully against the grain, watching as the hairs jumped up. Afterwards, the stubble lined the sink. He assessed his handiwork in the mirror.

'Fine and dandy.'

Then it was time for him to wash. His skin was quite rough, so he stirred Kaiser borax into the water with a wooden spoon. He snorted – 'Ouch!' – as he began washing himself. He stood with his legs apart, his breeches slipping down.

This was how he had washed back in 1914–18, at the Burgdorf farm: under a water pump.

There are such cute Belgians here, he had written. Along with: *What do you think about America? We've got no problem with having a little dust-up.* . .

I looked over to see if his breeches had completely fallen down. But no, they were somehow staying up.

'Don't you have to hurry?' asked my mother. 'You're the lieutenant colonel, after all. You're not allowed to show up late.'

'I'm ready,' he snapped back, running, bent over, to the wardrobe to rummage through his various shirts. 'Besides, I'm not going to be late. I'm never late. Punctuality is the politeness of kings. And here in Gartz I'm the ruler of all of Reußen. Do you understand?'

A new handkerchief was spritzed with cologne. (*Ritsch-ritsch-ritsch!*) He combed his hair and put on his watch.

'Gentlemen, here I am.'

Then, sitting in pairs in the wagon, we rode to see Schulz, the forester.

'He's a nice man, you'll see. He has rabbits and chickens, and he'll give us a proper meal.'

It was a cold April day with a sharp wind. We spread a blanket over our legs, which made it a more comfortable ride. The wagon see-sawed, and the trees glided past us one after the other.

'How's my skin doing?'

The smell of the horses.

'Funny how even while they're running they can still break wind . . .'

Who falls from the horse when it farts?

That's the Kaiser's cadet.[4]

'In the World War,' my father said, 'in the *First* World War' – you had to be more precise now – 'someone once stuck a piece of wood under my saddle. Well, when I climbed up, the horse bucked: kicking out its back legs before rising up in the front. Poor animal.'

My mother had her hat on – the one with the stuffed bird on it – and a thick netted veil in front of her face.

'Can't it just be summer? Does it have to be so windy? Typical that we have to travel at this time of year, of all times.'

'Why didn't you bring your winter coat with you? So foolish. It'll probably go up in flames in Rostock.'

At least it wasn't raining. Then we'd be completely screwed.

En route, my father inspected some of his men. ('Just drive in on the right.') We met an old guard accompanying five Russians, who were all chopping wood.

'Did you even load your rifle, man?'

'Yes, sir, of course I'll load it right away,' said the man.

'What do you mean?' screamed my father, and opened the bolt mechanism. 'This arsehole hasn't loaded it!' Turning to Kirmes, my father thundered: 'Look at this! He's guarding five Russians and his rifle isn't loaded!'

The man's hat sat high on his ears, and he had a Hitler moustache. It was like my father could smell the mistake on him. (The Russians continued working dutifully.)

'When the cat's away, the mice will play. What if they came at him with an axe, eh? A Thuringian through and through. Well, there'll be a new regime around here: no more taking it easy.

'And we're supposed to fight a war with idiots like this,' he concluded, climbing back into the wagon.

The lodge was exactly as I'd imagined it. ('This is very lovely!') It was in the middle of the woods, and smoke was rising from the chimney. The ranger's wife came out to greet us, along with their three daughters. None of them were married, it seemed. Likely because there was no opportunity to get to know anyone out there. (Plus, the smell of sweat followed them wherever they went.)

Inside there was a round table in a dark parlour, a leather sofa against the wall behind it. There were countless horns and antlers on the wall, and black curtains made of wooden beads in front of the tiny windows. Flowerpots hung from hooks throughout the cabin.

'Oh, Christ's thorn, how lovely.'

A partridge hound with dumplings between his legs sniffed at me. He'd probably been attracted by the smell of fire. Instead of wagging his stubby tail, he scurried around in front of me, running this way and that. He was a very friendly dog.

Finally Schulz shuffled over to us too.

'You've got it pretty good out here!'

'Do you think so?'

He was knock-kneed, and would straighten himself up from time to time.

'Have you heard anything from Rostock yet?'

'No, nothing was coming through,' he said. 'I have a bad feeling.'

At noon there were flawless scrambled eggs. They were nice and moist, with spring onions folded into them.

'Now make sure you eat it all up . . .' Frau Schulz said to me.

Afterwards she served cake with warm milk, and my father handed out Old Gold cigarettes, which he'd got from the prisoner of war camp.

'She must have run up those stairs a thousand times,' my father recounted, 'fifty steps each time. And it might have been for nothing.'

My mother then spoke of how she'd been overcome with despair when she saw the burning city. And my father said: 'Shame you didn't bring your firebombs along, boy. You could've shown them off here.'

The conversation moved on:

'There's nothing but Thuringians in the company. I can't stand it. They're a complete waste of space. Take the one today: he's guarding a bunch of Russians and hasn't even loaded his rifle!'

Then he lowered his voice and cast glances around the room. Prisoners had been seen working in the neighbouring districts.

'"Keep driving and don't slow down," the man from the SS said to me. They looked terrible. "Concert camp," they said. "Those chickens will come home to roost."'

'But keep your mouth shut – are you listening, boy? – Herr Hitler must certainly know all about it, but I'm not sure who else is aware.'

It then struck my father that he had left his charcoal tablets at the Black Eagle, and so he needed to leave.

'Shall we see whether Robert's sent a telegram?'

When we arrived back, the innkeeper had a message waiting for us: 'Everything is all right.'

'It feels like when the elevator drops,' my mother said. 'What a relief.'

We'd heard reports that Rostock had been attacked again. The announcer had emphasised 'again', as though this time was one too many.

I looked into the mirror. What did the people who had been burned to death look like?

*

Next day we paid a visit to Pastor Vorndran. My ears and hairline were cleaned with eau de cologne before we left. ('What thick hair you have!')

There was a giant black cabinet in the hallway.

'Good day, Herr Lieutenant Colonel,' said Pastor Vorndran. 'I am glad that your lovely wife has come along too.' He held out both hands to us, radiating concern: 'Now everything will be good, Frau Kempowksi, now all will be well. It's funny how life turns out . . . I studied in Rostock, you know.'

His wife came in, wearing a thick gold necklace which hung down on her breast. ('A little much for a pastor's wife, but she seems kind-hearted . . .') She also held out both of her hands to us.

'Why does God allow all these terrible things?' my mother asked the pastor. 'What does he mean by it? Does God want us to burn?'

She had these thoughts going through her mind at all times.

I was locked away with the children in a room full of beds. In the centre was a gigantic table that you had to squeeze past. A white lacquered washstand stood in the corner, with a stoneware jug and bowl.

An older boy, an eight-year-old girl named Trudi, who had braids, and her two younger brothers were gathered in there. The two boys stood up as soon as I entered.

'No one touches anything here!' one of them said, and pointed to a microscope that was standing near by. He walked out through a door into the rain.

Trudi was doing her homework. (I had it easy in that regard.) She sat there, her back bent, and swayed back and forth, dozing. Little individual hairs curled up from her blond plaits. She was supposed to be copying out a poem:

> Young Siegfried was a proud boy,
> Rode down from his father's castle . . .[5]

At the top of the page was a woodcut: a knight, his horse trotting on Death's head. Trudi gnawed on the cap of her pen, copied out one word, then returned to dozing.

A clockwork miller made of tin stood on the table; he would raise a sack up on to his head. As soon as he'd got it up there, and was standing beneath it, the sack would fall back down.

In Trudi's workbook: 'Cave Children in a Stilt House', let's see, what's on page 210.

When Trudi was finally done ('Close the book now, child!') she got her things together and said, 'I'll go get Gila.'

Gila was a black-haired girl, her eyebrows grown together. She held her pointy knees and tumbled on to one of the beds. Someone needed to come and resuscitate her, she said, looking towards me. I didn't move, and she soon leapt up and declared that she wanted to play spin-the-bottle.

'Whoever the bottle lands on has to say who they're in love with.'

'Hermann Göring' was the first answer, then 'Gila.' With this, Trudi started acting strangely.

'Whoever the bottle lands on,' she said, spinning the bottle, 'is in love with – with the time?' She posed it as a question, looking off into the corner of the room, where a clock stood.

Trudi was lovely, we said afterwards. ('Did you see her eyes?') And the pastor too ('a kind-hearted man'). My parents commented on the cabinet too, noting the inlay. Now that was really something. Did it belong in the parsonage?

Maybe after all this we'd buy an old mahogany table and a decent carpet. Ours were really frightful.

'And a car,' my father chimed in. 'Once the war is over, of course.' In any case, he was never getting on his bicycle again.

By this point, my mother couldn't hold out any longer: she'd fought it off, but she had to go home. Hopefully nothing had happened.

*

Robert came to pick us up on our arrival back in Rostock. We carried our trunks through smoking streets strewn with rubble. He'd left his bicycle at home because of the glass shards carpeting the street. Hose lines stretched out of the dykes.

'How is this even possible?'

'Not a single weed has grown since the last attack,' Robert said. He thought the next bombardment was already hanging in the air above us, like a Sword of Damocles. And the clean-up at home was a job for the fifty daughters of Danaus; my mother should prepare herself for that.

But when we got into the apartment she threw both hands over her head anyway. She steadied herself against the door jamb.

'It looks awful! An ungodly mess. You work your fingers to the bone, and all you – well, you let everything rot.'

It was the Polish in our family that was coming out: the laziness, the sloth. When she was a child her mother had beaten her because she hadn't wanted to say grace. But this was beyond that.

'You beg, you plead, but no, you refuse to do it. Are you a simpleton? You could at least have washed the dishes, or mopped up! There's not a single clean cup!'

We got the best mineral water – crystal clear – from Dr Krause, and heated it up in the laundry tub. Herr Kröhl replaced the broken window shards with X-ray film and cardboard. The glazier would have enough glass to repair it properly the following week.

Water, gas and electricity: one by one, they would definitely come back, she said. The Nazis were much too clever for things to stay like this. We'd see, the wheel would turn, things couldn't go on like this.

Where were all the sour cherries?

'You said we could eat them . . .'

'Not *all* of them!'

When I saw Manfred, he was dejected. The Main Cooperative's safe had survived the attacks, and his stamps had been saved, but there was a little brown dot on each of them. In other words, they were all ruined. Even the Munich-Riems.

He wondered whether we'd get medals for the attacks, and pondered who in the city had lost the most money from the damage. Perhaps commemorative stamps would be circulated, he wondered aloud: St Peter's on fire as a 12er; 5 pfennigs for the churches that had been damaged in the bombing. St Mary's Church had a really great view now that everything around it was gone.

By the way: 'Did you know the school burned down?'

19

The Nazis locked up Sörensen, one of the Danes from the harbour. 'He's away on business,' it was said. But everyone knew that meant he'd been imprisoned. ('The poor man . . . Did they beat him?')

We heard that he'd been marking destroyed property on a plan of the city while in the Hotel Schröder. He'd sat there, scratching out burnt-out buildings, checking off where rows of bombs had fallen, for anyone to see. He wanted to get 'an overview', he'd said. ('It's just outrageously careless. He's obviously gone completely crazy . . . What an idiot.')

This type of stupidity had to be punished, and sure enough, one day a soldier came at him with his sidearm.

'Come with me and don't make a scene,' he'd said.

The hotel owner had just about spilled his beer, staring goggle-eyed. We all felt it was a wonder they didn't strike Sörensen dead right then and there.

'As if a spy would just be sitting there in the middle of the bar,' said my mother. That alone was proof of his innocence.

The other Danes were dismayed at the news. Jenssen sat on the sofa while Berg walked back and forth shouting: 'But they can't do that!'

'Do you have any idea what they can do?'

'We have to telegraph the King right away.'

'Slow down, now,' said Jenssen. My mother didn't think very much of him: he had such womanly hands, she felt, and was always looking around so furtively. She could imagine him being a spy far more readily than Sörensen. Jenssen slid the curtains to the side and looked out on to the street. 'Slow down. The important thing is to remain calm, cold-blooded.'

My brother agreed: 'Cold blood and warm underwear.' Then he spat some tobacco remnants on to the carpet and suggested putting a record on. ('Deep in the Heart of Texas'.)

'Leave it,' Jenssen snapped, before regaining his composure. 'It's probably not the thing to do at this moment. Sörensen might not be alive. We shouldn't be holed up having a good time.'

The next day my mother made herself up and took hunter's sausage sandwiches to the Gestapo.

'Hopefully he'll get some of it too.'

'He'll get some all right,' said the porter. But he couldn't pass the forget-me-not perched on top of the sandwiches along; it could mean something.

'It's *supposed* to mean something,' my mother answered.

She wasn't deterred though, and kept pushing until she got to the Gestapo's führer.

'I'm German,' she said, 'and my husband, previously a shipping agent, is now a lieutenant colonel. He fought through the whole World War without getting a single wound, despite always being on the front lines.

'I know Sörensen to be a completely harmless boy. He's from a good family. The business with the city map was an immature mistake, nothing more. You can believe me. Surely you know how young people are: impulsive, mercurial . . .'

'No,' said the man from the Gestapo, cutting her short. 'There's more to it.'

It had been established that on 9 April Sörensen had worn a black ribbon.

'On the 9th of April? Well, yes. It was the anniversary of the German troops' entry into Denmark. It's completely understandable,' said my mother, 'and a patriotic love of his homeland and his king isn't directed against Germany . . . The Danes still love their king, just as we love our führer, or as I loved the Kaiser in my youth. Please, please, let him out!'

The official smiled to himself and looked around the desk, as though perhaps something was out of place. Then he got up and walked over to the window.

'What do you think, Frau Kempowski,' he said, looking out on to the street, 'how many bad people are out there? It's said that Germany is crawling with spies . . .'

'Please let him out, we'll vouch for him,' she replied, ignoring his question. 'He's innocent, please believe me.'

But it was to no avail. In the end our employee Denzer steeled himself and visited the Gestapo, too. He spoke of Sörensen's circumspection and his devotion to duty, pointing out that he was irreplaceable: Sörensen worked on the eastern tonnage deployment. It was a serious business, they could believe that.

And so, after fourteen days Sörensen reappeared. Visibly emaciated, he sat at the living room table and told us what had happened.

Spring lets its band of blue
Flutter through the air again.[1]

He'd been crazy with fear. Stood against the wall of his cell, he'd kept repeating the Lord's Prayer . . . ('Boy, go get the cheesecake out of the pantry!' my father told me while Sörensen was talking.)

During his interrogation, the Gestapo man had made clear that the window was too high for him to jump out of – 'Don't do anything rash,' he'd said – and there was always a guard stationed in front of the door, so there was no point in running. They asked him what intelligence agency he was working with, which accomplices he could name. They wanted him to expose the whole network, then he could go back home right away.

But strangely the Gestapo man had let up on him fairly quickly. He hadn't expected that.

'When was that?' my mother asked. 'On the Thursday, or had they already eased up on Wednesday?'

'I'm not sure,' Sörensen said. 'Either the Thursday or Friday. It might have been Friday.'

And did he get the bread? Yes, he'd got the bread.

('Thanks, son. Now fetch the apple juice.')

'Did you also get the forget-me-not? The porter thought he couldn't pass it on. "It might mean something," he'd said. Isn't that hilarious? Did you get it?'

He had, there had been a flower with the bread.

'What was it called? Forget-me-not? That's a funny name.'

If the slightest thing should happen, he was in for it, the official had said when they let him go: 'Be careful, Sörensen, we're not messing about.'

'Maybe the jerk picked on you because you look so Germanic,' my brother suggested. 'In any case, Denzer must have been the deciding factor. He's well respected. He lost a leg in the last war, which is nothing to sneeze at.'

'What did you do all day?' my mother wanted to know.

'I kept looking out the window, to see if someone had seen me,' Sörensen said. 'I made signs, but no one looked up, even though they might have thought someone was looking at them through the window . . . The truth is that no one cares about you when you're sitting in there. No one. You're written off, done for.'

'I wouldn't be able to stand more than three hours in prison . . . It's beyond me,' my mother said.

'What do you think a human being can withstand, Frau Kempowski?' Sörensen asked.

There were nineteen nationalities represented in there with him, Sörensen continued. He had deciphered clippings from illustrated French magazines with a Frenchman.

'I've always regretted not speaking French – it's such a lovely language. I'd much rather speak French than German. You can really see how it might come in handy.'

'He's really quite bitter,' my mother noted, such that he didn't hear, 'but the wheel turns, and in time everything comes back to its proper place. He'll be cheerful again before long.'

'And then, on the second-to-last day, they put a Russian, of all people, in my cell. Unbelievably filthy. It was probably a joke for the guards.' They'd had to untie twine together. They had shucked, and then eaten, ears of corn. He had woven himself a belt from the twine, because his trousers were constantly falling down.

'Could you see a system to the destruction on the city map?' my brother asked.

'As far as I can remember, there was less than I thought there'd be, and it was seemingly random. Some here, some there.'

He didn't want to hear a word about it ever again though, he said.

He had saved his last bread ration. He'd keep it till the day he died.

'"Give us today our daily bread": that's what I learned. God, above all else, is what's really important. And culture, too. You have to keep up with concerts and the like.'

Since his home had been bombed, we took him in. Ulla's room was free, after all: she was on work detail. Her room had a wide view over the city.

My father was on duty again and wrote to us, stressing that it wasn't very seemly, but we disregarded this; it was only 'as far as he was concerned', after all. And so her confirmation cross was packed up, along with the cork containing the three tiny dice. The floral curtains remained, though. As did the tablecloth and lampshade made from the same material.

Once we'd prepared the room my mother and I heated up the bathwater, leaving Sörensen to make himself at home. He needed a proper scrubbing to get all the filth off. There might even be fleas, we had no idea. Afterwards he got supper in bed. ('Salt, please. And where's my egg? What kind of service is this!')

Before long, however, Sörensen went back to Denmark to regain his strength. He returned to his father, who lived in a white villa with a park and a private beach.

'But you're going to come back?' my mother enquired. They'd struck up something of a friendship; it would be a shame to tear it up. All that suffering bound you together. 'Please don't think all Germans are bad. Nazis and Germans: there's a difference.'

*

Since our school had been destroyed, we attended the lyceum with the girls. ('Our lovely old school!') The charming yard and the seven lindens, lost for ever.

The lyceum was a modern building from the System Era. It was originally called 'the Chest', but the Nazis were getting rid of 'foreign bodies' and had built a pointed roof on it. There was a giant clock on the wall – with dashes instead of numbers – that was always showing the wrong time. The doors were fitted with toughened glass.

The classrooms were bright and airy. ('Everyone whose home has burned down, please stand up.') We all found it funny to think that girls used to sit on the chairs. There were no urinals in the toilets. The girls were in a different section of the building now, and the hallway that led over to it was full of desks and old benches. We weren't permitted to use the big outdoor staircase to get into the school grounds, as we might run into the girls; we had to go down the main staircase and then go around the building instead. But the girls were also forbidden to use the outdoor stairs. They too had to go round the outside of the building. And so we met them anyway.

'Have you seen the Köster girl?'

She was sixteen and the ends of her hair had been curled. Apparently her parents were extremely strict.

The invisible barrier between the genders ran through the playground, from the second window of the gym up to the bicycle stand. It was not to be crossed. The girls were shooed away by their teacher on their side, and we were discouraged from looking at them by ours. ('Pick the paper up.') The girls linked arms and practised the Lambeth walk or whatever it was; we stood all herded together and grumbled. ('You're like animals.')

Occasionally you would be grabbed by schoolmates and taken over the border by force, no matter how hard you fought back. ('Blomert, can't you help yourself? Go inside and report to your professor.')

I was now combing my hair back. It looked flattering in my mother's mirror. (But was my nose a little crooked?) Where before my hair had waves on the top and the sides, I now ensured it was perfectly straight. ('What lovely hair you have . . .') I also wore new horn-rimmed glasses, which helped make my head look less round.

'Is it better like this or like that?' the optician had asked before putting the lenses in the frames for me. My grandfather had worn glasses, as had my father, and now I was the latest to need them.

'We've made that optician a fortune.'

'Wow, they give me a headache,' my sister said after trying my new glasses on.

My brother on the other hand thought they were fake lenses. He'd had polished sunglasses made. Zeiss Umbral: they were crazy expensive, much like Michael's.

You had to follow the curve when you wiped them. How were you supposed to get the greasy bluish film off the lenses?

'It's going to be really hard for you,' said my brother, 'now that you're wearing glasses you're pretty much disabled . . .'

Things weren't going too well with my schoolwork. (You didn't raise your finger to speak any more, but casually raised your whole hand.)

'What's wrong with you?' my mother asked. 'It's enough to drive you to despair . . . First things first, I'd get my bum on that chair: now that's an idea!'

Though if she was being honest, she hadn't always done such a good job herself. She'd been too emotional. One time she'd run away from home with her shoes unbuttoned. But back then it had been different: learning didn't play the role it did now.

'Reading books – there just wasn't anything like that.'

She'd only picked up a book for the first time in the early years of her marriage. She said my father was as lazy as a sack of beans, too; that he only bucked up once Lehmann, a senior teacher, had rapped him as hard as he could with his spoon. Then it all came together.

Drawing class was pretty painless. They called the teacher Audax, because his name was Kühn: bold. I had it good with him, because I was constructing churches instead of painting pictures on subjects like the poems of Matthias Claudius. He was however always amazed that I drew my towers so small.

'Which of you communists made that mess?' he demanded when someone had knocked over some cans.

The gymnastics teacher was called Edmund Ballon. ('You put the emphasis on the first syllable.') He always had everything ready for us. Once we'd marched into the yard, he paced along the row and tapped each of us on the chest and sent us off to grab something: 'Pole, pole, pole, rope, rope, dustpan, rake, broom, key . . .' Standing by the climbing bars, he complained about the toilet seat being left up.

Latin was bad. Instead of learning vocabulary, I prayed to my private deity Santa Claude. But it didn't usually help. Even my solemn vow not to step on cracks in the pavement amounted to nothing.

The teacher, Jäger, banged on the lectern with his flat hand: 'Hang it all, you hear! You've fallen out of the correct case again!'

He had a spot on his back that he would scratch. His shirts were always torn there.

'He's overly nervous,' my mother would comment, 'a complete degenerate.'

That *contra* meant against (in the hostile sense), and *vae victis* meant 'Woe to the conquered!' stuck in your head. But it was far more boring to try and remember the second-person-singular imperfect subjunctive of *amare*. ('Kempowski, help me here . . .') I laid down my arms at *velle, nolle, malle*.

Robert was appointed to be my assistant. ('You haven't paid it the least attention until now, have you?') Helping me pass my Latin exam was something of a risky undertaking, but he gladly took on the task:

a) because he was getting money for it, and

b) because . . . well, it would be a pathetic display if we couldn't manage it, and he didn't want the shame.

Not long into working with Robert, I realised that Latin wasn't quite as useless as I'd first thought. Take 'uniform', for example – if you knew Latin, you could understand a word like that right away. And it was easy enough to use a word like *merito* – worthy – in conversation. If someone said something you liked, you could just answer, '*Merito*,' and then the other guy would stare at you like an idiot.

He himself hadn't wanted to learn it at first, but Koch, the teacher, had shouted: 'I won't let you be lazy!' It still gave him strength today. It really was a shame he'd been drafted.

He gave me a column of vocabulary to translate, and sat facing away from me, listening to records.

> The cross-eyed cowboy
> With the cross-eyed horse . . .[2]

'Again!' he said when I didn't know something.

For mathematics they gave me to Matthes, the tutor who lived next door.

'He'll be happy to teach you,' they said: 'the poor man has only a very meagre pension. And he's always with his wife. It can't be easy.'

I remembered him from the air raid shelter, but also knew him from the skating rink. He would find a quiet corner for himself and make figure eights in that spot until red bits of brick from the tennis court under the ice showed up in the grooves. Once he'd accomplished that, he would unbuckle his skates and go home.

Matthes sat at his dining room table. He had a little red lamp instead of a doorbell because he was so sensitive to sound. Before we started ('a to the power of zero equals one') he made himself a supply of cigarettes with a tube-shaped device that loaded tobacco into pre-rolled papers. He took the tobacco from a wood-panelled metal case on which Egyptian slaves were carrying huge stones. As he made his cigarettes, he let the little flakes of tobacco fall back into the case.

'When did you start wearing your hair combed back?' he wanted to know. 'Is it supposed to be a rite of passage into manhood? But one that doesn't really hurt?

'In the old days, you wouldn't have had it so easy. In Ancient Greece, for example, among the Spartans, a boy once had a fox under his robe. Out of honour, he didn't tell anyone it was mauling his guts.

'Holding your hand in fire, that was also no small thing. In Tibet the monks even let themselves be walled up . . . That was taking things too far though. Where does it end, after all?'

In spite of his Jewish wife he'd been permitted to travel to chess games in Spain. He'd actually been able to buy oranges there. They grew on trees, like apples did here at home. And before the war he'd once eaten plums in Lugano. ('a to the power of minus one.')

He knew a method to count the grains of sand at Warnemünde, if you wanted to. That was very interesting.

In his view, the war could no longer be won. It was running towards a 'stalemate'. The opponents were drawing back to their borders and then everything would be the way it was before.

'"It was butchery, not a battle," that's what later generations will say.'

'And what else do you have going on?' my mother said when I came home. I always had to have something going on. But before I could answer: 'And did you do your piano practice? Honest?'

She begged and pleaded, which was always most unpleasant.

The frame of my bed was fairly wide, so I used it as a road, driving my trucks back and forth along it. There was a new bus toy available, one without the radiator that smelled like machine oil. I wanted three or four of them. But unfortunately there were no more in stock.

Through bullying and trading, my Halma army had grown to over 500 pieces. Setting it up took half an hour. I made myself a fortress out of the feather duvet and the comforter and from there I fired on the army with little rocks.

'Now come on and put your crap away,' said my brother, 'I don't even know where I'm supposed to walk any more.'

But then he asked for a few stones and shot them at the soldiers below, like I did. And he was happy when they scattered under the bed.

The army had been registered in several schoolbooks, it had been counted and organised over and over. The names of the officers had even been determined, and their salaries – little balls of silver paper

– had been fixed. The king – the Halma piece that had a knot in the wood – lived in a drawer of my desk.

At night I read science fiction novels under the covers with a torch or, when the battery died, with two small lights in the shape of flowers. *Thin as an Eggshell*, for instance, which featured a piece of twine that was as strong as a steel cable, along with all manner of screens and gently humming machines. And *The Destruction of Berlin in 1936* by Major Helders. I thought: 1936, how funny, that was six years ago.

*

Sörensen returned soon enough. I came home one day to find huge Danish newspapers lying around the house. They were inconceivably extensive. ('Quality.')

'It's amazing that you can get these here, really . . .'

The *Rostocker Anzeiger* was meagre by comparison. (Lost & Found was one section.) It was lying on the stairs.

Decisive Battle near Karkiv

He'd brought back technical equipment no one had ever seen: a device – 'made in England' – that sharpened razor blades; a flashlight with a generator; and a bunch of pipes (thirty-two of them, in fact). Delicate ones and some as thick as tree trunks. One was shaped like an ear trumpet.

'You can only use each pipe once before letting it cool down again,' he said. He only took one pipe with him into the office, however.

'And breaking it in right. Not everyone knows how to do that. It can be dreadful. It burns your tongue . . . The tobacconists smile to themselves if you buy a pipe for the first time, they know. And so later you smile too.'

He smoked pressed tobacco. He cut a corner off the disc, rubbed the tobacco between his hairy hands until it blossomed up into a cloud. Then it was rolled back together and stuck into the pipe. He ran the lighter over it, so that the flame curved down, while he held the pipe between his teeth.

'Hm, that smells really good,' said my mother, 'like plums, or honey.'

In the early days of their marriage, my father had also smoked a pipe, but it didn't smell as good back then, it was more for workers.

'A pack lasted a whole month, no?'

'Hydraulically pressed,' said my brother, 'if I'm not mistaken, open and shut case.'

The tobacco probably smelled better than it tasted, I thought.

Sörensen wore checked jackets, shirts with stiff collars, and tiny ties. He also owned a trenchcoat with epaulettes and leather buttons, which he wore with the collar turned up.

When the weather was hot he donned a straw hat. All Englanders wore a straw hat like that in the summer. The Danes dressed according to the English fashion, without exception; they were the leaders in Europe after all. English wool was the best in the world.

I inherited a dark brown double-breasted suit from Sörensen, with big lapels and packed cotton in the shoulders. It was first-rate and fitted me well.

'I got it from Denmark,' I said in school. 'A Dane lives with us. A Dane from Copenhagen.'

At that time every conversation began with 'A Dane from Copenhagen lives with us . . .'

Against my mother's protests he helped me set a loudspeaker that hadn't been working down on its back. But we never got it to work. We didn't have a hammer, so we hit it with scissors.

'The cord is probably too long,' Sörensen said, 'we'll have to switch it later. Maybe we need to add an amplifier in between, too. We'll see.'

He produced electric sparks with a brush and newspaper. That was the right way to understand electricity: you start with these small sparks, and then later you power machines with it.

'Boys should be allowed to do this – to tinker,' Sörensen said. He'd been allowed to do it when he was young. At school he'd even learned to patch his own stockings.

As a boy he'd put messages in a bottle and thrown them into the Little Belt. One answer came from Holland. I looked up how far away the two countries were on the map. I wanted to try it out. But I was unsure whether it was forbidden now.

We exchanged stamps too. Together we pored over the Hitler 1936 collection.

> Whoever wants to rescue a people
> Can only think heroically[3]

Sörensen, however, always misread 'rescue' – *ritten* – as 'ride', *reiten*. I laughed.

'Whoever wants to *ride* a people,' I said, 'can only think heroically.'

'Hey! Don't let anyone hear you say that!'

I had to teach him German swearwords: *Arsch*, arse, and *Scheiße*, shit. You couldn't find them in any dictionary. *Satanslord* was the worst Danish curse, he said, or just *skidt* – shit.

'But there must be other curse words in German?' he asked.
'Worse ones, too. What you do . . . down there.' Did I understand?

'Sure, shitting . . .'

'No, that's not what I meant.'

'Pissing?'

'No, not that either. Don't worry, I'll ask your brother.'

We agreed that the best language for swearing was English. *God damn!* That really blew off steam. What was *verdammt* compared to that? Way too tame. No, the Germans couldn't swear.

'And *rødgrødmedfløde* means "red berry compote with milk"?' my mother clarified.

'Yes, it's like *Fischers Fritze fischt frische Fische*, or *der Cotbusser Postkutschkasten.*'

'Oh, you can do those? Fabulous! You learned things like that in Denmark?'

He had one tongue twister that was completely original, though: '*In Ulm, um Ulm, um Ulm herum,*' he recited, and we all cheered.

My mother could prove she had a Danish great-aunt. She had photos, thick brown ones, dated 1893. Her name was Löfgren, her husband was a sugar refiner.

In turn, Sörensen showed us a picture of his parental home: the villa with its own beach. There was white garden furniture on the lawn, and a long driveway flanked by huge trees.

Even as a child he had received an allowance, meaning he had to pay for everything himself.

'May I have eight kroner for my new schoolbook?' he'd ask his parents.

'But why? Don't you get an allowance?'

But he never bought school supplies with his allowance. Instead he bought fishing equipment and a camera. He and his friend directed a film using it, a crime movie. They often went sailing too, he told us. They made it as far as Sweden once. For Danes this kind of thing was only natural.

'But you couldn't do that today,' he said.

'Yes,' said my mother. 'Lovely. But the whole pulling the fish off the hook business . . .? I couldn't do that.'

She'd actually met her husband while fishing – 1913, in Graal – but he'd never caught anything. The whole time they were sitting in their beach chairs he'd wanted to kiss her, but she'd fought him off, thinking it would get her pregnant.

'We were so innocent back then. Shame.'

After every meal Sörensen marched around the table to my mother and expressed his gratitude with a handshake: thank you for the food; thank you for the coffee; thank you for supper.

'That's how it's done in Denmark,' he told us. 'Politeness is the most important thing there. You say thank you for everything several times. First you express gratitude in writing, for an invitation, for example. Then again in writing, before the event, on the evening itself. And finally once again when you see one another for the first time after the event. Then you're done.

'And when you encounter a lady again for the first time after an initial meeting, you have to wait to see if she wants to be greeted. It's embarrassing, truth be told: you're always caught off guard. But that's how it is in Denmark. In Germany, it seems everyone just shakes hands at the same time.'

'No, that's not entirely right,' said my mother. 'The lady has to extend her hand first.'

'Really? Well, that's refreshing to hear. As a guest one has to pick up the customs of the country or leave. The German soldiers in Denmark are always polite – they're famous for it. They stand up in the streetcars, and when the Danish King rode through the park, they saluted too. They'd probably been commanded.'

During the occupation though, a lieutenant had given him a slap. Sörensen had knocked over his machine gun. He'd never forget that the Germans had done that, for as long as he lived. He'd been mortally insulted. The slap and the imprisonment: he'd always remember both.

My mother bought herself a hat with a wide brim, with little tassels hanging from it. She had to lift the hat up slightly to see, which made her look a little like she was trying to peer into the future.

In the evenings she showed Sörensen the beautiful sights of the area. Together they went along the willow path where the Warnow flowed by, and where yellowhammers were singing, and both marguerites and poppies were blooming.

'It would be even lovelier, however, if there were peace in the world and all human beings got along with one another,' she said during one of their walks. 'Oh, how I long for peace: the neon signs, and all that.

'When I was a young married woman,' she told him, 'we would always walk here, and I would make myself up so pretty. But now . . . how would the business survive? And what would the children do?'

A white sign stood at a branch of the Warnow:

> POLLUTING THE WATER
>
> IS PROHIBITED UNDER PENALTY . . .

'That's typical of the Germans,' said Sörensen. 'A prohibitive sign in the middle of nature.'

20

It annoyed me that I had never been inside St Jacob's. Now it was too late; it had been destroyed.

'What? You never went inside St Jacob's? You never saw it from the inside?' At that point my mother broke down. 'How is that even possible?'

To have gone past it so many times and not once looked inside was an oversight that I could never undo. But I maintained that the teachers should have helped. We'd seen everything with them – the Stone Gate (six squares wide, twenty high), Peter's Gate, the Kröpelin Gate, the city wall (before and after the restoration) – just not St Jacob's Church. I found it utterly incomprehensible.

I bought postcards, all of the available variations – from the front, from the back – and went around the ruins with them. In the ashes I found hand-forged nails, which I took with me when I left, along with shards of the colourful windows. Was this looting?

I decided that I wouldn't let the same thing happen with St Mary's. It could be gone tomorrow, after all. I went to look at the great monstrosity again and again. Swastika flags hung out of the abat-sons.

Wake up, wake up, you German land[1]

Which of the two main entrances had been used in the Middle Ages, the left or the right? And why were they locked now? What did the sandstone piece in the middle tower signify? Had there been a rosette there once? And would they decide to finish building the original two- or three-tower design when the war was over? Cologne Cathedral and Ulm Cathedral had been built to completion, why wasn't that possible in Rostock?

'Without her sisters, the now-destroyed parochial churches, St Mary's looks even more colossal,' said Dr Krause. 'A masterly testimony to the German Brick Gothic, pointing to the east, and a clever counterpart to the similar architecture of Wismar and Stralsund.

'You didn't really notice this immense, compelling, powerful structure before the catastrophe. It was concealed by shacks and cottages. For my part, I never paid the least attention to it. I was caught up following the grim daily news of the war in the press.'

'Yes,' said my mother, 'it's so vast. And now, out there over the rubble, we have a surprising view: the radiating chapels of the cathedral's east choir, spread out like little chicks around their mother . . . If there'd been no catastrophe, we would never have seen it. Everything had to be sacrificed for the sake of this view. The entire Old Town destroyed and only the church untouched: like a symbol, like an act of providence.'

Bombowksi, the tower attendant, with his short-cut hair, gave me the key. It was thanks to him that the church was saved. Before the catastrophe no one would give him the time of day – they saw him worthy of only demeaning domestic work. Now, though, the superintendent had thanked him personally. Maybe he would even get a War Merit Cross.

I was full of excitement when I unlocked the church. Inside, blind Jahn was practising Bach's 'Toccata and Fugue in D Minor'.

I walked through the transept, amid the echoing sounds of the organ, taking care not to step on any of the cast-iron heating grates, which made such an ugly sound if you walked across them, so that the man upstairs would have heard me.

There were models of old sailors in the church's aisle, and heavy lamps hung down from the dirty, off-white vault. (It was four metres taller than the dome of St Mary's in Lübeck – now destroyed – and just two metres shorter than Cologne's cathedral!). It was the only church in the world where the nave was longer than the transept. ('It's really quite something for it to be housed in a city like Rostock.')

Climbing to the higher levels, I looked down on the giant whitewashed walls, all completely bare. A red fire extinguisher appeared tiny amid the empty space below. (I was surprised that one was permitted to just punch holes into the walls of such an old church!)

Were there frescoes under the white paint? Medieval allegories? Holy kings with arabesques, martyrs, and mystical symbols? Why didn't anyone try and scrape it off? You'd have to be a restorer, I supposed.

I crawled behind each wall, into the family vaults and arbours, thinking I saw art treasures and *vasa sacra* – altar crosses, chalices and thuribles – where there were only brooms and dustpans.

The astronomical clock was set into one wall, charting sunrises and sunsets up to the year 2047, as well as the phases of the moon and the constellations. Judas was perched at the top, behind a small door which opened at 12.00: a little figure not unlike the wooden conductor on the Mountain and Valley Railway.

I descended a spiral staircase to the ground floor. Boards were laid down where there were humps in the floorboards. And in the arch, a hatch. I lifted the cover and suddenly looked down thirty metres into the nave. In that moment I realised that the floor I was standing on was paper thin.

In the west front, above a canopy commemorating the Archduke of Mecklenburg, was the giant organ, reaching up into the vaults. Its structure was rounded off with a beaming sun at the top. Those visiting would gasp in awe when they turned the corner. Before the war Bauerfeld, the Wehrmacht's musical director, had stood up there with his military orchestra.

Now you all thank God . . .

My father had had his green leather gloves on because of his chapped skin and had sung completely off key. The music was gentle and soft, despite it being men who were playing the trumpets and trombones.

As I walked carefully along the gallery, the blind organist stopped playing.

'Is someone there?' he asked. He had a clock – lacking the glass, its face exposed – perched next to him; his senseless eyes rolled as he felt the hands. I said good day and gave him my father's cigars. ('Just for me.')

In exchange for the cigars Jahn agreed to play the highest pipes, which were as small as a match, and also rumbled the lowest pipes, which were I don't know how many metres long. He showed me the shutters of the swell box, and the bellows: vox humana, with a tremulant in every pipe to produce vibrato. The stop knob that was bottom left had NIHIL written on it. (I laughed so he knew I studied Latin.)

He played me Heykens's 'Serenade', which Gregor often played on the radio. Then he laid his head back and continued practising Bach. Sometimes he only played with his feet, his hands in his lap, like he was sitting on a garden bench. I climbed up on the balustrade and looked down.

'Are you still there?'

It was quarter to four. I listened on, hoping that he wouldn't be stopping any time soon.

Supposedly Frau Kröhl had long wanted to sing the Bach-Gounod 'Ave Maria' up there. Eventually she'd got to do so, with Jahn. This was long before the catastrophe. But apparently he'd reached out and groped her. Frau Kröhl, the tax officer's wife. She with her lovely alto, velvet soft. He'd suddenly screamed quite strangely, she later said.

'All the pain broke open in him suddenly. He'd been blind from youth, so you could understand why.'

She just kept singing, despite his crude advances, so he found his place and continued tapping at the keyboard.

'Ave Maria!'

I thought it better not to ask him if I could play. The little I'd learned with Frau Schnabel probably wouldn't have gone down well.

My sister was working in a munitions factory at this time. Part of the auxiliary units, she spent her days writing out addresses: 'To Army Ordnance Officer So-and-so.' (Even grenades had to be addressed.)

'Ugh,' said my mother, 'in the First World War, women's hair turned completely green when they worked there. The working conditions were so poor that many of the women got very sick, and lots of people quit.

'But those were the good ones. Many others went on strike. Oh, I can still see them, such Furies.

'Across the way,' she continued, 'in Wandsbek, one of the women lived with seventeen children, believe it or not. Seventeen! In a tiny apartment. If you brought them things, old stuff, you had to take a deep breath before going in, there was such a stink. But all of them made something of themselves, all of them became honest craftsmen. And then, touchingly, they supported their mother afterwards.'

Just remembering all of their names would be a struggle, she thought.

Sometimes Ulla came home on a Sunday, full and lethargic from eating so much of the soup they served there.

'A Dane?' she sneered when we told her about Sörensen. But

when she saw him she ran into the bathroom, scrubbed her face with almond flour and put on her fancy gem ring, the one from Grandmother de Bonsac.

'Fraulein Uhla,' Sörensen said, stretching his backside out as he bowed. 'Will you permit me to invite you to the movies?' (*My Wife Teresa* was showing, starring Elfi Meyerhofer – with her big saucer eyes and pillowy lips – and Harald Paulsen, playing a burglar who was constantly sneezing.)

Instead of looking at the screen, Sörensen gazed at Ulla's hands. The white cameo on her caramel-coloured stone. Light shadows cast over the wall.

> Today the whole world makes music for me
> A little love symphony . . .[1]

In the newsreel, they showed clips from American films.

'See how rotten the plutocrats' morals are!' cried the commentator, set against footage of mud wrestlers.

'There's bound to be stuff like that,' Sörensen said afterwards, unimpressed, when they were outside on the street. Flipping the collar of his trenchcoat high, he continued: 'You've got all kinds of things in the big city. Six-day races, for example, or naked dancing. People shouting and jeering. What's the big deal?'

When my brother heard about the wrestlers, he went to the cinema right away. He came back thrilled. ('Tadellöser & Wolff!') He'd been waiting for something just like that. It was just a shame the fights were always so short.

'The way they punch each other, just taking turns kicking one another in the arse. It's awesome! They should make a whole film about it.'

Recently someone had said to him: 'Want me to put your lights out?' He thought it was great fighting talk. 'I'll bash your head in so hard, you'll be looking through your ribs like a monkey in a cage' was also good, but the first one was better.

That made him think of Laurel and Hardy, the last time we were at the movies. 'Remember *Tit for Tat*?' he asked. 'A guy pours syrup on one of their heads and the other guy puts their watches through the centrifuge. Then some wheels and springs come out of the bottom . . .'

This in turn led us to fruit loaf with marmalade and our good grandfather. ('You could always beg him for some money for the cinema!')

'Maybe it's for the best that he died. There's no way he would've been able to handle the decline of the *Consul* and all that. And just imagine him putting up with the air raid sirens! How he would have cursed!'

We heard that Schneefoot had also died. I thought of the dictation from class:

> It astonishes me and almost makes me
> sorry, that you weren't
> more careful in your
> dangerous undertaking . . .[2]

'I can still see him sitting here.'

'Schneefoot?' Ulla asked, overhearing: she hadn't known. 'The one who tried to kiss me?'

'What sort of a person was this?' asked Sörensen.

No one wanted to talk about that now. It was over and done with; dead.

'He fancied Ulla,' said Robert. 'But, *de mortuis nihil nisi bene*.' Who was going to inherit the roofing-felt factory now, though? That's what he wanted to know.

Sörensen was amazed that the names of all of the fallen were printed in the *Rostocker Anzeiger*. It was a lot of names, all things considered. You only needed to count the Iron Crosses ('on the field of honour') to know how things stood. He had a good laugh at the line reading 'Whoever knows us, knows what we have lost.'

'It really should go: "Whoever knew *him* knows what we've lost,"' he said.

Michael wrote to us from Witebsk. In turn, Bubi sent letters from Odessa, saying how there were guys – ragged, dirty – sat on every street corner, begging you for a smoke. He included caricatures.

'These are practically works of art,' said my mother, and held the pages at a distance. Then Robert pinned them to the wall, with Tommy Dorsey and Ralph Arthur Roberts.

'Shame there are holes in the paper.'

'Come on! He's bound to send completely new ones. The war is going to last a while, after all.'

To everyone's surprise, my father came back too. When he rang the doorbell, I thought it was Manfred.

'Oh, it's *you*?' I said. How little he was, and how fat he'd grown. He stepped in, panting, amid a blast of cold air. He dropped his trunk with a crash, in the corner next to the open cabinet with Wolff's telegraph reports from 1914–18.

'What's this?' He was pointing at Sörensen's summer hat, which hung on a hook. 'Foreign crap! Get it out of here, and I mean right this second!' He hung his holster on the wardrobe. ('So that you don't go for my pistol!')

My mother hurried in. 'Karl!'

'Oh, come on!' he screamed. 'No one was waiting to pick me up at the station. No auxiliary forces, nothing! It's unheard of. Really, I've had it up to here!'

'But Karl, we had no idea you were coming . . .'

'That makes no difference!'

He'd wanted to surprise us. So he dragged the trunk by himself. How terrific, how crazy, I thought. It was heavy as hell . . .

'I ran into Dr Heuer, of all people. "Where are you coming from? Isn't anyone picking you up?" he asked. Idiot. Bet I looked like a moron: an officer dragging his trunk by himself. It just isn't done!'

He paused for a second, before the tirade continued: 'And what kind of sty is this?' he screamed. 'Pipes and newspapers everywhere?' (*Peng*, the piano lid was flipped closed.) 'Who can't put their stuff away? And turn off that bloody jazz!'

Robert got clear of the fray ('Oh Jesus, how the little mouse bites'). He was off, he whispered, he'd be back at six-thirty or thereabouts.

Then my father made his way to the toilet, to 'drop a proper load'. A scream soon erupted: 'Hideous and disgusting!' The windows were flung open. 'The seat's still warm! I can't even have a decent go on the toilet! In my own house! Wherever you look, there's grime and grit. The whole day down the drain.'

When he re-emerged, he was equally keen to know who had just been on the loo.

'Stop your yapping,' my mother said, 'I can't stand it! You come home and immediately start yelling! From now on, we'll have a guard posted at the train station to see whether the master of the house might appear. When he does, he can make a signal: "The master of the house is coming now! Be warned: he's in a bad mood, take him with a pinch of salt!" And then everyone can come running to receive him. Someone can carry his trunk, someone else can run ahead and shout, "Clear the street!" and another, behind him, will scream, "*Heil!*"

'Honestly, you work and work, you run yourself ragged, you work your fingers to the bone, only to get yelled at. It's enough to drive you to despair. It's unheard of!'

She ran into the living room, her pearl necklace swinging, and began throwing things around. 'As if you don't have things just the way you want them! Why don't you move into a hotel, maybe that'll suit you better.'

She charged upstairs, and shirts came flying out of the bedroom, their sleeves waggling as they unfolded.

'Mother!' cried Ulla, and grabbed her hands.

'Might as well grab a rope and hang yourself!'

My father put his holster back on and whispered to me: 'I'll be back around seven. Got to blow off some steam.'

When he came back in the evening he found a swastika flag hung over the door. Over his bed a sign read:

> WHERE THE WARRIOR SLEEPS,
> HIGH LAURELS STAND[3]

'Is this a fitting reception?' asked Ulla.

We could never tell when things were about to go south. But when he saw that there was bunting around the bed he laughed with a wry expression and said: 'That's enough now. It's all a little bit much, isn't it, Grete?' Everyone was still nervous.

'If you only knew what rained down on me day after day. Those Thuringians, God damn it. And then, nothing but Russians. Russians, Russians, Russians. No French at all. To hell with it. And then Frau von Eickstedt turned to me and said: "But Herr First Lieutenant, what should we do with these people?"

'But then, they *were* always slipping me eggs. Plus, I got to eat two saddles of venison recently.'

He then told us how he'd had to witness a military tribunal. It wasn't exactly pleasant.

'You're probably thinking about Morgenstern's writing, "What is not permitted cannot be,"' the military tribunal counsellor had said when my father had asked for clemency; an educated man, he was. 'I'm afraid not, my good man. These people will be finished by the time this trial's over.'

One of the delinquents kept shouting to the pastor – 'Just one more question!' – despite already being at the wall, just to drag the whole thing out.

'Now that's enough,' the officer had finally said. 'A word of comfort, then it's over.'

My father tucked a napkin into his uniform collar. My mother presented wholegrain bread with a victory rune on it. The long nickel serving dish was covered with hunter's sausage.

'And there's more of this,' my mother said.

'They taste like rubber tape. Where are they from?' my father asked.

'From Max Müller. We got them with the ration coupons.'

'Really?' He was wrong, then, they were good. They *had* to be good.

Artificial sweetener in the tea, such that it bubbled up. 'The tablets are so tiny . . . Where did they come from?' my father asked.

'From Sörensen, from Denmark.'

'Remarkable.'

'So, what's new here?'

'You're going to laugh,' my brother said, 'but Schneefoot fell.'

'Schneefoot? Oh – who would have thought. His poor father. And what's become of Warkentin?'

'He's a cadet now.'

'That's good.'

The city looked terrible. There was probably no chance of pulling through. It was still smouldering at Doberaner Platz, and the streets smelled like burnt flour. ('Like back in Flanders,' my father noted.) Who was going to pay for it all to be repaired? There was only a narrow path through all of the rubble on Kistenmacherstraße – 'and it'll stay that way for years, no doubt' – and there was nothing left of Rosinat. The lovely cigars, all hand-rolled, gone.

'But we've been lucky.'

'It's not something to be sneezed at.'

Professor Krickeberg had crawled from roof to roof, filming the whole city before it was damaged – exactly fourteen days before. It had documentary value now. And a man was on his way to Lübeck with a camera as we spoke. Remarkable, no?

'I want to photograph the *rubble*,' my sister declared; she'd already made up her mind.

'Don't get caught,' said my father, 'you know it's forbidden.'

> You've got no clue,
> You little doe, you!⁴

He looked at her carefully, spying traces of lipstick.

'Ulla, my child, were you drinking lemonade? If all your admirers were to show up at the same time, the whole street would probably fill up, eh?'

'Sit straight! Left hand on the edge of your plate!'

'Do you want any more roast potatoes?'

'By all means.'

A knife fell to the floor.

Ulla told us that at the war emergency service if you didn't have your hand on the table they'd say, 'Are you looking for a dog down there?'

Apparently Ulla's dance teacher had been heard on Radio Moscow recently. 'The voice of the other Germany', they'd said: he had deserted.

'He'd most likely been with a scouting troop when he ran into a clearing, waving his handkerchief,' Ulla relayed.

'It's remarkable that the Russians didn't shoot a turncoat on sight, as a precaution. It's very dangerous after all . . .' my father noted.

'And how is school going?' Then, without pausing for an answer:
'*Ut desint vires tamen est laudanda voluntas?*'[5]
He could still do it all, we should test him.

> *O si tacuisses,*
> *Philosophus mansisses . . .*'[6]

'*Esses*,' my brother cut in. '*Philosophus esses.*'

'No, it's *mansisses*,' my father said, 'otherwise it makes no sense at all.'

'Whatever you say.'

'"Whatever you say"? Is that another way of saying "Kiss my arse"?'

'*You* said it!' Robert answered, and held two knives against his cheeks, the blades pointing out.

'We need to have a private chat about school later,' said my mother. 'Something must be done. Robert has caught up in maths, he's just got a C. But our little Peterpump, the poor little fellow . . .'

And then she spoke French, and looked at me as she did so.

After dinner my father took charcoal tablets. They absorbed all of his stomach gases, but gave him black teeth. A gulp of water to wash them down. Then he got his wallet out of his pocket and let the crumpled-up travel marks flutter into his leather portfolio.

'Can I have them?' my mother asked.

'Can you? – Sure. May you? – No.'

My mother sighed. 'Why don't you ever bring any eggs? Or sausage, for that matter. Forgot, didn't you?'

'I'm living at the courthouse now, by the way, my Gretelein' my father announced. ('Doesn't she look like a countess?') Then he peered over to the pantry. 'Any biscuits left? Any last crumbs in the biscuit tin?'

'There are none left,' my mother said. 'If I'd known in advance . . .'

'Well that's that, then!'

We retired to the living room. The women cleared the table while my father cut the cigars. He tested the knife against his thumb.

'Robert, go get a bottle of wine. But don't shake it up too much. And fetch the nice glasses too.' They came from Wandsbek. My father remained extremely pleased that we'd inherited them.

'And the picture here of *Consul Discher*, my old flame, also very nice. Everything's so wonderful – children, how nice it is to be together again inside these four walls.'

'Hopefully there won't be any air raid sirens.'

The bookcase's glass doors were open.

'So much I've yet to read,' he noted. '*The Mecklenburgers 1813*, for instance. Maybe I'll take that along with me. Or *Forests and Peoples.*

'And here, Heinrich Mann, *Professor Unrat*. That really reminds

you of how things used to be. It could all be taking place in Rostock
– though it's Lübeck, of course. The way he describes the cobbler,
who is also a Herrnhuter. It's so well written, it's as if you really
know the people.'

Just then the doorbell rang three times, and Sörensen came in.

'Aha! What do you hear, what do you say? Everything all right
again? I heard about your entanglement with the Gestapo from my
wife . . . Something of a fright, eh? But all forgiven and forgotten
now, no?

'And what's the story behind all these pipes? Don't take this the
wrong way, my good man, but would you be kind enough to take
them back with you?'

Sörensen cut in to announce that he'd just realised our telephone
number added up to twenty-one.

'Twenty-one – two-one-oh . . .!' My father had been calling all
year and never noticed that it was almost the number of his
regiment.

'Have you served?' he asked Sörensen.

'Yes, with the navy.'

'Remarkable. Do you want an Old Gold?'

'Yes, thank you, why not.' Sörensen had nothing against smoking
cigarettes.

'Then put your pipe aside!'

('Boy, you have to go to bed!')

My father then launched into a monologue about finder's fees
and tons, dividends and foreign currency and bills of lading.
('Supply and demand is the rule of business. Anyone who can't
keep up gets flattened! No mercy.')

The women came back in at that point. My mother was wearing
a black dress that was buttoned all the way up, with sleeves made

of lace. Around her neck she wore a fine gold chain with her topaz. Ulla meanwhile wore the cross-stitch embroidered Russian jacket. Her hair was sitting nicely, nothing was out of place.

She started telling us about what it was like at the munitions factory, but it wasn't long before my father interrupted.

'Are you allowed to tell us about all of this?' he asked, and looked around pointedly. When she continued talking, he stood up and went into the dining room.

'Do you understand what I'm trying to say?' he whispered. We were to keep talking calmly, and he would stand near by. Did we get it?

'I assume you're not listening to any foreign radio stations . . . Robert, look at me, for goodness' sake!' he insisted. 'What if someone's listening? They'll get everything out of us. Cell Leader Kollwitz has his spies everywhere. The jerk. A real Polack. He even came from Torun.'

'In Danish the name Kollwitz means "cold fart",' said Sörensen. 'Koldfis.'

'Cold fart! Hilarious!' Everyone fell about laughing. 'Cold fart!' ('Boy, you have to go to bed.')

'Let me tell you what we've been through, Sörensen. My God, the bin men!

"To Adolf Hit—"

And then for a long while, nothing.

"—ler we have sworn."

'And they really do look like garbage men, in their shit-brown uniforms . . . Who'd have thought things would go this far? That bunch can't even speak German properly. Gauleiter Hildebrandt was just a herder before all this. And he still looks like one.'

Sörensen was amazed to hear my father speaking like this. 'Aren't you an officer?'

'Mister: I'm conservative to my bones, but that doesn't make me a Nazi.' With that, the difference between a 'German' and a 'Nazi' was explained to the Dane.

'I understand. Right or wrong, it's still your country.'

'Exactly.'

'Before the Nazis it was still very black-red-and-mustard here. I could hardly stand it,' my mother said. 'Honestly, the political meetings . . . "We have to get out of here," we'd say, "the fighting's about to start." And then they'd just go after one another with chair legs, cracking them against one another.'

'In peacetime,' my father continued, 'we read light-hearted things like Fritz Reuter out loud. And went to concerts. But we didn't really take advantage of that opportunity at all. Now the theatre is gone again. And it had just been renovated too . . .'

Once a year a dove comes down from heaven.[7]

My father sat at the piano and played the 'Arrival of the Guests'. 'Do you know it?' he asked Sörensen.

Ulla fetched a poetry album shaped like a heart. We all had to write something in it, she said. Someone had written *Koldfis* at the bottom of the page – 'cold fart'.

'Okay then, cheers!'

'You said it.'

'In Denmark you say *skol*,' Sörensen said.

This wasn't of much interest. In Germany you said '*Prost*', and that was that.

22

When my father next went away, I had to go to Aunt Anna. ('It's already arranged, so that's that!') My mother told me that Professor Maßlow's sons were also staying with her, along with Dirke Vormholz and just about everyone else from school. Schneefoot (the rascal) had also gone to her, if she remembered correctly. ('If you won't listen to the lesson, you'll definitely feel it.')

'Be happy!' said my brother, 'You're in for a good old-fashioned whipping! They'll sort you out there.'

Jäger, the teacher from whom I had to get extra tutoring, looked at me sympathetically. '*You* at Frau Kröger's? Is that really necessary?'

He had to note it down, as you received fewer points for an assignment completed with a tutor's help. When it came to your report, on the other hand, you usually got a boost overall, because Aunt Anna really worked to make sure you made the grade.

'My father always went to the toilet at the cadet school when things got dicey,' said Manfred. 'You could do that too. Oh, and dodge sideways when she goes to hit you.'

He also pointed me towards a student in the sixth grade: 'He's already been there for a whole year, he'll be able to tell you a story or two.'

'It'll be all right, you'll see,' my mother said during supper. 'It's not a beating, just a bop with a shoe brush. She's not so scary, she puts her trousers on one leg at a time, just like everyone else.

'But remember: not doing your schoolwork is no way to go about things. You can't be surprised when we lose patience.' That laziness was the Polish in our family coming through.

'You have no idea how good you've had it here at home,' she continued. 'In my youth I only had the Reformation – we were taught about Luther all the time, and not much else. Now, you really have a chance to learn something. Like French! What an elegant language. *Dans une coin est une papier à la papiere* . . . How pretty that sounds! And history – how things used to be, the opportunity to learn about kings and emperors. It makes me want to pick up a schoolbook myself.'

'Your mother's right: you can't get by without learning,' Sörensen said. He used to mix up the order of Christians and Fredericks, but he was so cunning that he'd managed to blag it. 'Do you think I'd be sitting here in Germany now otherwise?'

Robert said he still had it all up in his head. ('Here, the Battle of Issos, 333 AD, the Persian forces take a clobbering . . .') I could ask him whatever I wanted. His knowledge of history was flawless.

'That didn't just fall into my lap . . . "Don't let yourselves get lazy," my teacher always shouted. But it did the trick, and now I'm reaping the rewards.'

All of his friends had been drafted into the war. Thanks to his bad eyes, though, he was able to stay here. And soon he'd go to business school, my father had seen to that.

*

You had to arrive at Aunt Anna's by one-thirty, and we'd then stay until seven in the evening. We had five hours of lessons every day, even during the holidays.

My brother drove me to Warnemünde on that first day, and I remember being struck by the house: Anna Kröger lived in a fortress-like villa, with battlements, little towers, and green-painted knights on the roof. Two tall poplar trees stood to the left and right of the house, and there was a grotto made of wizened, glazed firebrick in the middle of the grounds. In all likelihood, no one had ever sat inside it.

Across the street there were three doctors' offices – Dr Ditten, Dr Düwel, Dr Dietz – a lawyer's office and the headquarters of the Luftwaffe. We always saw the girls who operated the telephone switchboards and radio equipment going in and out of there.

'That place is full to the brim with all kinds of machines,' my brother told me. 'If a bomb ever fell anywhere near it, the whole place would go up.'

A sign on the building's entrance read SHOES OFF! Laced boots and exercise sandals stood in a row by the door. You crossed the floor in your stockings. To your left as you came in there was a toilet; it was always ice cold in there. We would come in, and then stop and listen to see if she'd already started the lesson. ('All quiet: we're safe.')

Upstairs, on the first floor, she rented rooms to the retired. They were sons of landowners, for the most part. Occasionally we'd hear sobbing coming from above. I was told that the older retirees used to entertain guests in the evening. But that was in peacetime, back when you could still have roaring parties. To the right was her husband's room, Kohlchen as he was called. He always sneezed twenty times in a row.

Revision sessions took place in the dark hall. Aunt Anna sat at a long table at the head of the class, with a wooden spoon resting in front of her. Diamonds sat on her bosom, which was the same shape as her nose: a long, sloping plane. We resented that these precious stones were gleaned from our toil. They rose and fell with her breath.

'Did you do your assignment?'
   'No, Frau Kröger.'
   'Did you get any marks back?'
   'Also no, Frau Kröger.'
   'Did you get called on for it?'
   'Yes, Frau Kröger.'
   'And . . .?'
   'All fine, Frau Kröger.'

I would quickly find a place to sit, often somewhere at the back, before opening my book promptly. We'd cover our faces with the open book, ducking behind it to begin reciting:

> And how he beckoned with his finger,
> The wide enclosure opened up
> And into it, with slow step,
> A lion strode . . .[1]

The first blow landed to my left, on the boy next to me: he'd been caught stretching. He was from the Blücher School. His father was a low-level official, at the customs or in the police, I was never sure. He had a triangular head, and his trousers had buttons made of horn, and fringe on the sides.

'C'mere!' Frau Kröger thundered. Then – *whack! whack!* – she boxed him on the ears. We knew not to look over, otherwise we'd get the same treatment.

At that moment the door opened and one of our peers came in. He was extremely late.

'Where're you coming from?' (*Whack! whack!*)

Don't look up. Focus deeper into the book. Look like you're focused. I scanned the page: Antofagasta. (*Whack! whack!*) The boy's briefcase fell to the floor; his notebooks tumbled out. (*Wham!* A kick.) Just keep writing anything, even if it's only your name . . .

Around 4 p.m. someone brought her coffee. (Only three hours to go.) There was something like sympathy in the servant's mien, but not sympathy for us: he felt sorry for the poor Frau Kröger, she was always worried about something.

'That one there, he's not writing at all!' the servant pointed.

She hardly looked up. 'It's fine, everything's all right. You can go.'

She dunked her biscuit and finally looked up to check: was he really not writing? Was there mischief? Foolishness?

'What is it? What do you want?' she snapped, seeing that the servant was still standing in the doorway. At this he took his leave. And as she stirred in her sugar, our bowed ranks were assembled. Her bangle pushed up as she felt for the cream. Everything was as it should be: not a peep, absolute silence, bar the ticking of the grandfather clock.

*

There were about twenty of us in the class – sometimes more, sometimes less – including the pretty daughter of the stingy landowner Vormholz and the ugly daughter of Dettmann the district leader. She gnawed at her fountain pen.

'You can be rough with my daughter,' Herr Dettmann had said to Aunt Anna.

Edler von Salchow and Ferdinand von Germitz, two of my classmates, were good-for-nothings from the country. They had heavy leather jackets with diagonal pockets, and wore brown wool stockings over their breeches. They laughed whenever they got smacked: 'It serves us quite right! Oh, what stupid boys we are. We'll bring something with us on Monday to say sorry. We'll come with saddles of venison or a duck.'

At another table, sat together, were the Maßlow brothers – the sons of Professor Maßlow. ('Highly educated and intelligent.') There was more to be squeezed out of them. We had nothing to do with the brothers though, they were in a different category entirely. We heard that they played chamber music with their father in the evenings – cello, violin and piano. ('They're supremely musical, you know.')

We knew to sit tight when we'd finished our schoolwork; to look busy. Only fools hurried or let Frau Kröger know they were done. If you told her, you had to sit there and do it all again right away. ('Again!') It was common practice. She crossed the work out with a red pen, from the lower right-hand corner to the top left. The time had to be passed, after all.

If your vocabulary wasn't right, you got a smack on the ears with a book. ('*Velle, nolle, malle.* Here, I'll show you.') Pulled down by the ear to the table, your nose pressed into your mistakes. ('There!' *Whack!*) And one more clip with the back of her hand, just in case you thought it was over.

If you were dumb enough to let her know that you'd finished the work for a second time, you got something else to do: learning your work by heart, page by page.

Full many a wonder
Is told us in stories old,
Of heroes worthy of praise,
Of hardships dire . . .[2]

You sat there for an hour, dozing off to the sound of the grandfather clock, then: *bam!* She'd wake you and quiz you on your work.

Sometimes Kohlchen appeared at the side door, newspaper in hand, slippers on his feet. But she didn't let up on us on his account. She just shooed him away.

'Don't bother me now.'

'But it's urgent . . .' he whispered.

'No, there's nothing doing. Go!'

Under no circumstances were you permitted to laugh when he sneezed.

When everyone was in attendance, the room was often too full and the veranda was opened up. We could then see down to the yard, in which a laundry mangle stood. ('Draw a pipe organ.') We joked with one another quietly and carefully.

One of the boys pulled faces when Aunt Anna's back was turned. One time however, Aunt Anna was right behind him. He was beaten through the whole building. You could hear him bawling from floor to floor, including from down in the cellar.

The Maßlow brothers straightened their papers. Where had they left off? Ah, yes, up here, another line had to be drawn. In the evening they would play chamber music with their father again, the white-maned professor. 'Divertimento in G', Köche catalogue 201.

The *a* and *c*,
The *l*, *n*, *t*,
And *ar*, *us*, *ur*,
Are neuter.[3]

The one relief of this new system: no more Schnabel woman. No more etudes, no more Schumann. She was phoned and told I could no longer come. I was now at Hitler Youth for two afternoons every week, and there was just no time for piano lessons. She had to understand.

'It really is a shame,' said my mother, 'you were making such good progress. *Chants sans parole* . . . Well, it's all the same, it wouldn't have come to anything anyway.'

We also telephoned Matthes to say I could no longer come (plums in Lugano; mathematics at his dining room table).

'But I can still have a real influence on his education,' he pleaded.

*

My service in the marching band was practically time off. I now had three students under me. I had a silver chevron on my left sleeve. There was a victory rune on the right, along with our department triangle, with NORTH MECKLENBURG emblazoned underneath it.

Sometimes I had to accompany the flagbearer, Löffelholz, to the district offices or the public health department. I was the adjutant, so to speak, and carried a briefcase and a pellet gun. He took a shine to me. He'd also listened to records with Robert a few times.

'Say hello to your brother,' he'd say.

'Tell him hello back,' Robert answered.

For my birthday, a sheath knife lay next to the ring cake on one of the six side tables. But it didn't say 'Blood and Honour' on the blade. That wasn't allowed any more.

I sanded the lacquer off the blade, as was custom ('It's a lovely knife, boy!'), and opened the clasp. I reattached it a little lower, so that the knife hung at an angle.

'What do you have that dagger for?' asked an old woman on the tram.

Of the three scouts in my charge, one limped and another had a red nose, but the third was all right. He was the son of the family from Zeeck's, the department store. My only assignment was to pass down orders to these boys:

'Report to St George's School at three o'clock.'

'Polish your shoes and belt.'

'Wash the hand you jerk off with.'

When Löffelholz wanted to ascertain what kind of troop leaders we were, we once had to do exercises with our underlings. The other troop leaders drilled 'Eyes right' and 'Eyes left,' or 'Division, about face.' Klaus Bismarck Stüwe, who normally just sat in the grass, went completely wild.

'Get down! Up! Down!' he screamed. He acted as though he wanted to hit his subordinates.

'It's all for show,' I heard Eckhoff say to Löffelholz.

The girls watched from the wall. ('Pooh! Just our luck that we're not boys.') One did a silly imitation of our drills. Spotting this, the fat troop leader made an appeal to her conscience for her to cut it out.

I stood my three scouts in a row and played telephone. I knew it from the children's groups.

'Pudding bowl,' I whispered into the first one's ear, who would then whisper, 'Wudding bowl' or something else entirely into the next scout's ear. We had no idea what kind of nonsense would come out at the end of the chain.

I thought it was a shame we didn't have a table out there, as that would have greatly expanded the number of games we could play. We could even play *Wattepusten*, with two scouts on either side of the table, trying to blow a cotton-wool ball over the other's goal line.

> Am I not a young man in the world?
> Leaping like a little stag in the field?[4]

Löffelholz observed us from afar while we played, then drew closer. Soon he signalled to Eckhoff and stood next to me. It would be better if everyone moved over so we could all play. The girls with their white socks jumped off the wall to join in. I saw Gina Quade among them, pretty as ever, in her pleated skirt.

The troop leader had her recorder with her. We began singing as soon as she started playing:

> On a tree a cuckoo bird sang
> Simsaladimbamasaladusaladim . . .

Gina could sing the nonsense syllables especially quickly, she bopped along with her head:

> . . . on a tree a cuckoo sat.[5]

The others also moved their heads: head-bopping all round. And the troop leader got wet spots under her armpits.

'Your turn,' she said to Löffelholz.

He started a different song, indicating the pitches with a flat hand. A canon:

> The lazy man and the wanton man
> Are two peas in a pod.[6]

'From here to here,' he said, pointing to people, 'are the first group. From here to here: the second.' Singing in the round, a war of all against all. When we were supposed to stop he gave a special sign: one final round.

My mother thought I should go to Aunt Anna for another hour after band practice, or that I should start going on Sundays.

'It would just be so nice if you could make it to university. You'd be the first to follow in my footsteps: to finish high school, to study . . .'

'Yes,' my brother chimed in, 'it's up to you to end our family's dry spell!'

'Student life is the freest thing you can imagine,' my mother said. 'Oh, I still remember how drunk they were all the time! "My good man, you were staring at my lady," they'd snarl. And then they'd duel! They weren't supposed to flinch, otherwise the duel didn't count. The scars across their faces were stitched up without anaesthetic – to prove a point, I think.'

Afterwards I'd have the choice of becoming a paediatrician or a lawyer. I had to rethink the option of working for our firm, though. My brother was going to work there, and two members of the family in one firm had never gone well. So that came to nothing.

*

Sometimes Anna Kröger's old mother stood in for her. She tried to imitate the strict lady. She pointed to one of us with a kitchen spoon and said: 'You there, what's your name? Sit down properly.'

We moved like ice skaters over the parquet floor and laughed like mad the whole time. Von Germitz sat behind her and blessed her white head ('Holy, holy . . .'). I gave an impromptu lecture about 'sulphurusoxydialic acid', which was all complete nonsense. I had no idea whether such a thing even existed. ('It turns green litmus paper gold! Just try not to get too bogged down in the details.')

'Well, that doesn't make sense,' she said, before hesitantly returning my book. 'Read it again.'

She hadn't so much as smiled at the daughter of the district leader: Dettmann's daughter, the 'Child of Light' we called her, after her father's pagan speech. She had glassy eyes and dirty fingernails (which she used to scratch her pimples open). She was stupid; slow. The seats next to her were always free. (I would have liked to sit next to her, though. I wanted to find out whether she had a servant at home.)

'I have to leave very early today,' I tried once, 'my mother has entrusted me with something urgent.'

'No, that won't do.'

'Well, it's on you then . . .'

She grasped for her medallion. Then, after quarter of an hour:

'Okay, pack your things. That's probably enough.'

I threw my shoes on, jumped on my bicycle and got out of there at a mad speed. Past the three doctors (Ditten, Düwel, Dietz), cycling as far away as I could.

Once, on my way home, I stopped to watch the construction of the bunker at the station. Its walls were three metres thick. I saw the rush of *Ostarbeiter*, workers from the east, crowded in the express goods department, having just arrived: women with knitted headscarves, men with pointed flat caps. They all had wooden trunks, which many of them were sitting on, and each had a pot of soup. They were supposed to go to Heinkel to manufacture aircraft.

My gaze wandered back to watch the clearing of the rubble. A tractor with a steel tow cable at its rear; its loader bucket going up so high.

'Is this necessary?' an old man asked. 'Aren't the walls still completely stable?'

'No, it's been burned out,' a woman replied. 'They've just torn down the Gothic gable at the Wendländer Schilde, too. They're doing away with damaged property.'

There were advertisements in the cinema boxes for *The Great Love*. Zarah Leander was the star.

> I know, a miracle has to happen one time
> And then a thousand fairy tales come true[7]

Then I'd cycle on to Manfred's. At that moment he was being tickled by his mother as punishment. He'd lost their bread coupons. Again and again she grabbed her 'Swiss cheese little boy' wherever he ran for cover: under the table, in the wardrobe.

'I'm wondrous, aren't I?' she would coo to her dachshund. 'Isn't Mummy divine?'

Manfred collected maps. He cut them out of all the newspapers, he already had a fat folder full of them. They showed progress at the front; a spearhead moving in the direction of the Caucasus.

For his birthday his parents got him a map of Africa. He knew his way round it: two big splotches to the right and the left, marked in red, and above them two smaller ones. Those were the former German colonies, now 'under English administration'. They still belonged to us really.

Life under the English, as Manfred imagined it: sitting on the veranda, listening to the chirping of the cicadas, having your boy bringing your whisky; threatening damnation with the riding crop, auguring nothing good, unrelenting.

'Have you had a few knocks from Aunt Anna yet? Yes? With the wooden spoon? Or with her hand? On your head or on your back?'

'Two big students held me down,' I lied. 'They twisted my arms.'

'And what happened? What happened? Did Dettmann's daughter get a couple of clips too? No, eh? She wouldn't dare. She'd be dragged off right away . . .'

Around evening, I got up the courage to go home. I received an unexpectedly friendly greeting there, beyond anything I had hoped for. The Rosary Circle was meeting, and so marmalade cake and coffee substitute had been presented in real Meißner porcelain. Pumpkin seeds acted as a substitute for almonds on top of the marmalade cake. When I tried it, the cake tasted of rum.

'Well, my little fellow,' said my mother, and kissed me on the forehead. She looked me over: ears clean? ('And how's your widow's peak?') She dabbed eau de cologne on a twisted handkerchief and wiped me down.

'Oh, how big he's got!' one woman cried. She was the wife of Jäger, the teacher with a hairdo like a wreath cake. Frau Kröhl and Frau Professor Angermann were there too ('I believe her husband's going to put a bullet through her head, that's how dumb she is,' my mother had once said of her), along with Frau District Court Counsellor Warkentin.

'How is your piano-playing?' Frau Kröhl wanted to know. 'We should play together.' She had a wonderful alto.

'He just played such a lovely song,' my mother said, 'from Tchaikovsky. *Chants sans parole*. But now his piano lessons have ended. All over and done with.'

'How come? Is Mrs Schnabel sick?'

'No, his studies come first. He wasn't doing any schoolwork, the naughty little creature . . . Tchaikovsky, by the way, complained about his head being heavy. "I can't hold my head up," he always said. It's in the book *Beloved Friend*. I'd really recommend it. The author and Tchaikovsky had written to each other for years but they never met one another!'

She went on to say how Eugene Onegin's name was actually pronounced completely differently; it was Yevgin Anyegin. She'd always listened to it with such pleasure before, in the old theatre, she said.

'Ah, those concerts were wonderful. The music was so lovely. And so international! It went beyond all borders. I don't understand how people can't just get along . . .'

'My son doesn't have a head for music either,' said Frau District Court Counsellor Warkentin, sitting up straight. He'd been home recently, she told us. ('Ah . . . on leave?')

'Mother,' he'd said, 'you have to give me time, a lot of time.'

'Son,' she'd said in return, 'go over to the rose garden; try and think some different thoughts . . .' But no, he just sat at home.

'There's still half a melon in the kitchen, my little Peterpump. You take it . . .'

Its spherical surface put me in mind of Kurt Laßwitz's *On Two Planets*.

23

My confirmation lessons also served to disrupt my tutoring. We had to take part in sessions for two years ahead of the ceremony, and religion classes in school had been stopped.

> As the stag cries for fresh water,
> So cries my soul, God, to you.[1]

My parents didn't mind the disruption, they let me walk to St Nicholas's, out of an old sense of attachment; they had got married there in 1920. Plus all of their children had been baptised there, and my siblings had been confirmed there too. No matter what else was going on, when you were in the church you were standing on solid ground, you were protected.

Now and again on my way there I was stopped by children in the street. I had to take long detours to avoid them.

'Professor Knallaballa,' they shouted after me, like the pastor in John Brinkman's memoirs. In winter they threw snow at me.

My mother didn't go to St Nicholas's. She saw Professor Knesel at the cosy little Convent Church instead. He preached primarily about flowers and animals, drawing on sayings from the Apocrypha: 'The snow is miraculous rain,' or 'The bee is but a little birdie.'

'Is it bad that we don't go to St Nicholas's now?' my mother asked. 'It isn't as nice to sit in the white vestry, singing along to the harmonium, though. It's so miserable! And ever since the church was destroyed, Pastor Nagel has become more and more pitiable . . . The tower itself is also showing cracks, what are we supposed to do? And the people there! Good, upstanding people, but still: Old Town, crowded, working class.'

No, it was certainly more pleasant in the Convent Church. Even the walk there . . . Hopping over the wall, walking past the Palais and – admittedly – the prison. (Those poor people, I always thought.) Frau Dr Vegasack had once spoken of a woman who wouldn't redye her hair because her husband was doing time for abortion.

('Abortion? What's that?'

'They do stuff *down there*.')

And to think that Sörensen had landed himself in the prison; how funny . . .

The folding altar had been removed from the Convent Church, to make space for the air raids, but the intimate atmosphere remained. The charming cloister and the old gravestones were quaint. ('It's all just so sweet.')

And everyone knew each other. Fraulein Dibbersen from Viennese Fashions went, along with Fraulein Heß from the university library and Professor Guntherman. Professor Guntherman had his usual seat on the front row, right under the pulpit. He cupped his ear with his hand in order to hear better. District Court Counsellor Warkentin was always there too, his hair snow white now. ('Such a nice man. Sensible through and through.') That's how it was in the Convent Church.

Fraulein Heß had once made old issues of the *Rostocker Anzeiger* available for my father to read, though she wasn't really permitted to do so. They were delivered by cart, he recalled, and charted the ups and downs of local businesses; you could follow their fortunes so clearly in its pages: how Krüger's gourmet food store died off bit by bit, while Bölte came up in the world.

Meanwhile, Pastor Nagel at St Nicholas's always wore a black suit, with shoes that had leather laces. He was a good sort, but wasn't a German Christian. And he didn't preach about flowers and animals. He pronounced his vowels darkly (*oh – uh – uh!*), as if he were always warning us, or conjuring at the pulpit.

Before the bombing, when the church was still intact, he'd paused upon hearing the fanfare of the Hitler Youth marching outside and clearly, visibly, shaken his head.

The sermons he gave us were a collection of concluding remarks. You always thought: Now he's about to say Amen. But no, there was another detail, and yet another . . .

Now and again he launched attacks against Catholics in a squeaky voice. They weren't allowed to read the Bible. ('Can you boys imagine that? To never read God's Word . . . The Sermon on the Mount, for example, or Corinthians Thirteen, or the Twenty-third Psalm?')

> Thou preparest a table before me
> In the presence of mine enemies[2]

'The Catholics think they can command Christ during Mass,' he told us. 'They act like they can contain him in the church. But no! That's not for them to decree.'

'Some people say, "God damn me." Isn't that terrible? Whoever says that is willingly calling damnation on to himself. Eternal damnation! Just because he might have bumped into something!'

From a scholarly perspective, the sixth request of the Lord's Prayer – 'and lead us not into temptation' – seemed to him to require elucidation:

'It sounds as though God led us into temptation. Now, think about it. Your beloved God, who gave us His only son and let him be nailed up on the cross, would *He* lead us into temptation?'

No, the sixth request meant the opposite, just as the cross was not a sign of defeat but of victory. For us the cross was a heavenly ladder, that was certain.

When he was done, he kept us for a while longer: just this Bible quote ('Okay, now you can go . . . No, wait!') and now that quote. ('And that servant of servants is not to be mixed up with our contemporary understanding of a servant, back then they were completely inferior people . . .')

When you eventually got out to the street, you looked around to make sure he wasn't going to come running out after you with another quote.

*

I used to leaf through the Bible often – lying on the carpet, shoes off, crispbread with blackcurrant jelly. We kept a huge copy, with pictures, in the pantry, next to the cookie jar. For Noah's flood, the image showed bodies laid out on boulders and in the crevices between them, each of them naked. Further up the page, atop a mountain, there was the ark, and one further small but crucial detail: a dove. Another picture showed the waves of the Red Sea crashing down on some soldiers. On the far bank, clearly visible, the rescued children of Israel were shown to be grateful to the Lord. In my favourite, the shaggy head of a placid lion rests on Daniel's lap while a lioness tears her victim to pieces in the background.

My great-grandparents had got this Bible in Königsberg, from the dean in charge of their district. They'd received a medal too, for their golden anniversary, which was kept in my father's desk, next to the cover of Uncle Fredi's urn. (He had wanted his ashes scattered in the sea, but it was forbidden now; the Nazis didn't allow it.)

24

One night after dinner in the autumn of 1942, we all sat together at the table for a while. The sun shone in the living room, and the canary sang.

'This is so lovely, isn't it, children? So lovely,' said my mother as she watered the plants and snipped off wilted leaves. The myrtle was doing well, and the Christ's thorn also had new blossoms.

Ulla was now studying English literature. She filled page after page of her college notebook with clear handwriting. She was both thinner and more tanned than I had seen her before, and she spent every free minute lying in the sun. ('Isn't this a little silly, child? You look almost dirty.')

A university education had been Dr Krause's advice. The munitions factory wasn't right for a young girl with a high-school diploma.

'Someone like Ulla has to study! Art history or medicine, perhaps. And then she'll stand by your side, Frau Kempowski, in this difficult time.'

After all, who knew what was yet to come?

Robert was also home again. He was supposed to go back to Stettin, to the business school, the next week.

'It'll be the first whiff of business I'll have had,' he said.

He still didn't feel entirely at home there, but that would come later, he thought. When it came to handling money, he still hadn't learned all the tricks of Moses and the prophets.

Sörensen was stuffing tobacco into the pipe shaped like an ear trumpet. He sat on the chair at the desk, where my father liked to sit when he looked through the mail, groping through the telegrams with his fat fingers and scratching at the cracked backs of his hands.

'Oh, how cosy this is,' my mother used to say. And then my father would get up and sit at the piano and play.

> I have no father, mother,
> Brother, sister in the wo-orld any more . . .[1]

And my mother would sing along in falsetto.

'Your father couldn't sing the German national anthem at all,' she said. 'I mean, really, what an embarrassment.'

Sörensen yawned.

'Tired? Sleepy?' my mother asked.

'I just can't get used to the hot lunches here. I feel so full and sluggish after eating green beans in sauce thickened with flour.'

'My husband always used to lie down for half an hour in the afternoon,' my mother said, 'but afterwards I'd see him with his hand in the cookie jar, popping biscuits into his mouth. Do you all remember real coffee? Oh, how Daddy enjoyed that.'

Now she had a craving for real coffee.

Ulla put fruit loaf on the table, along with the floral cutlery and the nickel pot containing the coffee substitute. We made grimaces at each other, like the faces of the dying warriors sculpted in the courtyard of the Berlin Armoury.

'I have nothing to read,' Sörensen piped up. 'I recently picked up a copy of *British Classical Authors* at Leopold's second-hand bookshop. A miracle to find an English book, in Germany.'

'There used to be many English books in Germany,' my mother said. '*Captain Sorell and his Son* by Warwick Deeping, Taylor Caldwell's *The Day Will Come* . . . All English authors. *Gone With the Wind* too.

'It's a shame the Punch books were thrown out,' she continued, 'they made for good reading. I last saw them in Grandfather's apartment. Very funny, though; they'd certainly take your mind off things right now.'

My brother got the English print from the hallway, *The Hunter and his Horse*. It was framed in mahogany.

'Here,' he said, 'also English.'

And I rummaged around in my schoolbooks. An article titled 'A Little Hold-Up in the City'. ('You can read these if you want?' I offered.) The book also explained how English coins worked. Twelve pennies to the shilling. Rather strange . . .

My mother opened the creaking glass door on the bookshelf and, after thinking it over briefly, pulled out *Moltke* by Eckart von Naso. The cover was blue with red type.

'Moltke served in Denmark,' she said. 'The Great Silence, they called him. There is a connection there.'

'If I'm not completely mistaken,' Sörensen said, 'Moltke had no hair. Did you know that? Completely bald, but he always wore a wig, even in battle.'

'Is it right to speak of "Singing Germany"?' Sörensen wanted to know. 'You never hear any singing . . .'

'Thank God!' said Robert. 'That's all we need right now. If everyone were to suddenly get the idea to start singing.'

Out there in the distance
With a loud trumpet sound[2]

'At school I deliberately sang the wrong notes so that I didn't end up in the choir,' Robert continued. 'But I did learn a war song once.'

He could still remember it: with its references to bivouacking and all manner of shenanigans, it was a song of the Fatherland. Schulze, the music teacher, had stood on the podium and beat time with his leg hanging down.

'Otherwise, no music for me.' Jazz, it seemed, was a different matter entirely. He went to the record stand and pulled out one disc after the other.

'What should I play? "Grand Terrace Rhythm", perhaps? Or "Fate"?'

'Knock it off, boy.'

'We always had "morning singing" in the munitions factory,' Ulla said. 'Thank God that's over.'

And then it was time to say grace:

People eat,
Horses feed,
Today it is
The other way around.
Everyone – come and get it!

Although, when Ulla really thought about it, there was nothing wrong with her comrades. And they'd all felt connected somehow, and safe. A certain order was necessary, after all. Otherwise there'd be nothing keeping them there. They'd just jump the fence and bolt.

'Singing Germany, you say?' said my mother. 'Oh, I still remember how well Frau Kröhl used to sing. And my father too: he used to sing.'

'Grandfather de Bonsac?'

'That's right.'

'You never told us about that!'

> The fields are mowed,
> The gleaning wind blows,
> I love the one
> And kiss the other,
> Marry the third, listen . . .[3]

The doctor had prescribed the song to him because he spoke from too far back in his throat. But it didn't really do anything: he still spoke strangely, even today. She could still remember how his voice echoed down the corridor, though.

'I always tried to join in, but my wailing was deemed too oppressive,' she said.

'It seems Germany is the only country with two national anthems,' Sörensen said.

'No,' said Robert, 'we only have one. The second one has nothing to do with us.'

'Good,' said Sörensen. 'But all the same, I'm not sure I understand "from the Etsch to the Belt". The Belt is still in Denmark and the Etsch is in Italy, no?'

'It's not meant literally, you have to understand it figuratively.'

'The Germans are very hospitable, I have to give you that. You fell in love with half of Italy and half of Denmark, and deigned to include them in your anthem. But it made a bad impression abroad. A very bad impression.

'"*Deutschland über alles in der Welt*": "over everything in the world" . . . How do you know that you're superior to *everything* in the world? And what's more,' Sörensen continued, 'you couldn't even provide your own melody! It's from Austria!'

'It's from Haydn's *Emperor Quartet*,' my brother said.

'Precisely, from Austria. Haydn was an Austrian. And the Austrians and the Bavarians aren't really German. I learned that in school. They speak completely differently.'

'Good grief!' said my brother. 'It's just a dialect.'

'The Norwegians speak just like the Danes,' Sörensen countered. 'But I wouldn't say that they *are* Danes.'

'Did Norway occupy you once, or what?' asked Robert.

'Don't be so tactless,' my mother put in. 'In any case, we used to sing the old anthem – "*Heil dir im Siegerkranz*" – in a melody taken from "God Save the King". Oh, I still remember. We always had the loveliest view from our window when the Kaiser came to the races. I always thought the motorcade was the race, when I saw all the cars driving behind him! I thought it was odd that it was supposed to be a race but no one passed anyone else!'

'It would be better for us if we'd joined the English,' Sörensen said. 'That would be better for us, and all the people in the world.'

'Back then,' my mother said, 'in the First War, there were lists of the fallen. You don't hear about that any more. Don't hear anything, don't see anything.'

*

Sörensen spoke good German. Whilst he called my sister 'Uhla', said 'Schleger' instead of *Schlager* and emphasised the word 'humour' on the first syllable, he knew his way around special cases much better than we did.

'German is an ugly language though,' Sörensen said. '*Brrrruttorrregistertonnen* . . . What kind of sound is that? Ugly through and through. Like Russian or Polish.'

'But *Schmetterling* is a lovely word,' my mother said. 'You immediately picture a flowering meadow, *Schmetterling*. No comparison to the English "butterfly".'

We asked Sörensen if he thought in German.

'Yes,' he said, 'but only linguistically. Just recently I caught myself counting crates; saying *eins, zwei, drei* instead of *en, to, tre*.'

'That must have been rough,' my brother said.

My mother said that an acquaintance of hers – a captain – could count in Finnish.

'*Kaks, koks, kelwe*, or something like that. Oh, how funny that was, we laughed and laughed!'

It had been shocking for him, Sörensen went on, that he'd suddenly started thinking in German. What he was worried about was that his thinking would change with the language.

'After all, language,' he said, his fingers coming together into a point, 'is thinking.'

If anything, his character was being twisted away from the clarity and truth of Danish thinking into the mystical darkness of the Germans at this present moment.

'Another drink?' my mother said. 'It's a shame Daddy's not here. He would definitely have enjoyed this . . . How good we have it, being here all together, and healthy. We could have been burned to a crisp! Imagine, everything in ashes. But no, the sun shines. How wonderful, how lovely . . .'

'The Germans in Copenhagen were polite,' Sörensen continued. 'They jumped up to make room in the streetcar when a lady got on. But then they always walked on their wives' left-hand side, instead of walking where it was most dangerous; on the side of the street. It's completely unreasonable! That's just how it is in every other country.'

'You're right,' said Ulla. 'It's very stupid.'

'Just a moment,' Robert chimed in; it was time for his comeback. It was time for Sörensen to get as good as he was giving. He wasn't to take it the wrong way, Robert just wanted to give him a snappy comeback. 'As far as I'm aware, there's a deeper logic behind walking on the left. It isn't because of politeness. On the contrary! If I don't have it completely mixed up, it comes from the Middle Ages. Back then you walked on the left in order to avoid wounding your lady if you suddenly had to draw your dagger . . .'

'There it is again!' Sörensen shouted. 'Everything is about war.'

He had more to complain about, too.

'Answer me this: why are the titles on book spines printed upside down here? Everywhere else they print it so you read from the top of the spine down; it's only in Germany that it's the other way round. It's crazy!'

And on he went, speaking of how the Germans were a prideful people, complaining that none of them learned Danish.

'In Denmark, every student learns German. People there are more open minded. No one here makes the effort to pronounce city names in their original language. They say Düppeler Schanzen, and not Dybbøl skanser, for example. And a normal Dane has no idea what that's supposed to mean! I don't say Pierdknuppel instead of Rostock. There's no respect here for other people.

'Traditionally, a third of Danes have looked to England, a third to France, and a third to Germany. Since 1940 that has changed abruptly, as the German third went over to England. You have to understand that. All that comes from Germany is war; that was the reason.'

'Culture too, surely . . .?' my mother said. 'From the good old German fatherland.'

'Excuse me? Culture?'

'No, not culture, Mummy,' Ulla said. 'We stole the Gothic architecture from France. I think Rembrandt was German, but Leonardo, Raphael – they were all Italians.'

'Yes,' said Sörensen. 'And it's the same with music: Haydn was, as we said, an Austrian. Mozart too. And Beethoven was Dutch. Bach, however, was German. But he was also a lot older. Besides him, I can only think of one German composer: Mendelssohn; Felix Mendelssohn-Bartholdy. But you definitely won't have heard of him.'

'Oh, we have,' my mother said, straightening up in her seat. 'I know him. He wrote "Wedding March" and that charming music for *Summer Night's Dream*.'

Oh, how angry her husband had been, she continued, when years ago he'd wanted to see '*Summer Night's Dream*', only for the production to use other music. He'd been so excited. Oh, how he cursed! ('This piss music!')

Yes, she knew Mendelssohn. He shouldn't think we were dumb and uneducated. My father had so much fun at their wedding, throwing open the double doors (*bang!*) while the "Wedding March" played. And then they started dancing. Left and right, around the table.

'Listen, you shouldn't say such things. We happen to be Germans, and this happens to be our fatherland. We love it, even when things don't go the way they should, or as one wishes they might.'

'Well now . . .' said Sörensen, in English.

'And stop it with those ugly English words. We are at war, after all.'

'In England they never open or close their windows,' I said, remembering what Liesing had told me, 'and they drive on the left side of the road . . .'

'*You* keep your mouth shut,' Ulla shouted. 'Shouldn't you have been at Aunt Anna's a long time ago?'

Sörensen knocked his pipe out.

'No, Ulla, have some tolerance. Everyone has to be able to express their opinion. You Germans forget this too easily . . .'

And as an example of tolerance he mentioned modern music, the kind where the notes were all in a jumble, the kind we didn't have any more in Germany. In Denmark, people did often laugh when they heard that kind of modern music, but they also clapped. He'd seen it happen many, many times.

*

One Sunday I went over to Fat Krahl's again.

'Well hello there, lazybones,' his father greeted me. He looked out over his half-lenses, with his hand in his waistcoat pocket as if he were searching for some change. 'You haven't been here in a while.'

His wife showed me the hole that the firebomb had burned into the floor, along with the melted cupboards. I remembered how, in the air raid shelter, it was as if they'd been called by a higher power; how they'd leapt up and run upstairs to discover the mess. Just a quarter of an hour later and everything would have been lost to the fires. That had happened to the Haagens, who weren't at home when the bombs fell. They hadn't even been able to save the doormats; they had lost everything.

At the time Herr Krahl had said: 'You probably have a sixth sense.'

And his wife had agreed, saying she thought so too. She always had premonitions, she told us. She knew that something was going to happen. She just didn't know what.

On his desk Fat Krahl had a painted plaster landscape, on which he'd built a village made of little wooden blocks. The scene was replete with whole forests of Plasticine trees and tiny model tanks and artillery, which were excellently camouflaged. There were no civilians.

On one side of the model was a harbour. There Krahl had placed grey battleships and cruisers, with the Reich's war flag on the stern. (*Sea Travel Is Essential*, or so said the title of a novel by Gorch Fock.)

The tanks made sure nothing got past the ships, and the ships made sure that nothing got past the tanks. The *Scharnhorst* and the *Gneisenau* were side by side in the harbour, with rotatable triple towers and hydroplanes on their catapults. Krahl had destroyers and black minesweepers, as well as the *Seal* – a seized ship – which was sea green instead of grey. He also had some trade steamers and little fishing boats with paper sails. The steamers' smokestacks were sometimes in the middle and sometimes at the rear, depending on the model.

When the bigger ships needed to pull out of the harbour, it had to happen extremely slowly. Three tugs lined up next to one another, tied up to the ship's padded bow and ready to assist it.

The *Friedrich* looked similar to the model of the sunken *Consul* that I owned. We considered for a long time whether we should paint it grey and use it as an auxiliary cruiser. However, we weren't sure what we would have done with it in peacetime. It would be a lot of effort to repaint it again.

Klaus Greif wanted to bring along older, poorly made models. We considered it for a long time, before deciding that they couldn't be used. I suggested we could saw them off at an angle and use them as sinking ships, but Klaus wasn't keen on the idea.

Manfred, meanwhile, had two French battleships: the *Dunkerque* and the *Richelieu*. Both were extremely elegant, and together with the *Potts*, a German ship, were a picture of overwhelming force.

> The sea is the gateway to the world.
> Only a fool doesn't hold it open!⁴

None the less, we couldn't use them. They'd both already sunk off the coast from Toulon. It was a real shame. Though, in the grand scheme of things, we admitted it was also something of a blessing. The cannons on the French ships had a completely different calibre from the German ones. We would have had to make extra factories for the munitions. No one would have been able to handle that.

The water was crafted using silver foil, though we all felt that glass would have been better. We added another lighthouse here, a heap of coal there. For the battles, we lowered our eyes to the map's surface and looked around as though through a periscope. ('Just a little further left . . . Great!')

But we couldn't really do a lot with the ships. There was too little sea. One time we pretended the German fleet had broken through into the Channel. Then, since we didn't know what to do with them, the ships all sat there on the wharf, doing nothing.

If we'd had a film camera we could have taken a photo, moved the ship over a little, and taken another photo. We could have darkened some cotton wool with graphite and set it over the smokestacks. Then we could have shown the film and used the admission money to buy new models. But those would just end up lying around doing nothing, too.

('Did you all see New York on the newsreel?')

*

There was a dictionary on Fat Krahl's nightstand. We asked whether he had already looked up 'embryo'? ('And what about "pregnant" and "abortion"?') 'Arse' wasn't in there, unfortunately, and the description under 'fuck' only said 'rub back and forth quickly, north German'.

Greif, meanwhile, had a health textbook. Open mouths coloured with dark spots showed diptheria and tonsillitis. The caption noted how diptheria also gave the breath a putrid, vinous scent.

'How to get a foreign body out of your eye': the images demonstrated how you should flip the lid over a match (the man in the pictures wore a moustache). Further towards the back of the volume they showed something falling down towards a pregnant woman dressed in old-fashioned clothes. In the series of images, she kneels down to protect the foetus and ensure it isn't crushed. ('Does she shit the kid out?')

'There's tons of filth in Heinrich Zille too,' said Manfred. ('Mother, do I have breasts yet?' said the caption beneath one picture.) Unfortunately the book was in his father's desk, so he couldn't bring it along. We didn't believe what he said was in there.

'Have you guys seen a rubber yet?' You had to put them on or else it'd hurt all over, and you'd get bloody. Blausiegel or Fromm's were the best brands. ('Men protect their health.')

Manfred had watched a man who was walking bow-legged: he'd definitely been fucking, maybe somewhere in the cellar or in the attic. He was breathing heavily and staring with a glassy expression.

And the women! They couldn't walk for an hour afterwards! And even then, they had to do so very carefully. We just had to keep a lookout. In any crowd there were always two or three who'd just done it.

My brother's magazine was also brought out. When we were finished with it I laid it back in the same place, exactly as it had been lying before, so he wouldn't notice.

We also turned to Sörensen's illustrated Swedish magazine, which showed judo training on the roof. A woman (pretty) is cheating on her pushy husband (ugly – his ankles too thick). She holds him down until one of them comes.

'Do they talk to each other?' we pondered. 'What would they say?'

*

One day Sörensen said he wanted to show my sister how the sun 'danced'. To do that, however, she'd have to wake up at 6 a.m. and go hiking with him.

'Oh, how lovely!' my mother cried. 'I'll make sandwiches for you. Ulla, you can take the rucksack. It's very practical. And be sure to wear something warm underneath!

'Do you remember the walks we used to go on, Sörensen? The ones in the Warnow meadow, the Weidenweg . . .'

'Your father always had his knickerbockers on when we went hiking,' my mother continued. '"Whatever you do, don't wear your knickerbockers this time," I used to say. He has such fat calves, you see. But no, he always wore those atrocious things.

'"You don't understand, my little Grete," he'd say, "the suit is fine and dandy." He'd never let me say a word against them. And his boater, too! Out of the question!

'I have matchstick legs myself: much too thin, and unfortunately, these days, with plenty of varicose veins. You've got to take life as it comes, though; there's nothing you can do.'

They came back in the late afternoon. ('Tired? Worn out?') When I came into the kitchen he was there, holding my mother in his arms, their behinds sticking out, their heads together.

He was asking whether he might marry Ulla.

'With my whole heart: yes!' He could have her daughter. Another embrace and a clap on the back.

'But be reasonable. Do you hear?'

'Yes.'

'Your father will be furious!' she cried, turning to my sister.

'Yes, well. All right. All in order,' Sörensen mumbled, wiping his nose.

Later that evening they sat together on the sofa, under the autumn picture in which something wasn't quite right: old Sörensen had his pipe between his powerful teeth; and little dark Ulla was in her Brussels collar. They were nibbling on each other's ears.

> Mammy, can a daughter sneeze?
> Does beloved God drink beer?[5]

They were listening to a record they'd borrowed from Christa.

'Do you remember how you baulked when you first met him?' I asked my mother.

Yes, she remembered. 'And the imprisonment! Oh, my! The porter said he couldn't hand over the forget-me-not because "it could mean something". It was *supposed* to mean something!'

'Forget-me-not, a funny name,' Sörensen chimed in, he would always think of it. And the slaps that the lieutenant had given him in Copenhagen during the occupation; he would never forget that as long as he lived.

My mother cleared the map of Europe away. Russia – marked with the red thread – had grown, it now stuck out to the Caucasus. ('Better out of sight and out of mind,' she said.) She then fetched the family chest, which she put on the table.

'The two of you should look through it – it's very interesting to see how life goes up and down, sometimes fortunes riding high, sometimes not. There are papers, genealogies; a bone letter opener and a real Iserlohn tobacco box.' Its inscription read:

> Nothing is the same
> After war and blood is spilled,
> Let us by the grace of heaven
> Delight in the joy of peace.[6]

'What – it was buried in the chest?' Sörensen asked. 'Better set it out somewhere!' He went around the room, seeing how it looked in various locations. '"Perpetual peace between Russia, Prussia and Sweden", it says on here. Now that's a tragedy . . . Go get some Sidol, then we can polish it,' he suggested.

'Oh yes, great idea. Sidol makes everything shiny,' my mother agreed.

'And clean the autumn picture with some soapy water, then the colours will come out properly . . .'

There was another picture on the reverse. It had been hanging there for years and no one knew! But it was all blotted out . . . well, something wasn't right here.

'Hang it back up, switch on the table lamp so the light falls on it,' my mother instructed. 'Oh, yes, lovely. That's good. Daddy will like that, everything brighter. He'll throw a fit when he finds out. That all this time no one knew . . .'

'And this,' said my mother, rummaging in the chest, 'was my family's crest.'

She blew the dust off, revealing her family name, de Bonsac. She was descended from Huguenots. Her family were all pastors, and persecuted because of their beliefs by the French. But they managed to emigrate in time; arriving safely in Germany.

'This fragility – this nervousness – you can trace it all the way through to today. (Please turn the radio off.) Like noble, thoroughbred racehorses, which are highly sensitive and high-strung. Sometimes this purity is not good at all. But then again, at least they're tough; hard to kill.'

Aunt Silbi had come away with the birch furniture and the Rostock watercolours. But we had the lovely autumn picture and the *Consul Discher*.

'We're happy now, it's true, but who knows when an air raid will come and leave everything in ruins. Just think about how much must have been destroyed in the war so far . . .'

It was our own fault, Sörensen told us, we started the war. And we shouldn't forget all the things our army had smashed to smithereens, too.

*

We began receiving angry letters from my father. He didn't want to give his consent; he wouldn't agree to the engagement.

'How could this even happen?' he asked; Sörensen was a foreigner, after all . . . *And I am an officer in the field. They shouldn't forget that.*

Plus everyone will grow distant from one another; I might not be able to understand my own grandchildren! Danish Rødgrød med fløde. *You should think about that! Something like that could split a family apart.*

'He's always working himself up!' said my sister. 'Where did he get that idea?'

But then, he had always been easily alarmed, and he had no sense of humour. No one at the yacht club understood him either.

'Christa von Laßow's parents let her do whatever she wanted, even during the cadets' dance lessons, but I'd never get away with any of it.'

Then, just before Christmas he phoned for a lengthy conversation, and all of a sudden everything was hunky-dory. ('Heavenly.') He had spoken with Handke ('a very nice guy'), who had shown him a photo of Sörensen, which had been the deciding factor.

'He's a Northman after all – that goes without saying. And so that's that!'

And they'd come to an agreement on everything else, too. Sörensen could open a branch of the firm later, during peacetime, and Robert could go to Lübeck. Rostock-Lübeck-Copenhagen: it would be great for the finances.

He was sending *Streets of the Reich* over today. ('It's good that Sörensen wants to learn about Germany in such depth.')

'Father is a good guy after all,' Ulla said, kneeling on the armchair and bobbing up and down.

'Yes,' my mother agreed. 'You know what I think it is? Your father's just still so bitter about everything that happened with Aunt Silbi. It bothers him more than he thinks, and certainly affects how he sees the business. And that includes Sörensen. Some evenings your father will just lie there, thinking about the debt, and he'll say: "It could all be so lovely . . ."'

Oh, she still remembered how it all started.

'This person – unrecognisable to us – screaming, "I'm not your puppet" and denouncing your father as an "inheritance hunter", a "dog". Lost for words, he spat on the street, at her feet, and she ran to the chief burgomaster. "How did it come to this?" Father mumbled after she'd left. He was so shocked that she'd denounced him.

'The last time he and I were on holiday, he suddenly jumped up one night and started tearing the bed apart. "Snakes! Snakes"' he yelled, in a frenzy, turning on the light and tearing everything off the bed. "Karl," I said, "we're in Germany, there are no snakes here." "There are, there are, there are," he insisted, "here! At the foot of the bed, here, it's lying there!" He tore the whole bed apart: the mattress, the pillows, the whole thing. And who was left to get up and put it back together in the middle of the night? Me, of course.

'And to think, Aunt Silbi hadn't been so mean as a young girl. But she was raised completely wrong. She had a charming voice, but never developed it. I remember her singing "O lulala, o lilala, o Laila" in the spa garden in Oeynhausen. And she could be so funny on those days when we sat together in an alcove doing our needlework! We'd laugh so much! Oh, it really was a crying shame. And so sad. It was the Polish coming through there. But that had its upside, too . . .'

*

Now that the all-clear had been sounded, my sister started styling her hair and taking Danish at the university. (Her English literature fell by the wayside.) She soon learned some simple phrases – she was talented at languages – and early on she learned a joke: if someone didn't buy anything in a shop, then you could say, '*Mange tak for ingenting*' – 'Thanks for nothing.' ('It's polite and witty at the same time!')

She had to get used to the constant thanking, but that would happen soon enough. For now, she felt it was simply better to thank too much than too little.

'You notice it too. When someone gives you a funny look, you know that you've forgotten something. If you quickly say '*Tak!*' then everything is all right; the Danes don't hold grudges. They're nice and friendly and forthcoming. A good-natured people.'

Sörensen and my sister went to a lecture about the Danish countryside which included a slide show. Looking at the pictures of burial mounds on the heath, my sister concluded that it looked exactly the same as Germany, yet somehow completely different.

'Is it true that there isn't a proper beach in Gedser?' I asked.

'What? No beach? There's plenty of beach!' Sörensen said. 'It's quite the opposite: Denmark is, percentage-wise, the country with the most beach. Baltic, North Sea, whatever you want.'

There were mountains in Denmark, too. Most people didn't know that.

'I suppose they're hills, really. But very lovely things, none the less.'

The fact that Copenhagen had over a million residents was an impressive accomplishment for such a small country, when you think about it, he assured me.

During the lecture they met with various foreigners who were still in the city: the Spanish Consul and his wife; the Finnish Consulate Secretary; Herr Wennerström; and Mutén, the Swedish lecturer. The Portuguese representatives had just had to leave, they were told.

'A real shame,' Sörensen told me, 'they're such educated people, and art lovers too.'

After the lecture coffee was served in a side room, in celebration of St Lucy's Day.

'The Germans are truly disgusting,' Ulla told us. 'A revolting people. They carry on, not caring about who they're disturbing. It's typical that they'd stay on to drink the coffee. They invade other countries without paying any attention to foreign customs; they destroy the culture but want to eat their cake.'

She had, admittedly, been referring to a private first class though, she granted us that; perhaps he was just poorly disciplined. His arm had been in a plaster cast and he wore the 'Frozen Meat Medal' – commemorating his service on the eastern front.

'Regardless, he was so stupid! He kept saying that, for him, "Danish might as well be Chinese," looking around him for a response the whole time, even though no one was laughing. And it's this kind of guy who's our poster boy abroad!'

Herr Mutén – the lecturer – though, was something else. His delicate hands! Maybe he knew how to tell the Germans to leave!

'Na? *Fra konges vakre by?*' Mutén had said to Sörensen, asking whether he was from 'the King's beautiful city' (he meant Copenhagen), before clapping him on the shoulder. (*By* meant 'city'. For example, Landsby: Rural city.) But Sörensen had a remark ready, of course. Though she couldn't understand it; they were speaking so quickly. They were going back and forth – tit for tat – and neither of them ever fell behind. Or took anything amiss.

Really though, Sörensen had nothing good to say about the Swedes. Mutén was an exception. Danes and Swedes, they'd always been at odds. Not the individuals, but the populations as a whole. Take the Swedish language: it was so broad and rural. Both Denmark and Sweden delivered ore to the Germans, which was also part of it: they were competitors.

The Norwegians were a bit more cordial. But for their part they held a little grudge against the Danes. So the whole thing was a big mess.

The Finns were beloved all over, though. Even now, when they were allied with the Germans. They were also the only ones who had paid their debts to America after the First War, right down to the last heller and pfennig. That wasn't to be forgotten.

During coffee, each person had to sing a song. The Danish and the

Germans shared some songs; only the words were different.

> Are you sleeping? Are you sleeping?
> Meister Jacob? Meister Jacob?
> Morning bells are ringing, morning bells are ringing,
> *ding – dong – ding*
> *ding – dong – ding.*[7]

('Every language probably has that song,' Ulla mused.)

Ulla was really at a loss when it came to singing. Then, thank God, she struck on the idea of singing '*Sur le Pont d'Avignon*'. She'd have been pretty embarrassed if she'd defaulted to a German song.

Just when everyone had become warm and friendly, St Lucy arrived. The woman wore a long white garment, with an advent wreath on her head. She moved very carefully, so the wax didn't drip on her hair.

'A remarkable custom,' my sister said.

'How so?' Sörensen asked. 'Every country has its customs, and anyone who doesn't accept them should leave. Besides, it wasn't an advent wreath, it was a Lucia wreath. You shouldn't be so reductive.'

And then they'd all laughed like crazy while Herr Mutén and his wife performed a sketch. She played Frau Lundal, a character from the Swedish language textbook, while he played her husband. '*Idaghan har särskiltbråttom*,' he said: he was in a particular hurry. He had to get to the shop, and quick. But somehow his wife still managed to cajole him into helping her dry the dishes. She was a born actress; the whole thing was improvised, and too funny for words.

'Women!' he'd exclaimed at the end, a floral print apron resting on his belly. Oh, how they'd all laughed!

For our part, with Christmas on the way, we taught Sörensen about German festivities. That way he could experience the good things about the Fatherland; the things that really mattered.

'It's so cosy and devout,' my mother said. She thought Ulla should make sure that a little of that spirit went with her to Denmark. It could spread and shine and proclaim itself throughout the whole world.

'The preparations are the best part,' my mother said. 'The joy of anticipation. Lighting one more candle every Sunday.

'I can still remember my father decorating the Christmas tree – he'd always do it himself. There was a science to it. He would unbox wax angels, bought at Kordes – each one in a little crate, packed in cotton wool – and gather golden roasted nuts and baked apples. "Look, aren't they wonderful?" he'd cry, and he would take a large handful of the nuts and polish them till they shone, and then we'd sing.'

> Do you remember my little rocking horse,
> Malchen's nice shepherdess?
> Jettchen's kitchen with the little stove
> And the shiny-polished pewter?
> Heinrich's colourful harlequin
> With the yellow violin?

'And then after the festivities he'd gather his brothers to look at the Christmas tree, like connoisseurs. "When I think about it, we really *do* have the loveliest tree," he'd say.'

> Do you remember the big wagon
> And the pretty lead hunting scene?
> New little clothes to wear
> And the many little treats?[8]

'The Christmas tree was invented in Germany, after all,' she continued. 'They were used in the time of Luther, but the tradition began in earnest in 1812. In England, they have the medlar. What kind of Christmas cheer is that supposed to bring?'

Sörensen had to tie ribbons into bows, clear wax out of the candle holders, and put together the *Weihnachtsberg*, another ancient German custom. The candles were set below and then they rotated on their stand.

> Ring, little bell, ringalingling,
> Ring, little bell, ring![9]

There were whole mines on the model – replete with overseers and miners – with the Christ child in its centre.

'It's like a carousel,' Sörensen said.

'Please don't belittle it,' my mother replied. 'We love our fatherland, you must understand that.'

A bowl with brown ginger nuts stood on the table. We had sacrificed some sugar stamps for the syrup. Now and then you reached in and took one.

Ulla went to the piano and played a Danish song that she had been practising in secret.

'Hey, what do I hear?' said Sörensen, and took out his pipe. 'All the dumb farmers in Jülland sing this song. But please keep playing. It just reminds me of a particularly dim friend.'

My father had to spend the holiday with the troop, unfortunately. But he sent a duck in his stead, from Frau von Eickstedt, with his best regards.

In an accompanying letter he told us that a social evening had been planned ('nothing to be done'). Afterwards though he would

go to Schulz the forester, with the sled. ('Impeccable thing, that.')
He was already excited about it. ('Saddle of venison or roast goose,
I bet.')

Next year, though, it was his turn to have some time off. Handke
had promised him that. If it wasn't already long since peacetime by
then – and it certainly looked like it would be.

He was able to share some good news with us, by the way
(*someone told me . . .*): he was about to be promoted to captain.
(*That's something to take away with you!*) For that, he was prepared
to accept much inconvenience. (*If you work hard, it all pays off.*)

Robert came from Stettin, though. He arrived home and dashed
straight to the bathroom. His journey had been terrible: he'd had
to wait for hours in Pasewalk, and it was completely full of soldiers.
This was his first chance to have a proper shit. But he soon returned
to join us, wearing a fresh shirt and a wine-red bow tie.

'Gentlemen, I have arrived!' he said, rubbing his hands together;
his hair lay in his usual thick waves. 'Well, brother-in-law . . . Do
you have a cigarette for me?' (North States, 5⅓ reichsmarks.)
'You'll be rewarded later in life. In the meantime, many thanks.'

Stettin was a terrible city, he told us.

'Nothing but squares, with streets leading off, and each of those
streets only led to another square,' he said, pacing back and forth
through the parlour, spitting shreds of tobacco throughout the
room ('Must you do that?').

'And at the centre of it all, the harbour, which is just full of
steam. City-planning like that could only be the product of a
diseased mind; it's such nonsense. And the people? Nothing but
crooks. One of them gave me the wrong directions on purpose . . .
On purpose!'

At this, he sat down next to the radio. He had bad news about his friend Michael. He had been in a military hospital, and had lost both of his legs. He couldn't stand up any more. If his parents had known, they probably would've kept the doctors from cutting them off. He had died not long after the procedure.

'Thank God they have a daughter too,' he said. 'But she had such bad teeth. So unfortunate. You have to wonder whether Ulla's dance instructor didn't pick the better side when he ran over to the enemy.'

'I don't think it's that simple,' my mother said.

Sörensen looked at Robert and asked: 'Enemy? What do you mean?'

'Well, the Russians, they are our enemies.'

'What difference does that make?'

*

Together, we went to the Convent Church of the Holy Cross. On the way, we passed the burnt-out Monastery of the Brothers of Common Life, as well as a Reichspost wagon. I watched as the postman opened the official's door in the back and carefully laid the packages in there.

Sörensen walked out in front with Ulla. My mother and I followed behind. Robert had stayed home – he'd wanted to listen to records again so badly. ('Don't take it the wrong way.')

Fresh-fallen snow lay on the ground, like rice pudding ready to be dusted with cinnamon and sugar. As we walked past the prison Sörensen turned round:

'Second floor, third window,' he said, directing our gaze: 'That's where I sat back then – together with a Russian – if anyone had bothered to look up!'

My mother with a wide brim on her hat. 'Those poor people, to be in there, alone, at Christmas . . .'

'Do you still remember what you learned at Aunt Anna's, the school tutor? You'll see, my Peterpump, you'll get back on track, step by step. It'll all be quite lovely afterwards.'

Professor Knesel ('a wonderful man') stood in the pulpit and described a triptych that no one knew. He chose his words carefully. He'd seen the image years ago – in Zurich or Lucerne, he wasn't completely sure – but it would never leave him. He still remembered it perfectly.

'If I had to hazard a guess, it was in Zurich. I don't know if you've ever been to Switzerland, but it's a wonderful country, with snow-covered mountains and a pious, hard-working population.'

He had followed in Goethe's tracks, so to speak, coming from Italy.

'This is not to say that there aren't good paintings in Germany too – the German museums are full of them, and one can make many good discoveries, if one were to seek them out. But the image I'm talking about had been hanging in Zurich, in a side hall of the museum there, unnoticed by the greater masses. It was a picture of the birth of Jesus Christ the Redeemer, but it contained a complete exegesis of Christ.'

He went on to tell us how the Christ child lay on the shining stone floor, not comfortably bedded in a crib; how the shepherds' staves crossed over the child. An inexorable fate.

'He who is left alone, who is always far from us, ungraspable, already marked out at birth. We have no conception of how lonely the saviour was. But that's how it is for us too, in our everyday lives. Some thoughts move our hearts – we hold questions, doubts – that we never speak of out loud, not even to our best friends, for whatever reason. And we feel that if we truly tried to share them, then the whole world would back away; that abysses would open up in the earth around us.

'It must have been in Zurich or in Lucerne . . . No, no, it was Zurich. Now where was I . . .? A lovely country, Switzerland.'

We lit the lights when we returned home. The process was made a lot easier by using a telescopic tube with a candle stuck in it. ('Old Knesel, boys, he's certainly got spirit!') I was in my Danish suit with the wide lapels, while my brother wore a striped suit whose jacket was a little too short for him. A clamp held the tie in a constricting buckle.

My mother read the Book of Luke while playing with her topaz. The handkerchief embroidered with blue lace lay in wait: the tears would come soon enough, just as they always did at this time of year.

The gifts were amazing. Where did they all even come from? I received the *Köln* cruiser and the *Leipzig* cruiser, as well as a copy of *Through the Whole Wide World*. There were notepads, letter openers and, tucked away in a corner, a microscope – we didn't notice it at first. We immediately used it to look at hairs and salt crystals in detail.

'Shame no one has a flea,' I said.

There were brown cookies and an orange for everyone when we got to the third chapter of Luke. I had tried to copy all the famous Germans out of the encyclopedia for Sörensen, but I hadn't made it past the letter *A*. Sörensen sat hand in hand with my little sister, and watched as the candles slowly burned down.

Robert was excitedly holding a pressing of 'Night and Day' by Svend Asmussen.

'Mother used to bake white ginger nuts,' he said to Sörensen, 'but they were gone before you'd even turned around.'

'That's right, my boy,' said my mother. 'I couldn't do anything about it, though. They need so much fat, and your father couldn't get hold of enough.'

It was always this propriety with him, she said. He'd rather bite his tongue off than ask someone for something.

'In Denmark the Christmas tree is stood on a stool,' said Sörensen. 'And then everyone holds hands and dances around it. It's all rather funny; it's far more serious here. You do everything backward! Christmas is sad and the New Year, which is an occasion for mourning, is a time of fun!'

'We celebrate Christmas with a different kind of cheer,' my mother said: 'a deep inner cheer. You must let it work on you.' It would be a shame if he didn't get any of it. 'Now, children, time to turn in. Then tomorrow we can get back to it.'

You couldn't see the stars outside, as the sky was cloudy. Otherwise, the darkness would have been nice.

Suddenly, out of nowhere, as I was getting up to go to bed, Ulla pressed up against me from behind and stuck a cigarette in my mouth. I would never have had the idea to start smoking if it weren't for that.

25

The whole family was together again at the wedding in May. We celebrated at home, because we'd had to source the food on the black market. It gave us the opportunity to use the white china for the first time: a set for twenty-four people that my parents had had since 1920. They had yet to have an occasion to use it. ('A joke, really.') We brought the mother-of-pearl silverware out, too. It was lying in the cellar. It also catered for twenty-four people, but was lacking fish knives, strangely. And they were exactly what we needed for the meal.

It was also fortunate that they'd been gifted sixteen chairs for their wedding, as they all came in handy now. The table could be extended on both sides, which created just about enough room for everyone. ('That should do it.')

Cornelli, the wine merchant, took care of the wine. He'd been racking up debts with my grandfather since he was a young man, so we decided to call them in. Dr Krause, meanwhile, gave my sister and Sörensen apple juice as a present; he'd managed to get his factory going again. ('Just don't call it cider. He'll take that as an insult.') He gave them a whole crate, most generous.

'It's pressed through 360 filters, and made without any added sugar. Hard to believe, really.'

'It's first class!'

For the cooking, we borrowed Countess Bodmer's housekeeper. She was so strong that, if someone held the bowl for her, she could beat an egg with each arm simultaneously. However, she was also easily insulted, so you had to be careful. It was best to say nothing and not go into the kitchen.

The police forbade sending cards, as it was deemed a waste of paper, but my father saw to it that we sent them regardless.

'Do you want to invite someone, Robert?'

'And who might that be, if you please? Should I create someone using one of my ribs? Everyone I know is gone.'

'And could you pick a few nice records out? Nothing too intense, though!'

*

Slowly but surely the guests trickled in. ('Hello! How's it going?') The men hugged each other with tears in their eyes. The telephone rang off the hook, and endless bouquets of flowers were brought in. ('Do me a favour and go inside.') Oh, I thought the roses were lovely.

Our vases were kept in the pantry, and so we were forever running through the kitchen to fetch them. We hoped the house-keeper wouldn't notice: she already had steam coming out of her ears. The water boiled. ('Eel or perch . . .?')

'Walter, come on, look who's here!'

I had to kiss an old lady who was perched on the sofa.

'I don't know you,' I grumbled, which was met with laughter.

'It's Aunt Hedi,' my mother said, 'from Fehlingsfehn, my boy. You used to play on the swing in the garden at the back of her house. Among all the flowers . . . Do you remember?'

'*I* do! He used to shout, "That's all mine!"' Aunt Hedi said. ('That wasn't Walter,' my mother chimed in, 'it was Robert.') 'He used to run through the flowers and shout, "That's all mine!" while the butterflies fluttered overhead.'

Grandfather de Bonsac was there too, he'd travelled up from Hamburg. He was six feet tall, with a narrow head, and came from an old Huguenot line (they had all been pastors).

'You're tempting fate!' he had shouted at the sky, shaking his fist, when he saw the first bombers flying overhead. But then he'd learned Italian at the age of sixty and how to drive a car at the age of sixty-one.

He told us how, at Wörther Lake, Hitler had greeted him in a motor boat. He had been standing, wearing a leather helmet.

'A fabulous man, truly.'

My father arrived later that morning, red-faced, carrying a heavy trunk. We'd taken precautions this time, and travelled to meet him at the station. Numerous auxiliary troops had been called in to help with his luggage. ('Why, thank you. How's my skin doing? Any pustules? No, don't touch my pistol!')

When we arrived home the trunk was set down in the kitchen right away. 'There are more coming from Jagel. Things for the evening,' he said. 'It'll probably be enough.'

There had been another man with him on the platform, my Uncle Richard. He was yet another person I couldn't remember, but my father basked in his splendour; they'd travelled together in first class. Uncle Richard had crimson lining stitched into his trousers and smoked a cigarette from a holder. He had been based at the Führer's headquarters, since he spoke French and English

fluently. His language skills were sterling. ('He's a real big shot.')
His head stretched eagle-like out of his collar; his face had a yellow,
leathery colour to it. He had been in India for a long time, he
told us, before going on to say that, on relocating to the Führer's
headquarters, he had become responsible for setting up new
barracks and ensuring they were equipped with washbasins. He
had guided Romanian and Hungarian gentlemen around too, and
ensured that visiting generals got up at the right time in the
morning in order to travel back to the front. They always got
plastered.

He called me 'Walting'.

'Well, Walting?' He pronounced it with a Mecklenburg accent.

After asking permission from my parents, I was allowed to
accompany Uncle Richard to the Hotel Rostocker Hof. Together
we walked past the bank and the secondary school (I hoped
someone would see me walking with such a distinguished officer),
and I pointed out where the city gate used to stand.

'It was torn down in 1860,' I told Uncle Richard.

'You don't know the Führer like I do,' he replied. 'It will be
replaced. The plans are almost certainly already in motion!'

He became distracted by some of the granite slabs in the
pavement.

'They must have cost thousands,' he murmured. 'And this fence
here . . . It's so solid.'

'What is going on with your troop? Are you the leader yet?'

His son, Hartmut, had already received his Medal for Service to
the German Youth, he told me.

'Is Ulla really happy?'

He wanted to wish her happiness, but these foreigners were all vultures.

'They hate us. They're just waiting for their prey to fall . . . Then again, a Dane is always better than an Italian, or a slack-jawed Saxon.'

When we returned home for the festivities, he complained about the crowd. I had to put his coat in my parents' bedroom. That way it wouldn't be rumpled.

Rita, his daughter, played a sonata for everyone on her violin while the telegrams continued to pour in. ('Be quiet, all of you!') She wore a dress made of Bemberg silk with giant poppy flowers all over it.

The recital began only after she had plunged her hands into warm water. At certain high points of her performance, she curtsied. The teacher had already told her she had to shake that habit, Uncle Richard whispered to my mother. ('She's overly nervous.') She didn't eat crispbread, like we did, but Rowa crackers, which were supposed to be easier to digest.

*

The ceremony was held at eleven. ('Your ears are clean, yes, boy?') The bride and groom arrived back at the house in a white coach, with myrtle wreaths hanging from the windows. It was drawn by one horse instead of two.

Ulla wore a floral dress. ('No sense in buying a white dress you can only wear once.') Sörensen, meanwhile, wore a dark blue suit.

'Have you thought carefully about this? You're going to lose your German citizenship!' the civil servant had warned her.

'I wanted to shout, "Thank God!"' my sister recounted to us later, 'but instead I played dumb, for appearances' sake. "Oh that's such a shame . . . can't something be done?"' She mimicked ignorance, pulling a wide-eyed, troubled expression. "'I'll keep my nationality though, right?"'

She had wanted to throw out Hitler's *Mein Kampf* right away, she told us, but Sven said no.

'It might be worth something later . . .'

(It was called *Min Kamp* in Danish.)

And of course she made a mistake when writing her new name: Ulla Sörensen.

'It's a funny feeling. Everything you have to give up as a wife . . .'

'Yes,' my mother agreed, 'women always have to give in, always.'

Professor Knesel had spoken about the living bread of God.

'He also felt it worth mentioning that a travelling Danish queen built the convent, with all its structures,' Sörensen noted. 'A remarkable providence, for sure.' A plaque in there read:

THIS CONVENT, FORMED BY GOD'S GLORY,

BY MARGARETE OF DENMARK

He'd also offered for them to go through to the cloister, in which a picture of the Queen hung, after the ceremony. ('There's a little chest in her hand . . . What could be in it?')

The organ player had also recognised that Sörensen was a Dane. He teased us during the singing. He would suddenly play faster and, when we caught up to him, he'd slow right down again.

After the ceremony we were told to take our seats, and my father played the 'Wedding March' while we all squished in at the table. ('You're sitting here; the best place for you is over there. Has everyone found a spot?') A fat uncle was the cause of some disapproval because he wiped down his plate with a napkin. ('The cheek!')

I would have liked to have more of the clear broth, but it was followed by eel, and boy, was it good.

'With the troop you only ever get slop,' Uncle Richard told us, already heaping forkfuls of eel into his mouth. 'They use a soy filler to make any food go further. It's nothing on this . . . Did you know that, to catch them, someone will put a horse's head into a canister, into which they'll have punched holes with a chisel, so that the edges of the hole point inwards. Then they'll sink it into the water, and the eels will be able to get in, but not back out. When they pull the chest back out after one or two weeks, the horse's mouth and nostrils are crawling with the fattest eels.'

'Genius. They can get in, but not back out . . .' said my father, returning to his food.

'If I could only eat with the same appetite as Karl,' my mother sighed. 'He's so healthy . . . And meanwhile, *everything* upsets my stomach; none of it sits right. Oh, when I think about the future, everything gets so dim. Maybe it's good that you don't know what's coming in advance . . .'

('Just don't knock the salt over,' I heard someone mutter, 'that's all anyone needs.')

Braised meat stuffed with pickles (nothing to sneeze at) was then served, while my brother made faces into the nickel plating on the serving dishes. He was annoyed about having to sit with the kids: with Kalö, who was always talking about school; with Franzel, who was always hitting his teeth with his fork; and with me. Consequently he spoke somewhat louder, so the adults further up the table could also hear him.

The men clinked their glasses and gave speeches to teeth-whistling and cheers. Grandfather de Bonsac recalled his father, who in his early years travelled across Norway in a two-wheel *fjordkarren* ('in clogs, mind you . . .'), and Uncle Richard mentioned that his oldest son was manning a flak cannon in Skagen.

'Ah! Another Danish connection in the family!' my dad cried out: 'A son in Denmark, and the other in the Hitler Youth.'

Uncle Richard chuckled in agreement before going on to tell us of how Rita, his daughter, held the fort on the cultural front. 'She'll start field hospital duty soon, tending to the wounded, but as a girl, she has a big advantage over the male violinists of her generation. They have to do military service, and in peacetime all their hands will be useless. A shame to think of it, really. A generation of young men, up and coming in the world of music: all finished.'

The wine from Cornelli was a proper Franconian wine (*Bonum bono*, good things to the good man), though it wasn't befitting of our station, really.

'We had a Château d'Yquem at our wedding,' my mother said. 'It tasted so good; it was smooth, like olive oil. I kept returning to the head waiter for more . . .'

At this, her face darkened. Her stepmother had shown up as the unlucky thirteenth guest and wished her unhappiness, she continued. Just because the woman hadn't wanted to take off her feather boa. My mother thought she'd looked like she'd just walked out of a brothel.

'Sometimes I believe all of the difficulty that came after, everything with Aunt Silbi and so on, could be traced back to that one curse.'

Real coffee, from Denmark, was served after dinner in tiny cups. Unfortunately it was a bit overroasted and smelled like cat turds. Undeterred, the men lit Old Gold cigarettes and held forth, discussing the political situation. One cigarette stuck out further into the middle of the table than the others.

My father announced that he would soon be a captain. It hadn't been confirmed, but he had heard some noises about it.

'And how is it going otherwise?'

'I'm living like a hedgehog. No one sees me during the day, but it does mean that I'm that bit more cheerful – and excitable – in the evening! I had saddle of venison twice in one day not too long ago! Not bad, that. I just can't hack the company food any more.'

'Just you wait and see whether we have any duck left over,' Frau von Eickstedt whispered knowingly to her sister.

Uncle Richard told us about Hitler.

'Handshake hard as steel. Eyes like Frederick the Great. You have no idea what kind of supplies the man has stockpiled. We'll be able to continue in this war for years and years. It's tremendous. Every gymnasium in Poland has been commandeered to store them: crate upon crate of supplies; whole towers of them!'

Then he waited for the right moment – when the groom wasn't standing near by – and whispered:

'Things will be going our way again . . . I have access to secret sources: the whole strength of the Reich is being concentrated in order to force the outcome this year. A single, powerful blow. Thousands of tanks in the east. The world will tremble, that's for sure.'

It had been a great mistake to rely on Romania and that entire rabble, someone else further down the table conceded.

'A bunch of crooks! A real lesson for the leadership.'

That my brother said 'Gobiles' instead of 'Goebbels' annoyed Uncle Richard.

Those of us who were younger stood around a schoolfriend of Ulla's. She had come from Indonesia, and had returned home via Siberia just three weeks before the Russian campaign.

'Why are you staring at me?' she asked. She was plump. We didn't say as much, but she somehow understood. 'It will go away with time. We only had rice to eat in the internment camp there.'

During that time her father had built an organ out of tin cans, she told us.

'I would have done the same thing, believe me,' said my brother. 'You certainly have time in a situation like that.'

*

Eventually it was time to take Ulla and Sven Sörensen to the station. They were to catch the D-train to Copenhagen. The other guests stayed at home while the family made the journey down Bismarckstraße, under the linden trees.

'Now look around you . . . soon you won't see any of this again,' my mother said. 'Our lovely Rostock.'

Or maybe they would, I thought. Maybe we would see each other again sooner than anyone thought.

At the station, we had to wait twenty minutes for the train. The Olympic rings were still hung there. ('By golly, how long ago that was.') They carried two trunks with them, which held the necessities. The other one was being shipped for them.

She had left behind the letters from Esau and the hollowed-out cork with the three tiny dice inside. ('It's time to put an end to those old flirtations. You have to be able to forget too.')

Ten minutes to go. The two of them boarded the train, and looked back at us from the window. Steam poured forth from under the carriages.

'We used to travel to Warnemünde from here,' my mother said. 'Me and your father used to make crying baby sounds so that no one would get in the compartment with us.'

Apples, pears and oranges,
Have the most tremendous vitamins . . .[1]

No one felt like going to the beach any more. Not since the time when an English fighter plane fell out of the clouds in broad daylight and tore along the shore. The tea pavilion was gone now; the fronts of the houses painted grey.

'Do you remember, Sven, how we walked along the willow path together?' my mother said tearfully. She then turned to Ulla: 'If at first you think the marriage isn't working out, have patience: before long everything will be quite lovely. And if you have arguments, be sure not to go to bed until you've made up.'

'Very true,' said my father. 'Where tears flow, nothing can work out. Those who want to make it must be happy.'

Five minutes to go.

'If things get bad, you've got to keep your eyes peeled. I might not be able to write as much as I want to,' my mother said. Perhaps she'd draw a cross after the date on her letters, then Ulla and Sven would know something was the matter. She'd think about it.

We shook their hands. ('Till next time!' said Robert.) Sörensen ignored me. ('He is our führer after all,' I'd said.)

'Now come on,' said Ulla, 'don't be that way. You see, you're hurting him . . .'

He let me grab his hand. Limp.

'Well,' he turned his lapel up, 'why'd you have to go and say that?'

Then the train started moving.

'Off you go! Time to leave, my little Ulla!'

'For them, the war is over,' my father said.

Ulla wore a little golden medallion around her neck with a tear-shaped diamond on it. A picture of all of us was held within.

'All the things we did wrong,' my mother wept into my father's shoulder. My father was really quite small.

'It'll turn out okay,' he said.

26

As a 'long-serving student', I now sat next to Aunt Anna on the veranda. I was still studying with her five days a week. A boy called Ulli Prüter sat next to me.

> Skinny and pretty, a little black boy
> In a sky-blue apron brings
> Cool air and sweet spices . . .[1]

He was easygoing, though he was the youth troop leader in the Fanfare Procession and always came in his uniform. He wore epaulettes on his shoulders that had green braids hanging from them, and carried a trumpet mouthpiece in the leather knot of his neckerchief. His eyebrows had grown together into one long dark line of hair.

Because Ulli wore a uniform, he never got hit: he was protected by the Führer's Garb of Honour. ('You wouldn't dare,' he'd say.)

Biology, geography, we had to learn it all by heart. (The division of amoebas.) But his gaze always drifted over to the evergreen oaks of the untended garden outside. He couldn't do it. He could barely finish his schoolwork, he was so unable to concentrate.

We spoke in whispers about what was 'dumb' and what was 'fun dumb'. All the while, we'd shoot constant precautionary glances at Aunt Anna to ensure we were in the clear. The Juno ad copy, for instance, was 'fun dumb':

> Why is Juno round?
> Because only this format provides the best, most even
> Ventilation of the cigarette and thereby the
> Unusually pure taste of the fine Juno blend.
> Juno's round for good reason!

Ulli could recite it back without hesitating, which he did pretty often. He'd learned it on the toilet. ('You've got time there.')

The movie *Jenny and the Man in the Frock Coat* was also fun dumb. That was the one where Paul Kemp is constantly running everywhere with his stamp collection, and Oskar Sima says: 'Everything has two sides, even a stamp. A front side and a back side . . .'

We watched through the glass as Aunt Anna grinned at Dettmann's daughter.

'Is your father's leg still broken?' she asked.

'He'll be able to get up again soon,' the Child of Light responded. 'He could do with a little food.' When Aunt Anna turned away she returned to gnawing at her fountain pen and pulling glassy bogeys out of her nose.

Ulli told me that a plumber had been repairing the district leader's john when he found cartons full of French soap.

'The high and mighty. They're all in cahoots.'

One day Aunt Anna announced that she was moving to the Black Forest, in the south. She had earned enough to enjoy the peaceful twilight of her life. She would go for walks, and take in the fresh air.

We waited for the furniture wagon to pull up – it was Bohrmann, the removal man, of course – with its little wheels and the horses with brasses on their bridles. (Across the street, the offices of Ditten, Düwel and Dietz.)

Her husband was now free to peer in through the glass door as much as he wanted: there was no one there to tell him not to.

After Anna Kröger's departure her mother, Grandma Kröger, had to substitute. She sat at the front of the class and scratched her head with her knitting needle.

'You there, what's your name again? I'll pull your ears till they're nice and long!' she'd shout, but no one took much notice.

I got licorice sweets from Ulli, and ate them until my stomach started fizzing. We stuck them to the backs of our hands and licked them. Or swallowed them, chased with a gulp from the cough syrup bottle, like schnapps. ('Cheers!')

'Now don't get an inferiority complex,' Ulli would tease, when I decided I didn't want any more.

We then returned to playing dots-and-boxes, and battleships. Ulli was the master at dots-and-boxes, I really had to give it to him. His trousers smelled like varnish.

*

My mother and I sat alone at the table.

'We're a very small family now, aren't we, my Peterpump?' she said, somewhat forlornly. 'Why don't you turn on the radio.'

Father always used to like having music playing. And there were the concerts he used to take us to too. Anton Bruckner was becoming well known – you'd hear more and more of him on the radio. My father didn't rate him very highly though. Robert and I used to play his music four-handed, until my father finally said: 'I can't take this any more!'

The Christ's thorn was blooming profusely, and the canary was singing.

'The sun is so wonderful. Summer is so much more lovely than winter, don't you think? If only I didn't have these stomach pains . . . Could you bring me a hot-water bottle?'

My mother told me how this pressure was constant, how it meant she had no appetite at all.

'The maids used to be totally unable to tell abdominal pain from stomach problems. They just said: "I've got a tummy ache." And I'd say, "Right, but *where* does it hurt? Up here or down there?"'

Before long, she was in a bad way. She really wasn't feeling well. Everything tasted bad; she had to choke down every bite. It wasn't a good sign.

'I feel miserable in the mornings, and I know I still have the whole day ahead of me. The laundry, heating the old cauldron, and everything that follows.'

She blamed it on the stress of the attacks, the strain on her marriage and the uncertainty of it all. She blamed it on not knowing how things were going with Ulla and Robert, whether they were safe.

'If only you'd make up some ground in school!'

She couldn't understand how I was such a simpleton. The Maßlows had no difficulties, she said, pointing to the success of young Warkentin too ('He was always top of the class!').

'We beg, we plead, but no, you just won't do it.'

On the other hand, she said, Egon Warkentin was at the front now, and could get killed at any minute. It could all go down the drain. ('Almost laughable, really.')

Dr Kleesaat visited her and tapped her stomach. ('Oh, oh, not good.') He then had her X-rayed and analysed the stomach acid before he gave his diagnosis.

'You have a gastric ulcer.'

My mother was aware of this though; she'd been taking bicarbonate of soda for it.

'Oh, that helps at first, but then it makes everything worse. It's not a long-term treatment option. How long have you been taking it?'

'For years.'

At this, Dr Kleesaat decided it was beyond his remit and that he'd have to pass her on to Professor Peters, whose verdict was clear: my mother needed surgery.

'The most radical solution is the best,' he said. 'You have to get the illness by the roots. The quicker it's done, the quicker it's over. It'll be like you were born again. You'll arrive wilted and hunched over and leave feeling fresh and young.'

My father agreed with this decision, as did Professor Knesel, and so it was decided.

'Okay, let's do it then.' Her jaw was clenched. She was scared stiff.

In the days leading up to the procedure, she spoke of how my grandmother had once twisted her foot by stepping into the hole left by a stake – all her toes were hanging off – but that she remained brave. My great-grandfather, too: he fell off a horse and had to stitch up his own cheek.

'And there are all these new instruments today. It's all so much more comfortable. And the clinic is new; the most modern in all of Europe. And Professor Peters is famous.'

The only thing left to decide was where *I* was supposed to go. To Anna Kröger? No, who knew where she was now. And Dr Krause wouldn't work either, what with the factory being under construction and his wife away in the office. Frau Kröhl had her hands full, and the Warkentins' living conditions were already cramped. ('Aunt Kempi, you have to understand – I'd love to otherwise.')

'Something will turn up soon, it'll all work out.'

Instead, it rumbled on. There was even talk of Aunt Silbi at one point. ('Any port in a storm.') The Quades, too, came up for debate. A bolt of lightning shot through me at the suggestion.

'But if you really think about it, we don't know them at all . . . We're offering you out like sour beer. It's enough to drive you to despair.'

We'd always been there for everyone, come hell or high water, and now, when it came to the crunch, there was no one in sight. We were over a barrel.

My parents were even considering sending me to the Hitler Youth camp at Neukloster. But then Frau Prüter – Ulli's mother – called.

'And we hadn't even considered reaching out to her! She called off her own bat! I couldn't believe my ears. You live in a totally Evangelical city and it's the Catholics that end up helping you out . . .'

With Aunt Anna gone, this solution meant that I could continue to work with Ulli. Two birds with one stone. Plus, my father knew Ulli's father from the Reich Association of German Officers – they'd had a beer together at some point. ('Yes, I know Dr Prüter. A fine man: educated, reserved. He's a doctor, after all.')

My mother could rest easy now that she knew I'd be taken care of. But this was also a lesson for her – she'd remember this.

'Let them try coming to me for help again! I can't wait to show them the door . . . We've always been there for everyone, and now, when we need them: no one! They all played dumb, gave it no mind.'

She really could understand the Communists when she saw people treating one another like this. Oh, she could have been one. Totally.

Ulli helped me pack my trunk, while my mother dragged the valuables down into the cellar. The apartment would be sitting there completely empty, and if there were an attack, everything would end up in the ashes. The papers, the account book with the paid-off debts, jewellery and silver: everything was moved down there.

'Can you take my flak shards and firebombs down?' I asked as my mother shuttled back and forth. It was as though something snapped: she suddenly stopped, sat down on the stairs and began crying.

'It's all too much. I work my fingers to the bone, but no, I can't do this – not for the life of me.' Then she lay down on the chaise longue and burped. 'Oh, the pressure, the pressure.'

They'd also be taking this opportunity to remove the ganglion on her wrist.

*

To get to the Prüters' I had to take the number 4 bus. I had never taken the 4 before. It was a funny feeling. The house stood outside the city, at the edge of the forest, with green trellises for the roses to grow up, and a cherry tree. It all looked rather pretty.

Rostock lay down below. A new silo had appeared on the horizon, it was taller than the remaining stump of the church spire. 'What did it look like during the attacks?' I asked.

'Like fire and magic.'

Taking photographs of the wreckage was forbidden, in case they were found. None the less a photo did exist, but no one knew where it was.

The Prüters' house had more rooms than I could count, and each of them was stacked with junk. Heaps of books, records, cups with cigarette ash, dirty dishes. There was even a bicycle in the living room – a white bowl sat next to it, with water for patching the inner tube. The tyre pump sat atop the piano. Various coats and suits lay on top of one another in the hallstand: they'd probably all have to be brushed before being worn again.

'Don't touch anything, or everything will fall down,' Ulli warned me.

'Where are all the ration coupons?' Frau Prüter asked. 'Children, could you please look for them? Quickly!' Then after a brief, futile search, she declared that it was fine. We had my coupons for now, and the others would certainly have turned up by the time they ran out.

The household was something of a shambles since the father had been called up. His wife couldn't maintain it and had let it slide. She sat at the window, smoking and playing patience – both the version in which the cards fell like braids and the one where they looked like a harp.

'Is the five o'clock bus late?' she'd ponder, staring out of the window, shuffling her cards. 'Oh no, there it is.'

When Dr Prüter came back on weekend leave, the tables were quickly swept clean and all the clutter was hastily crammed into one cupboard or another. Frau Prüter sped from the top of the house to the bottom, scrubbing the washbasins and taking the flowerpots out of the bath.

'Have you already picked out books for the Library of the German People?' Dr Prüter asked.

'We've set aside *Friedemann Bach* by Brachvogel and *Two People* by Voss,' Ulli replied.

Dr Prüter wore rimless glasses. He was an officer, and I thought his braided epaulettes looked better than my father's, which were plain and flat. But maybe my father would still be promoted to major, if the war lasted long enough.

For lunch we ate 'steak' made from oatmeal with green beans. It was served at one on the dot, not a minute later. We sat together at the big round table in their dining room, under the Virgin Mary. Little Brigitta – Ulli's sister – prayed with real fervour. The first time I heard her, I thought it was a joke. But I soon learned to sit and listen with polite reverence.

'How is your mother doing?' Ulli's father asked.

'Good, thanks.'

'What do you mean, "good"? I thought she was having an operation?'

He didn't think very much of the men under his command.

'At muster,' he said, 'you used to have guys who looked like they were chiselled out of marble. Not so good now. They're all puny. Everyone's gone to pot: sunken chests, knock-kneed. There's no real joy in it any more.'

As soon as he left, the junk began to pile up again. Lunch was served at four. Everyone took a jacket potato and sprinkled some Maggi seasoning on it.

One time, we all shot sparrows together. Those we hit were plucked, wrapped in ham and fried. They were then served in roux, such that you could hardly find the meat, but it tasted good.

In my room there was a kneeler for praying. I made the bed myself: smoothing the sheets, fluffing up the duvet and spreading it out. ('Like that, my Peterpump.') I always slept with an open window.

In the mornings you had to fend for yourself. No one woke you up. Suddenly there was movement throughout the house, a crash as though a cabinet had fallen over. And so I'd take off like someone had pricked me, running around getting ready. Before I knew how or why, I'd be on the bus, headed for the city.

We had a lot of time together in the afternoon. We didn't have to go to Anna Kröger any more; she was gone. In those uninterrupted hours we stood in front of the mirror, pushed our hats all the way back to our necks and pretended we were playing the drums. Ulli would then play a fanfare on his mouthpiece (*toot-toot*) while I banged a rumba beat I had taken some time to learn on the cover of the typewriter. Or we'd practise falling on our behinds without bending our legs, or do handstands in the parlour.

Ulli played the piano beautifully, his big, always rather scruffy hands flowing over the keys. (*Bum-da, bum-da, bum-da . . .*) He even had time to conduct and to sweep his hair back while he played 'Lovely Is the Time of Young Love' or 'Two in a Great Big City'.

On occasion, he'd put sandwich paper on the strings. When the piano's hammers struck the paper, the instrument was transformed into a drum. I'd hit an imaginary cymbal. I knew the motion; I'd seen it done since I was little.

I wrote the lyrics, and he made music to them. That's how it worked.

Your love is like a riddle to me,
And I don't know what I should make of it –
Sometimes you're sweet,
Sometimes you're mean . . .

Hoff, hope, would rhyme with *schroff*, mean ('while I still hope'?), but I never finished the song.

'We could make a ton of money like this, old chap,' Ulli said.

We played the piece again and again, and hoped that the rest would come to us. We could send it off to a record company.

'Soon there'll be no more hits,' Ulli said, 'every melody will be exhausted, and all the progressions used up. Then they'll be happy to have something like our song as a back-up.'

27

'Oh my goodness,' my mother said, once we were both back home and she'd heard the details of my stay. 'You've been so understanding . . . Jacket potatoes with Maggi? How is that even possible?'

The operation had gone brilliantly. Already after fourteen days she was tiptoeing across the corridor. The doctors couldn't believe it, they were all amazed.

'You're one tough broad,' one doctor said.

All of them had laughed when she'd said that she'd 'lent out' her little fellow.

And impeccable care. Great. No Nazi nurses.

'Do you want to see the scar?' she asked me.

She was to go to Graal now, for her recovery. I was therefore to travel to Hamburg, to stay with Grandfather de Bonsac.

'It'll be a holiday,' my mother said. 'It'll be lovely.'

The station staff gave me paper and a pencil to take with me so that the ride didn't get too boring.

'Write down all the stations you pass through,' they said. 'Then afterwards you'll know where you've been.'

I pressed my nose against the window for much of the journey. Maybe going to Hamburg wasn't so bad.

Just before we arrived, I stood in the aisle for a better view. If you looked out for it, you could see my grandfather's house from the train. On previous trips they would stand out back on the compost heap and wave to us. It was a big house full of cousins. One of them, a boy, was quite proper; the rest were all pretty girls.

Grandfather de Bonsac built the house with a single year's surplus from the textile export business. In 1902 every man in Japan just had to have a dark blue suit. All my grandfather had had to do was pass on the orders and pocket the commission.

The house had a timber-framed gable, and a round window on the ground floor. This was situated beneath a cantilevered roof, from which they hung a flag on either the Kaiser's or the Führer's birthday.

The black family clock stood in the front porch. It had been a wedding present from Uncle Bertram, dated from 1885, with the carved crest of the family de Bonsac on it: the grapes and chalice.

Bonum bono, good things to the good man.

Next to the clock there was a cast-iron stand with brushes on each side, in which you could clean your shoes. It was chained up so no one would steal it.

The cousins wanted to play a game called war right away, so we went out into the garden. ('You're not to jump over the vegetable beds,' my grandfather said.) Next door, their neighbour pottered around in his private bunker. He was a pensioner, my cousins told me, so he didn't have anything else to do. He carried logs inside – all of which had been cut to measure – and climbed up on the roof of the shelter, bouncing up and down to ensure it wouldn't give.

Together my cousins and I walked on wooden stilts over the damp garden paths. Seeing us, my grandfather knocked on the window with his ring. The stilts were leaving deep holes all over his garden. His mouth opened and closed behind the window; we couldn't hear him, but it was clear he wanted us to stop.

My cousins left the next day. They were travelling to East Prussia, to their father, who had a very different situation there. And I was left alone in the house with the old man and with Schura, the Ukrainian servant girl.

It was a real shame, I had already begun to imagine that I might seduce my cousins. I'd have said, 'Let's attack each other, for fun' – or something like that.

With his departure, I moved into my cousin's room. He had looked around the room one last time before he gave it up. His pencils lay like a pipe organ on the table and the books on the shelf were arranged by size. A light rust-red eiderdown lay on the bed, and the mattress was very soft. Next to the bed was a crystal radio receiver, with headphones, mounted on a cigar crate, as well as a signal clock from the German Office of Hydrography. Outside my new window, the train to the suburbs rolled by.

Next door was one of the girls' rooms. Floral patterned curtains. A teddy bear on the window seat. There was also the big doll's house, from my great-grandmother who had lived on Ritterstraße. The father doll was at the piano but appeared very casual, almost lying down rather than sitting.

I ate breakfast with my grandfather on the red slate terrace. He sat there in his velvet jacket and chewed endlessly; his hands were always folded in front of him while he did so. His hair, barely showing signs of grey, was oiled and cleanly parted. A single curl hung down on the left. He would however burp now and then.

There was a young birch tree in the corner of his garden – a lithophyte – which had been pruned back so as to avoid any of the plants coming too close to one another. The garden was made up of two large oval lawns. Looking down on the garden from the veranda, the second, rear lawn was almost entirely obscured by a hedge. ('Oh, there's more? Is that all yours?') They'd have to cut out the roses and the weeds in the lawn, I noticed: they were beginning to get the upper hand. The potato knife and the canning jar were standing at the ready.

Schura, the Ukrainian, poured milk into my grandfather's tea. There was news going around that mass graves had been discovered in Vinnytsia again. Representatives of the Swedish Red Cross had already begun the official excavation.

'You hun'ry?' She meant, was I hungry?

Schura served us small circular loaves, *Rundstücke*. We called them rolls. We'd add either nut butter or Vitam-R to them: a brown paste that was served in stoneware bowls.

'Vitam-R is a pure wheat product,' my grandfather said (taking a bite, chewing and swallowing before continuing), 'whose good taste is achieved by separating the wheat cells' (bite, chew, swallow) 'and by killing off the microbes' (bite, chew, swallow) 'living in the wheat.'

When he bit his own tongue (which he did fairly often), he'd sit shaking his head for a long time. His big hands felt around, shaking roughly, at his temples, the little finger bent with gout. 'It's enough to drive you to despair!' he said.

My grandfather asked me how long, in my opinion, he still had to live.

'You're seventy-six? I replied. 'Maybe another ten, fifteen years?'
He was quite content with that answer.

'My heart works just fine, I get a lot of fresh air, my digestion is

good too – I always chew thirty-two times, once for each tooth!'
Vitam-R, nut butter, and pepper powder: these were his secrets, he
told me. 'They eat peppers all over the Balkans, and people there
grow to be as old as the hills.'

400 tanks destroyed in Belgorod!

He was squinting at the newspaper with his good eye, trying to
find out how his stocks were doing.

'Our boys are lying in trenches' (bite, chew, swallow), 'a wide
plain in front of them . . . The enemies coming from the east, and
our guns go *tak-tak-tak*, shooting them down.'

That was how he imagined the war.

'We provide the munitions, the Russians provide the tanks. Like
two rollers moving towards each other. Woe to anyone who gets
caught between them. It's a battle of attrition.

'That's 752 Soviet tanks destroyed . . . I'm surprised they had
any left.'

There were always interesting stories in the Miscellaneous section:
a fire in a room caused by neglect; a slip and fall; a story of a little
boy in São Paulo who was killed by a wild swarm of bees; and in
Auschwitz, at Kattowitz, a bloody marital drama had played out in
the street.

'The tragedy of the German people . . .' my grandfather sighed.
'I once heard a lecture about how everything turned out like this.
It was a long time ago, mind. It was about the disunity of the
German rulers, and the constant aggression from France over many
centuries. When you thought about Frederick Barbarossa, that he
of all people, a leader who could have done great things, had to
drown . . . And as for the World War, after the assassination in
Sarajevo, what was the Kaiser supposed to do? He was bound by
his promise.

'Hitler really is a piece of good fortune. A fabulous man. What is a country in our position supposed to do without him? It's just a shame he can't leave the Church alone.'

When he'd finished eating he wiped his beard mechanically with his napkin, and rolled it into the shape of a mouse. He then covered his mouth with his hand while he used a short, knife-like object to clean the gaps between his teeth. He always carried it with him; it hung in a silver Tula sheath on his watch chain. Occasionally he would pause and suck breath in through his teeth, to assess his progress.

'What are you planning to do today?'

'I thought I'd visit the art museum,' I said. (I'd have to leave the house quickly, otherwise he'd try to scotch my plans.) A pause, in which he was distracted by his teeth again ('Hm, something isn't right back there'), before he made his disappointment known.

'Then I won't be able to put you to work in the garden, I suppose. How frustrating. The lawn needs your attention, and I thought you might help with replanting the lilies-of-the-valley. But it seems that's not going to be possible. Haven't you already been to the art museums, though? I have to say, I don't see what good will come from your visits.'

Schura came and began clearing the table.

'Either way, go ahead. You can visit the art museum every day as far as I'm concerned! You'll see what good it does you. And why are you always cutting more bread?' he suddenly snapped, turning to Schura. 'You never learn!'

At that, he picked himself up and hurried into the garden. ('I have to do everything myself!')

*

I took the rattling suburban train into the city. The S-Bahn was easy enough to navigate, but the subway system in Hamburg was more difficult to use: it was already quite extensive.

A poster saying VICTORY OR BOLSHEVIK CHAOS stood on the iron grate of St Peter's Church, and there were camouflage nets draped over the Inner Alster Lake; they were there to confuse the planes. The Damm Gate Station appeared as a mountain. It was also covered with nets, and they'd added small trees on top of it to further confuse the enemy's orientation.

I had the museums listed on a piece of paper. As soon as I arrived I began working through them one by one. In the Kunsthalle there were only reproductions, as the originals had been evacuated to safety. I went through the exhibition rooms slowly at first, then faster and faster.

In the Natural History Museum there was the skeleton of a whale. Up above on the first floor, where you weren't allowed to go, there stood hundreds of cases with mounted insects. All in rank and file, one after the other. And yet they were all different, which you learned when you looked at them closely.

In the Museum of Ethnology I noticed three shrivelled chestnuts. They were in the section for 'Superstitions', under an explanatory note that positioned them as 'a folk remedy against rheumatism'.

Wounded men stood around on the streets of the city. *Kriegsversehrte*, as they were called – the 'war-damaged' – their arms in slings, or heads bandaged. I saw one with a rerouted oesophagus, like a handle.

The wounded disappeared behind the iron gate, which said ENTRY FORBIDDEN TO MINORS. When they came out they were fumbling around at their flies.

You could find more in the shops here than you could in Rostock. Actual Märklin model cars and Auto Union Record Cars, in which the seats were situated further forward than they were in a Mercedes. All sold for 2 marks apiece.

I visited a bookshop, and leafed through titles called *African Mosaics* or *Unforgotten Cameroon*.

'Do you have books about architectonics?' I asked.

'I'm assuming you mean architecture?' replied the bookseller. Yes, they had some, *German Style* and a volume of Wilhelm Kreis's *War Memorials in Europe*. It contained charcoal sketches of angular columns with eagles and braziers: one in Narvik and one on the Volga; for Tobruk, he'd included a memorial that looked like a desert fortress. They were supposed to be built when the whole thing was over, in memory of the heroic struggle of the German nation.

In *German Style* I found pictures of the new plan for the capital of the Reich. It had been published by Franz Eher Verlag, the Party's publishing house, and included plans for the Soldiers' Hall of Honour – it'd be 300 metres long, a ribbed barrel vault – as well as the Congress Hall in Nuremberg, construction on which had already begun, using Swedish granite. There were blocks of stone lying all around the site.

After I'd visited the city a few times – enough to sufficiently scour all of the museums – I visited some relatives. Aunt Hanni, for example. She was a fine woman, delicate yet always busy.

Her husband was a colossus of a man. He was a commander at the city's airfield, and wore a white uniform jacket, with a coveted badge from his service in the First World War, on his breast and, somewhat strangely, on his breeches too.

I could still remember him visiting us in Rostock. He'd stopped off while travelling somewhere, and had sat on our balcony eating layer cake made from a one-cup recipe. He'd admired the Christ's thorn and the lovely view.

'How nice of you to stop by,' my mother had said. He was always so warm and convivial.

Walthi, my cousin as well as my namesake, nestled up against me. He was a cute child, only three or four years old – the baby of the family – and had blond hair. He wore a thick scarf on account of always having a sore throat. His name was spelled with a *th*, Aunt Hanni told me, because the name came from *Herrn des Waldes*, lord of the forest, rather than from *Verwalter*, steward. He was Waltherr.

Together Aunt Hanni and I climbed the cherry tree, and sat in its branches for the whole afternoon. When I told my grandfather about it, he was furious. ('The lovely cherries! They could have been canned!')

Walthi approached and wrapped his arms around the trunk. He appraised a hollow, and braced a leg against the tree, before bursting into tears: he couldn't reach us. The other cousins played in the adjoining garden, but they didn't speak to me. It might have been the Polish in me that bothered them, or maybe my curly hair. They may also have thought that I was from landed gentry. The last syllable of my surname – 'ski' – meant 'of'. Someone had figured that out back at school. *Kepa* meant 'river', which might account for the opening syllables of my surname. Kempowski: 'of the river'. *Kepa* could also mean 'corner' or 'sponge', though. ('Lord of the sponge'.) So maybe I was part of the lower echelons of the Polish landed gentry? Who knew. Instead, they settled for laughing at my Mecklenburg accent.

'Well, Walting?' they called up to me. I went down to join them, but they ran away when I got down to the garden.

The other aunt who lived there was tall and gaunt. She wore the de Bonsac crest on her finger. (*Bonum bono*.) Seeing me, she opened the terrace door. I thought she simply wanted to greet me, but no, I was supposed to tell Aunt Hanni that a letter had come from her eldest son – from Normandy.

You weren't allowed to say 'Oh God' around Aunt Hanni. On the open writing desk lay the Book of Common Prayer – a black book with a golden cross on the cover – Bible quotations written out by hand, and the parish newsletter.

'How is it all going to turn out?' she said, worry in her voice. 'The young vicar has also been drafted now, and Pastor Eisenberg too, despite being old and decrepit.' She had always admired him, ever since she was a young girl, she told me.

When I had eaten enough cherries and wanted to go home, Walthi held me tight and kissed me. After he was told to let me go he said that he had to squeeze me one more time and pressed his hot face against mine again, sniffling the whole time.

Even after I'd left, as I was turning the corner at the end of their road, he ran after me, and his mother had to come and fetch him. He came charging after me, with his hasty stooped steps, smoothing his hair, which had fallen out of place ('Just one more time!').

On returning to my grandfather's, it was evident that the garden had been taken care of. The old man had seemingly been out there for the entire day.

'Look, Walter, this rose, isn't it wonderful?' He grasped it with his big, trembling hands and held it out for me to see.

> On which instrument are we strung?
> And which player has us in his hand?[1]

He then showed me a lily with thirty-three blossoms, and the yucca, which had won praise from a gardener who otherwise never said a word.

'How do you even do it?' he'd said. 'You could put it on display.'

In the autumn, nets were stretched out under the trees so that the fruit didn't land in the grass and bruise. He would clean each apple individually, place them all on a grate, and turn them periodically to keep them from bruising. Before his orchard had been planted, he had corresponded with a woman in Mecklenburg who used to send him apples. Together they had carefully chosen the cuttings with which he'd started.

'She always sent different varieties of apple, and they were all delicious!'

I lay out in the deckchair and worked on my novel, which was about an elephant. Next to me, weighted down with a stone, was enough writing paper for the job.

I told my grandfather, who was digging up the lilies-of-the-valley, sighing and groaning, that this was schoolwork: an essay comparing the formation of the English and Japanese Empires. He kept glancing over at me while I worked.

I hadn't been working for long when I realised I had to get up and fetch a stool from the kitchen to put my feet on. It would make writing easier.

Then, a little later, I noticed that I had left my sunglasses inside (they were new, made by Zeiss Umbral). What's more, my head was lying too far back – I needed a cushion, which required another trip inside. So, up again.

In the veranda I found a cushion that looked old and faded, such that my grandfather wouldn't come running. ('For God's sake, boy, not the Chinese one!')

It had to be about the last elephant of the herd, that's how I imagined my novel. Things were going quite badly for him: he was surrounded by pygmies who wanted him dead. If they caught him, his legs would be hollowed out and sold as waste-paper baskets to white farmers. Unfortunately, however, the writing was slow going because I didn't have enough knowledge of the subject.

I stumbled through the house looking for an encyclopedia. My Uncle Richard's bookcase was locked. Fine Chinese silverwork lined the shelves, set in front of the gold-printed spines: the pictures, brought back from Hong Kong, showed junks and coolies. There was also a pine cone on the shelves, though that came from Ohlsdorf.

At the very bottom, visible only if you pressed up against the glass, were the de Bonsac papers. Our family was ennobled in the fifteenth century, but, as with racehorses, the line was thoroughly overbred. None the less, there were transcripts from Gotha – in Thuringia – and correspondence with other people named de Bonsac, all of whom testified to the de Bonsacs being of the most noble blood.

My grandfather's dining room had twenty-four chairs.

'Here's where your grandmother used to eat her corn flakes.' She had struggled with stomach ulcers for the last years of her life, and half her body had been paralysed since 1918. She then lost her ability to speak, except for a few words. She couldn't write, couldn't read. Upon first noticing her deterioration, she'd hit herself in the mouth out of frustration. ('Oh terrible, you little . . .') But the language centre was soon no more.

'Not easy for her husband either,' it had been said. He was in his best years. But she continued to knit the most lovely coffee-pot covers, all with her left hand.

'And oh! How angry she could get when the girls polished the silver. "You little!" she'd cry. It was *her* job, after all . . .'

I still remembered the guests at her seventieth birthday, sat round that same dining table. My mother had forgotten to pack my father's frock coat. ('Everyone wearing formal dress, and him in his green knickerbockers!')

They'd all been invited for stew and so it was to everyone's terror that a giant pot with pea soup was set on the table. ('How is this even possible? Pea soup! For a seventieth birthday!') But it was followed by ice-cream cake, with little paper umbrellas and small dolls on every slice, which felt more fitting. I got a harmonica-playing monkey on my slice.

A conservatory, made entirely of glass, had been built on to the house in 1936. There was a big maple tree in it. It was attached to a stake to hold it in place. ('It's almost *too* impressive.') It stretched up to the glass ceiling and then back down the opposite wall.

A little protrusion had to be made in the dining room wall to house the mahogany buffet table, because of its size. On it sat a large glass bowl full of water; there in case someone was thirsty. A crocheted runner was draped across its surface, held in place with hanging pearls. This too was the work of my grandmother.

Hung above it was a winter landscape of Schnars-Alquist. The foreground was dominated by fields, all of it white. My cousin once tried to see if you could write on it with pencil, then erased and erased some more, and now there was a light white spot on it. The picture had had to be restored, to the detriment of my cousin's savings account.

In the cellar my grandfather had his workshop, a workbench with a vice and a glue pot. He made flowerboxes and rabbit hutches in there. The garden and the cellar: this was his reich.

Unfortunately, partway into my stay the weather took a turn for the worse. Heavy cloudbursts came, and it wasn't long before the cellar flooded. We had to bring up the air raid case and lay everything out on the floor to dry: long underpants and the girl cousins' panties.

I wanted more rain, like in Elise Averdieck's *Children's Stories*, where Karl sails around the kitchen in a bathtub. My mother often used to read it aloud in the evening before bedtime, back in the old apartment – the one with the lilac wallpaper and six ovens. ('It's certainly not a fun story when the whole apartment fills with water . . .')

I dried off the silver with Schura. Forks, knives, big and small spoons, all cushioned on velvet. ('Worth a fortune.') The lovely cases they were kept in were all soaked through. Burglars had stolen the centrepiece back when Wandsbek was still part of Prussia, my grandfather had told me.

'Back then, you could only follow the thieves as far as Hammerstraße. That was where Hamburg began, you see. A cobbled stretch in the middle of the street marked the division. The thieves made it across, stuck out their tongues and made V-signs.

'They always shat on the typewriter, too – it was their calling card. A shit on the table as a parting gift. They broke into one house after another throughout the year; you could practically set your watch by it. Things like that don't happen any more, mind. The matter was resolved quickly. They crack the whip now.'

Schura was actually named Alexandra. She was an ample girl, and sang the songs of her homeland in a bright voice. My uncle had brought her with him to Germany back when Hitler's headquarters were still in Ukraine. He'd had to promise her mother that he would keep a good eye on her.

'Vinnytsia was much lovelier than here,' Schura said. 'But in 1936 there was a big famine – many people died.'

They'd had a lovely cinema, as well as a palace. There were two cinemas there but, being a Slav, she wasn't allowed to go to them.

To my grandfather's chagrin, she had glued ugly postcards to the walls of her room upon her arrival. What was more, she never remembered to leave the knives to dry off. Instead, all of the teatowels were ruined.

Sometimes other Russian girls visited, and sat around with her in the kitchen. There was Vera, the larger of the two, with fake fur around her neck, and the small, dishonest one, Natasha. They worked in a nearby factory.

On one visit, a man with a pointy flat cap came up to the garden gate. He wore a badge reading OST: *Ostarbeiter*, a worker from the east. He would stand at the end of the garden and look around for a while to check whether any police officers were coming. My grandfather soon shooed him away though, before he could make his approach. He looked as though he were shooing sparrows away from his peas. The Russian didn't go far, though. He merely went to the corner and continued to watch the house.

Later he was back at the garden gate. Standing there watching. I found it all quite creepy.

'Oh, it would be bad if he ever got the upper hand,' my grandfather said. 'He'd beat us all to death!'

It was a rude awakening. The Russians were rough, brutal. They were like cats. You couldn't get rid of them either.

Schura always ran around in her Russian clothing, but the *Ostarbeiter*s had nothing. They went to the Business Office with her, where Schura tried to help them:

'But the young girl needs something to wear,' she implored.

'She doesn't need anything!' came the reply.

They had to stand against the wall in the office, they weren't permitted to step forward.

'Thank God we'll soon have a separate nationality badge for Belorussians and Ukrainians.'

We knew that from Uncle Richard. It meant that at least they'd be able to be distinguished from all the others.

*

One night there was a heavy air raid. We sat all together in the garage, which had been rebuilt as a bomb shelter. It was a real rat trap though: there was only one exit and it went into the house. It was a wonder it was even permitted. I had helped bring my cousin's Schiffer piano down into the shelter so we'd have it to pass the time. However, it stayed shut. 'Black Eyes' went unplayed.

A great whistling sound encircled us, and we all fell to the ground – and then it hit. Schura screamed shrilly and my grandfather hit his head against a support beam.

'What a stupid and impudent boy you are!' he screamed over the crashing, holding his head with both hands.

When everything was over we climbed into the house through the shattered doorway. The roof was gone; the red sky hung above us. The family clock lay on its face and didn't make a single sound. (*Bonum bono.* Chalice and grapes.) I stood it up, pulled the weights high and set the pendulum in motion. I set the time to three-thirty.

In the meantime my grandfather went to check whether his workspace was still in one piece, and found that all of his tools had fallen off the worktable.

All the windows in the house had been blown away, and rubble, dust and mortar lay a foot deep on the carpet beside them. A single cobblestone lay on the desk next to my uncle's marble writing implements, and all the silver junks and coolies had squished together in the bookcase. (The upside being that you could reach the books quite easily now.) The snowscape, meanwhile, was speckled with shards of glass, and the frame had lost a wing.

My grandfather pulled glass shards out of the windows of his conservatory, sucking his teeth, and tied the maple in place again. On the street the macadamia tree had been torn out, he said, and showed me a piece of it. He'd switched on the lamp, which still worked, surprisingly.

'Fabulous,' he said, 'everything turned upside down except the grandfather clock.' It ticked on, unmoved.

Schura straightened the chairs and I brushed the ash off the table with the silver crumb brush. I swept it carefully on to the floor, so as not to ruin Grandmother's crocheted runner. It would be cleaned up later.

A gigantic sinkhole had opened up behind the house. The flowerbed with the lilies-of-the-valley had disappeared, and all the roses were covered in ash.

Next door, the garden bunker had been destroyed by a direct hit. Thankfully there had been no one inside. A pair of Grandfather's long underpants hung in the bush. (That too was 'fabulous'.)

Where had the other bombs fallen? I wondered.

It was only then that we became aware that the villa across the street was burning. There was a horse bucking in the front garden; it had become tangled up in the wire fence. Behind it, the flames raged. The wind was strong and caused them to burst out of the windows.

We were called over to see if anything could be salvaged. In the living room we found heavy green armchairs. If they had been smaller, someone might have pulled them out. Instead I grabbed a model ship from a chest and brought it out to the owner of the villa, who stood outside among the few possessions that had been saved, meek and quiet. There were table linens in the chest that were more important.

'But thanks anyway, my lad.'

We saw a political leader dragging beds into an arbour. ('Everyone at Krammon's is dead,' I heard someone say. 'And Poststraße has been completely destroyed.') Where there was once a bridge over the railway lines, there was now a yawning hole. The security and emergency services blocked it off. ('Now you can't get into the city any more . . .') Everyone was angry. ('I'll kill them all myself! Dropping bombs here for no reason!') Sternstraße was still intact, for the most part, I noticed.

Then a time fuse exploded. All of the windowpanes burst out into the street. At first I thought it was just paper being thrown out. ('Why is everyone throwing paper out the window at the same time?') It was only afterwards that I heard the explosion.

I saw black clumps in the front garden. I thought they might be corpses, so didn't explore any further. ('Careful! Don't step on the wires!') Blood sausage was handed out to everyone, but I soon escaped the street to pack my trunk.

'I can understand why you're leaving,' my grandfather said. He fished a 5-mark note, one of the new ones, hesitantly out of his wallet. On the front there was a young German soldier with Brunswick looming behind him. ('Since the outbreak of the war the demand for paper money in small denominations has been constantly rising,' the paper had reported.)

My grandfather probably thought it was his fault that I'd experienced a raid here. He was giving me money out of guilt. It made me feel sorry to leave him sitting there like that.

At Wandsbek Station, refugees sat and waited. There were hundreds of them. Why they hadn't left already was a mystery to me. There were women in tracksuit bottoms – wearing two coats, one on top of the other, with kerchiefs on their heads – and old men too. Each sat with a pot of soup.

A double-decker train stood empty on the track. I got in, paying no attention to where it was going. Getting out of Hamburg was the main thing.

It turned out to be going to Lübeck. The only passenger besides me was a young man.

'These double-deckers are so draughty,' he said, 'that's the downside. Wherever you sit, there's a draught.'

Why did I choose to spend my vacation in Hamburg? Who would come up with such an idea . . .

When we arrived in Lübeck the sky was dark. The trees were covered with ash, blown over from Hamburg. Book halves lay abandoned in gardens. They had such nice little bunkers in Lübeck, I noted: they had timber frames, and were camouflaged as towers.

'Oh heavens!' my mother said, when I called to update her. Her whole recovery was down the drain now. 'Typical.'

28

We were no longer grouped with the girls when on duty. That would only happen again after the war, we were told. Then culture would flourish again, and we'd be singing in the best regions: in the Acropolis, in Brussels, or in Copenhagen. (Perhaps I might nip over to visit Ulla, I sometimes thought. I was pretty sure you needed some kind of pass to do that though.)

In one of the meetings we had a small party to celebrate my father's being conferred the War Merit Cross.

Löffelholz was gone by this time, and no one sang at Eckhoff's any more. He was always busy with his maps.

'Mountains are like sliced potatoes,' he said, 'layered. Every potato slice signals a ten-metre elevation.' That's how we were to picture it. As if the mountain had been cut into slices. That was why there were rings on the map. He also showed us the difference between coniferous forest, deciduous forest and mixed woodland in the maps' markings, and how to make sense of the scale (1:25,000).

'There isn't a measure less natural than the metre,' he said. 'It doesn't exist anywhere in nature. Ell, pace, foot: *they're* all natural measures. People knew where they stood with them.'

Eckhoff told us how the original metre was stored in Paris. It was made of plastic and preserved in alcohol, so it never changed. If we were to lose access to it, no one would know how long a metre was. One degree hotter, the thing would swell, and then the cars outside would have to go slower.

'Every ruler manufacturer has to travel to Paris to see whether his yardsticks are the right length.'

After the final victory the original metre would, of course, be brought to Berlin. ('Then they can come to us. As is only proper.')

In the field we had learned that, if you held your thumb against the horizon and looked at it with your left eye shut, and then switched eyes, your thumb would jump to the right, signifying a distance of one kilometre ('that's a thousand metres'). We'd already mastered the technique when we showed up for duty; the petty officer was happy he didn't have to teach us anything.

'One jump of the thumb to the right there's a house.'

(Orient the map north. Who-what-where-when-why.)

There had been lessons in camouflage too.

'Don't climb the trees!' That was dangerous. When camouflaged, make sure there's a swell in the ground behind you, 'otherwise you'll raise your head against the sky, and you'll get it good'.

We all crawled forward. Whoever was spotted had to go back.

I never wore my uniform when I showed up for duty with the Hitler Youth. It's not like we were throwing ourselves around, after all. Instead I put on my best suit.

'Why don't I ever see you in uniform?' asked Eckhoff.

'It went up in flames in Hamburg,' I lied.

'Do you at least have your member identification on you? Yes? Then let me see it!'

If I gave him the least trouble I'd be thrown out of the troop, out on my ear, then he'd transfer me over to the 'Line Group' of the Hitler Youth. (They called it that because they 'brought you into line' there.) Or perhaps weekend detention in Kröpelin. (Pulling grass from between cobblestones: that would also do me good.)

Klaus Bismarck Stüwe was now the leader of our German Youth subsection, and his gaze was as penetrating as Eckhoff's. He checked to make sure my thumb was cocked when I saluted. 'Press through with your palm!'

He walked around me. Heels together? Did my feet form a ninety-degree angle? (It had been a while since we'd sold WHW medals together.)

I was constantly writing excuse notes to get out of service.

> I can't report for duty on Wednesday,
> because I have bad stomach pains.

I wrote the note myself and threw it, hopefully without being seen, into the mailbox of Nickel, our leader in the Hitler Youth. It was a good reason to give. 'I had to do my homework' was not. In the service bylaws it said:

> There is no furlough from the Youth Service
> due to your sudden bad standing in school.
> Members of the Youth must be the best students.

To switch things up, my mother also sometimes wrote me a note, which I dictated to her. The fact that I always looked like 'buttermilk and spit' came in handy.

'Do you actually have stomach pains?'

(Always this pressure, oh, the pressure . . .)

'Are you sure you're not exaggerating?'

But then again, perhaps it was the French in me: I was as noble as a racehorse, but sensitive too – perhaps hypersensitive. Who knew?

*

Every day I biked over to Ulli's right after lunch. To get there I cycled down the Mühlendamm, which was no trouble at all. But the ride back was less pleasant, a so-called 'slow rise'. And it was almost always against the wind. The most miserable-looking sheds I'd ever seen lined both sides of the street, and St Nicholas's loomed ahead of me, all burnt out.

Ulli was usually leaning against the fence waiting for me when I arrived.

'*Zack mi seu!*' we said when we greeted each other. 'Kiss my arse.'

Ulli wore a light grey suit, and his trousers were long in the leg; they folded down, covering the tops of his shoes. I wore my Danish jacket with the wide lapels. It ended at my waist, with thick cotton pads under the shoulders.

'Subhas Chandra Bose': that sounded nice when you said it out loud. (He'd given a radio address in Berlin against the British imperialists just last year.) Ulli said it twenty times in a row, then continued mentioning his name at every opportunity. 'Subhas Chandra Bose.'

We had begun lifting weights together. We'd challenge each other to fall forward, without bending our legs, into a press-up, throwing our arms up at the last minute to stop the fall. Or we'd dance to jazz records in front of the mirror, and continue to write hit songs together.

A little working maid, who made a fool of me,
A little working maid, who gave me what I need . . .

We could put a drum solo in there, or loop back to the start ('Once more from the top!'): we'd figure it out later.

At other times we'd sit around in the garden, shooting the breeze.

'Why do girls wear dresses and not trousers, like us? How bad do they stink, that they need fresh air down there all the time?'

'What's the difference between a muzzle and a haemorrhoid? One holds you back from biting, while the other bites your backside.'

We'd do impressions of our teacher too, and wonder what the chances were that they might be walking by, just at that precise moment. Or we'd discuss various rules of etiquette. I learned that one used 'the most honourable' when introducing an esteemed guest, not 'the most honoured', as I'd previously thought.

I also learned that when you shook hands with someone ('Here, give me your hand . . .'), instead of squeezing you had to wrap your fingers all the way around the other person's hand so they were pointing back at you. ('That one there . . .'). Or you could bend the third finger and scratch the other person with it. That was obnoxious, but *good* obnoxious.

Then there was the 'barber grip': that involved holding your thumb up and pressing it against the other person's as you grasped their hand. It only worked if you'd agreed it with them in advance, though.

Sometimes we killed time trying to catch couples at it. It had been described to me by Ulli as being 'especially interesting'. (Who-what-where-when-why.) But it was dangerous; you really had to be on your toes. You had to run away immediately if either of them noticed you, Ulli told me. The guy would definitely beat you to death if he caught you. He'd come at you with a knife, without a second thought. He'd flay your back in a blind rage. ('Honest, he would.') So we decided that we'd run in separate directions. ('Then he won't know which way he's supposed to go, and he'll stay where he is.') You had to work something like that out beforehand.

We crawled around the forest, using our knowledge of camouflage. (One thumb jump to the right, one to the left.) We found cigarette packs in the bushes, sometimes a barrel cap, but no couples.

'Funny . . . They're usually lying around here and getting each other off. But today of all days, when I wanted to show you, there's not a dick in sight. Typical.'

The man got hard in the run-up, that much was clear. But he didn't know whether something happened with the girl . . .

'Women are much lewder than men, by the way,' he told me. 'When they tell jokes, even the most hardened soldiers blush.'

Other times, we rode the streetcar all day. The cars jumped up and down, clattering along the tracks, as they zoomed by. While we were on the number 11, the driver got out to stretch his legs at the New Cemetery. Mourners came running towards the tram standing at the platform: they thought he was about to leave again.

'Thank God! We just made it,' they said, and looked around happily. (As if we cared.) 'I thought I wasn't going to make it!'

Then they'd remove their top hats, dab the sweat off their foreheads, and join us sitting in the carriage and watching the others come running, all while the driver tore chunks of bread from his loaf to have with some ham and gulps of coffee substitute.

We always stood at the back of the platform. The only people who stood at the front were those who wanted to see the steam-powered crank that powered the trolley. They'd gather round eagerly, but you could never predict how it was going to move. It always started right when you weren't expecting it.

When we were in motion, you'd see those same people staring as though they had to keep a lookout along with the conductor. Nervous and jittery, they'd leap up and pull at the emergency brake before anything had even gone wrong. If an accident were to happen, they'd be there to witness it.

Buses were beneath us. We only used them if we had absolutely no other choice. On top of each bus were sacks filled with wood chips. After every trip the driver had to leave his steering wheel, which had a loud little horn, and put wood in the carburettor. He'd then poke around in there with a rod, which clicked while yellow liquid leaked down.

No, *we* rode the tram, you couldn't beat it. When it drove through puddles, they sprayed out to the sides. And whoever got run over by one was done for. And what an outrage whenever there was a wagon on the rails, blocking the way. The conductor stamped his foot.

'Whadda you want? Brewery coachman, half drunk, huh?'

He pulled the tram closer and closer, clanging the bell. The passengers all angry, too: what an outrage, the coachman probably had a screw loose.

The seat next to the door was Ulli's spot. (PLEASE DISPOSE OF VALIDATED TICKETS HERE.) We didn't get on if someone was already sitting there. We waited for the next tram instead.

*

We were always on the lookout for girls. Particularly Gina Quade or the Köster girl. Ute Vormholz too, though no one had seen her lately. She had such thick legs.

'Move up, I think someone's got on.'

It was Helga Witte. But she was getting ready to get off again. A shame.

'Is she hot?'

'No, she's uptight.'

'She needs a good shag.'

'Yeah, she definitely needs a good shag.'

'The little minx.'

We'd drink cough syrup like schnapps, wearing trousers with a crease that touched our shoe. Left foot perched on the opposite seat, right leg dangling down. At our stop we'd jump smoothly off the streetcar and dance a few steps, as though we had too much swing. Then we'd jump on the number 2. At the next stop we'd hop back out. Always moving, always cool, with money clinking in our jacket pockets. On our lapels we wore a miniature German Youth Service badge.

'They'll be blown away when they see: "They're so cool, but still German Youth Service," they'll say.'

Annoyingly, the only way to stop the badge from pricking you was to use a safety pin. But then it always hung at an angle.

I always carried a Danish newspaper around with me. The *Berlingske Tidende*, of course, not *Foedre Landet* ('They're so loyal to the Party, you might as well buy the *Völkischer Beobachter*').

'*Tak I lige måde*,' I'd say when someone got on. I wanted them to think I was Danish, that I'd been sailing all day. ('Damn it, what are the Germans doing in our country?')

We'd stop off at the train station to see the bunker they'd built there. Its walls were three metres thick, but that also meant it was an ugly block. They could have made it a bit prettier, I thought – more like the bunker at St Jacob's, which was shaped like a house. Or they could've introduced exposed concrete struts, to make it look as though it were already burnt out. That way they'd think it had already been bombed, and so wasn't worth bombing twice.

Then back into the centre of Rostock, to Blutstraße. The street was so damn narrow: only one track, with a blind curve, so the driver had to lean right over to see whether something was coming the other way. Inching the tram forward bit by bit, peeping round the corner. 'Everyone get back in case of emergency!' he cautioned.

The bronze statue of Blücher in Blücherplatz was faded with time. He was originally holding his staff much higher, and so had once appeared far more dignified ('sublime').

A general in the Napoleonic Wars, Blücher was Rostock's most famous son. There was Blücherstraße and Blücherplatz as well as Hotel Furst Blücher (though it had been destroyed in the bombing), all named in his honour.

Other than Blücher, Rostock only had Paul Pogge, the African explorer. We couldn't find anyone else to claim. At some point the city was home to the biggest naval fleet in the world, and we had the fifth oldest university in Germany, but these weren't quite right to celebrate. Ulrich von Hutten had caught syphilis in Rostock, but again, it was rarely mentioned.

Kaffee Rund-Eck was a *Pißbude*: a piss booth. (MEN, PROTECT YOUR HEALTH!) The toilet at the Hopfenmarkt was far more comfortable. When it was being built, the citizens had thought Rostock was getting a subway. There was yet another public toilet at the Saarplatz, which matched the style of the houses there.

The founder of the streetcar was a Jew and he had put stops in front of his friends' houses. They were all Jews too, of course. How was that even possible?

The young female conductors enjoyed having us on the trams. They came from the Rhineland. We were always wondering when 'Dumpling' would be on duty. Liesbeth, too, though no one had seen her for a long time. She was a bit of a tramp, but very nice. When she was on, you could yank the emergency brake – usually out in Barnstorf, when she wasn't looking – and get off scot-free. (Ulli, of course – never me.)

The conductors lived in a barracks. You couldn't get to them though, as there were always soldiers standing around. We never saw the women off duty. Not even Ulli, although he always claimed he had. A fat SS officer also lurked around the barracks.

'Hey, boys, where is there a cathouse round here?'

*

When the air raid siren sounded we biked back to Ulli's house, in Fredersdorf, just outside Rostock. Gravenstein apples lay in the garden; ham sandwiches and cold milk in the dark; cool floors cobbled with brick. We would do our homework (translate and note) in the evening.

I had won over Frau Prüter, Ulli's grandmother, because I'd kissed her hand as a joke.

'What a nice boy,' she said to her grandson, 'a nice boy, this

Kempowski, bring him round more.' She gave me written confirmation that I'd done farm duty without my having to do a lick of work.

We would lie in the garden under a blue sky, eating apples and watching the glittering clusters of bombers. The flak cannon didn't move though: it stayed perfectly still, and the barrels were quiet. The silverfish above us looked back down.

We pointed two fingers up at them, aiming over our thumbs, as though we were going to shoot one down. We'd scream, whistle or wave, and nothing bothered them – so it wasn't long before we were sticking our tongues out, or flipping them the bird. We kept our pocket mirrors tucked away though; otherwise one of them might've broken ranks and made a quick detour.

After the all-clear was given, we crept around a little.

> Girl, you shouldn't be alone tonight,
> Girl, together, the world could look so bright.

'You just try and hold me down.'
'Careful, don't step in the cowpat.'

> Hello, girl! Hello, girl!
> Can't you see?[1]

One time we drove one property over, to the Schulze-Heidtorfs' place. They had 4,000 acres. On our way we passed the flak dummies: they'd been shoddily nailed together using tree trunks.

Ulli rode out in front and I always followed. Stay on the turf, don't get stuck in the sandy track, or you'd tip over. Then you had to speed up to catch up.

Ulli recognised – from signs totally invisible to me – that we were on Heidtorf soil. ('This cow here definitely belongs to them.')

I had heard that the Schulze-Heidtorfs used to have famous parties. ('Oh, I remember it like it was yesterday,' my mother would say.) They used to have Chinese lanterns and punch bowls in the garden. Now the concrete dance floor outside was overgrown with bushes.

Anneli, with her blond curls, came out of the dusty glass veranda, which had nearly been consumed by ivy. She stood in the door and smiled at us. A Belgian who worked for the family stood next to her, holding a pitchfork. He spat his cigar butt on to the floor next to him. He called me 'Kempi', and would squeeze my hand so hard when greeting me that it brought me to my knees. Could *she* hold me down instead? I wondered – picturing the girl doing judo in the *Swedish Illustrated*.

We went inside, and Ulli began to play hot jazz on the piano. It was brown, and slightly out of tune.

'Your left hand goes down the keys like this, one note after the other. When you get the hang of it, it sounds deceptively like the real thing.'

> It was always so lovely with you,
> Why did you do me wrong?
> And what'll I do without you?[2]

Meanwhile Anneli sat by the window, at her mother's sewing table. She was trying to catch the end of the windowshade cord in her mouth.

Then she rose sharply and said she wanted to go and have a look at 'the mother hen' – a big black metal screen that covered the chicks. It had to be warm and cosy underneath it; if you forgot to turn off the flame below and left it on too long, they all died.

When she left the room Ulli immediately jumped over and snuggled into the imprint she'd left on the seat. He wouldn't let anyone take that from him.

Later we found some cold chicken in the pantry, and sat at the kitchen table and tore it apart. We all drank out of the same bottle of mineral water: first Anneli, then Ulli and then me. ('Subhas Chandra Bose!' Ulli said.)

Anneli butchered the chickens herself. She'd learned how to do it from the Belgian, Jean. She held the chicken between her legs and slit its throat, from bottom to top, like she was cutting a willow flute. She told us that you had to hold the chicken down and let it flap its wings until it tired itself out; you had to keep your knees together, otherwise it would get away.

'How strong do you think they are?' she asked us.

From the way she'd been talking, it sounded as though you could fly away with it, like Munchausen on the cannonball . . .

We never went to the other neighbouring property, the Schulze-Karlstorfs, even though they had *two* pretty daughters. One of them had once said that I was a pale imitation of my brother, and I didn't like that. If I had seen her at the Heidtorfs', I would have left right away.

'You wouldn't do that,' Ulli said.

I would. I probably would, I thought.

*

'Walter, are you doing your homework?' my mother asked. 'No one ever sees you doing it, and you never say a word about it. Do you swear on your honour and your conscience? Look at me!'

It would be a shame if I lost everything Aunt Anna had built up, she said. She had no idea what to do any more.

And she didn't like that I was already wearing one of Dad's ties, either. ('He isn't dead yet.') My father had relocated to Lomza, in the north-east of Poland: it was a partisan region. We heard that someone had put a mine in his predecessor's bed because he hadn't wanted to give out any fishing permits.

'Better get yourself a machine gun,' his men had advised him. They were all based at the stalag. 'And always give out fishing permits. Don't be stingy.'

My mother had travelled with him as far as Stettin when he'd finally been deployed to the front. He'd looked at her so seriously, and she'd said:

'Why have you been this way all these years? You're so nervy.' At which he'd just stared off into the distance, the poor man.

'You'll see, he's going to get killed,' she told me.

I looked the region up in the atlas.

29

In October, UFA was shooting a movie in Warnemünde. We were back in school when we heard the news. It was going to be called either *Step into Life* or *Young Eagles* (it was yet to be decided).

It was to be set among a group of German youths – 'a sworn community', as the Party had begun to call them. Only someone throws a spanner in the works. One boy moves in fancier circles, and he can't get with the programme. The film then follows how he's melted down and forged again. The Holy Ghost doesn't visit him in the night though – instead they bring him round through the art of persuasion, with a lot of hard stares and pressed hands.

The lead, Albert Florath, gives a rousing speech: 'This business of being comrades is no easy thing. You can't just pick it up, like a pack of shoe wipes. It has to be earned.'

We saw Weidenmann, the director, at school. He was sauntering around the corridors with the head, dressed in a long leather jacket. He looked like Italy's Count Ciano, while the principal resembled State Secretary Meißner. They walked together like they were in the long, high-ceilinged hall of the new Reichs Chancellery. They were careful to keep an even pace. Cautious, even. Then they'd stand in place, looking at one another, before resuming their stroll.

Sometimes the crew brought up a light between the windows to see how it would look, or mounted a heroic sculpture, a frieze of the fighting troops.

When we march side by side[1]

'Young extras are needed,' Weidenmann announced, 'for a few days' work. Can anyone help out?'

'Extras?' all of the boys murmured.

'What did he just say?'

'What are you talking about?'

('Pick up that paper!')

'Did he say extras?'

Strapping guys from the upper classes were presented to the pensive Weidenmann. They stood up in groups, like in a roll call: those who'd received a medal for service in the Hitler Youth in front; those who hadn't, at the back. They all wore tiny shorts, their thighs like pink cucumbers, and had closely shaved heads, which they had absolutely under control.

Then Troop Leader Menge was presented. He was a real giant. He threw a bat from one end of the playground to the other. But no, Weidenmann was looking for yacht club types: groomed, in plain clothes, with long hair.

'Laid-back types, you understand? *That's* who I'm looking for.'

In response, the Hitler boys took him to a preparatory school for flight technicians (the Young Eagles that the film was about) at the Heinkel aeroplane factory. (A sworn community of boys.) Weidenmann was spoiled for choice there. He found what he needed.

He then returned to us to look for degenerate snobs. But we only heard about the second visit after it was too late.

'Shit, we took our eyes off the ball!' The casting call said:

You must be able to play the piano . . .

We got on the train right away. Maybe something could still be done. ('Do you have a comb on you?')

We arrived at the squalid beach in Warnemünde, the houses on the promenade painted in camouflage. Barrage balloons and fog canisters in the beach facilities, and there were some light flak cannons on the pier. I made sure to wear all my badges, including the one that read THE SAAR IS GERMAN.

Here, years ago, I had eaten Black Forest gateau under the open sky, the sound of the piano and a violin drifting out from inside: *In the Hall of the Mountain King*. My mother had put eau de cologne behind my ears.

An express train with Finnish boys arrived shortly after us. They were going to the World Summit of Fascist Youth. They were scouts, of a sort, like us. They didn't look particularly sharp though, some of their caps were worn to the right, some to the left.

Would everyone in Rostock be drawing their curtains closed, like the Poles did back when Elke and Lily travelled through the Corridor? (Whoever looked out was shot.)

Ulli and I walked back and forth in front of Café Becklin. He was always one step in front and to the right of me, such that I was diagonally behind him.

> Only the sun's for ever young, it alone is beautiful for ever. [2]

We paced in formation until someone approached us.
'Do you have any free time, boys?'
'Yes! Sure! Lots!'

He only really wanted to take Ulli, with his soft gaze and his eyebrows that met above the bridge of his nose. I paled in comparison, with my curly hair and glasses. I was also too little, and the hair on the side of my head was standing out (it was usually combed flat). Or perhaps it was because I didn't grin enough.

'No, you either take both of us or neither of us,' said Ulli. Now that was comradeship.

And it worked! They wanted to shoot another few metres of film before the sun disappeared completely. The two opposing camps assembled on the beach promenade: the strapping Aviation Preparatory Schoolers on one side and the long-maned boys in white suits, their skin painted brown, on the other. The light and dark of National Socialist society.

Together we ran to the film's hair stylist, who worked in the Hotel Hübner. (Ulli always a metre out front.)

'You too?' the stylist asked me.

While he put bronzer on us, we looked out over the sea. Denmark was somewhere out there. (How was it that the waves beat against the beach both here and there?)

> The sea is the gateway to the world.
> Only a fool doesn't hold it open![3]

A lovely country. Maybe we'd travel there later, when all of this was over.

(Aunt Silbi used to stay at the Hübner when she came to Warnemünde. She kept her eye on us using her opera glasses, tracking whether we were on the third or fourth landing, covered in tanning oil. She took our exuberance as a sign that we were doing well.)

Just as we were supposed to start filming, it began to rain. The shoot was called off and everyone crammed into a nearby bar. They sold frothy desserts for 20 pfennigs. Everyone sat around, wondering who might have to jump into the water in the cold. For that was how the script framed it: 'Tumbles into the water, enraptured.'

'Do you all come from Munich?' someone asked.

When the weather cleared the three most handsome boys were lined up on the harbour in front of some draped nets, arranged according to the golden ratio. They had to act like there were rowing boats down below and scream: 'Theo! Theo! Theo!'

Hundreds stood around them while they were filmed. ('Theo! Theo! Theo!') Then, just like that, it started raining again.

At the end of the day we got 10 marks. We came back again a little later, because we'd missed the bus, but the filming was over. Everything else had been filmed without us, and now the film people were gone again.

With the 10 marks, I bought a book about India. The author was named Mazooruddin Ahmad.

*

After our experience on set we began wearing white scarves, and decided to let our hair grow long too. I longed to look like the Dutch actor Johannes Heesters.

> You can see it by his walk
> And by his hair
> What Stenz
> And Louis were[4]

It had to be a white scarf; there was no question about it. I found one in my mother's vanity table. There was a group of boys who wore them like that in Berlin, too. 'Edelweiss pirates', they were called.

When I bumped into Manfred in the street one day he stopped still and asked: 'What on earth do you think you look like?'

He was still wearing shorts, I noted.

We always went to the barber in pairs. Ulli coughed to let the barber know he was cutting too much off. Your hair was supposed to reach over your chin when you combed it forward: that was the right length.

The Frenchman in the theatre barracks did a particularly good job. He only trimmed it a little bit. He more or less left it alone.

'Just clean it up, please,' we'd say. 'Just a trim.'

He held his finger underneath the smock when he tied it around us, so as not to tie it too tight.

One time he asked us why we wanted to leave it so long. We couldn't understand that at all. As a Frenchman, surely he could understand. Remarkable, too, that he didn't react at all when we hummed jazz while sat in the chair.

'Child, if you only knew how ugly you look!' my mother said. 'You look like some poor apprentice. It's not very becoming at all! Someone needs to bash you over the head with a mirror, then maybe you'd get it . . .

'What did you just say?' she snapped. 'Did you just grumble something hateful? Look at me! Be honest!'

I had, in fact, been thinking something like: Just let the old bag talk.

She'd recently seen young Eckhoff, who wouldn't have a hair left on his head before long. ('Can you believe it?') Only a bit of stubble.

'And he used to look so nice and friendly . . .'

After a while we switched from riding the streetcars to loitering by the cinemas. We'd stand around looking at the posters, and meet up with other guys just like us, with long hair and white scarves. There'd always be six or seven to a group. We'd dance 'hot' on the pavement. Our booming laughter could be heard streets away. ('Animals.')

One guy had a duck's arse; the hair combed back. His hat brim had been moistened and rolled over a pencil. It reminded me of a butterfly's proboscis viewed under a microscope. When he greeted you he always held your hand so firmly that you couldn't let go. He'd squeeze until you fell to your knees or had to bend left or right.

> The jellyfish sails through the world,
> It squeaks when you fuck in the sea.[5]

His hair was the colour of piss, slicked back with brilliantine.

> The most lovely of all ladies,
> I'll do everything you want,
> If you fulfil my wish,
> And be my one and only![6]

An SS assistant dressed in a trouser suit was always positioned in front of the UFA-Palast cinema. She stood on the highest step, and everyone had to file in around her.

One time they were showing the Swedish film *Her Melody*. The main actor was called Sture Lagerwall. We laughed ourselves silly at his first name: *sture*, stubborn. Meanwhile Sonja Wigert, his co-star, was incredibly beautiful. She writes him a note, but the piece of paper floats into the fireplace, and she's left thinking he doesn't want anything to do with her any more. Peppy music played at the end of the film, and the projectionist turned it up extra loud.

'When compared to the Swedish product, one can see how high a level the German cinema operates at,' we read afterwards in the newspaper.

You could sneak into the Kristall cinema through the toilets. The owner wore the golden Party badge, and he always stood around out front. ('Isn't it great what films we Germans have?')

There were two bathtub-shaped light fixtures on the ceiling of the auditorium. *Gong, gong, gong!* They turned a different colour each time.

The White Dream: it starred Wolf Albach-Retty and had Olly Holzmann playing an ice hockey player who pretends she doesn't know how to skate, and so is forever falling over.

> Maybe a prince will come to her from the moon,
> Or a millionaire?[7]

Hans Olden played a theatre director and Oskar Sima was the owner of some racehorses. Olly Holzmann is hired to join a revue and haggles over her salary:

'How much?'

'Double!'

Ulli mimicked their facial expressions, and their tone of voice when they argued, as though he himself were an actor.

'My dear sir, I am the theatre director . . .'

'I couldn't care less who you are!'[8]

(There were only fifteen minutes left of the film, a real shame.)

We always sat in the front row.

'Down in front!' we'd scream, even though no one was standing there. 'Lights out!'

Before the movie started we left jazz records in the projection room, which they played during the commercials. ('After You've Gone' by Turner Layton.) They always sounded completely different. The cinema had wonderful acoustics.

'Always with this nigger jazz,' a woman sitting two rows behind us said. She was scowling up at the projection booth. Stupid bitch.

MINORS NOT PERMITTED.

It was dangerous to see forbidden films. There were still four whole years until I was eighteen. When we went out, one of us was sent ahead to see if there was a patrolman standing outside the cinema. If we got in, we'd then tiptoe along the corridor – lined with blue plush carpeting, with large-scale photographs of actors on the wall – and sneak into the toilet. The idea was to wait until you'd left another film with the crowd, and then push your way into one of the forbidden films with the next crowd.

This was a lot easier for Sigi Herbst, a brutal guy who never hesitated to throw a punch. Or Menge the troop leader, the one who threw the bat from one side of the playground to the other.

'Where's your Hitler Youth badge?' he asked me once in the school yard. 'ID, please.'

> White scarf,
> Beat him down.
> Stiff hat,
> Beat him dead!

The white scarf particularly irked him. He tore it out of my collar, folded it up and stuffed it under my jacket. You had to laugh along, otherwise he might report you.

We managed to catch *The Vacation Child*, as well as *Two Worlds*, which starred Marianne Simons as a skilled horse rider. We saw both of them back to back, at three and then at five-thirty. When they were over we were wildly excited: we screamed and imitated all of the actors simultaneously.

> Today there's a hooplah at the cathouse.
> The police are on their way . . .[9]

The guys with the DAs started to sing in a strained voice, telling someone where he could stick it. We were all standing right in front of the youth detention centre. Passers-by in black coats, holding umbrellas, walked around to the side, shaking their heads. ('Utter animals, these boys – they need more schoolwork.')

Afterwards we stormed into an apartment building. We unscrewed the fusebox ('Is it a power cut?') then ran down the stairs to the floor below.

'Help! Fire!' Ulli screamed at the top of his lungs.

We knocked over water buckets and threw sand sacks between the landings, where they landed with a muffled sound. We then rang the bell somewhere else. A woman opened her door holding a ring cake.

'What a lovely cake you have!'

'It is, isn't it?'

We laughed about that for hours. 'It is, isn't it?' was a fun dumb question.

'Someone should have smashed that cake on her head,' said the guy with the duck's arse.

Another time we marched down Kröpeliner Straße in goosestep, one leg in the gutter, one leg up. Each of us held a human bone. We'd dug them up by the Stone Gate, where St John's Cemetery used to be. Thigh bones from the Middle Ages.

Fritze wanted to go fishing,
Stood up to his belly in the water.
Fishes played shenanigans
And bit him on his sac.
Oh yay, oh yay![10]

'Did you see all the people? Everyone was staring!'

'Did you see the old guy with the glasses?'

It was also fun when the air raid siren went off. All of us would pile into the bunker.

'If an alarm comes this afternoon when we're out, everyone go to the shelters in the city wall . . .'

We were always together.

The radio warbled in the streets: the enemy's air position was announced, along with where the squadrons were approaching and what direction they were taking.

'An enemy bomber group in the area of Perleberg': that wasn't dangerous.

'A group in flight over the Baltic. It has been confirmed that the machines are flying with open bomb-bay doors': that was somewhat more worrying. The district leader made the announcement himself.

'Citizens are asked to maintain order': an extremely Mecklenburgish attitude.

Whatever bunker we ended up in, we mostly stood watch by the door. We shouted, 'Oh!' when girls arrived, and danced 'Ring-a-ring-a-Roses'. An assistant police officer pulled three of us out of the bunker. We had no idea what he wanted, but he soon told us it was because we were being a nuisance. He took us to the guard.

'Someone should flog you good and proper,' said the constable.

'They should pull your trousers down and beat you with a thin cane. It'd do you good.'

Unfortunately for him, things like that weren't done any more . . . You could see that it pained him. A streetcar passed by outside.

'Can we make it up somehow?' asked the guy with the DA. 'We could do sentry duty or help old people? Or we could carry satchels and take ammunition to the front?'

30

In the summer of 1944 I went to visit von Germitz, one of my classmates from my time with Aunt Anna. His parents had some land by Plauer See in Brandenburg.

There was a coachman waiting for me when I arrived at the village station. He was wearing a cockade on his lacquered top hat. He took our bags and set them on the wagon before draping a blanket over our legs. ('Ho!')

We flew through woods, the horses swishing their tails, the cart bouncing. We were perched on a light hunting wagon with white rubber coating on the wheels. In the back there was a grate for tying on dead deer. A buzzard circled over us for the whole journey.

After two hours, a white manor house loomed into view. It had a grand driveway and an outside staircase, just as I'd imagined it. It was a far superior house to the Schulze-Heidtorfs'. But the columns at the door only supported a thin balcony. (Above it was a plaque that bore the crest of the family, painted red and gold.)

A panting dog ran up to us as we entered the hall.

'He's extremely horny,' said von Germitz, and took him between his legs. 'Are you going to behave?'

My room was on the second floor. I went straight over to look out of the window, and saw lawns with elderberry growing at the fringes, among old trees. Horses with pale manes were grazing in the tall grass.

I washed myself more thoroughly than usual, to help shake off the road dust. I had plenty of time. I opened the drawers in my room, and then put everything back exactly the way it was. (*Dear Mother, I feel very happy here.*) On the wall was a guitar. I fetched it down, but my fingers were too short to play with any skill. My brother said I had 'spider fingers'.

In a book called *Africa Waits* I'd once seen a picture of a man who had hands that were exactly the same as mine. It was entitled 'Negro playing the recorder'.

I heard doors slamming throughout the house – both close by and further away – but there wasn't a soul in sight. (*The landscape here is passable.*) They should have hung old portraits in the hall, I thought. Paintings of men with light beards, holding weapons, with a dog at their feet, perched up, alert.

Though in Paul Eipper's *The Yellow Dog Senta*, the dog bit him when she found herself cornered between the bed and the wall. She snapped at him quickly but then started whimpering right away, and leaned against her master. But it was too late, the offence had already been committed. It's not so easy getting on with animals. You need a great capacity for empathy and a lot of patience.

I stayed tucked away on the gallery and looked around a little, watched constantly by the dog, who had followed me to my room, and then hadn't moved a muscle.

Next to the door that led on to the balcony was a gun cabinet, which had several triple-barrelled shotguns in it. An obvious idea, when you come to think of it, inventing something like that. (*It's like a proper castle, dear Mother, a castle with all the bells and whistles.*)

> In the Tyrol, at Lake Inn, it so happened that,
> as the forest warden for the region was out for a walk
> early in the morning, I encountered a so-called fish eagle
> with its offspring, whose young at that moment a large
> bird of prey was seeking to steal, and in fact took away.[1]

('Buckshot', the word popped into my head, along with 'poacher in socks'. Summer days spent in the forester's house.)

A door opened, and a girl went into the room below me. She was about sixteen, with dark brown hair. She looked at me and turned round right away. A little later, Ferdinand von Germitz finally arrived.

'Why don't you come down?' He presented his grandfather, who was a bow-legged man with a beard and a pince-nez. He looked up at me, down the length of his nose. (The girl had been pretty.)

'What kind of soil do you have?' I asked.

'It's quite loamy up to the lake. Then around Harselfeld it's moderately heavy, and in the enclosure it's light to gravelly,' he said.

Before he'd finished speaking I asked about the harvest, how it was shaping up, and whether the livestock were healthy. At that he turned away without a word. Von Germitz winced as though he'd been burned.

'Ouch. You really put your foot in it there!'

I met the girl again in the study. It was dark in there, because of the columns in front of the house. She was kneeling next to a dachshund, which was running riot. A small basket with an opening in the front was on the floor next to her.

Her name was Margreta; she was my friend's sister.

The dachshund sneezed. I crouched down to it too. Its snout was warm.

'Should I get some cold water for him?' I asked. ('The good comrade'.) As a wire-haired dachshund, he probably yapped all the time.

There was another sister, called Rosalinde, who was twelve years old. Everyone called her *das Roß*, though: the horse.

'Do you play table tennis?' she asked me.

'No. I don't have anything against sports though,' I said. 'With football, for example, I'm always in defence; that way I can read the newspaper, and when the ball comes I just fold the paper up and stand in front of it with my arms outstretched.' That made everyone laugh. 'I even considered setting up a chair once.'

'*Mange tak i lige made*,' I said, changing the subject. 'Oh yes, my brother-in-law is Danish, by the way.'

'So there's not a whole lot going on with you then, is there?' the horse said, throwing herself on the sofa. It seemed she thought I was boring, maybe even stupid.

An officer came into the room. Von Germitz told me that he suffered intense headaches because of a brain injury. He'd been a Stuka pilot, but had been permitted to recover here. When he saw me, he immediately turned round and left the room again.

'You could have asked him how many bombs he dropped each time,' von Germitz said.

Then came two young women, one blonde, the other dark-haired. They were von Germitz's aunts, as it turned out. They arrived alongside a grim-looking inspector who had a Party badge. I could tell he was looking down on me ('apprentice'). He walked over. He wanted to stand in the exact spot where I was, it seems.

'Make room, now.'

Finally the mother came in. She was gentle and kind. Her wavy hair framed her wrinkled face. She stood under her own oil portrait, in which she was ten years younger. It had been painted using a palette knife, she told me. Should I kiss her hand? I wondered.

'A pleasure,' I said, remembering Ulli's advice: to always be pleasantly reserved and unassuming.

'What a nice boy he is,' she said.

I pulled some coupons out of my bag.

'My mother sends her greetings,' I said.

'There's no need. Put them away,' she said.

We gathered around a big dining table. Von Germitz's mother served fried liver with mashed potatoes (no kidneys, thank God). We all had whole milk, too, which I hadn't had for a long time.

We ate quickly and plentifully. Everyone was focused on the task at hand. The horse snatched bits of meat from her brother's plate. He kicked her in the leg in retaliation.

'You must be prrrroper at the table,' the grandfather growled. He had been shoveling away, but he was so displeased with their manners that with this he paused, holding his fork aloft for a moment. His teeth were tiny, set within his large head.

'You should take a good look at young Walter,' the mother said, 'what a well-behaved boy he is. His elbows bent, not resting on the table. What a splendid young man.'

'Yes, but why is his hair so long?' the blonde aunt commented. 'It bulges out on the sides, look. How disgusting.'

'Can I have another piece of liver?' I asked. 'It tastes so very lovely.'

She'd have to see. 'I don't know if there's enough to go round. Hold your horses.'

(The cutlery was all alpaca silver.)

'Besides,' the horse cut in, 'liver can't be "lovely". It can be "good" at best . . .'

'It can too,' I said. 'This liver tasted "lovely". I deliberately chose that word, because food is above all an aesthetic matter.'

'What kind of nonsense is this?' The Stuka pilot held his head in despair. He couldn't bear it. 'Would it be possible for me to eat separately, maybe in the workroom?' he asked.

After the meal I went out through one of the narrow French doors and down the wide, sweeping staircase. (*They've got a proper park here too.*) I held my hands behind my back and walked up and down the garden: Prince Walter of Aquitaine. (*In the English style, I would say.*)

The washed-out path was full of weeds. The horses raised their heads one after the other and drew closer to me. 'What do you want?' they seemed to ask.

When I looked back at the house, the whole family was standing there. ('What do you want – walking back and forth out there?') Upstairs, the Stuka pilot shut his window and drew his curtains. He couldn't catch a moment's peace.

In the evening I discovered that each of the girls had a room opposite mine. Their doors closed; the sound of giggling. The toilet that we shared hadn't been flushed. Was that the horse?

*

Von Germitz got me out of bed at four the next morning, on account of it being 'the most lovely time of the day'. He had breeches on and his riding boots, along with a green loden jacket that had diagonal pockets. A thick book was tucked under his arm: Praktikus's handbook for wine merchants. I thought he was joking. But no, he was completely serious.

When we got outside, everything was shrouded in fog. The horses appeared as no more than shadows. I saw a traction engine in the bushes. That too had been an achievement once. Von Germitz trudged through the wet grass, Praktikus under his arm, looking neither left nor right.

Finally we came across a hunting hide. Once we'd climbed up into the hut, he opened the book. A hole had been cut into the pages. There were cigarettes inside. It was his secret hiding place, and he came here to smoke.

'I'll need to replenish my supplies soon,' he said. 'But my parents are always on the lookout, along with my aunts, my grandfather and my sisters. I'm meant to read from the Praktikus every day.' With this he narrowed his eyes and scrunched his face. 'This is how I'll look in thirty years.'

I put the cigarette too far into my mouth, and the paper softened up. But things went more smoothly with the second one. I wiped my lips with the back of my hand to ensure it stayed bone dry.

'Why are your sisters like that?' I asked.

'Greta? Well, she's just dumb. She's always out to get me.' The aunt even hit him, he told me. His mother didn't, but the aunt did.

'Which one? Is it the blonde one?'

On the way back we met the steward. I was about to say good morning when he snapped at us:

'What are you doing here? Scaring away all the game, eh? You knew I wanted to go hunting, and you did it to spite me, didn't you . . .'

He turned away. I nudged Germitz and laughed. But the steward looked round again.

'I saw that. What are you laughing at? You probably think this is funny! Do you think you're better than me? You have your nose pretty high in the air, don't you . . .'

We walked on, and once some distance was between us I burst out laughing again. 'How strange!'

'Stop that!' the steward called back, now even further away. 'Do you think I'm blind? Or deaf? Or both?'

> On which instrument are we drawn
> And which player has us in his hand?[2]

'Or maybe you just think I'm stupid? Oh, you've made a big mistake, boy. I saw and heard everything.' He continued to shout across to us. There was a fire ditch between us, with some old buckets placed near by. 'What's the name of your Hitler Youth leader? I'm sure he'd be very happy to learn what an upstanding young man you are! To deliberately scare away the game and then laugh at someone who'd fought in the World War? My, my . . .'

Only later, after I'd made *very* sure that he couldn't see us any more, did I allow myself to laugh a third time.

In a shed, von Germitz showed me two ferrets. They were running about excitedly over the firewood. He picked one up and showed me its teeth. ('Like pincers.') It clambered all over him. Under the window there was a vice and a metal bucket filled with carbide.

Once we'd had coffee von Germitz fetched some beer bottles. He filled one of the bottles with the carbide, and we went out into the forest. Once we were a good distance in, he added some water, closed it up and threw it.

Silence. It should have exploded. We had to wait for the boom. 'Should we check on it?'

'Better not. You can lose an arm, or go blind.'

A cyclist came past us. He had ridden right past the bottle. And so finally we got up the courage to approach it. The fastener hissed: it hadn't held shut, it was probably no good.

The next attempt was better. There was a nice bang. Followed by another (*bang!*). We threw one into the stream (*whoosh!*) and pushed one down a rabbit hole (*boom!*). We then bundled three bottles together and blew up the entire burrow (*crash!*).

'I reckon they're all gone.'

'Clear!'

When the carbide was all gone, we shot staples. Von Germitz had a rubber catapult, too. He hit the metal bucket with it.

'If I were to shoot it at your leg, it could reach the bone,' he said. 'Should I try it? I could make you dance, like the fur trappers used to?'

He told me that he wanted to do a raid the following evening. There was tobacco hanging over in the Häusler barn and he wanted to steal it.

'Will you come along?'

'I'd better not . . . You know, what with being a guest and all . . .'

*

When the sun came out we sat on the balcony. There was no garden furniture, so we carried chairs from inside. (*The weather here is tolerable, dear Mother. That's as it should be, don't you think?*)

I checked my reflection in the window. My hair was sitting well. I was wearing my Zeiss Umbral sunglasses, along with a watch that I'd inherited from Robert. I wore it inverted, with the watch face on the inside of my wrist, the fastener facing out.

We played all sorts of games together. We threw rings at a bottle. We fell forward, without bending our legs, and saw who could catch himself.

Think-fast: Name a bad behaviour. Name something everyone has. Name something that annoys you.

We shook hands with a barber's grip, or one of us scratched the other person's hand with our middle finger; we squeezed each other's hand until one of us fell to our knees. And when the other person squeezes, squeeze back just as hard, that way it only hurts half as much. Wiggle your ears, right and left separately. 'Wow, incredible what you can do . . .' they said.

'We can do that because we come from the ooze,' I said. 'We developed gradually, up from primordial cells. Life must have come from somewhere, after all.'

'Do you think there are still people with tails?'

'No, but there are people with hair all over their bodies. In Krausnitz there were workers from the east, and you'd think they were wearing a sweater.'

'The workers from the east are really primitive. It isn't easy to kill them. Apparently they feel completely fine at forty degrees below freezing. While our machine guns are jamming, they just keep shooting . . .'

Imitate-the-teacher. ('Take your hand out of your trousers, boy!')

Can you? – Sure. May you? – No.

Tadellöser & Wolff.

'Tadellöser & Wolff? What's that supposed to mean?' everyone wanted to know.

'Well,' I tried to explain, 'it means everything's perfect, *tadellos*. That's how people talk in the city. "Goodmannsdörfer." That's another saying. When you think something's good, you just say, "Goodmannsdörfer." Or 'Badmannsdörfer,' or 'Stinknitz & Jennsen.' In Berlin they have completely different sayings, though. They're much harder to understand.'

With my long hair, I felt like Moses breaking the tablets, just like in Doré's drawing. See? I could break the law just as well as my old schoolfriend Blomert.

The horse brought a comb and a mirror, and gave me a centre parting and braided my hair. That was funny. We laughed until it felt like we were going to be sick.

'Shame there isn't any film around . . . That'd be some picture!'

The Stuka pilot was sitting down by the beech tree, on a white bench, shaking his head. ('My God, my God!') He'd put his life on the line, all so that we could comb our hair. ('Deplorable.') He shut his book, stood up and headed back inside.

Then the evil aunt – the blonde one – arrived. She wanted to know whether Greta had put the laundry away. Once again, Rosalinde hadn't dried the dishes.

'Did you think they'd dry themselves? And what're you doing out here, anyway? Feeling full of beans? Who braided your hair? Certainly not Greta, I hope?'

She didn't feel it was right that I was always hitting her on the behind.

*

Two days later von Germitz was sent to Hannover, to an uncle on an estate, so as to 'get some fresh air in his lungs'. I couldn't be happier. I was always deathly scared when he forced me to come along on our nightly undertakings. I would have preferred to get a good night's sleep and pick currants with Greta.

> Is she the fairy?
> The fairy from Odelidelase?[3]

She always wore a lot of perfume. ('Does it smell good?' she asked. *Ffft – ffft – ffft.* Just a little more, to be safe.)

The younger aunt – the one with black hair – picked up a bucket in each hand

> Yes that's the one
> Who blows forth planets from the grass[4]

She was the good aunt. She also knew Morgenstern; she read him with amazement. She accompanied me and Greta on walks through the meadow grass, and read the beginnings of poems which I then finished off.

'Why are you wearing your good jacket, Greta?' she asked. 'And your perfume: it's much too much . . . You only need one drop, behind the ear. Lovely out here, isn't it? Hopefully the weather will hold.'

The horse called us 'the couple', she told us. But she hadn't known who we meant by 'the horse' at first. Now she understood, though.

'Greta, Greta, the two of you are up to something.'

In the afternoon Greta and I went swimming in the lake. It was difficult to shake the horse, but we managed it. I thought we'd have to walk for hours to get there, but it turned out the lake was just behind the house; only a short walk through the woods, and you were there. It looked like the lake in *Immensee*, the UFA colour film starring Christina Söderbaum.

We could see the edge of the forest in the distance, marking the opposite bank. The sounds of the wildlife were scarcely audible in the clearing. A silver bluebottle drifted past above us. (Friend or foe?) There were ospreys there too; I saw two or three eyries in the higher branches.

Felled tree trunks lay on the bank. Greta told me that they'd been sold five years ago, but still hadn't been picked up. Incomprehensible, really, that they had the money to waste. I set myself down on one of them and shooed away the horseflies.

Greta wore a two-piece with an image of a buoy on the bottoms. Sometimes she swam on the surface and sometimes underwater.

'Hoo-hoo! You should come in, the water's warm!' she shouted to me, splashing. I remained where I was, though. There was no way I was getting my hair wet.

But then I decided to go in the water after all. Surprising myself, I leapt up and left the tree trunk rocking back and forth for a while. We swam out a stretch, then swam back again. (What else were we supposed to do?) I would have liked to take her on my shoulders, but then my hair would have been gone for good.

On our way back we came across a carthorse with thick feathering over its hooves. Greta climbed on the fence, and mounted the horse from there. Her thighs spread wide over its back, her tiny knees jutting out. (*The Hunter and His Horse.*) At times, various parts of the animal's body would tremble – sometimes its legs, sometimes its long neck – but it kept grazing unconcerned.

After a time Greta dismounted, and we continued on foot. We decided to make a short detour. We noted how the clouds were moving across the sky, and I told Greta of how the storks were dying out. ('It's a real shame. Owls, ravens: they're just about gone too . . . And it's a disgrace what's happening with the whales.') I told her how they'd found a mammoth under the ice in Siberia, and how the flesh was still edible.

'Can you slaughter chickens?'

'I've never been allowed to watch.'

Then we sat in the cornfield under a cherry tree, and Greta wove me a wreath.

*

On Sundays the fireplace was put to use. This was something special for everyone. The good aunt lent us a gramophone and some records. *Sweet Music Man* by Nat Gonella – he was almost better than Louis Armstrong, I thought.

'Why this racket again?' the evil aunt said through the door. 'And don't use *all* the wood.'

The grandfather also peered in briefly.

'Have you stacked the logs correctly?' He checked, and shook his head: it had to be a pyramid.

I reeled off my brother's records, asking whether the good aunt knew each of them. She was delighted. Then she began quizzing me in turn. That way we were even. Pound for pound.

We spoke about how Art Tatum was blind and Chick Webb crippled, that Artie Shaw could play classical for a whole night, and how laid back Teddy Stauffer was when conducting, standing with one hand in his pocket: we were always in agreement.

'Where do you know all this from?' Greta asked.

Occasionally I went over to the piano. I'd play Eddie Carroll, 'Harlem at Saturday Night', smooth back my hair, and conduct at the same time. Playing the bass keys for 'It's Always So Nice With You'. (If you knew the song, it sounded right.) Though I'd play up high sometimes too; as Robert had said, there are keys to use up there as well.

My fourth finger was the weakest. With people who practised a lot, their thumb muscle bulged out. They also cut their nails very short, which was hard for me to do as my nailbed jutted too far out. My mother could move each of her fingers on its own.

'There's someone over there who recently had two fingers lopped off,' Greta said. By 'over there' she meant the barracks where the farm workers lived, hidden behind a hedge.

'Come back here!' the horse shouted. 'All of the wood has burned away, what a waste!' Greta and I were huddled under the bearskin, amid Greta's perfume, nice and cosy, staring into the dwindling flames. As was only proper.

. . . so unite in the flame – may you all make ready.[5]

We added more wood to the fire. ('Not so much, or she'll complain again.') Outside, there were definitely bats flitting around. The aunt went to the gramophone.

Anytime you're Lambeth Way
Any evening, any day . . .[6]

The horse could do a kind of tapdance. The chandelier clattered as she leapt up and down. She could dance the Krakowiak too – she had seen the Russians 'over there' doing it, and had watched to see who could dance crouched down like that for the longest.

The evil aunt came over. She'd had enough.

'What's going on here? Were you raised in a barn? Such an ugly noise! And why are you still not in bed?' She glared at the horse. 'Quickly now. You've turned the whole room on its head. The fire is roaring, you've put far too much in, and no one has an eye on it.' Finally she turned to me. 'And when are you supposed to go home? You've been here for ever!'

'Tomorrow,' I said, right away.

'Well, no need to leave quite that quickly . . . I didn't mean it that way.'

'No, tomorrow. That's what I was thinking.'

The good aunt also said I should stay for a few more days. ('It needn't be for ever.') She said she'd take care of it. But I held firm.

I found sweets on the bedside cabinet when I went to bed. Greta came to pull down the blinds, which she never normally did.

'Oh, what's this?' I said. 'What have I done to earn this? How can I thank you?' (Her curly hair, her glasses smudged.) I took the guitar from the wall. A string was missing. Maybe I could get one in Rostock, I thought. (Spider fingers.)

I told Greta how we always found records at Löhrer-Wessel among their second-hand things.

'You wouldn't believe what you can find there.'

There was rumbling in the distance. It was Rechlin: new weapons were being tested there.

*

I got up at five o'clock, and found Greta already in the kitchen. She spread schmaltz on bread and poured me a coffee. Then she handed me the confirmation of my mandatory service – three weeks of labour in the country – to show the school.

Her mother told me I should write something in the guestbook: a real honour, as not everyone was permitted to do it.

> Silen rides homeward and plays on his beloved flute.
> All sorts of things of course, but mostly doot-doot-doot.[7]

That was what I would have written. But the guestbook was nowhere to be found.

It wasn't the coach that showed up to collect me, but the milk wagon: a crudely thrown-together cart. Also it didn't pull up at the house. Instead it just idled over by the reaper barracks, and I had to go down to meet it. The coachman was beating a calf in a sack. The long, stalky limbs resisted and the cane cracked. The horse raised its tail.

Greta waved for as long as she could. She stood under the colonnaded balcony. The crest hung on the wall above her. At the edge of the forest we saw a man wildly gesticulating from afar. It was the pilot. He came closer, his face contorted, so the coachman stopped.

The pilot then brought one foot up on to the running board, leaned in and took my head in both hands.

'See you,' he said. This would have been a perfect time to ask him how many bombs a Stuka like his dropped, and what it was like to pull up again after he'd dropped them. I only thought of it once it was too late.

'Where did you disappear off to?' my mother wanted to know. She was very irritated about the coupons, which I must've dropped somewhere. 'It's enough to drive you to despair! You couldn't have posted them or something?'

It was only then that she asked me how it was. She told me I looked completely different.

'You're still my little Peterpump, though. You know that, right?'

I wrote a letter of gratitude the very next day. (Was it 'most honoured' or 'most honourable' Frau von Germitz?) I asked after the dachshund; whether he was doing any better.

A card came back quite swiftly: *You'll have to come back if you'd like to learn the answer to your question . . .*

31

My father returned home on leave again in October 1944. He was very large by this point, and arrived with a red face. ('That's the day down the drain. I'm completely done in. And look at my skin! Everything's sore.') But he was taking Vigantol now – vitamins, often given to babies – which helped.

'You go from doctor to doctor, run from Pontius to Pilate, go to Aachen, smear yourself with tea, sulphur, sludge – rack up one bill after the other – and all to be given baby vitamins by a simple military doctor . . . And so here I am: a grown man, forty-seven years old, taking baby vitamins. Just imagine that. It's enough to make you laugh!'

Life with the troop was becoming a bit of a joke. They'd been assigned a lieutenant who had worked his way up from a private. You could tell right away, my father said, because he was always talking so loudly. ('For now accept my thanks.')

'And he's always sticking his nose in everywhere . . . He needs to remember it's dark up a Moor's arse.'

Hempelmann, the old lieutenant, had been completely different, my father told me. He was heavily decorated: he even had a Romanian Knight's Cross. ('"Comrade," I said to him, "if I may be permitted to ask . . . such a highly esteemed distinction . . .?")

'"Kempowski," he always said to me, "things don't always turn out how you think they're going to." He knew which side his bread was buttered. From a good family: they worked in exporting coffee.'

'Still, it's no walk in the park out there. The train line to Minsk was blown up by partisans. Then came the Russian offensive, with no warning. Everything is over-organised. We didn't get an order to retreat, and ended up having to crawl through a cornfield.' They'd just made it. Another minute and they'd all have been finished.

He pushed the pencil under his wedding ring and spoke in French. He no longer mentioned Lomza. And the only food mentioned was green beans and potatoes. 'It's been a bad year. But soon I'll be promoted to captain: "It's your turn," Simoneit told me, "and it's 'bout time." A big lush, that Simoneit, to be honest.'

'Maybe they'll send you as part of a relief detachment to Hessia? Because of your skin?' my mother asked.

'It might suit them,' my father said. 'They probably want rid of me . . . Then again, the Hessians say *gockel* for cockerel and *hinkel* for chicken; that nonsense is the last thing I need.'

'But isn't it safer there?' my mother asked.

'Safer? What am I, an idiot? What use is safety when I'm stuck with a bunch of Hessians? No thank you. Pilot, get me to land! In any case, no, I'm not going to Hessia. The unit is being taken over by the Greater Germany Division. No matter that we're only a construction unit. More shenanigans . . . "Then everything will function better," they said, "it'll run like clockwork."

'"Greater Germany Division" has a ring to it though, I'll give them that. And I'll get an armband. When all's said and done, that's not something to sneeze at.'

He took a crumpled-up ration card from the leather sheaf in his wallet. His sausage fingers struggled to grip it. His nails were long, curling round the tips of his fingers.

'Is there pudding?'

'No, but we do have *migetti* soup. It's made from a dairy substitute. With noodles, it's not bad at all.'

'Just incredible what they manage to make from milk these days . . . Soon they'll be making suits and chairs. They'll make things to wear out of milk and then maybe they'll make milk out of things you wear! Substitutes are often better than the real thing, Gobiles said. But it *can't* be. Otherwise it wouldn't be called "substitute".

'It's the same nonsense as that "either-or" philosophy,' my father went on. 'I read about it earlier. Kierkegaard says that it's only "as if" a table is here in front of me. It's not really there, you just imagine that it looks that way. Completely Dumbmannsdörfer. You can bang on a table, after all! Oh, and Oswald Spengler, that's another one who's full of hot air. He's predicted everything, so they say. You can read the news and look it up in Spengler right after. *The Decline of the West*. I borrowed the first volume, but made neither head nor tail of it. Now I'm curious. It's all a race between cultures, he says, and right now the Africans are winning. But the way he says it, it's more complicated.'

'And what's new here?' my father asked.

'Well, the pretty birches at Krause's have all been cut down.'

'Really? Is that true?'

'Yes. The roots were reaching into Merkel's garden. He noticed it because his carrots weren't growing, apparently.'

'Disgusting behaviour, not very neighbourly. And Merkel was in the Party, too. And what kind of guy has only one name – Merkel?'

'Frau Kröhl has been completely beside herself recently,' my mother continued. 'Their lovely view is completely and utterly gone now. She'd planted the birches herself, with love and care. She fertilised, nurtured and cared for them, shared joy and sorrow. In times like these, when people are so desperate for something beautiful, she has to go without. Unbelievable. But I've said she can use our throughway, just to save herself having to walk a few metres.'

'Krasemann's been locked up.'

'Krasemann? He's the one with the pince-nez, right? The one whose arms flap behind him when he walks?'

'That's the one. He'd also got more and more careless. Used to be a Social Democrat, very black-red-and-mustard, and never kept his mouth shut. He was always giving everyone a piece of his mind. He sent his son to Hitler service in a coat, for goodness' sake. It covered his uniform! That wasn't going to turn out well. And all instead of being happy that he didn't have to go to war. "So what?" he'd say. He always used to come late to political meetings too – so everyone would notice him.'

'Both of Heinemann's sons have been killed,' my mother continued. 'Tragic, really. First the family was bombed out, and now the two sons are dead. They only have one little daughter left. But the workshop is still intact, thank God. He's a good man, Heinemann. Catholic, you know.'

'There are new tenants downstairs?' my father asked.

'I think he works at the gasworks . . . Do you know him? Nazi?'

'Her, yes, and he's under her thumb. Just be careful, for God's sake. Don't give yourself away at the last minute.'

'Boy, bring me the ashtray and the carbon tablets. It pays off later in life, absorbing carbon.

'How's Ulla? Any mail come?'

Ulla's clear handwriting, crossed out in blue by the censor: was there sensitive information underneath?

'The brave lass.'

'Things are going well for them, and they've sorted out all the things they need for winter. They've wallpapered the whole apartment and painted it too. She's a good child,' my mother reported.

'Have you asked about Löfgrens yet?' my father wanted to know.

'You shouldn't picture bad things like that. Everything's completely different over there. They only speak Danish now, for example, not a word of German.'

'Why?'

'Well, they hate us.'

Robert had been drafted now. (Robertus Capulius.)

'The poor devil. Well, at least he's only a driver! Still, it's hard to even turn the wheel in those giant things. But the main thing is he's behind the front line, taking care of supplies. Things aren't nearly as bad as they seem there. Plus, he'll be able to drive a car when the war's over, assuming the qualification is still recognised. Who knows what that might be good for . . . Brave lad. You needn't worry about him. Small as he may be, he's very sharp. And tough. Hard to kill.'

'And so there's only little Walterli home now. Our Peterpump is left holding the fort, standing by his mother's side.'

'Everything fine in school?' my father asked, but didn't pause for an answer. In his youth, he told me, they were in school well into the late afternoon. 'Kempowski, hold me up . . .' the teacher would say, it was so hot. Twenty-five degrees in the shade and the flies thumping into the windowpane. 'Kempowski, hold me up.'

At the end of the day he climbed up on the post wagon at the

Kröpelin Gate, and sat on the coachbox in front. Then he jumped off just before the post office. He liked to annoy Plückhahn, who was the porter there. '*Schindobbri*,' he'd shout after my father. He came from somewhere or other in the east. (*Schindobbri* must be the same as 'good day', but in Russian or some similar language, my father thought.) He wore a red hat with PORTER punched into a brass plate.

'Do you fancy a cigarette, Walter? I wonder if you'd like it . . .'

'But Karl, he's only fifteen!'

'Well he has to start sometime! Look at this beautiful headful of hair. Could you give me some of it? He looks a bit like an artist!

'Why don't you say "*Nieulenant*" again, like you used to? Just one more time? How cute that was!'

I had to become a lawyer, he told me, that way I could clear up all the legal questions that popped into his head.

'Robert in Stettin or Lübeck, Sörensen in Copenhagen, and you here in Rostock, at the central branch. Completely feasible financially. I could sit out front and you can take the glass box, until it all pays off. We could rebrand as "Kempowski & Co.". Or maybe it'd be better to keep the old firm name, "Otto Manger". It's established, after all. Tradition is nothing to look down on!'

Otto Manger, everyone knew the name.

'How about a biscuit after dinner?'

In the living room there was coffee substitute and cakebread, but only the last crumbs of it. It didn't taste quite so bad when you spread it with marmalade. You could also mix it with cottage cheese to help with the flavour.

'Get out the Meißner serving bowl, we use it far too seldom. Careful though, don't chip the pot!'

The Meißner sat alongside the lovely silverware with pearl

details. Grandmother had taken care of it. It was pretty valuable. Very heavy in your hand. A good portion of the total weight was real silver.

If you scraped the knife on the fork, the sound was unbearable. It cut through to your core. Like nails on the blackboard, or touching wool: disgusting! Just thinking about it gave me the shivers.

Emmi Goedel-Dreysing was on the radio with her children's choir.

'Turn it off right now. That "plink-plink" music is unbearable. Makes you wonder how anyone listens to that dross. You might as well just end it now.'

'Finally, some quiet. A chance to sit back and savour everything,' he said. He drew our attention to the picture of the *Consul Discher*: his old flame. ('One day *you'll* get that . . .' he'd said to me.) And then towards the net curtains, and how the light flooded through them. ('Or would you rather have the autumn picture?')

'How cosy it is in here! And to think we used to always have your lovely ring cake, the one with I don't know how many eggs in it. Right, my Gretelein? Thirty-three eggs for a mark! Or pudding in the form of a grapevine. Everyone wanted to have the grapes, no one wanted the leaves. "Children, it's the same pudding," we'd say. But no, everyone wanted the grapes. And who had to go without? Your mother.

'"Man trains himself with austerity," your Uncle Schorsch always used to say, and then he'd take Aunt Silbi's overfull plate away from her and set it on top of the oven. Oh, how she sobbed and stamped her feet . . . She also ate bonbons all the time but never went to the dentist, she was so scared of hearing the results. A completely warped woman. A crying shame, really. She could be charming on occasion.'

'And she did such wonderful needlework,' my mother chimed in. 'And that voice! But no, everything's gone to pot.'

'Another piece of Uncle Schorsch's wisdom: only eat plaice in the months without an *r* in their name,' my father recounted.

'Do you remember the little fish woman with her stand under the city hall?' my mother asked. 'Why does Karl bring a fish home every day? I used to ask myself. Your father never brought anything else home. Not even during the inflation. I prayed and begged: "Karl, the minute you have the money in your hand, please go to the store!" But no. It was enough to drive you to despair! I'd be down on my knees, pleading – but no, only ever fish . . .'

'And remember when Stribold stepped in the butter, Gretelein?'

'That was some beast.'

'Poor dog fell from the balcony . . . Well, now he's dead, we thought. But nope: he was soon standing at the door, wagging his tail.'

'"Anna," your father had said, "come down and get the matches from under my coat." He'd hidden the puppy in the pocket. Bought him at the Whitsuntide Market. Good man, dead six years now, mind.'

My father wanted to know how we were fixed for food.

'We're making ends meet,' my mother replied. 'Siedler Reppenhagen said he'd bring potatoes this year though, he's already agreed. He might be able to double the amount, too.'

We got some salsify from him last time – it tasted like asparagus. ('Why haven't we eaten this before? Take note! Tadellöser & Wolff!')

'Better to have too much than too little,' my father said. 'You have to stay on your toes. The main thing is not to burn through it: go to someone else's house if possible, and be sparing when you go into the cellar.

'It's a good thing that Rostock's already completely destroyed: they probably won't come back again, it'd just be a waste of time. They can hit Berlin, Leipzig or even the Ruhr, as far as I'm concerned, just not Rostock.'

('The worst of it is behind us,' Dr Krause had said recently.) 'The faster it comes, the faster it'll be over.'

'And remember the trips we all took together?'

'Oh, the Rostock heath was always so lovely. Remember how Walterli used to look up at those great trees, and how he always wanted to climb them. He even asked whether there were wild boar there once!'

'But on the way back, the people in the villages were incredulous. "You're going to Rostock by horse?" They just stared at us and shook their heads.'

This led to a discussion of how Hitler drove through Rostock once. He was followed shortly after by Mussolini, in 1936. Both of them were passing through for the autumn manoeuvres.

'"Abyssinia! Abyssinia!" our Walterli shouted, the little Peterpump.'

'But there was only icy silence from Hitler. He just stood there, steely, behind a high pane of glass. Remarkable. He's always had it in for Rostock. He gave a speech here once, back in the System Era, and all of a sudden these leaflets fluttered down that said, "Nazism is complete nonsense," or something like that. He never forgot that.'

'But the Anschluss of Austria. You have to give him that.'

'And the Sudeten Germans, for that matter.' ('We're holding out.')

'And what he did in Wandsbek, with the communists. Pow! He got the troops to shoot into any window where the light was on. They sprayed every house.'

'Oh, what we've all lived through,' my mother sighed.

*

'I fancy going for a walk. You coming, boy?'

Our beloved home town. The ugly owl still stood in the cellar window of Wernicke the potter's. Robert always wanted to buy it and smash it to pieces.

'Soon there'll be nothing left standing on Friedrich-Franz-Straße,' my father said. 'Afterwards they should clear it and build a park there. It's the right thing to do. Tear the rest away, flatten it and make a park out of it.'

Trenches zig-zagged along the city wall. All the trees were covered in ash.

'And no children! Where are all the children?' he said. 'Remarkable. This is where the little girls used to sit feeding the ducks. And over there, next to the public toilet, was where the little bronze girl was positioned, the one who drank out of a seashell. Also gone. Probably housed inside somewhere, I'd wager.

'There used to be lantern festivals here all the time, with everyone dancing, and everything illuminated. You'd get turned around and then walk smack into the face of a complete stranger.'

They had begun to sell special stamps in the barracks post office. ('The Art of Goldsmithery'.) They were dark green and dark brown-carmine.

'Would it make you happy if I bought you one?' my father asked. They had GERMAN REICH written across the top. At one point we had had stamps with the Germania head on them –

misprints from the Weimar years, the Old Germany. They had to be somewhere. Probably insanely valuable now.

The Soldier's Memorial was still standing, and they'd walled Blücher in, to protect him. ('Quite commendable.') St Mary's was still in one piece too. A relief, really; she'd already been through so much. To the south of Blücherplatz was the sundial. ('Let's see if it works. Ugh, a cloud. Typical.')

My father was constantly saluting everyone, and every kid saluted him in turn.

'Just don't tip your hat any more. Now the only thing recognised is the German salute. Throughout the whole world military men tip their hat, except in the German Army.'

In Blutstraße the shop windows were boarded over. Peering through tiny peepholes, I could see that there was nothing left inside them. The shelves of the shoe shop were completely bare. Now we had shoelaces made of sheep intestine, and footlets for stockings, as they couldn't be mended any more. We had leather patches to mend shoe soles, too.

> Think when you take every step
> Your soles protect a soldier.[1]

Graffiti was scrawled on every wall:

THE PEOPLE TO THEIR ARMS

It would never come off. Everywhere you looked:

DOWN WITH TRAITORS

STRUGGLE TILL THE FINAL VICTORY

'Pack of philistines,' my father muttered. 'The whole city ruined.'

In the Brünnengräber pharmacy we bought Inspirol, Sparta cream and a little bag of licorice for me to chew on. There was nothing kept under the counter any more, really. Herr von Brenning came in ('lovely!'), with a face like an old boar, his hat worn at such an angle that the brim rose high above his forehead. He grabbed the flashlight that my father wore on his coat button, with a dial for red or green light.

'Well look at this! Did Kempowski get another medal?'

'Run along, Walter.' My father said he'd be right behind me.

*

There were only four more days till he had to go back. A giant chest full of laundry sat in our hallway. It was painted grey, and had PROPERTY OF KEMPOWSKI written on its side. We were to send all of our belongings to the country for safekeeping, so they wouldn't be destroyed at the last minute.

We were to itemise the furniture too, in a list. ('My goods and chattels.') Everything had to be quite precise. West, the second-hand dealer, would say as much, my father said. ('Don't forget to detail *sixteen* chairs. And don't forget the crystal.')

We'd buy a real rug in peacetime, my father said, to run between the dining room and the living room, to join one carpet to the other. Money would be no object. ('First we win the war, then we'll sort it out.')

The lamps were in good condition. We could take them back anytime. No regrets with those purchases. ('How's my skin doing?')

My father paced the room constantly while my mother asked whether she could finally do the big wash. It was just sitting there in front of her, waiting.

Meanwhile, I was to clean my father's books. ('Dust is the

adversary of leather,' he said.) I was to leave his white uniform jacket and the 'letter opener', his officer's dagger, alone though.

'And don't touch the piano,' he told me. (I still recalled how he used to play 'Rustle of Spring' – that was all over now.)

The bookshelf still smelled like chocolate. I pulled out the lovely Bruckner book; the sheet music in the back had been stolen: we'd lent it out but it had never been returned. ('Who could have it?')

Also on the shelves was the ranking list of the whole Prussian Army. A Major Krempowski, Ulan, was listed in the back. (If I put my thumb over the *r*, it was correct.) And then there was the charming book about Strindberg: *Marriage*. ('That was a nice one. He wanted to go to the bar and found it closed. He doesn't know what to do, but that's how he meets his wife.')

'Perhaps I should read a newspaper,' my father muttered. (*Berlin Rom Tokio*.) 'We had to be talked into buying it, you know. And it's certainly a flawed paper. You got a big piece of cardboard inside every time. Before long, the cardboard was the best thing about it. The old *Rostocker Anzeiger*, however, now *that* was good. You could read all about everyone's ups and downs: how Michael Krüger's gourmet food store slowly died off, while Bölte came up in the world. Supply and demand. Only the strong survive.

'All they have in here today are reports about "energy criminals". There are so many, they've even made up a character based on them to use in posters and advertisements: "the Coal Burglar". It's actually pretty good . . . The Nazis certainly understand a thing or two about propaganda. They can organise, you have to give them that.'

The radio announcer read with a reassuring voice. He was saying something about withdrawal movements and a planned straightening of the front. But in between his statements a horrible voice crackled: 'Make Hitler cold, then you'll be warm in your living room!' Just like that, disrupting the peace. That wouldn't have been possible before. Where were these people? Maybe at Timm, the butcher's, in the attic? ('Don't give up when you hear that voice!') Something had to be done about it. The voice would scream so hoarsely, it was repulsive. It seemed to take such pleasure in our suffering, as though it were glad about all the dead. If only the enemy were a bit more sympathetic, then people might be open to discussion.

'As you can see, I'm just about ready.'

'Perhaps you should take another picture of Ulla with you?' my mother said. 'The one of her in the Harz – where she's picking flowers in the meadow. It really was the loveliest time. And one of Robert. And of Walterli, our tiny boy, with his knapsack.'

She held a picture of me in which I was wearing my old itchy coat. Behind me Hahn's houses, all burnt down.

I transported the suitcase to the station on a handcart. ('Watch out when a car goes by. Make sure you stop and get up on to the pavement.') Then my father bought his train ticket from the machine. (Ten pfennigs.)

My father in a stiff coat, wearing buckskin gloves. His red face and thick glasses. He had toilet paper tucked inside the cuff of his left sleeve, his travel order was in the right.

'Quick, hide behind the poacher's shack.' Dr Heuer was coming. That was all he needed. ('What's he doing here?')

He was getting cold feet.

'Everything's so bleak,' he said softly, 'and there's so little hope and cheer. But you'll see, everything will turn out splendidly. Everything will turn out fine.'

Where tears flow, nothing can succeed,
He who wants to create must be cheerful.[2]

'Everyone puts their trousers on one leg at a time. You build it up in your head and then, in the end, it's not so bad.'

Steam came out from under the train.

'Watch out, do you hear?' my mother said.

'Yes, yes.'

'And be careful! Promise me.'

'On my life.'

We watched him climb aboard, then he appeared at the window.

'Be careful, Karl . . .'

When we got home, my mother suddenly burst into noisy tears at the table. She was taking gulps of air, and had covered her face with the napkin. She washed laundry for the whole afternoon.

'There isn't a healthier person than him,' she said in the evening. 'But then he's always so proper . . .'

32

In November 1944, I was called up for mandatory service. We'd stand and sing with Eckhoff on every street corner:

> We take rags, bones,
> Iron, paper and knocked-out teeth.[1]

And then we'd go into the buildings and ask for scrap material.

Arthur Milchsack, a tax attorney, had what looked like a kind of marble gutter running down his office's stairs, in lieu of a banister.

When Mutén, the Swedish lector, opened the door to his office by the Bridge of a Hundred Men, his face was chalk white. He probably thought the pogroms were starting. He was wearing a kind of housecoat. Perhaps we had woken him from his afternoon nap. He told us that all his things were in Sweden, and that he was sorry; he had no scrap for us.

'*Mange tak for ingenting,*' I said: thanks for nothing. The scouts were proud: the boys of the German Hitler Youth knew foreign languages. It wasn't long before Mutén left for Sweden too.

Frau Dr Von Eschersleben, an old teacher who wore a black band around her neck so her jowls didn't hang too far down, gave us stacks of old newspapers.

Die Woche, with Grand Admiral Raeder on the front page, and the *Berliner Illustrierte*, which carried the headline *The Beacons of Stalingrad*. The front page was divided in two, split between Paulus and Seydlitz, the defenders. They probably didn't have a picture of the two of them together.

A clock ticked within its glass case. Diana slaying a deer was framed on the wall.

'Why aren't you wearing a uniform? Well, at least it's a Hamburg suit. And what's your name? Kempowski? Then I suppose you're probably Körling's son?'

She rummaged through her bookshelves, then held a copy of *Prospecter of Duala* against her chest for a moment, her bracelets clinking.

'I want to give you a book. A special book. When you've read it to the end and understood it completely you must give it to someone else: to a good friend, or a student, as the case may be. It should go from hand to hand until maybe, one day, it'll find its way back to me.'

She leafed through it one last time with her wrinkly fingers. They were covered in rings set with old, coloured stones. She then handed it to me.

When we returned, the scrap material was weighed in the school basement. We were forever banging our heads against the heating pipes down there. Schulze the music teacher was in charge. ('Shame on you, sit down.')

> Eat what's cooked,
> Drink what's clear,
> Speak what's true.[2]

Schulze peered down through the lower part of his glasses when he looked at the pointer sliding along the decimal scale.

'Well, that's the whole afternoon down the drain,' he said, disappointed. 'And today of all days! Never any peace around here. Don't shove like that or I'll give you a good whack.'

Dr Krause offered me a wagonload of used bottle tops. To be on the safe side, I brought only one back to Schulze at first, to show him as an example. When I handed it over, he fiddled with the cap.

'Could you please tell me how you're supposed to get the iron out of the cap? Maybe I ought to do it? Perhaps I should work through them, one by one, pulling it out with a knife?'

We accrued points based on the amount of material we collected. You got five points for rags; just one point for iron. The students who got the most points received books. Dr Krause knew I wanted to win – that much was clear to him – but he deemed me a shabby sort of winner.

'Quiet down there!' he cried, distracted by the racket. 'Who is it that's constantly banging back there?'

'The Knocking Ghost!' either Struck or Stuhr shouted back, and got a slap in the face.

The awards ceremony took place in the classroom because the gym was full of homeless people's furniture.

'You boys really threw yourselves into this, you made it your number one priority,' the dishevelled director said. 'And that's why I am proud of you.'

In physics, which he had to teach now, the director tackled such conundrums as how to tell whether a cyclist was going forward or backward, simply by looking at the bicycle's tracks; or why tealeaves all gather in the middle of your cup when you stir them.

'Perhaps you still remember the lovely golden-brown colour of real tea, with sugar and cream . . .? Now, why do the leaves all gather in the middle? They should have been pushed to the outside, no?'

He taught us that the layperson could most easily recognise fake gems by their cheap metal settings.

You could distract him from classwork by asking him for a description of the battle at Tannenberg. He'd then regale us with how they came from behind, and the thin line that had to hold out against the entire attack. ('When shooting, always crawl zig-zag with your rifle: then the enemy will think there's a bunch of soldiers lying there!') He was more than happy to tell us about it over and over again.

'Even America will get a taste of our next miracle weapon, I'm officially permitted to tell you that.'

I also had to gather potatoes for my mandatory service. I'd run along behind the harvester, bent over, in the rain, picking potatoes out of the sludge one by one and throwing them into various baskets, depending on their size. If you didn't grab them fast enough, the machine came back around and caught up with you. The angry farmer then had to stop, otherwise he'd be burying his own potatoes.

One time the farmer reprimanded me because I'd kept my gloves on. ('Gathering potatoes with gloves on? A thing like that just isn't done!') He'd never seen anything like it.

'Gathering potatoes is anathema for my career as a pianist,' I said. I'd be putting my hands out of commission for months at a time thanks to this work.

Manfred meanwhile had made himself a nail-stick, like the litter pickers had. He speared the potatoes and stripped them off into a basket with two fingers. He stomped any soft or mouldy potatoes into the dirt like they were beetles. He recommended I bring wooden tongs along to help protect my hands.

Together with Liesing, our class rode to gather beechnuts in the forest. We found a spot where they had just been sown: it was like a bottomless barrel. You didn't have to look for very long, you could just sweep them together in the furrow.

'The good old German forest,' said Liesing.

Then he gave us instructions with expansive gestures and disappeared.

On the day of the invasion, Liesing had laughed loudly and rubbed his hands together. 'The Americans have landed in the Seine region,' he announced. 'We finally have them by the scruff of the neck and we can annihilate them. How stupid are they? They've come over the water and run straight into us! I hope they continue to send us more and more troops. It's like they're running into an oven: we'll keep incinerating them until the iron glows red hot!'

For a long time we tried to find the 'Seen' region of France on a map, but we couldn't find it anywhere.

While we were filling our sacks with beechnuts, a forest ranger and his dog came along. He was smoking a long pipe.

'You can't gather just anywhere,' he said.

Because he had such a strong Mecklenburg accent and said 'just anywhere' so stupidly, someone shouted: 'Shut your mouth, you old bastard.'

He went away but came back fifteen minutes later with two eastern workers, the two of them whistling as they whittled down their long sticks. On the ranger's command the two of them advanced slowly on us, striking the air with swift, exploratory swings. Yes, it was about to go off.

'Well, where shall we start? Who's first?'

We made it clear to the man that he couldn't have Slavic *Untermenschen* beat up German scouts. He should think about what he was doing! Seeing our point, the attack was called off.

We returned home on foot, as we thought that would both toughen us up and ease the burden on the public transport system. (The empty train caught up with us later.) We walked along the Warnow, Liesing behind us on the bicycle.

'Enjoy it!' he shouted now and again. We should enjoy the landscape. ('They can't take that away from us!')

The black river rushed without seeming to move. Fat Krahl kicked a can into the water, and his shoe flew in after it. Accepting his fate, he threw the other shoe in and continued in only his socks. With this, Liesing abruptly stopped, leaned his bicycle against a nearby willow tree and shouted:

'Get over here! You have defiled the river and wasted valuable footwear.' (*Whack! whack! whack!* Three slaps.) 'What were you thinking? Huh?' (Liesing's lower jaw jutted out.) 'Well? Are you happy? Huh?' (*Whack! whack! whack!* with the back of his hand.) 'You won't be doing that again, will you?'

At this point Klaus Bismarck Stüwe began throwing burrs at my head. Annoying as it was, I swore to myself that I would stay calm. I just picked the seeds out and made no sign that it bothered me. But then Stüwe pressed a handful of them into my hair. For that, I pushed him into a ditch full of stinging nettles.

'Ow! Hey! Ow!' he screamed, rolling around, struggling to get out. 'I'll put his lights out,' he said to the group, and tried to organise a gang to back him. But I had my friends too: Fat Krahl, Klaus Greif and Manfred never left my side.

'Were there thistles in the ditch too?' Manfred wanted to know. 'Or dog roses, perhaps? I can only imagine how badly they must've burned . . .'

If only there'd been a few broken bottles in there too, he went on. Or a pitchfork. They would've skewered him like Wilhelm Busch.

'I just read about how they roast live dogs in India,' Manfred recalled. 'First they stuff them with rice, so that their stomach is taut, like a drum, and then they roast them – alive – on a bamboo rack. The explorer who described that had been attracted by the yowls and wondered what they'd been doing. Imagine stumbling across a scene like that.'

At some point, thanks to all my diligent work gathering beechnuts, my mother got a voucher for a pound of margarine, as well as a coupon for a hundredweight of potatoes.

'Nice work, son. How many did the others gather?'

*

The next time we reported for service, Klaus Bismarck Stüwe had to stand at the podium and recount what had happened. As Eckhoff noted everything down, Stüwe's face was turning red. But then afterwards Eckhoff clapped his folder shut, took out a piece of paper and one of his six pencils, and turned to me:

'No, this isn't going to work any more, Kempowski, you have to go to the remedial Hitler Youth instead. You never show up to service, you have a non-military hairstyle, you sit in Café Herbst eating frothy desserts, and probably go to the over-eighteen films too, I'd wager. I'll write a transfer right now. It's done. I'm calling it a day.'

Stüwe was dancing for joy.

'Oh! They're going to rip you to shreds!'

In the remedial Hitler Youth, we only had service in the evening. Musters were at the Ulmenmarkt, where Ulli and I had once overturned the air raid buckets in the staircases.

> When the colourful flags are waving,
> The ferry must be going over the sea.
> If we want to see a distant land,
> It's not hard for us to say goodbye![3]

I was now with locksmith apprentices and boys from the shipyards.

'When did you crawl out of your mother's crack?' I was asked by one boy. They were asking for my date of birth. ('You look like a woman. Why are your lips so red? Do you wear make-up? And what about the waves in your hair, eh?')

I was sent with some others to a barber, who reopened in the evenings. He was already cleaning the mirror and straightening the chairs when we arrived. I was to be given a bowl cut, like a soldier about to go off to fight at Ypern or a prisoner on his way to St Quentin. A fellowship leader accompanied us, walking out in front, as a kind of guard.

On our way back, I ducked behind a linden tree in the Old Cemetery. I stood there, where the prisoners from the Franco-Prussian War were lying, and let the others go on. When they were out of sight, I headed home through the cemetery.

I peered into the mausoleum as I passed it: white coffins stacked on top of one another with pieces of wood between them so they didn't rot. Air needed to pass between them.

There was a gigantic sinkhole in the graveyard; a passing jet had torn it open. As Manfred told it, the pilot was trying to knock the cupola off.

My great-grandmother's grave has to be around here somewhere, I thought. The gravestone was polished black granite with gold lettering.

She had never been quite right. One time, she had shown up at our house in her nightgown in front of all our guests, got up on the table with a gas lamp in her hand and sung children's songs. She had gone hungry for much of her childhood, it was said, that was where that streak came from. She had learned English and French, but never had enough to eat.

Once home, I looked in the mirror. I tried combing waves into the hair on the side of my head, but it just came out straight again: Prince Walter of Aquitaine. A real shame.

'Oh God, you just walked away?' my mother said. 'When everything was going fine? You shouldn't challenge these people! They have the upper hand.'

I was picked up and taken to the next session. I had never been picked up. It was certainly an unusual occurrence. I had already thought of an excuse: constant stomach pains. I had wanted to telephone, but I just couldn't work up the nerve, no matter how hard I tried . . . The doorbell rang.

That's definitely a stranger, I thought right away, he rang just a little bit too long, and I could hear him fumbling around at the milk hatch.

'Walter? Someone's here for you!'

It was Loetke; his father was a cabinet maker from the shipyard. 'Heil Hitler!'

I leapt up.

'Heil Hitler!' I echoed. In the rush, I had only managed to get one slipper on. His handshake was forceful. (Definitely not one to try the barber grip with.)

'I'm here to pick you up for service,' he said with a lisp.

'How nice of you,' I said, 'how nice of you to pick me up. In a new unit one is so distant and lonely – you don't know anyone, you seek out comrades with whom you might, perhaps, outside of service . . . Anyway, really nice of you to go out of your way. By the way, the record that's on, it's a piece by Chick Webb: he's completely crippled. And Art Tatum is blind, and Artie Shaw can play classical for a whole night. Do you want to listen to a record?'

'No, we have to go now.'

One of my father's clay pigeons was in the hall (he'd shot twelve on that trip). A relief of a steel helmet, made of soft metal riveted on to black wood, was on the wall. I drew Loetke's attention to both, as well as the sabre, replete with a blood gutter.

'You can try and put the spiked helmet on if you'd like, but it doesn't fit anyone anymore. You see, people used to have much smaller heads, you can tell from the helmet . . .'

'No, we have to go.'

Loetke smelled like shoe cream and corduroy. He swiftly affixed a pin to my lapel.

No one usually saw the district führer, the head of all the scouts, but he was reading a speech in the Hall of Princes at City Hall that day. He wore a little red braid on his uniform, which was a mish-mash of styles, incorporating the Party's design, as well as the Hitler Youth's. (It probably annoyed the Hitler Youth higher-ups that the Hitler Youth badge was so small.) A flagbearer of the nation and a Lansquenet drummer stood behind him.

Everyone was motionless, sat in rows. (No one dared break rank, not even to bend forward and tie their shoes.) His speech lasted a long time. He cursed the 'damned family', saying that it had to be destroyed.

'The Third Reich hasn't gone so far as to completely do away with familial bonds, unfortunately. They're fetters. But you'll see, after the war, flattery and coddling will be stamped out and we will be forged anew in a shower of sparks. The red-hot iron will take its form amid the strong blows stipulated by the Führer . . .'

> Comrades shot down by the Red Front and reactionaries
> March in spirit
> Within our ranks.[4]

Outside, in the market, my new führer stopped me. He was called Bobsin, and he was very friendly.

'Don't you think you should participate with a bit more enthusiasm? You should think of the soldiers out there on the front: grenades exploding between them and the mud flying high . . . Or the miners, who bore holes deep into the earth, like inverted cathedrals, day after day so that the factories in the city and the countryside have coal. Or the farmers, walking with heavy step over the earth. That's also not so easy. You should spare a thought for them all. For here we are, in our soft beds, protected by our mummies, with porridge, and scarves around our necks, and even a hot-water bottle. Do you think that's fair? Well?'

In that moment I was ready to do what had to be done. With just this short speech, he had me ready to donate all three bulbs from our sprawling dining room lamp at home, and to report to the agricultural detachment to help plough soil. I saw myself as Essenholer Trinks – who I'd read about in *Exciting Tales* when I had scarlet fever – hopping from one bombed-out crater to another, carrying bread and cookware forward, or as the last man on the *Cologne*: clinging to its balcony and crouching when an English destroyer came by, to avoid being taken prisoner. ('Death before slavery!')

Bobsin was still waiting for a response. 'Well? Can you promise me you'll shape up? Definitely?'

No one had shown up at the marketplace in some time, so Bobsin kept looking at his watch and at the clock on City Hall. The time was marked in Arabic numbers on its face, the Roman numerals having been replaced.

Was it time? Yes, it was finally time: he could let me go. Whistling loudly, I walked by the Stone Gate – now severely damaged – and along Richard-Wagner-Straße. '*Amorcito mio*', from Theo Mackeben's *Anita and the Devil*: if anyone who lived on the street knew the piece, they'd be sure to notice that, not only could I whistle particularly well, but also that I'd mastered all of the song's finer points, right down to the last detail.

I crossed the Reiferbahn, which was lined with beautiful thick trees. Number 17 was on my left, where Christel lived. And just beyond it was where Antje and her strict father lived.

> Antje, Antje,
> Don't you hear the ship piano in the distance?
> Antje, Antje,
> This song is a greeting from me to you.[5]

Her father had been the director of the municipal utilities or something. He'd probably had no idea when he named her that there would be a hit song like that later.

Whenever Antje came out of the house someone would always be looking out of the window to make sure nothing happened to her. Behind her house there was a shack where she kept her bicycle. Sometimes she attached her bag to the back of it: she'd stand with the back wheel between her legs, pull up the clamp, rest the bag on it, then let go of the clamp. (*Clack!*) She always stood for her first three pumps on the pedals (*ratsh, ratsh, ratsh*). Then, with a flourish, she'd sit down and the seat would disappear under her dress.

The Köster girl had recently begun to walk too stiffly. She had a new mouse-grey ski outfit made of quilting. And Gina Quade was no longer so good-looking. I'd noticed something flabby about her face when I last saw her in the bunker. Quite strange. No, Antje was the best. As far as I was concerned, she could be dumb, get straight Fs and have filthy fingernails, it was all the same to me.

Walking home in the moonlight, I approached our house. KRAUSE: the lettering on the roof clearly visible from afar. I had once sat in the *A*.

'What a menace,' people said to my mother, when they'd seen me up there. ('Can you believe it?') Even the butcher's wife came out from behind the counter to have a look.

The Woldemanns had left, and there were new tenants on the first floor now. They weren't very pleasant. ('Good day.' – 'Heil Hitler, my boy.') The man always wore checked felt slippers with metal buckles, and they always left their apartment door open so the stale air wafted into the staircase.

Just as I was making my way towards the building, the key ready in my hand, four or five boys came running at me through the gateway, handkerchiefs covering their mouths.

'There he is!' they shouted, grabbing me. One took a pair of scissors out of his pocket and began snipping at my hair. They were pinking shears – a kind of sewing scissors, the kind you'd maybe use to make broderie anglaise for coffeepot covers at the Rosary Circle. I turned my head to the side a little, keeping away from the place he was cutting. There was no help in sight: no sign of the butcher's wife.

Then I saw Matthes further down the road. At first it looked like he was coming to help me, but it became clear that he knew something was up. He scurried by as though it were raining and locked the door behind him. The bolts clicked – once, twice, three times – but then again, his wife was Jewish: you couldn't expect anything from him. I saw him part the blinds in the staircase. He wanted to take part in what was happening on the street – this kind of manly ritual – if only in secret.

'Lights out!'

He quickly closed them again.

Because I didn't defend myself at all, only turned my head a little, they let go of me.

'What is it? What's the matter?' one of them said.

They began to question whether they'd made a mistake. They'd set everything up so well – planned it meticulously – but something was wrong . . . A big building across the street, in shadow, its doorstep bathed in a pale luminous colour.

'Better get out of here, quick!'

Once they were gone I bent over and picked up the bits of hair as best I could, not knowing whether to cry or scream.

I made my way inside and looked at myself in the mirror of the red wardrobe.

'You beg, you plead,' said my mother, 'but no, you do nothing.'

She straightened out the *Wolff's Telegraph Reports* in the open cabinet. *Poisonous Fish and Fish Poisons*, still unread. Wiped the red leather volumes of *Mecklenburg's Sons in the World War* down with a duster. 'Well, now it's time to pay the piper. You only have yourself to blame. Oh, so stupid, so stupid!'

The next day in school, they were waiting for me. They were already standing at Weinrebe, the paper merchant's, and began laughing as soon as they saw me. One of them ran out in front to tell everyone inside I was coming: 'Kempowski's here!'

They received me lined up on the stairs, all bent over the banister, head to head, all of them grinning. Some others walked next to me as I ascended, as though they had to film me.

'Not entirely successful, was it? His hair looks pretty much the same.'

'He screamed,' said one of them. He'd probably been there. I looked at his face: I had to remember him.

I went to see Dr Jäger, my teacher, immediately. He was standing at the window, watching as an apprentice engineer on a locomotive let off too much steam again. I showed him the hair that had been cut off, taking it out of my wallet.

'My mother sends her regards. If you should hear anything . . .' My mother had told me how he'd always played Bruckner back then, when Bruckner was really making his mark. He'd borrowed the records from her, along with Johannes Kessler's memoirs. He had been there for their tours on Rostock Heath too, when Stribold had stepped in the butter. But Dr Jäger just let out a mirthless laugh.

'What? They cut your hair off? It's nothing but a prank! A silly boyish prank . . . Cheer up! Just keep your head down. We all have to try and get by.' Then he clapped: 'Okay, inside, inside, inside! It's high time we got going. Why are we all standing around?'

I became a hero among my cinema friends. Ulli, who was on furlough from duty manning a flak gun, looked me straight in the eye and took gulp after gulp from the cough syrup bottle. Night was falling placidly across the country.

He wanted to hear the whole story again and again. ('How many were there? Did they hit you?') Then he looked at himself in the mirror, to see where he could lose a little weight from his hair, so it wouldn't happen to him. But it would never happen to him anyway. He was already halfway into the army, and they weren't nearly so strict.

*

I still went around with long hair regardless, and at one point my mother registered a complaint with the district. She couldn't send her son to service without something happening to him. Even her husband at the front was getting nervous. She walked over to the district headquarters with the cut-off hair in a blue envelope. Frau Kröhl had said that registering a complaint might set her at ease: 'You have to draw the line somewhere.' Even Frau District Court Counsellor Warkentin had agreed, and she had always been sympathetic to the Nazis, and Professor Knesel too had said: 'That's just a bridge too far . . .'

But in doing so, she rattled the cage. And so I got a summons from the army.

'He has a summons,' they said, 'Kempowski has a summons . . .'

'It's about time! They're finally going to whip him into shape.'

'I knew his luck was bound to run out sometime.'

'I have a summons,' I said to the handful of my cinema friends who were still left – most of them were on flak duty. They told me that I should go to Ernst Papenhagen, in Class 7A: he had also been called up, and could tell me which way the wind was blowing over there.

Three days before the hearing, two days, one day. I counted down the days at school. I was screwed.

'You should take a good look round and see what kind of encouragement you're getting from your fellow students!' Dr Jäger said. They were all shouting and whipping the air. He shook his head and knocked with his knuckle on the logarithm table. 'You want to be an officer, don't you? Well, you have to exert yourself then! This is no way to be!'

Before leaving, I smoothed my hair down with water so that it was lying flat, like a helmet. I polished my shoes one more time, washed my hands – ugh, drops on my shoes – polished my shoes again, washed my hands again, and took one last look in the mirror. (Tragedy in the House of Aquitaine.)

'Son,' my mother said, 'promise me you'll come back home and tell me what happened . . .'

The army service station was in a villa not far from the conservatoire where I used to have piano lessons. Bombs had fallen in the area in April. They were supposed to hit the train station, but they all fell right next to it. There were craters twenty metres deep along the street. Dr Felgendreher's house had collapsed – the roof perched above the rubble, like a hat. The telephone had rung from within: Felgendreher, who was on holiday in the country, wanted to know what had happened.

Aunt Anna's house (she had been gone for some time now) was completely intact, as were the Luftwaffe headquarters across the street (the brain). My grandfather's house was also still standing, a metal chimney sticking out of the window upstairs on the second floor. Some kind of engineer for Heinkel was living there now.

An apprentice locksmith rode by. His pannier fell off the bicycle's rack, and pliers and wrenches danced all over the cobblestones. I ran after him.

'Thank you, that's very kind of you.'

'Oh, it's nothing. Maybe one day I'll drop something and then you'll come running after with it . . .'

A tuba was lying on top of the lockers in the waiting room of the district service station. Hitler Youth leaders were shadowboxing; a female führer sat on the table.

There were ink spots all over the room and a chalkboard on one wall detailing first-aid procedures: how to set a broken bone with a walking stick; how to get water out of the mouth of a drowning-victim; instructions to open the window in case of gas poisoning.

We the summoned thronged together.

'Why are you here?' we asked each other.

'I was in the cinema, loitering, smoking.'

'I skipped Hitler Youth service.'

'I was still on the street after eight o'clock.'

'I showed disrespect for the flag.' (He had stuffed it, rolled up, under his bed. He was embarrassed that it had to happen to him, he hadn't meant to offend anyone.)

Someone came out, someone working class, very 'Old Town'. He had a stutter. 'What happens in there?' we asked.

'Someone sits there and g-g-gives you hell . . . Then you just fly right out again!'

'What did you do?'

'Sm-sm-smeared shit on a doorknob . . .'

I was next. I entered a sunny room with bay windows, parquet floors, and stucco on the ceiling. But where there should have been a chandelier hanging there was only a lampshade made from plywood covered in agricultural emblems.

The secretary, at her Sönneken writing desk, looked up at me, full of hate. In front of her was a Mercedes typewriter with a wide carriage. (*Cling!*)

In the bay window sat a lieutenant colonel called Lühns the Nazi (a nickname). He was immediately friendly, courteous. He probably had to gather his energy first, I thought.

'Now that we can talk in peace, tell me, what happened? What silly things have you been doing? I have it in this report: your hair is always too long, you're never at service, you've been seen sitting in the jazz club and at the café, eating mousse . . . You can't be doing these things, loitering at such a difficult time.'

'Me? In Café Herbst?' I was completely taken aback. I tried to explain: 'There must be a mistake . . . My brother looks exactly like me, only with bigger glasses and thicker waves in his hair, and he often sits around there. But he's already nineteen, so he's allowed to. Plus he's a driver with the military. Only the other day someone shouted, 'Hey there, Robert' to me in the street, confusing me for him . . .

'In any case, I have to wear my hair long because my head is a funny shape, in front and at the back. Otherwise my side hair tips forward. Here, would you like to see?' (I meant that in all seriousness.)

Lühns the Nazi listened to this very calmly; he almost smiled. But then, out of nowhere, he threw a pencil against the table. It went clattering across its surface, almost hitting the picture of Axmann.

'Now that's enough!' he thundered. 'Things are grim. People like this get to live and Schiller has to die? Damn it all! These goddamn foreigners flying over us. And you goddamn Edelweiss pirates. Film buffs. Dandies.' He screamed louder and louder, the veins bulging in his neck. Surely he's reached his limit, I thought: I'd never heard someone scream so loudly before. He held on to the back of the chair, as if he wanted to keep himself from leaping up and screaming from the lampshade above us.

Then, as suddenly as he'd started shouting, he stopped again and began arranging his writing utensils. But then he continued unabated: 'I will say this as clearly as possible. You will go to the barber *today*, otherwise I will tear your arse apart! Now, out!'

My mother had to pay the police 50 marks for dereliction of custodial duty. And then, one week later, a notice came: I had been demoted to junior comrade. Thank God I was still *something*, otherwise I would probably have ended up in weekend detention. I'd get my hair cut the next day, or maybe the day after. After all, one more day wouldn't make a difference.

33

My 'stomach pains' got worse. I was in no condition to show up for duty. They also impaired my ability to go to school, so my mother entrusted me to the care of Dr Krause, who sent me to the university clinic.

'It has to be investigated thoroughly,' he said, picking up the telephone and switching to the local exchange, 'you can't let the reins go slack. In my business, for example, I had only manufactured mineral water and apple juice, but now I've also turned to bouillon paste and sauerkraut. I might even branch out into syrup and pickles soon. Sickness has to be torn out by the roots.'

At the clinic, nothing could be ascertained. Perfectly healthy, they said.

'Remarkable, really, because the boy is so pale. He looks like buttermilk and spit.'

I was doubled over, and, as we passed by a merchant called Paeper's office, I suddenly couldn't go any further. Even Frau Kröhl confessed to not knowing what was going on with me.

'Maybe it's the constant sirens,' she said. 'Whenever you hear the sirens, the blood from your body sinks away, like when you're falling. And having that happen in the middle of the night certainly can't be good . . . We've all been so nervous for years now.'

Once we were back home I was sat in an armchair again, and given a hot water bottle, when an unexpected visitor arrived: Greta von Germitz, 'just passing by'. I threw the warm bottle into the waste-paper basket.

We shook hands. (Oh, I got to touch her thumbs.) Both of us said, 'How's it going?' simultaneously, and both answered, 'Oh, fine' together. (How lucky that I still hadn't been to the barber's! How would it have looked, my misshapen head; high in back and in front . . .)

Greta wore a dark sweater and a pleated dress – like Gina Quade – as well as shoes with a buckle that covered the laces. 'Too sweet,' my mother said, 'what a nice child. You hang on to her, my boy . . .'

She poured each of us a coffee and took her leave. Only to return again with fruit loaf and marmalade. Then she left once more, before coming back to ask whether we needed anything else.

We stirred our coffee. The cups were Arzberg porcelain with a violet pattern.

'Unfortunately the pinions in the gramophone are bust, so it's impossible to play records,' I explained to Greta. 'But I have the whole catalogue here; up to date, as always. At least you can take a look at that.'

'You have almost all of Nat Gonella's records . . . One, two, three, four, five of them! Only "Sweet Music Man" is missing. I'll have to worm that out of my aunt.'

'Is the property still as nice as it was back when I was there?' I asked. 'Oh, and the big park!' I hastily sketched a plan of the house from memory: the white bench over here and the stairs in the back. 'Is the copper beech still standing? And the wood in the lake: I assume no one's picked it up yet?'

'How do you still remember all that?' she said. 'What a memory you have.'

And that was just the beginning . . . I even drew in the furniture – the worn-out sofa, her grandfather's desk with Waldmann's little basket next to it.

'The dachshund had such a bad temper back then . . . Only, I can't remember where the reaper barracks were . . . How many were there? There was that big hedge in front . . .'

Then it was quiet.

The gramophone absolutely refused to move. She turned it by hand, and then it yowled. A voice on the radio: 'This and that for your amusement.'

'So,' I said, 'you can have a look round the flat. See how we live here. It's on the third floor, sure. But still comfortable.'

The white ivory mouse on the bookshelves, and the oak chest on the floor: 'These would look good in your manor house,' I told her.

From the balcony I showed her the stub of the tower at St Jacob's. 'See this postcard? That's how it used to look.'

'Shall we go out for a little, we could take a look at the city?'

I stuck a Danish newspaper into the pocket of my coat, but left my white scarf at home: it would be too dangerous to go out wearing it. Greta set a dove-grey men's hat on her head; it had a little white down feather on it. There were red-edged oak leaves on her hunter's coat.

'Ready to go, as far as I'm concerned. Let's do it!'

We were still in front of the house, debating who was supposed to walk on the right and who on the left, when a man stopped before us, blocking our way. He appeared to be a gentleman, and had a portfolio folded under his arm, as though he had come right from the rations office.

'Don't take this the wrong way,' he said to me, his face twitching. 'It's just you look exactly like my son who died in combat.' He walked on, before circling back. 'My son used to look exactly like you.' He grabbed my sleeve.

Then he took his leave again. He half turned towards us as he began to walk away. We watched as he approached the Mecklenburg Peasant Women's Association shop, where the *Mettwurst* sausage used to hang. Once there, he turned to look at us again, as though he still couldn't get his head round it.

At that point we turned a corner, and Greta immediately began to laugh. When she saw that I looked serious, she became serious too, but then I laughed.

I didn't point out Tinkel and Pott, but we saw the memorial for those who fell in 1890. She thought the burnt-out post office was a church. I showed her the Stone Gate too – (SIT INTRA TE CONCORDIA ET PUBLICA FELICITAS) even though it was also burnt out.

MAY THERE BE COMITY AND
PUBLIC HAPPINESS WITHIN.[1]

'You have to add "these walls",' I told her. *Muros* was the word.

I had brought other postcards along, so she could see what the destroyed churches and gabled houses used to look like. The postcards brought it all to life. You couldn't bomb a picture.

'Professor Krickeberg filmed everything a few days before the raids. Funny, no? I think it's lying in some archive. The important thing is that it's safe now.'

'And what did the city hall used to look like?' Greta asked. 'Do you have a picture of that too?'

'Why, it hasn't been touched. It remains the same as it was before.'

'Don't look to your left,' I advised her. Frahm's, the medical supplies store, lay in ruins in Hopfenmarkt: bedpans, vomit bowls and so on were strewn across the square.

The Great King, starring Otto Gebühr, was showing in the Union Theatre. On screen Frederick the Great would be declaring: 'If only, if only, if only . . . If only the Prussians hadn't fled at Kunersdorf . . .'[2]

Then to the Metropol, to see what was playing there today. There was a film called *He Who Is Beloved by the Gods*, with Hans Holt. We asked around to find out how the rest of the saying went before committing ('is called back to them early').

'You're going to have a very hard time of it,' Mozart says to Beethoven, after he plays something for him.

'I think so too,' Beethoven replies.

The dying Mozart conducts a choir dressed in black from his bed.

The 'streetcar general' stood by Café Rundeck. ('It always smells like singed flour here.') As ever, the number 1 didn't come far enough forward, so you had to walk back a bit to get on.

'These Dutch drivers!' someone hissed. 'How are old women supposed to get into the second carriage? Maybe they do it on purpose . . . Do they want to end up in a concert camp?'

I showed Greta how to ride the streetcar, and together we went to the business school. We stood at the rear, one leg dangling off the seat, before jumping down off the tram and dancing away ('In the same direction as the tram, of course'). I thought it a shame I hadn't brought any cough syrup.

Then we rode back, though I told Greta that we were journeying onward, so that she'd be impressed by the size of the city. But she caught on immediately.

'Haven't we been here already?' she asked.

At the Ulmenmarkt, in the UFA Theatre Palace, where the political meetings used to take place, there was *Herr Sanders Lives Dangerously.* ('Good flick – I've already seen it twice.') It was too late to go in, but I could recount the plot for her instead.

'It's about a real pearl necklace and a knock-off version of it. The whole time they think they have the real one, but it's actually the fake one. And when they think it's the fake one, it's the real one. The film is real Goodmannsdörfer.'

*

'I don't want the lousy dog any more, he's screwing up my whole unit,' Bobsin said.

My transfer to a 'mandatory fellowship' with the Hitler Youth came in November. The fellowship was made up of truants and so-called nancy boys. At first it was called a 'disciplinary service fellowship', but then a steady stream of parents had complained. 'Mandatory fellowship' sounded more neutral.

As Admiral Nelson said, 'England expects that every man will do his duty,' so too would we learn what Germany expected of us. The Hitler Youth was finally taking drastic measures, cracking the whip. They'd stood by for long enough.

The first meeting of the mandatory fellowship was on a Sunday morning, at 8.30, out in Barnstorf. It used to be a destination for our family outings. ('Today we're going to *Bernstorf*,' my father finally said, because we didn't want to go to Barnstorf any more.)

I rode out there a half-hour early to avoid arriving late. There were already some people standing in front of the nailed-shut kiosk. Boys in naval uniforms and some from the Air Scouts. There was a red-haired boy and even one with polio; some nancy boys arrived in civilian clothes.

An acquaintance, Gert Brüning, was among those already there.

The son of the bank director, he was quiet and delicate; his black Hitler ski cap sat straight on his head, not even a little crooked. He would rather be lying around on a sofa or crafting submarines out of tin cans. He was shocked to see me. He gave me a baffled smile.

'It must be a mistake,' he said, 'you don't belong here at all.'

After the last raid, on a whim I had helped his parents cover the roof of their house with all of their pots and pans, to help protect against bomb fragments. Frau Brüning had passed us sandwiches through the rafters and shouted: 'Oh, children, how diligent you are!'

'When my father returns we'll see what can be done,' Gert said. 'He's captain of the reserves, someone will have an idea. It's a mistake; it'll certainly be cleared up soon.'

We stood, freezing, on a narrow traffic island and waited. The graveyard gang, dressed in black, looked out at us from the window of the tram. Dumpling nodded at me from the doorway. As the tram drove on, I stopped to think what a funny bunch we must have looked. What *was* I doing there?

The leaders came out of the service barracks. The fellowship leader wore white and green epaulettes, while the main leader's were black and green. There were also men of lower rank from various other units. They were all upright guys, and were more or less all blond. Eckhoff and Klaus Bismarck Stüwe were among them.

'This is the lovely Kempowski . . .' they said. 'Oh, how lovely he is! With his red lips and his artist's locks!'

'This is some reunion, huh?'

In school we'd heated shoe buckles with a magnifying glass and swapped trading cards: Glorious Chapters of German History. And in Hannes's class old Stüwe had been sent to the 'inquisition chamber', where he was beaten.

'Now be a good boy and scream,' Hannes had said, banging with his stick on the desk.

'Step forward,' the leaders shouted. They swarmed around us so that no one could run away. They tugged at someone's shirt and checked his haircut.

'Make a note of him. And you, you're probably a communist, right? I know you though, where have I seen you before?'

Names were read out loud. ('Here!') Brüning stood in front, in the second rank ('Here!'), he had his stick with him in case anything happened. At least I wasn't alone; we were in it together.

We still hadn't started, though. Who was in charge?

'Should I begin the march, or do you want to?'

'You start, and then afterwards I can take over.'

Then the order came: 'Right turn!'

We marched out into the forest. The leaders forever correcting one another's orders.

> Left, left, left, two, three, four.
> Left, left, left, two, three, four!

Now and then they'd walk backward, studying our formation. ('You there, further forward!') They were like dance instructors. One of them walked his bicycle, and its bell rang when it went over a tree root. Sometimes he walked to the left of the bike, sometimes to the right; he switched the bike's luggage carrier without breaking his stride.

> And left, left, left, two three four.

His left hand on the seat; his right on the beat.

We were told to stop at the Thingstätte, an amphitheatre where folk dances or deployments normally took place. The granite stage appeared like a sun wheel, with the silhouette of the city hanging over it between the poplars. It was so warm.

The leaders kept conferring. ('Do *you* want to, or should I?') Each had a whistle on his lanyard.

'Give me your whistle.'

'Oh, this one's better.'

'Have you seen the new ones, with the double whistle? Or the ones that the navy have?'

'They're only two marks fifty at Lohmann. We can go there tomorrow.'

'So what, do you want to lead, or should I?'

'Let's let Kippie Hook do it; he's the best at it. Look, he's already laughing like the devil. Come on, Kippie!'

The boys from the Hitler Youth Navy, as well as those in the pilot greys, and the red-haired one and the one with polio, all nudged each other and laughed.

'Oh, oh, old Kippie! We know him, he's a complete savage. Come on now! Grind us down! That'll serve us right.'

Kippie put his service book away and buttoned all of his pockets. No button remained unbuttoned. Only the topmost shirt button was left, according to the decree, so that he could get some fresh air; so that he could move. (Even though he looked sloppy as a result.)

He had a silver lanyard, which rested on his pitch-black uniform. On his chest was the tiny swimming badge, which as everyone knew was very valuable. Adolf Hitler was also modest: he could have covered himself with medals, had he wanted to, but no, he only wore the Iron Cross 1. The Party badge was worn over it, on occasion, and sometimes the wounded soldier's badge from the First World War too. He was simple, loyal and unyielding.

'Mandatory service fellowship, listen for my command.'

It started harmlessly enough. Left turn, right turn, whole-division turns: a kind of survey. 'Eyes right. Eyes left. Stand up straight. You there, shit heel. Move forward, and you, pull your arse in.'

They circled us one more time. ('Not too bad.') They were hard but fair.

'You'll see, you won't recognise yourselves when we're finished with you . . .'

Then all of a sudden something was off: perhaps someone had quietly fallen out of step, or some words had been whispered. Whatever it was, it seemed that someone had been feeling just a little too cocky . . .

'Aha! You don't want to do it the easy way, I see. Well, now you can all get to know me properly.' He stood tall, his hands pressed against the seams of his trousers. His face was set differently now, his back muscles were taut. 'You'll see what that kind of behaviour gets you. You've got only yourselves to blame.' Old Kippie wasn't laughing any more. He was hard as steel.

He gave the dive-down command, then called for us to get up again at a near-frantic speed. Eventually you just gave up on throwing yourself down; you were hardly halfway down before you were being told to stand back up again. Some of the boys just made little bows, very solicitously.

And that was just the warm-up. Soon we were on to the second part: jumping. This was even less pleasant: we were to hold our hands in front of us, with fingers outstretched. ('Shame we don't have any carbines.') For the third exercise, he got us to do split lunges; one leg behind the other, bending our knees in stages. These were Kippie's speciality.

'One!' You were to stand with bent knees. 'Two!' You were to bend forward, like a hired servant, bum still high. 'Three!' Like you were crouched down, ready to shit.

Now and then he'd call for us to march 'to the horizon'. He practically sang it, so you only heard 'To . . . zon . . . march!' But you knew what he meant.

Eventually he'd call, 'At-ten-tion!' and we were supposed to stand in place. (He always emphasised the second syllable.)

After several rounds of exercise we noticed an SA man climbing down towards us. The steps of the amphitheatre were unusually wide, so he looked as though he was walking in parade step. He couldn't quite take two strides per step, so he was attempting to cover them in one long stride.

We were called to attention. We stood in place. The leaders watched and we did too. We all noted how the SA man was charging down the steps, a one-man demonstration of vigour.

There were a lot of steps and it took some time for him to reach us. His name was Hornung, and because of the thick lenses in his glasses I thought he looked like a mean frog.

He was shouting something and gesticulating wildly. The leaders cupped their hands to their ears ('All of you be quiet'), straining to hear. As we fell silent a plane thundered overhead, further obscuring his cries. ('Fucking hell, just what we need.')

'Drill!' he screamed as silence fell, 'drill until the water in their arses boils!'

Okay, *now* we could understand him.

While we were lying on the ground 'pumping' ('Let your stomach hang out, then it's not so strenuous'), he came up to us and unhooked his shoulder belt.

'Oh, I'll get you,' he said, laughing to himself. Then out of nowhere he turned and hit Brüning, who had no idea what was going on, in the back. ('Ow!?') Brüning jumped up and dodged additional jabs. Hornung was right after him. ('What? How dare you?') *Whack*: another one across his back.

And so the pumping stopped: we all stared. The führers watched on, too. Hornung kept lunging again and again, but Brüning kept dodging him, step by step. Eventually, he started running. Hornung charged after him, and almost caught him with the shoulder belt.

The chase went over the hustings – you could only see their heads and the swinging belt – then down the other side. Some eastern workers collected on the highest benches, sat down and started watching the chase too.

They came back, breathing heavily.

'Have you had enough?' Hornung asked.

'No, I'm fine,' said Brüning, wheezing, and we all laughed.

Before we knew it we were all due to be beaten, because we'd laughed. But first he instructed us to take off our neckerchiefs, along with the SS insignias. ('I've thought about it, and there's no need to dishonour the clothing of the Führer.')

Taking our neckerchiefs off was easy. But how were we supposed to get the SS insignias off? They were sewn on. Soon though everyone was helping one another using their penknives.

I was a little unsure about what I was to do. I was in civilian attire; I didn't have a neckerchief on. Should I remove my father's tie?

The other führers suggested that the district triangle should also be removed. Then they fell into a protracted conversation again, correcting one another and questioning the lines of authority. Some held on to their lanyards fondly, while others joined in with stripping the insignia off their uniforms. Others were hunting around for sticks, before gathering at the front; they didn't have shoulder belts and so had found an alternative.

They decided that we were to step forward in two ranks and look at one another: we were supposed to beat ourselves. ('No getting your hands dirty, though, and no grabbing.') But before the details could be agreed upon, another emissary jumped up, waving for us to stop. We were to go to the Sports Palace now instead: the district leader was there and wanted to see us.

'What? Now? What a shame . . .'

*

At the Sports Palace we were told to stand completely still. The führers prowled around us to make sure no one was moving. Then came the district leader: brown jacket, black breeches.

'Heil Hitler!'

'So these are the boys . . .' he said, and went along the column. 'What's on the duty roster?'

We were all perplexed. What duty roster?

'Sing a song!' one of the leaders said.

It was only then that the district leader noticed we weren't wearing our neckerchiefs. He took the SA man to one side. While they were gone, the führers consulted with one another about who was supposed to lead the rehearsal now. ('Do you want to or should I?') They decided that we should put our neckerchiefs back on first, and then sing the song:

> Holy Fatherland
> In danger,
> Your sons
> Flock around you . . .[3]

The district leader came back over and inspected us again. ('That's much better.') Those from the Hitler Youth Navy were collected together in one bunch, those from the Hitler Youth Pilots in another. ('What, only five? Shame, if there were six there'd be two equal rows.')

Those of us in civilian clothes were stood in the middle. We were told that they'd rustle up some uniforms from somewhere. They recognised that it couldn't be any fun doing the drills without a uniform.

The boy with polio was sent straight home.

'Aren't you Kempowski?' the district leader asked me. It turned out he used to go to dance lessons with my brother. They had also listened to records together. 'Come with me.'

Together we walked along the chestnut-lined avenue – him on the right, me on the left, a half-step behind. Just a suggestion of lockstep, otherwise he'd think I was trying to curry favour.

'You're the last person I would've expected to be here,' he said.

> In the shade of an old apple tree
> Where the love in your eyes I could see . . .⁴

'Just for a second, think about our soldiers at the front. And think about our enemies, too. Don't be so stupid. You'll end up in an SS juvenile detention centre. I don't want to see you here ever again. Do you not stop to think about your father? About your brother? Does he have any idea about this?'

My eyes filled with tears. They were de Bonsac tears, they came automatically at stirring speeches like this one.

'A Hitler Youth, crying? It's unheard of.' After a moment of silence he fished a letter out of his breast pocket and pressed it into my hand. 'Can you take this to the train station at the park for me? Understand? If we're not here when you get back, then you can go home.'

I turned to leave, but he called me back. He didn't think they'd still be here; I should just head straight home.

*

I slept for the rest of the afternoon. I only woke up in the evening. I took all my clothes off and had a wash. I put on fresh underwear, my ochre-coloured shirt and a tie from Father's cabinet. ('He isn't dead yet.') I took a new handkerchief, wiped my glasses, and tried to think about something else.

The two of us sat at the supper table, our spoons quietly clinking in our cups of tea.

'Be a little careful with the butter. Next week there will only be butter schmaltz – a substitute . . . And don't eat too much bread. Starting tomorrow, we'll have a bowl of soup beforehand, or roast potatoes, if you're lucky: that'll fill you up.'

With any luck it would remain cloudy. The bombers usually arrived around 10 p.m., or much earlier in the afternoon. A run at 8 p.m. would be unusual.

We made sure to leave on time to be certain to get a good place. The autumn air was crisp. The year was already over, and everything was dying off; bare branches were poking up into the sky.

'Caspar David Friedrich painted it all so wonderfully,' my mother said. (*The Ruins of Eldena Abbey.*) 'Trees are much bigger than you think. There are as many roots under the earth as there are branches above it; a root for every branch, so to speak. And people chop them down without a second thought . . .'

'We must be thankful we're still sitting in our cosy apartment. The central heating is unfortunate, yes – an oven would be more practical – but think of all the poor people who've lost their homes. Those poor, poor people.'

She brought me up to speed on how everyone was doing: 'Nice to hear Ulla is working on those summer dresses. I couldn't be happier that she's over there. Robert's now near Kolberg though, guarding prisoners of war, which can't be easy. But good to hear that your father has finally been promoted and is going to get the clasps for his Iron Cross.' It'd do him good, she felt, and would lift his spirits: he did love his fatherland after all, and he took everything to heart.

A lot of work to do, he'd written. What kind of work did he have to do? What work was there to do in a war?

'Oh, I've got myself into a bad mood now,' she continued. 'What human beings do to one another! It's all so pitiless and disgusting. And these young guys have no manners at all!

'Frau Eckhoff – totally miserable herself – can't do anything about her boys: they're completely out of control. I just saw her on the street. Before I had a chance to even say her name, she was waving me away and beginning to cry. The poor woman . . . But the wheel will turn, and everything will come around again. You'll see.'

St Mary's Church was still intact, and large as ever. There was already a light in the loft. Fraulein Heß from the university library was there, as well as Gunthermann (gosh, he'd gotten old). The young Warkentin too, furloughed to complete his studies. He had his exams in February. It seemed that his probation at the front had worked; he was looking far more together.

> It is certainly at that time,
> That God's son will come . . .

The organ music started off plainly enough. At first the organist played with just one finger, and then slowly began introducing the others, one finger after another, until he was moving up and down the keys and you thought: How is he managing to do this?

> Laughter will become quite dear
> When everything goes up in flames.[5]

A premonition: maybe we were hearing the organ for the last time? Perhaps a raid was coming? It was Rostock's turn again, really. The tower guard certainly wouldn't make it through another raid. He'd got older too. And you can't just pack an organ away. You could maybe screw a few angels off, and take the sun down from under the vault, but that was about it.

The blind organist's hands disappeared into the keys just as Boldt the coachman used to delve into the oat chaff. The cascade of notes streamed on, unrelenting, but all of them were in their right place. Each trill would certainly come back. Yes, everything was in order.

The people in front of us kept looking at each other.

'Oh, he's so good, so good.'

'We should come and listen to beautiful music more often. It really makes you feel lighter.'

During the intermission the pastor thanked his god, that He was so wise and that He ruled everything so splendidly. Then, bang! The light went out. The sexton brought a candle, but no sooner had he lit it than the light came back on. He blew out the candle and read on.

'What does the reading have to do with the concert, I wonder?' my mother asked herself. 'There must also be those whose faith differs in the Church – perhaps we might bring them over to our side with music like that . . . What an opportunity. Music, oh, how lovely it is!' But I couldn't help but think that these readings had to be driving people away – those unused to the Word.

Bang! The electricity went out again. ('The enemy's doing it on purpose, of course. Chicanery!') The candle was lit again. It was good that he wasn't playing the organ just now, at least the pastor could go ahead and read a little bit by candlelight. And then the light came back on again. Better not blow out the candle this time. Perhaps it was time to wrap the whole performance up . . .

There was some Max Reger in the second half of the concert. ('Very difficult,' my mother said.) Then some Liszt. The music kept halting and then it grew softer and softer. I couldn't tell if the piece had finished or it was still going . . . Hopefully the power wouldn't cut out again, not when the music was fading out, flickering out into nothingness.

The organist held the final chord a little too long for my taste. It felt like he was trying to say: 'This is how things are, and so they will remain.' But the way he did it, it came across more questioning: 'Will they remain so?'

But still, the music was beautiful. So adamant and unambiguous. We stayed seated for a long time, to rest in that beauty for a little longer.

'How thankful we must be,' said my mother as we went out, pulling her fascinator up high and wiping her snub de Bonsac nose. 'But these supposedly important people in charge of everything – they're just letting it all go to ashes. Oh, I could smash all their heads together. They think this nonsense up, the high and mighty, and we're the ones who have to pay for it.'

34

We sat in the kitchen through the winter, to save coal. The four and a half kilos were supposed to last us as long as possible. After all, who knew what next year would bring?

The coal was therefore stored away in an open shed by the cellar stairs. I always felt that this was a temptation for the neighbours. It wouldn't be difficult for them to take it. All they had to do was raise the hatch and it would clatter down the slide.

We moved the floor lamp into the kitchen, along with the radio. There we'd listen to *Rondo for Piano and Orchestra* by Prince Louis Ferdinand of Prussia. Classical music wasn't nearly as boring as people thought it was; it was something you could straight-out sing along to. But it was hard to like chamber music – it was too scratchy. Who knew, maybe I'd get a handle on it later.

My mother pottered around at the stove while I sat in the kitchen reading a fat book about the expedition to Tibet undertaken in 1940 for the German *Volk*. The firewood from Dahlbusch sat on the balcony; we had yak milk and musk-ox meat. ('We're still golden.') The built-in sink, and the large kitchen dresser with many bays, a shattered milk-glass pane in each. The view on to the yellow building next door. When out on the balcony, a man would come into view now and again as he retrieved scallions or kindling. We would wave to him.

'Well, how's it going?' he'd call up.

We'd run into Frau Matthes now and again, the poor woman. Frau Merkel too ('really a stupid turkey hen'): she had all the birches cut down – a whole bunch of them – but it wasn't her fault, it was her husband's idea.

Behind their houses was the Catholic church, with the bell that always rang so loudly. It had been damaged, but was already rebuilt, strangely enough. ('Where do they get it from . . .?')

It was a good thing that Dr Krause hadn't had the kitchen tiled. It would certainly be very cold underfoot. ('A sweet man.') He gave us a pot with syrup and a demijohn of molasses. ('I thought maybe you could do something with it.') They were a welcome supplement to our provisions. Every day we'd dash a little syrup or molasses into the roux. But not too much, otherwise you might go blind: it was poisonous somehow, my mother insisted, and so was to be enjoyed carefully.

We got a Danish Christmas package from Ulla and Sörensen, including sausage and cheese. ('Darning yarn is also very scarce, my dears . . .' my mother had written to them.) The sausage was salty, but it tasted good served in thick kale from the Schulze-Heidtorfs.

We had plenty of potatoes: four kilos, and more kept coming. ('Oh thank heavens – what luck!') It would soon be enough to see us through winter. But then again, who knew how it would all turn out?

A photo of a woman stood in a vitrine at Fredensdorf & Baade:

I am a pest to my *Volk*, I squirrelled this and that
away in my cellar and for that I am now being sent to a
concentration camp.

'They'd better not look in on us!' my mother said. We had a kilo
of carrots and twenty punnets of green beans, we had celery, a
pillowcase full of dried peas, a tin biscuit box filled with lentils
(where once there had been Petit Beurres), and a barrel of sauerkraut,
all buried in the ground.

'Still, it's better to have a stockpile of everything . . . If your
father were to come back, he eats like a horse, and Robert can put
it away too.'

When there was buttermilk my mother made cottage cheese from
it. Buttermilk cottage cheese with syrup. Or buttermilk cottage
cheese with thin marmalade.

Salt was the scarcest ingredient, though; we couldn't get it
anywhere. They always cited transport problems. And before the
war no one had thought twice about it – there'd always been salt.
How were we supposed to know that soon we'd be going without?

Another substitute came from Hamburg: an uncle sent cardboard
barrels filled with powdered ice cream. You could cook vanilla soup
with it too, but if you ate too much you got heartburn so bad it felt
like your chest was fizzing. The cardboard barrels were good to use
for storing the provisions you hadn't used in summer. ('Hopefully
the oats won't go mouldy.')

The gas only turned on at certain times, and when it was on there
was little pressure. There was always the mortal terror that there
wouldn't be enough for the soup, so my mother would be up early
in the morning, cooking at six o'clock to ensure she caught it. And

then she'd store it in the cooking-box, which kept it warm until evening.

In the middle of January came threatening reports from the east:

> As expected the Soviets opened their offensive
> after several hours of gunfire . . . Bitter fighting flared up
> along the entire front.

Aunt Silbi was down there, near Ostenburg. But we didn't see or hear a thing from her. What was she doing? Was she still alive? I felt extremely sorry for her; that we'd abandoned her. I still remembered the lovely Biedermeier room with the bronze clock under its glass cover, and the Rostock watercolours.

'Quick, write that they can come. In any event,' my mother said. 'She always used to be so happy . . . Such a tragedy that she didn't end up in better hands. The transformation when she screamed at your father: "I'm not your puppet!" He couldn't just stand by and take an insult like that . . . She threw a chair, too. And then ran to the Party. But now, now we need to circle the wagons. In times of need, these things must be forgiven and forgotten.'

In his last letter, my father said that he had become the local commander near the headquarters of the military leadership. His tour at the front was now over; he'd spend Christmas Eve in peace. They'd sung the magical, beloved Christmas songs together, and the commandant had given a speech that had touched everyone's heart.

The state was being very considerate too. Everyone had received cigars, cigarettes, acid drops, toothpaste and a good book for Christmas. Then for New Year they'd had some lovely punch, a bottle of champagne, and advocaat.

The letter was dated 2 January. That was weeks ago now. Where could he be?

Robert was still safe. But for how much longer?

And what about us? Weren't the Russians heading towards us?

There was an endless stream of refugees along Friedrich-Franz-Straße, they were there both day and night, constantly. From Dr Kraus's living room you had a great view of them. But we always sat behind the curtains, so they didn't see us.

The horses nodded, steam coming from their mouths. Sometimes there would be two or three of them in reserve behind the wagon, all in impressively good condition. Little cabins up on top of the carts, hastily thrown together, containing hay for the horses. Dogs ran along under the axles. We saw young girls, on foot, with children holding their hands alongside them on the pavement.

The procession moved in columns: they appeared to be people who belonged together, probably country estates or village communities. (Years ago, in the old apartment, we'd seen a gypsy caravan that looked the same. 'They steal little children and colour them with walnut shells.') There were also cars and tractors among them (where could they have got the petrol?), including an Opel P4 with a full tank in the back. I saw a man who was pulling a two-wheel cart himself. No one came out to help. All of them marched on, mute save for the squealing of the wheels. No one from the Party came to bid them welcome.

The women went into the houses looking for clothing and food.

'Oh, what things you have,' one of them said to my mother. She began pulling open drawers ('Oh, what lovely placemats'), before opening the parlour door.

'That woman was repulsive,' my mother said. 'Out for what she could get; eyes like cobbler's lamps. I couldn't keep up with her.'

The schools were closed. Dr Finck quelled the students' storm of applause with nothing but a vacant stare.

'What is all this? Is something wrong? You're all like animals. Laughing, at the moment of greatest calamity . . .'

He left the room, shaking his head.

We all had to register at the district. Hundreds of boys enlisted to assist the army. The tram rang like crazy.

One time we had to shovel snow: the big bend at the Petridamm was blocked. I only had my child's spade from Warnemünde. When I arrived there was an SA man screaming. He'd totally lost control of the situation, in completely over his head. He dashed back and forth beneath the meteor shower of snowballs launched by the boys.

Russian prisoners of war were put to work there too. (One of them threw a shovelful of snow at my feet.) It grew quiet when the district leader drove past in a Horch. However he got stuck – he didn't have snow chains – so we ended up having to give him a push.

Afterwards Manfred and I piled up an old woman's wood for her. She'd requested the two of us specifically. That seemed funny to us. We got cramp from laughing so hard.

Manfred had seen a newsreel about the Gumbinnen offensive, which had shown a woman who had been raped by the Russians. Furniture was overturned, laundry everywhere, beds stripped. And amongst it the woman was completely naked, you could see everything.

Nail them to the barn door, cut off their dicks – it's the least we could do to the Russians, Manfred and I decided.

Another time, we were enlisted for station service. We were to pick up refugees and transport their luggage on trolleys. New ones were arriving constantly.

Only refugees came by train now. Most of the other trains were being redirected. Whoever had relatives or acquaintances in Rostock was supposed to get off the train. Occasionally a train filled with wounded soldiers would pass through – nothing but sleeping-cars all in a row – in which case we were shooed away.

One evening, a woman stood with a boy in front of the station entrance, a piece of paper in her hand: they were refugees from Elbing, here to stay with us.

Instead of greeting me with 'Good day,' the woman simply said: 'Everything's gone.' She had got off the train to get something to eat, but the train moved on, with her four children on it. The boy was the son of her neighbour, who'd also got off.

'Oh!' cried my mother. 'Come on! I'll warm up some water for you. You can have a quick wash. Where's your luggage?'

'On the train, that's the thing. I have nothing, not even a nightshirt.'

'Well, we'll get you one.'

The boy staying with us was blond and wore a black Hitler Youth hat. ('What does *Rehbaum declatrus* mean?' I asked him.) The woman was seemingly calm – she didn't wail, she just kept asking, 'Where could they be?' and telling us that she had only got off the train to get something to eat.

By the end of the month, however, she had lost my mother's good will. ('Why didn't she just stay on the train? Honestly, at a time like this, why did she have to get off?') She'd said, your knives will get you to Paris. ('My lovely knives!')

35

I was drafted on 17 February. My mother just stood there, in shock, her hands empty.

'Well, this is a fine mess. To give my Peterpump away . . . I just don't understand.'

'What?' Dr Krause said when he heard the news. 'But he's not even sixteen!'

The conscription order was in the attic, next to the dead geraniums – the envelope had been opened. Why hadn't they put it in the mailbox? Was it a prank? Had my mother tried to hide it?

As members of the Hitler Youth, we were supposed to work as couriers for the Henkel factory. We were briefed to pick up important files or substitute parts. You couldn't rely on the mail any more. Every letter had to be sent by courier, it was the only way to ensure it would arrive.

'Courier': that didn't sound so bad. Adding a division wouldn't hurt – first class? – and perhaps a special band on my uniform too . . . ('I'm a courier, could you please open the door?')

I had to wear bulky boots and a ski cap, with a sharp-looking fold in the brim. These were supplemented with a thick sweater and a long warm coat. No cuffs on the sleeves, unfortunately, otherwise I could have stuck toilet paper and tickets into them.

My belt had the Luftwaffe eagle on it: that was important.

We were supposed to wear our Hitler Youth badge on our caps, as well as the Hitler Youth armband. We'd have much preferred to be standard soldiers though, so we bought Luftwaffe eagles, or traded them for our badges. We'd take the armbands off whenever we could; they were already pretty rumpled.

We lived in a school all together.

'Aha! Secondary schoolers!' the sergeant said when he came in for the first time. He was already delighted with us. Then he turned to me and said: 'Why are you standing there like you just shat yourself?'

While *he* was putting his neck on the line at the front, we were busy lying down like cottage cheese in a shop window.

My hair had to go right away, of course. The upside was that no one would bother me about it again. And I wouldn't have to carry a comb all the time, worrying about what would happen if the wind were to blow from behind. I'd been keeping my head tilted to the side all this time, to make sure nothing like that ever happened.

We washed all together, with our chests bare. It was of no interest to the sergeant whether we ever washed our feet. There was only one washbasin for all sixty of us, and it wasn't even really a basin at all; it was a tap.

'We'll be getting a basin soon,' said the sergeant. The request had already been submitted.

In the mornings we had training. We were taught methods of camouflage. We learned that ditches played a central role, and that trenches were to zig-zag, so that the invading enemy couldn't just shoot along the line with a machine gun. They also taught us the correct way to dig foxholes: that it was best to have a small mound behind you, otherwise they'd take your head right off. I was hoping that he'd ask about thumb jumps, so I could prove my worth, but it never came up.

Tunnels had been dug underneath all of Paris, according to the corporal. They were laced with dynamite. The residents had no idea. At just the right moment Adolf Hitler would push a button and they'd all go up in smoke. All the chic Parisian girls would be goners. (I'd heard that you just about came in your pants when you saw them . . .) Maybe they'd be looking out the windows and thinking: We're rid of the Germans! And then: *boom!*

Everything down the drain.

Things were only so bad in the east because we had been too careful with our construction. The corporal went to great pains to make this perfectly clear to us. We had built the tanks too carefully, with the high-quality workmanship expected from German manufacturers. There were even hooks inside for hanging hats and canteens, with little enamel signs labelling each item. The Russians, on the other hand, were slapdash. They didn't even polish their tanks; they let them rust. But they drove well. By the time we were polishing our second tank, they'd already made their third. It didn't matter – we were men and could take it – but still it was worth knowing.

In other areas, attention to detail was our prize quality. That was probably the reason the Russians didn't have any good aeroplanes, the sergeant hypothesised: they just didn't know how to do it.

'Our researchers take time. They sit in huge laboratories, about ten times as long as this classroom here and six times as wide, with bigger windows. Some are underground, with great ventilators.

And they work in total peace in white coats and think up the newest weapons. If ever you find yourself thinking that the war's not going our way, just know they'll have weapons ready to turn the tide: acid bombs or who knows what. We can't imagine much beyond rifles or planes. We'd be amazed by what they were thinking up.'

For lunch, we had to march four kilometres to the canteen and four kilometres back. Using the tram was forbidden.

> Where walls fall,
> Others are built before us;
> But they all yield
> To our victory march.[1]

We always marched along the streetcar tracks through the shipyard district, past factories and warehouses. (Nothing had been destroyed there.) Eventually the mothers – including the wife of the district administrator, whose boy was part of our troop – started complaining about it. Often, after all that time spent marching, all the food was gone by the time we got there. As a result, they started taking us to the canteen on buggies.

'Is this acceptable to you?' the sergeant asked. 'The Herr Secondary Schoolers are satisfied, yes?'

They made the son of the district administrator ('Where is that dweeb?') step up to each transport and confirm that everything was in order.

In the afternoons we'd practise manoeuvring through fields laced with explosive devices. We used little cartons that exploded like grenades. (The women who lived near by swore about the noise.)

Or we had to aim a Panzerfaust grenade launcher at a tank that had been painted on to one of the walls of the school. But we were *only* to aim. We were to set the Panzerfaust up sixty to eighty metres away. A hundred and twenty metres was its optimum distance; it was easy as pie to use from there. That was the whole secret with the new weapons: they were effortless to use.

'You can really see the shot burn through the metal when you get a direct hit. It bores into the tank and explodes inside,' the sergeant told us. We would all get to experience it, he said. 'Then they'll open the hatch, and half the upper body will come out, and it's goodbye . . . But before you fire, be sure to look and see whether anyone's standing behind you: the stream of fire that shoots out of the rear of the chamber burns everything. Not a few people have made that mistake.'

In his glory days it had made sense to climb up, open the hatch and toss a grenade inside. You couldn't do that any more though; now they locked the hatches from the inside.

He showed us the exact place on the tanks where they would have to put the adhesive charge in order to blow the hatch open. ('They'd have to place it at exactly the right angle, too.') We could be quite sure of that.

I didn't manage to get a bed. My straw mattress lay on the floor. I had two covers though, so it was cosy regardless. Lights-out was at nine o'clock. We swept the trash under the straw sacks lying around on the floor.

'What are you doing?' screamed the sergeant.

'You said to sweep it under the beds!'

'This isn't a bed though, this is just a sack mattress. Your Sunday leave is cancelled. Is that clear?'

Some boys went into his office and said they thought their comrade had a point.

'That's your Sunday leave cancelled too!'

*

In the beginning of March we started travelling. We didn't care where we were going – the main thing was to get away from Rostock. Each of us had a linen rucksack that hung down by our arse, and a blanket.

Someone got a trip to Ulm. Everyone was jealous. (Ulm sounded nice.) I would have liked to go to Cologne. The cathedral there hadn't been destroyed yet. Although recently the air pirates had attacked it once again – it had taken 650 years of human labour to build, yet now they were trying to strike it with firebombs and explosives.

The trains were so full that each time one arrived I thought I was better off waiting for the next one. But at some point someone pushed me from behind, so I climbed aboard. Once I was crammed in, I wondered how I would ever get off again.

The only seat I could find for the journey was the toilet. I had to twist my way out whenever someone needed to use it ('No way around that'). For some stretches, I would ride on the wooden boards of a converted freight wagon, and for others I'd catch a ride on a truck, if the tracks had been hit. There were always delays, but I always got there. We'd ride among the cars or cockpits for the new jet planes or sacks containing rubber gaskets. Sometimes I had to help them unload the carriage. When the people saw me dragging the sacks, they held the door closed from the inside and looked out the window, as if they had no idea why the door wouldn't budge.

I took pride in my ability to fall asleep anywhere. I felt like

Essenholer Trinks. In the troop quarters, waiting rooms or bunkers – the less comfortable it was, the more fun I found it. My ideal spot was the doorway of a building, but I often had to settle for less.

One time, I slept in the gutter. When I woke up it was already afternoon. (I felt it was a shame it wasn't raining. I wanted to get soaked through to the skin just once, so that later I could say: 'I didn't have a dry stitch on my back.')

In Neustrelitz I slept in a park. Out of nowhere, a cow loomed next to me. But as I roused myself I realised it wasn't a cow at all; it was a white stag, one that belonged to the Grand Duke's park.

In a tunnel in Heidelberg, I saw some of the troops' entertainment. The soldier who'd been instructed to forage supplies was putting together rations for the march: hunter's sausage and margarine. I begged him for a little, but he didn't give me any; I was Hitler Youth after all, not a soldier.

'You have your own coupons,' he said, 'you should buy yourself something.'

'Yes, but it's Sunday. All the shops are closed.'

'Well, you should have thought about that before.'

'Please, just a little piece of sausage?'

'No.'

I took long walks while stationed in Berlin. SA men wearing red belts stood in front of the Reich Chancellery on little wooden pedestals. (Did I have to salute them?) The buildings across the street had all been destroyed. On the tram I saw a Hitler Youth leader wearing a white scarf.

In the bookshop at the Friedrichstraße station I came across a copy of *Nature and You*. I thought it would look good on the second shelf of my bookcase, next to Zischka's *Inventors Break the Blockade.* (*The Motor and You* was also for sale, but I already owned it.)

In an elegant restaurant, with gigantic framed pictures over the sofas, I ate the house meal for 90 pfennigs. No one had any marks.

No one should go cold or hungry.[2]

I ate cabbage with thick pearl barley. There were two girls at the table next to me. One table over from them were two flak soldiers, their luggage extending so far out into the aisle that the waiter had to go all the way round it. I watched as one of the soldiers stood up and asked whether 'the two of them' could join the girls. They could, one of the girls responded. They were both wearing hats with colourful feathers.

The front is hard as steel.
Stand your ground![3]

The soldiers proceeded to drag their backpacks over, and then the four of them sat around the table, knees together. They were polite, quiet; it seemed they didn't know what they were supposed to say. I meanwhile left half of the house meal on my plate.

'Did you not like it?' the French waiter asked.

Always know where your next waypoint is. I moved from bunker to bunker, just as Roald Amundsen had trekked from depot to depot. High-rise bunkers were the best – the comfort was just Tadellöser & Wolff – but tunnels were also not to be sneered at.

One time I landed in a trench shelter, which was covered only with thin concrete plates.

'Don't you want to cover it up with dirt before the invasion begins?' someone asked.

*

In Osterode a butcher's wife gave me half a liverwurst. I stuck it between two slices of bread. Afterwards I had a cube of sugar with margarine for dessert.

In the town, a long road led uphill to the factory. It was extremely steep – you wouldn't want to walk up it twice – but a little river ran alongside you the whole way. There were lodgings for travellers built into the mountain itself, which was where I was to camp.

I had been told that I had to go to Vienna. But the man in the transport office just shook his head.

'To Vienna? No, no, that belongs to the Russians! It's completely out of the question. If you go to Vienna, it'll be on my head!' He took a quick look at the other people in the office. 'I can't believe we're just sending *children* off now . . . Do you still have a regulation for sleep hours in the Hitler Youth? And do you at least get special ration coupons? No? Well, isn't that just wonderful.' He let out a laugh. 'You should stay on another day, then tell your troop leader you missed the train.'

A woman got bonbons out of her bag for me. I didn't tell her that I would have preferred a cigarette.

But I couldn't stay. I caught a so-called 'Führer train', which was painted light brown rather than the usual grey. The lettering on the coal car (WHEELS MUST TURN FOR VICTORY!) had been painted as though they'd been in a rush. There was a wagon loaded with light flak guns situated right behind the locomotive, to protect against the Lockheed Lightnings with their twin-boom.

They'd been instructed to look for any sign of movement, and to shoot around whatever they saw. A farmer in the field, for example: he was trying to get away, with the shots falling all round him, then he ran to the left and then again to the right. Behind him, at the top of the field, was a lovely, up-market white house.

Bet he wished he'd stayed inside, I thought.

'Everyone off the train!'

The command came in the tiny village of Oberhaid bei Bamberg. Low-flying enemy planes flitted through the sky, but they weren't shooting. The flak gun was also silent, since it was just a dummy. We ran as quickly as we could into the shelter of a nearby forest. During the second fly-over the train was destroyed.

When the air had cleared I went back through the village. It was lovely: I noted the name down in the hope that I might return in peacetime. A woman I met gave me a pot of 'blue kraut'. I didn't know what it was when she first said it; we called it red cabbage. I was to write to her and tell her how things were going, she said.

I found my flask in the train compartment I'd been in, a hole had been shot through it. When I got back home, I'd tell them that I'd had it around my neck, of course.

In Mannheim-Ludwigshafen the hundredth air raid had just ended. When I arrived they were still tidying the rubble. To mark this milestone, the residents were to receive fifty grams of real coffee and an extra allotment of cigarettes. I found it completely incomprehensible that there might still be people living here: there was not a single house to be seen any more.

While there, I ran down to the Rhine. (Just so I could say that I'd been by the Rhine.) But I had to run back quickly as there were warnings that they might be starting the next run.

Sheltering in a shop cellar, I lied and said I'd been there during the attack.

'So how about that coffee?'

'Sure, you might have been here for *this* attack, but you probably weren't here for all the others.'

In another shop, I found some salt.

'What do you want with four pounds of salt anyway?' the shopkeeper said. 'Do you have a bag with you to carry it all?'

In Mühlacker the sun shone down amiably. I sat in a café, which was really more of a refurbished parlour. When the waitress turned her back an old man stood up and took a piece of cake from the buffet. (Rye flour cake; one ration coupon for fifty grams of bread.)

'That won't do,' said the waitress, who spotted him right away. 'You mustn't do things like that.' I expected her to throw him out by the ear, or publicly denounce him. But then she said: 'Don't do that again, Grandpa, do you hear?'

'Yes, yes, I hear.' It sounded almost like he was singing the apology, and he continued chewing, rocking back and forth a little and from side to side.

In Plauen, the bunker teetered. It was almost a metre off the ground, and rocked back and forth like a ship. A number of trunks fell down the stairs. Some Canadians had gathered in there to take shelter too.

'Take it easy, boys, comes other times,' I said to them in English. But they didn't move. I assumed they'd probably been deafened. Either that or they didn't understand my English . . .

'Take it easy, boys, comes other times.'

The guard didn't understand it either.

Later, at what appeared to be a completely destroyed station, there stood a train due to depart for Karlsruhe.

Why not go there? I thought. There had also been a light cruiser called *Karlsruhe*, Fat Krahl had had it. May as well go to Karlsruhe, because who knows when I'll get to go again . . . There had to be mountains around there somewhere too; it was pretty damn far south.

At the station in Kiel, I saw prisoners who were housed in the concentration camp pushing wagons over the rubble. A *Kapo* beat them with a thin bamboo cane. Each time the gaunt, skeletal figure would curse: 'Knock it off!' or something like that. Female prisoners holding fishermen's bags and wearing headscarves stood there with their children.

A man ran up to the SS officer who was patrolling the area.

'Am I allowed to give them something to smoke?'

No answer. The man made his way through the wreckage towards them, pulling out a leather case from which he removed four cigars. He gave them to one of the prisoners. ('Just for me?' the prisoner replied.) After he'd made it back out he brushed down his trouser legs and turned round to see the fat SS officer beating that same prisoner.

I would wake up whenever the train I was on came to a stop. (What's going on now?) One time, however, the leather strap you used to pull the window shade up had been cut off, so I had to leave my compartment to investigate further. I went out and stood on the empty track for hours. It's not that I was in a rush, but still, you never knew when you'd end up in an air raid.

I saw soldiers playing cards (17 and 4) on their rucksacks. Among them were three Indian men standing silently on the platform in SS uniforms. (Subhas Chandra Bose.) They each had a tiger on their sleeve, and turbans on their heads that read FREE INDIA. They'd probably had something very different in mind when they learned they'd been stationed in Germany.

When I returned to Warnemünde the people said:

'What? You're back already?'

But when I told them about the bombed-out tracks, and the bunkers and the Lockheed Lightnings, they fell silent.

'What this boy's been through!' my mother said. 'He's like a grown man. And lovely that you brought me back some salt, my Peterpump.'

*

Sometimes a whole week would pass before my next trip. We were supposed to rest in that time, so we sat around in the school and played skat and chatted about everything we'd gone through. Sometimes we played think-fast.

'What's a mountain range that begins with an *S*?'

I knew the answer: Sinai. When that question came up I always guessed it first.

'Name something that happens in summer.'

'Name something you feel when you think of life.'

'Name a nice hobby.'

It reminded me of Greta's. (Is she the fairy from Odelidelase?)

I'd teach the boys to fall forward without getting hurt, catching themselves as they fell, or tell them about how Art Tatum was blind and Chick Webb crippled. And always press firmly when shaking hands.

The clown of the group was up for anything. We'd get him to sit on the radiator with no trousers on (though it was only lukewarm), or we'd blindfold him and see if he could tell the difference between sugar and salt. Another time, one of us pulled his trousers down and got up on a footstool.

'Okay, now you just have to come forward a little. Great. Now lick real good!'

We always had a matchbox at the ready to test whether a fart could be set aflame. We hadn't learned about that in school.

Our military training was abandoned because half of us were always absent. ('I always have to explain everything twice,' our sergeant said.) Plus, there was no ammunition for us to practise shooting with.

Some of the others got food parcels, and they often gave me their supper bread. Once I ate twelve slices of it. I just lay back on my sack, wrapped up in the covers, with the packets of bread next to me, and ate one slice after another.

'What're you reading there?' the sergeant asked.

'*The Prospector of Duala.*'

The next day he gave me furlough.

'Furlough!' he cried. 'Why is it that all of you are always on furlough . . . I never get furlough.' He then charged me with finding a birthday present for his bride: he wanted me to get her a book. I managed to stretch that furlough out to a whole week.

'I still haven't found the right thing yet,' I said every evening. 'I'll have to go out again tomorrow.'

I ran around the city in the first warm days of spring. Now, whenever I saw Helga Witte or Gina Quade they looked at me with more interest: the uniform looked good on me.

I saw Antje at the Hopfenmarkt, and I greeted her out of politeness. She only gave me a friendly nod, but I knew she did a double take: I saw her turn round for a second look, thanks to her shadow on the cobblestones.

Antje, Antje,
Don't you hear the piano on the distant ship . . .[4]

I went home as often as possible. ('Are you allowed to do this, my Peterpump?') I'd sit in the parlour and listen to records. Reginald Dixon's 'You're an Education' on the Wurlitzer. As it played I'd think about the nice times with Heini, how he'd lifted himself up in his seat and farted, and how my brother shuffled the cards for solitaire.

'You can't put that card on there . . .' he'd cry before clearing all the cards away out of exasperation.

I thought of Michael too. But he was dead now.

When I looked out of the window I would always see a soldier or two headed towards the west. ('They come in dribs and drabs.') Some were wounded, but there were also plenty of healthy ones; a mixture of infantry, pilots, and engineers from Organisation Todt, a construction unit.

There were always soldiers in Kotelmann's, the drugstore, too. Again, all headed for the west. One of them wanted to requisition the bicycle of a woman who was queuing. But she noticed just in time. None of them visited Café Drude.

Aunt Silbi had written: she wanted to wait and see; to stay put for now.

'It's probably best for all involved,' my mother said. 'I hope she's still alive, though. Things happen quickly . . .'

While in town I saw the woman from Elbing again. She had found her children. ('Thank the good, great, gracious Lord.')

She had left our apartment, and a young woman now lived with us instead. My mother had met her on the street, where she'd been wandering around with a horse and her fallen husband's Iron Cross. She'd sheltered the horse at Dr Krause's.

She could be a wife for Robert, my mother had thought.

'My name is Stoffel,' she said to me. 'Funny name, isn't it?'

She wore big pearls in her earlobes and was always smoking.

It was really remarkable: the Russians were so close to her family's estate that she could *smell* them. They had all tried to flee north together, but the father had been taken prisoner. She'd only just escaped.

'I have to have a little smoke to calm me down,' she said, 'just a couple of drags . . .'

'I feel so uneasy,' she said one morning, 'I have to get out. I want to go to the station. If I don't come back, know that I've moved on.'

And she never came back. The horse was left at Dr Krause's.

She'd only just left when Grandfather de Bonsac arrived to stay with us. ('Well, I'll be a monkey's uncle.') He shook his head, his trembling hands at his cheeks: 'It's totally bombed out.'

'What is? Your house?'

'Yes! Everything's gone. It's all burnt up.'

The canister had burst in through the roof and skidded into the garden. The house had burned down from the bottom up. He'd managed to bring two trunks with him; they were full of nut butter and Vitam-R.

'You should have saved your silver instead,' my mother said.

('It's a good thing I had to let Schura go . . . What would we have done with her?')

We moved a white-painted bureau and a leather armchair into Grandfather's room, and Dr Krause sent over a book by Peter Rosegger: *When I Was Still the Forest Boy.* ('Dust, cinders, ash, mortar and smoke . . . Everything burnt up.')

For him, the fact that he hadn't brought his sock garters along was perhaps worst of all. ('My copy of Brehm's *Life of Animals* was burned too. It would've been a nice thing to read now.') Over and over he'd continue in this way, whenever something else popped into his mind.

Letters went back and forth between Uncle Richard and my grandfather, detailing what had been lost. Whether the poultry shears had been found was central to these dispatches. Uncle Richard had asked for them, as he had nothing else to remind him of the house he'd grown up in.

My grandfather should have his picture taken, my mother suggested: who knew what was going to happen? When the picture was ready, his right ear hadn't developed properly. It looked as though it had been cut off.

My grandfather had difficulties finding a new confessor. (*I'm spiritually homeless*, he wrote on every postcard.) Our parish priest wasn't his cup of tea. He wore glasses like Harold Lloyd, and sometimes sat in the front room with us, the sun warming his feet, to talk about politics.

A confirmand had said to him, '*They* elected Hitler and now *we* have to carry the can for it.' Those words still haunted him.

'For my part, I'm done with the Third Reich,' the priest said. 'Hitler is a hypochondriac, I can see that now. And Hermann Göring, the Scharnhorst of German aviation? Ha! Were we all blind?

'If it really were a matter of total war – and this is just my opinion

– then they should have been logical: get grenades in every kitchen. Take me, for example; what am I doing sitting around here? Whichever way you slice it, I should have been at the front a long time ago . . . *If* you take total war seriously, that is. You understand me, yes?'

The Japanese were different, he felt, they weren't so prissy. They were the real Germans: even more fanatical than we were, and not so sickly. A young *Volk* unto themselves.

My grandfather listened and nodded, the tartan blanket covering his legs; the very blanket that he had brought us from Italy, back when you could still do business with the Italians.

'The Italian sky was so blue! Never since have I seen a sky so blue. Oh, and it was boiling hot. I wore Egyptian cotton underpants . . . They're burnt up now, mind. Everything cinders, ash, mortar and dust.'

After a pause he started exclaiming something about the tomato stakes he kept in the shed. We were to write to Richard immediately to ask if they were still lying there.

'And such bad news from the bank . . .' he went on: the market was failing. *But please, no more speculation*, he wrote, *I can't take it any more!* Every word was individually underlined.

*

I kept combing the bookstores. Finally I bought a book by Kurt Peter Karfeld: *Drowned Cultures*. It was about Mexico, with colour photos – and only 24 marks. The sergeant himself liked it, and he thought it was just the thing for his fiancée.

On 22 March I had a medical examination.

'So, you're Körling's son,' the staff surgeon said, as he pressed my arm. (I thought of Ulli's father: 'You used to have guys who looked like they were chiselled out of marble.') My shoulderblades protruded, he noted. I told him about my stomach pains and the constant pressure in my head. ('Oh, the pressure, the pressure.')

'Yes, yes, I know, I know,' he replied. I was deferred until October 1945; that included work service. 'Get strong. Play sports regularly. Then it'll be all right. Cod liver oil will help too. You'll have to see where you can get it, though. Ask around. And nutrient chalk too.'

A few days later some SS canvassers dropped by.

> Bright the glasses clink,
> A cheerful song we sing . . .[5]

A completely new division was being created, and we would be the first ones in it. All us boys had to do was sign up. We could even pick out our own weapons. It would be best if we all signed up then and there, they said, then the whole gang would stay together. (It was an organisational advantage too though – all the paper would be on one staple!)

'I can't wait to see the look on my squad leader's face,' one of the canvassers said, 'if we return with the news of another sixty boys voluntarily signing up.'

The news would be sent to the Führer, and similar news would come from every corner of the Reich.

'Here are the weapons,' they'd say, 'now, get to it!'

'I have to go to the army,' I said, 'my father is an officer there, and his deepest wish was that I should become an officer in the infantry. Having the white stripes on your trousers is something of a family tradition.'

'You can do that too,' said one of the canvassers. 'Just fill in these same forms, and we'll just write "army" underneath.'

But I held my ground. And since the son of the district administrator was also being stubborn, they couldn't do anything: we didn't sign up.

'Everyone's reporting for duty! Except you two, that is.'

The canvasser told us how Hitler had succeeded in uniting the German *Volk* and how we now had to defend it.

'You know,' he said, not a little miffed, 'I wouldn't be surprised if the two of you were to come to me later today and say, "We *do* want to join." You want to sign up, I can see it shining in your eyes. But you know what? I don't think I'll want to take you after all.'

36

In the middle of April, the dentist tasked me with retrieving medicine for his patients. He looked at me anxiously.

'Do you understand? You'll be helping many poor people.'

I was to collect it from Maßmannstraße, in the capital. I'd never been to this area of Berlin before. (It'll be interesting to be on Maßmannstraße, I thought.) I sat in the corner of the sofa in his office, the stained grandfather clock ticking, while he leaned on his writing desk, whose colour matched the clock.

'Or perhaps it'd be better to just leave it . . . What do you think? And how much money would you need? Two hundred marks, perhaps? Would that be enough?'

'That's a *lot* of money. You know that, right?'

'Yes, yes. But listen, my boy, be careful.' When I reached the door, he asked again if I'd prefer to stay put.

'What?' My mother couldn't believe the news. 'You have to go to Berlin? Now? Oh, I don't know about this at all.' The Russians had reached the Oder River, so the other couriers weren't being sent out at all. 'He should go himself, the fat wretch! Here he is, sending a young boy. I just can't even. No!'

She gave me the addresses of people I could turn to, were anything bad to happen: Frau von Globig from Sophienbad, who she'd known back in 1939; the Woldemanns and Aunt Herta too.

'A good woman – so nice, and always so funny! How we used to laugh! She lived in England as a young woman, in a boarding house. She's so sharp and capable. Oh and Uncle Heinrich too; he's also very nice.'

My grandfather whispered into my ear, asking whether I could bring back some hair oil for him.

'Yes? And sock holders? Everything burnt up, burnt up, burnt up!'

It was growing late by the time we were pulling in to Gesundbrunnen Station. Just as we arrived, however, there was a major attack. The doors closed and the train started moving again, eventually coming to a stop just beyond the station. The barrage lasted a long time before it finally came to an end: red flare bombs sparked, the tracks illuminated by their light.

The passengers all dispersed and I went on alone, with my brother's barber bag under my arm. I had left the rucksack at home, it looked too silly on me.

'These are England's last throes,' a man was saying as I entered a nearby bunker.

> Our walls may break,
> But never our hearts!'

The bunker had a conical roof. The bombs were supposed to slide off it. ('But I just saw him yesterday!' a woman wailed.)

The next day I resumed my habit of taking long walks through Berlin. There were soldiers wherever you looked, and the women

wore tracksuit trousers under their dresses. I lost count of the
number of burnt-out businesses I saw, all with their grilles down.
A smell like wet mortar and burnt paper hung in the air, and there
were bomb craters filled with sewage water in the middle of the
road. The work details had begun the clean-up.

I heard one man say that the bombs had been as big as Litfaß
columns, and that they'd always fallen in pairs.

The bookstore at the Friedrichstraße station was still open. I picked
up *The German Philistine's Magic Horn* and *Steps* by Christian
Morgenstern. An inscription inside the latter read *Don't forget St
Blaise's Day*, dated 23 October 1928. It was bound in blue cloth
with a golden star. The book was made up of lots of small paragraphs:

> Nietzsche, the Pole, gained spiritual depth when he
>   embraced his German identity. He lived from 1871
>   until 1913. No war in his lifetime.[2]

The Woldemanns' house was burnt out. I'd walked halfway there,
asking everyone I came across, until I got an answer. On my way I
saw O. E. Hasse – the film star – in a streetcar, wearing a fur
waistcoat. He stood right next to me, but I paid no attention to
him, to demonstrate what a good upbringing I'd had.

I'd called the Woldemanns during my last stay in Berlin.

'Yes, come,' they'd said, 'you old rascal.'

Ute wasn't there. She was in Chemnitz, in the country, but she'd
be happy that I'd come by all the same, they said.

But now it was too late. The garden gate was locked with a chain.

I couldn't decide where to turn next. To visit Frau von Globig
– a good-hearted woman ('I'm an old biddy, aren't I?') – or Aunt

Hertha ('Hertha, oh boy, when she gets going . . .') with her pretty daughters.

Better, I thought, to go to the soldiers' cinema. It was a kind of Chinese theatre, everything decked out in black and gold. They were showing one film after the other non-stop through the whole night.

In *Immensee*, Kristina Söderbaum held a water lily in her hand: 'Water lilies . . .' she said, as if in a dream. When they showed the distillery they'd built on the lake, the colour film really showed what a blight it was on the landscape. But that was fine. Tadellöser & Wolff.

She and her lover meet again later, when their affair is long over, but the water lily still stands in a bowl on the table.

At other times I caught some of the troop entertainment. There was often jazz music there: Kurt Widman and his orchestra, or Stathis the Greek with his electric Hawaiian guitar. If Widman was in the mood, he took a cymbal from the drummer and hit it with his head. Every night the drummer would threaten him with his drumsticks, and every time the soldiers would laugh and nudge each other. ('Did you see that?')

The 'Tiger Rag' was dead, Widman said. Instead he played 'Black Panther'. There was no difference really.

'Could you give me a few marks?' the cloakroom attendant asked. She got paid just as many marks as everyone else. But she probably thought I didn't know that.

I was staying in the Excelsior; 'the biggest hotel in Europe', as it was known. There were mirrors that ran the length of the corridors. You were supposed to think it just kept going and going. I had a lovely double room on the fourth floor, with a view over the whole city. (Both engines, full steam ahead, *ring, ring!*)

I live in the Excelsior, I kept thinking. Now, you never thought you'd be here, did you, Walter?

Looking at myself in the mirror, I wondered how you should look when you lived in the Excelsior. (Prince Walter of Aquitaine.) Maybe I'd just stay at the Adlon next time? Or the Delphi? (Though where was the Delphi?)

Whenever I wasn't sleeping or sitting in the bunker I gathered the medicines on the list. A bottle here, a bottle there. Each trip took several hours. The windows of the wholesaler were all completely destroyed, but the shelves were still standing.

'Shouldn't you be going straight home?' a woman asked me. And she was right – that *was* what I should have been doing. Instead, I kept going to the movies.

Sitting through one film after another, I often fell asleep in the cinema, snoring propped against the shoulders of my neighbour.

I saw *My Gentlemen Sons*, in which a father plays cowboys-and-Indians with his sons (the mother isn't there for some reason). Every time he wants something from them he addresses them in baby-talk: 'Does the big boy want to drink any milk?'

I caught *For Your Sake* – in which a jazz band meet in a hotel room, and even a film star like Ernst Legal is soon dancing 'hot' with them – and *Our Girl the Professor* too, starring Jenny Jugo. During her *Abitur* exam, the principal asks her for the name of a particular philosopher. In response she takes a Leibniz cookie out of her pocket. And when she's asked what laws made him famous, she drops a handkerchief. The law of gravity.[3]

One morning there was loud crashing, but no sirens wailing. At first I thought it was a storm, then that someone on the street was throwing boards in a pile. But I soon realised it was artillery. From my window I could see streaks of dust in the sky. It was the Russian field artillery, a 152mm.

People were standing in their doorways, looking up.

'Artillery can only blast a small hole at best,' they said. 'That's not so bad. Bombs are a lot more vicious . . .'

I bummed around the city centre, the barber bag with the medicine tucked under my arm. I wandered along Friedrichstraße in one direction, then doubled back, walking down on the opposite side. I contemplated swinging by the bookshop again, but when I got there they were folding the grille down in front of the store.

And where was the Church of Thanksgiving, I wondered? It had such a fabulous bunker. It was like a big gasometer. You hardly noticed the attacks in there. And it had its own electricity and water.

It was then that it dawned on me how close the Russians were: they couldn't be very far away if they were shooting into the city with artillery. I felt as though someone had just shouted, 'Get out! Get out of here this second.'

At Stettin station a chalked notice read: ALL TRAIN SERVICES CANCELLED AS OF TODAY. Shit on a stick. They had still been running the day before: I had seen queues twenty people long at the counter.

There was nothing to be done at any of the other stations either. (ALL TRAIN SERVICES CANCELLED AS OF TODAY.) I ran around the whole day, hoping that somehow it would work out. I tried returning to the hotel, but found myself forever looking out of my window at the columns of smoke. Restless, I studied the service map in the tram, and then made my way to the bunker again and asked people for guidance. They simply shrugged their shoulders. Ten thousand German tanks had been gathered together somewhere. Perhaps I could stay in the bunker until they were deployed and then I could ride back home first class.

I stayed in the bunker that night. I didn't have the courage to leave. 'As early as possible tomorrow': that was my plan. At around 4 or 5 a.m. I'd make a break for it.

'Yes, early tomorrow morning,' the people I spoke to said, 'that's what you should do. We'll all get out of here early tomorrow morning.'

A French civilian showed me his wedding ring and asked if I'd give him a slice of bread for it.

'It's got no seal at all,' he said, and clinked it against the concrete floor. 'Solid gold.'

I lay under a bench. A girl pushed her way in next to me, acting as if we'd known each other for a long time. She had a hole in her stocking, but I didn't mind it. Suddenly she kissed me and said: 'Let's go, kiss me, kiss me!'

She wanted to tell me something, but only in a whisper, and, when I bent forward to listen, she slipped her tongue into my ear.

'Do you understand?'

No, I hadn't understood. So again I leaned in, and again her tongue slid in my ear . . .

'In the back, we can do it there. Yes?'

I told her I had to leave, that I'd be right back, but I never returned to the bench.

I waited until exactly five o'clock the next morning. (Five more minutes, then I'll go.) I stole a sleeping soldier's steel helmet in preparation, to protect my head when they inevitably shot at me. He was a flak soldier, so the steel helmet was blue, which matched my uniform. I took a final look at the man. Perhaps I'd owe him my life . . .

I tightened my belt, went to pee, and then stopped and looked in the mirror again: so that was what I looked like.

Perhaps I should empty the barber bag, throw out the medicine? I wondered. No, better to keep it all: I could show it to the military police as proof of why I was here; then they'd have to let me through. It might even help if I were to meet the Russians: they might consider me under the protection of the Red Cross.

Okay. I'd wash out my mouth, then I'd go, once and for all.

I took the metro as far north as it would go. (That's the right direction for Rostock, at least.) I knew it was a long shot. The carriages were all completely empty. The back yards of the tenement blocks were washed in the morning's light.

When I arrived at the last station, I saw burning houses and heard shooting. Solitary soldiers stood with bloody bandages. I had to try to get further west; I couldn't pass through here.

> It astonishes me and almost makes me
> sorry, that you weren't
> more careful in your
> dangerous undertaking . . .

To Tegel, then. Before I left I spoke with the station manager. I wanted to lighten my load, but she didn't want the books. I laid them out in front of her but she simply said, 'No, put them away.'

Santa Claude, I prayed, help me just this one time, you don't need to help me ever again. But there was nothing doing in Tegel either, so I travelled back to the city centre, and then to Spandau, to the west. There I got out and went on by foot. I was relieved that I'd left my clunky boots at home; it was much easier going in my light shoes.

The bridge hadn't been blown up yet. I'd been told by the station staff that it was being guarded by military police, but there was no one to be seen. I crossed it in no time.

A new key battle line had been drawn in the forests just outside Spandau. I saw paratroopers unloading provisions. I should go ahead and lend a hand, they said, offering a piece of sausage as a reward.

Paratroopers   the strong movers of the battle's fate![4]

'You want to go west?' one asked. 'Then head that way . . .' They laughed and each one pointed in a different direction. ('He's a good sport! Holding up okay, yeah?')

Seeing a thin line of soldiers from the Territorial Army, I tried my luck asking them how to get to Nauen. They were family men, so they pointed me in the right direction.

'But the Russians are there,' they warned me.

I jumped over their trenches and ran across the battlefield like Pierre Bezukhov. (Who-what-where-when-why.) A raven flew out in front of me, and gave a warning warble. (*Markwart*, they were called in Plattdeutsch.)

I marched hour after hour without seeing a single soul. At first I walked next to the road, hidden in the forest, but then I moved on to the highway itself. Now and then I heard the sounds of tanks in the distance, but there was no trace of any Russians. Strange clouds hung in the sky, shaped like bottoms. Occasionally I toyed with putting the steel helmet on, but I couldn't see any reason to: there was nothing going on.

I came upon a house at the roadside. It was silent, with blossoming forsythia and a wooden fence. I held the barber bag under my arm, Morgenstern's *Steps* inside it along with medicine bottles, a jawbone chisel and wax plates for taking impressions. I wondered if there was any creeping bugleweed in the garden.

I travelled the next stretch of my journey on a freight train. It was transporting milk to a dairy wholesaler in Nauen. When we arrived, I encountered a man in the yard who seemed to be in a hurry.

'Could I get a gulp of milk?' I asked.

'Take what you want! We have milk, butter, cheese by the hundredweight!'

(How was butter even made? I wondered.)

There was another train standing in the station.

'Where is it going?' I asked the station manager.

'To Rostock,' he replied.

I got on, and found myself surrounded by refugees and soldiers. I told them I was coming from Berlin, that I'd only just made it out, that the artillery was already shooting into the city, and that we were supposed to just up and leave, otherwise the Russians would come. I told them how I'd heard great jazz music in Berlin, and seen non-stop movies, and that it was a miracle I'd made it out.

'It's also a miracle that this train is going to Rostock of all places, not to, say, Wismar or Stralsund . . .'

'Shut up,' said a soldier. He'd already stood up halfway through my story. He probably wanted to sock me.

The train was fully packed by this time, but still we didn't leave. It remained standing there as night fell, and at midnight I resolved to carry on by foot once more. I'd follow the tracks home.

'Don't take the ones that go off to the right,' a train official advised.

Still I carried the barber bag under my arm. As I neared a small station an armoured train crept past me, so I climbed into the ditch.

> Germany, Fatherland,
> We're coming.[5]

What would Eckhoff say if he could see me here? I wondered. The excitement was hurting my stomach. Better relieve myself, I thought. And just as I settled in, I saw lights in the distance, growing closer and closer. It was my train! It chugged slowly ever closer, following the armoured train. I'd never got into my trousers so quickly. (Crapnitzdörfer & Jenssen!)

The train approached very slowly, and came to a stop exactly at my feet. But by the time I got on to the running board it was already moving forward again. I stayed put, and rode on the running board all the way home. The other passengers said, 'come in, there's room,' but I stayed there. I owed Santa Claude big time.

Just in case, I threw the medicine bottles overboard: I didn't want to push my luck any further. I watched as they tumbled out of sight.

I kept the books, though.

> Philosophies are life preservers,
> Made from the cork of speech.[6]

They'd made it this far; I could take them home.

On 25 April the train came to a stop at Platform 3. Manfred and I had left for Warnemünde with Robert and his friends from this very platform, all those years ago.

> LAXIN PURGES, IT'S VERY MILD.
> TAKE IT AND YOU'RE GOOD TO GO.[7]

I hoped no one would see me, or I'd have to report for duty right away; I wanted to go home, to relax for a day or two.

I walked along Bismarckstraße, past all the pretty green linden trees. The magnolias on the corner of Roonstraße were in full bloom, as they always were at this time of year.

I passed the burnt-out concert hall, Kotelmann's pharmacy and Timm the butcher's, with the steel helmet under my arm. I hadn't needed it at all. And then I saw that familiar sign loom into view:

> Whether out in the woods or snug in your den,
> Enjoy Dr Krause's Mineral Water.

(I once sat in the *A*.)

'Thank God one of you is safe,' my mother said, once she'd got over her initial shock. 'You're a sight for sore eyes.' She'd thought that all of her men had disappeared.

('Oh, and you brought butter. My lovely Peterpump.')

Aunt Silbi had written, from Kudowa. She wanted to come after all.

'But it looks like she's called it off again,' my mother said, 'she just can't do it . . . Still, it would have been a real old-folks' home here had she come.'

At that moment my grandfather came through, asking whether I'd brought him the hair oil he asked for.

37

I stayed at home for three days. I cleaned my ears, wore fresh underwear every day, and ate cake bread with marmalade. The canary trilled and the sun shone on the doily for the coffee pot. I lazed around playing records. ('You're an education for me . . .')[1]

On the third day, the telephone rang. It was a long-distance call.

('Twenty-five thirty-eight?') There was giggling at the end of the line.

'Is it you?' It was Greta.

Someone shouted in the background though, and she hung up quickly.

I played through all the pieces of Irene Bien's *In Mozart's Reich* again. I used the transposing lever to shift them into a new key. As a child I used to hang my teddy bear from the lever.

'Don't stand so close to the piano,' the Schnabel woman had once said, 'otherwise you'll ruin your hearing.' ('B major? When do you think you'll be able to play in B major? It has five sharps!')

I went to the dentist that morning too.

'You only brought the tooth wax? What a shame.' That was the one thing he didn't really need. 'And nothing else at all? Where did you leave the other things? You can't just throw them away like that!' He hoped I had at least rung the doorbell of another dentist and offered him the medicines. ('And the money? Where's all the money?')

After he'd run out of questions he sat down and asked what I thought of the political situation.

'Do you think the Russians will come to Rostock too?'

'The German soldiers are known for standing their ground. We can be sure of that,' I said, because I knew he was a big Nazi. ('Just be careful, my boy.')

'Shame that all we have is that little bit of wax . . .'

After I left his office I went to Warnemünde. No one there had any idea what was going on any more.

'Go home,' one of them said to me. 'We'll let you know. The courier unit has been disbanded.'

At the airfield they were testing new planes. The He 111 Z, which looked like two bombers that had been sewn together at the wings – there was a fifth motor where they connected. There was the Mistel too – also known as the 'father and son' or 'the piggy-back plane' – which was more or less a fighter plane positioned on top of a bomber. In case of emergency, it would be loaded with dynamite and steered at a target. They told me they were going to blow the Strelasund Crossing sky high with it.

An empty hospital train stood at the station. Next to it a heap of fur vests. I would have liked to take one – there wasn't a person in sight – but I thought it might be a trap. Maybe someone was sitting somewhere and watching to see if anyone laid hands on them, so that they could arrest them . . . Or maybe the fur vests had lice. Why else would they be lying around?

I went back home and didn't show up at Warnemünde again. It was very cosy in my little room at the back of the apartment. It was just a shame that no sun came in there.

I ordered new books, and began a log for whenever someone wanted to borrow something from me. The date went in the first column, the name of the borrower in the second and the due date in the third. I changed the date on the stamp in preparation: 29 April 1945.

'Stay here, my boy,' my mother said, 'and if the Russians come and take you with them to Siberia, I'll pack you a nice bundle of warm clothes. There are good people everywhere, you can take comfort in that.'

> Take delight in the Lord,
> And He will give you the desires of your heart.[2]

Frau Warkentin had once told my mother that all boys aged twelve and up had to enlist.

> Silver bells of corn sway in the grass[3]

But her son was in the middle of exams.

'If everything goes wrong, Mother,' he'd said, 'and if this is the end for Germany, then we still must do only that which is good.' The ethical, he'd said, was an end in itself.

Manfred and other boys from the neighbourhood had to report to the district. ('Your son does too, Aunt Kempi . . .') They were given Panzerfausts and sent marching. This time I didn't search the house for draft notices though.

I heard Goebbels on the radio. He wasn't looking at our situation through rose-tinted glasses, but it was better to face an end with terror than a terror without end!

'Well then, get to it,' my mother said.

The district leader, also on the radio, said that he'd single-handedly turned a woman who lived on Parkstraße over to a concentration camp. Letting refugees stand waiting at your door while you're off at the coffee shop? 'There is no room in the *Volksgemeinschaft* for such subjects.'

My mother went to get supplies, as the rations for the next week were being given out in advance. ('If anyone rings, boy, don't answer.') She dragged a washing bowl full of sausage stuffing back with her. A proper roast was being held. There'd been a bowl full of meatballs in the kitchen, and whoever felt like it could take one.

She also brought twenty pounds of flour and a bottle of cooking oil, along with more bars of hard soap, and money from the bank: 5,000 marks. It would probably be enough. We would hide it behind the glass in the vanity table.

'We might be better off getting some more?' I suggested.

'But then it might get stolen. Damned if you do and damned if you don't.'

She said that Herr Kerner from Deutsche Bank had said, 'We're always there for you, Frau Kempowski,' but that it was best we kept our silver at home. He knew father from before, and had long admired his propriety.

Should we stay in Rostock, or were we better off leaving? The question haunted us. The map was pulled out again, with the colourful drawing pins. ('Verdun fell – my goodness!'). The Russian spearhead was now aimed directly at Rostock. ('That's us.')

I drew thick red Russian arrows from the east and the south. In the west, the green arrows were the English. The lines from above had already been taken care of, though. (*Boom!*)

The steamship *Friedrich* sat in the harbour, full of wounded soldiers from the dental clinic. All you had to do was get on it. But then the enemy might sink it.

Denzer came to our place saying that he wanted to leave by steamship: he had already pulled out his boxes and crates, and had bribed Schröder, the infantryman, on the gangway. As a shipping agent he would definitely be able to get on his own ship.

'There's still time for you to join me, Frau Kempowski!'

But my mother couldn't make up her mind. What would her husband say if she just left everything behind? One day he would walk up to the flat to find someone else's name on the door. ('Kempowski? No, we don't know him,' they'd say, and shut the door in his face.)

'No, we're staying here.'

'We're all staying here, Frau Kempowski,' Dr Krause said too. 'There have to be people here when peace is declared.'

Quade said that leaving was the worst thing a person could do. Without noticing it, he said, we'd fallen victim to Germany's propaganda, which had the Russians carrying out all kinds of atrocities. Tchaikovsky and Gogol were also Russian, but they were highly civilised. (*The Government Inspector*, it really was extremely funny!) And Petersburg was full of baroque castles. In any case, the Reichstag had been convened: things would come to an end quickly now.

'How lucky we are to have Hitler! He's the only man who can achieve peace with dignity in this muddled situation.'

But then suddenly Dr Krause left. The doors clapped in the wind.

He simply vanished into thin air with his horse and his wagon.

'The rats are leaving the sinking ship,' said Mother, 'can you believe it?'

Liesing – Dr Finck – had also been seen leaving, a cigarette burning in his hand. He'd simply raised his arm and waved. And the shipyard director had left for Sweden on his yacht, the *Lucia Warden*. ('Oh, he knows which side his bread is buttered. The sly fox.')

Fraulein Othanke was Baltic, so she knew the Russians.

'Oh, Aunt Kempi, just go! Your steamship is in the harbour: it doesn't get any simpler than that! I lie awake at night, hour after hour, and all I can think of is burning. Wherever the Russians go, no stone is left upon another.'

She'd taken part in quite a lot, back then in Riga, but she had been coerced. The city councillors had been stabbed and thrown into a stream.

'But that was a different time. It was the 20s, and the Communists were all still wild and bloodthirsty after all the oppression. You could understand it, really.'

'Oh, communism,' said my mother. 'If you have nothing, then of course you'd be a communist!'

When had Heinemann the paper merchant unscrewed the sign that read THE GERMAN SAYS HEIL HITLER from his door? He had to have chosen the moment carefully . . . I thought too of the sign at the yacht club that read:

NO JEWS ALLOWED

The woman from the Woldemann apartment came to visit my mother. She looked like an old Käthe Kruse doll.

'I haven't been for Hitler in a long time,' she said. 'Oh, not for a long, long time.'

('She probably just wants to cover her arse. Dumb as a sack of beans!')

A little pointy-nosed lance corporal rang our doorbell, asking whether we had anything to eat. I gave him four apples and one hunk of bread, plus two meatballs.

'Can I also stay here for a night?'

'No, no. Go on, go on.'

The French family from across the way left for the west with red lanterns on the front and back of their wagon. My grandfather went into the vacated apartment and brought back bedcovers and a cardboard box full of something crystal-like.

Was it soap powder, perhaps? Hängolin – an aphrodisiac? I examined it under my microscope, but still couldn't tell. Perhaps Kotelmann the druggist could figure it out.

They had set up a church for themselves in a garage, he said. A Madonna stood in there. ('Oh, right, Catholics.')

In the afternoon, I went out after all. A division of singing Hungarians marched along Hermannstraße, with a trumpeter out in front: they were our allies.

Barricades were set up at the Schwaan Gate. One of Bohrmann's furniture wagons, full of bricks, stood on iron girders: they were makeshift tracks. In case of emergency, it just had to be rolled forward. We were going to defend everything down to the last man: no stone was to be left upon another.

Klaus Greif approached me from the other side of the street.

'I'm telling everyone to stay put!'

He'd had appendicitis, and had just been let out of hospital. But there was fortune in his misfortune: he hadn't had to go along to Neubrandenburg, which was now under Soviet control. Five Messerschmidts flew over us. They were probably keeping watch to ensure that everything was in order.

The old slaughterhouse, where they'd been storing grain and other goods, had been abandoned, but a paymaster was still around, brandishing his pistol to make sure no one plundered what was left. He shut the gigantic gate. I had no idea how he was supposed to hold the gun while he did so.

We had better luck on Kröpeliner Straße, where we managed to get into a warehouse. We picked up vests and underpants, as well as one pair of wooden shoes with split soles. An auxiliary police officer was waiting for us outside. We had to show him our receipt, but he barely looked at it.

'Fine,' my mother said, 'it's fine, my Peterpump. Just don't worry.' She cleaned the windows and beat the armchairs. 'One thing I do wonder about: where are all the children coming from?'

It was true, there were children everywhere. They'd probably sent the evacuated children home from the KLV evacuee camps, I said. Aunt Annemi, the kindergarten teacher, had returned with them.

> Whoever wants to be with soldiers
> Has to have a gun,
> Has to have a gun . . .[4]

I saw her walking backward in front of the children.

'Maybe the British will come,' my mother said. That was starting to look more and more appealing.

Others weren't so sure; 'The British? Some of them will want to take their anger out on us . . .'

For emergencies, we buried a crate with mason jars out back in Dr Krause's garden.

'Bury the medals too. And take down the targets. They don't break easily. Your grandfather will have to get at them with an axe. And throw out the sabre. And the winter relief posters, they have swastikas all over them.'

> To your brothers in a besieged land –
> A warm heart, a helping hand.
> The People's Federation for Germans in Foreign Countries

It was good that we hadn't bought a picture of the Führer, I thought.

'And don't forget your uniform, boy!'

I carried it all through the hole in the cellar wall into the empty building next door. We could leave Dad's uniforms hanging; he wasn't here.

*

In the late morning of 30 April there was the patter of feet in the street: there were soldiers everywhere. Some of them were running, some on horses and some on bicycles. There went our army, in full retreat: it was every man for himself now.

'Oh, God,' my mother said.

They came in a wild stream, their uniforms unbuttoned at the top to help them get air. There were some solitary refugees among them.

'What if we sent you away after all? To Lübeck to Frau Susemiehl? There's still time . . .' my mother said.

Now that his leave was over, District Court Counsellor Warkentin's son folded into the crowd, carrying his certificate of examination. But he couldn't do anything for his mother now; he had to go.

'Mummy,' he'd said, 'it wouldn't have been the worst thing if I'd messed the exam up . . .'

A munitions train detonated in the distance. A few stragglers rushed over towards it, then the street was empty.

Ulli Prüter emerged from the stream of fleeing people. ('Subhas Chandra Bose!') He wanted to get his civilian dress, some old trousers, before leaving . . . ('Go, go, quick!' his mother shouted.) He had to run towards the Russians and get the door shut before they got there.

'Enjoy the war,' he shouted, 'the peace is going to be terrible!'
(*Zack mi seu.*)

In the night I switched the light out, sat at the piano and improvised, the corners of my mouth turned down, in minor. Russian planes droned lazily overhead. It sounded as though there were sewing machines running throughout the building. They were probably surveying their spoils.

I could just switch on the light, I thought: take a bomb on the head and have everything over with.

Some prankster called our phone.

'What should be done with the women's corpses?' a man asked.

'With the women's corpses? What do you mean, the women's corpses?'

'Well, the women's corpses that are going to pile up here over the next days.'

'Who is this?'

'This is the Bone and Fat Recovery Service.'

And then such a repulsive laugh, like 'Ha-ha-ha!'

*

May 1 was a wonderful day: 'a day for laying eggs', as Ulla would have said. My mother, my grandfather and I sat on the balcony together – with the Jew's beard, the tradescantia – and drank a bottle of champagne. We drank to the war that had been won.

My mother in her blue pelerine dress – almost not warm enough for this time of year – the lacework between her fingers. Grandfather de Bonsac wore a gigantic knot in his tie. His hair still had hardly any grey in it, and it was cleanly pomaded and parted. Though there were two or three tiny bits of dandruff on his collar, he looked like Edward VII.

His velvet jacket with the hussar rope had been burnt up, burnt up, burnt up, along with his ivory letter opener – the one from Uncle Bertram zur Nedden – his lovely down blankets and his crates of camphor.

'Everything rubble, ash, dust, muck. Burnt up, burnt up, burnt up.'

'There's an eerie stillness over the city,' my mother said. 'Could it be the calm before the storm?'

It was said that the terms of surrender were being negotiated at the gates of the city. (The surrender of Breda.) A citizen's delegation had made their way out there with white handkerchiefs around their arms.

'What is there left to negotiate?' I wondered, 'the scales are tipped pretty well to their side . . .'

Why didn't we go to Lübeck now? We'd heard that the British were there. And they had been greeted completely differently: they were welcomed, as liberators. The city had rung the church bells, streets were lined with garlands and flowers were scattered. The lovely old black-white-and-red flag had been raised once more. Our good kaiser.

'We have to go back to the time of the Kaiser,' my mother said. 'No more of the black-red-and-mustard, and those constant political meetings. Oh, I can still remember today . . . In the philharmonic Professor Klee, conservative to his bones, quick-witted, had an answer for everything . . . Ah, they were all angry at him! The behaviour in all those movements was disgusting. Beer glasses and chairs flying all over the place, no one able to hear the steward's ringing. And then groups of people in the audience would grab the functionaries off the stage and throw them into the crowd . . .

'Kaiser Wilhelm knew how to keep the peace, though. I still remember holding up my doll when he drove by, and the Kaiser's wife nodding at me. "You good child," she said.'

Those poor boys – Manfred, Struck and Stuhr – were armed with hand grenades and Panzerfausts and sent to Neubrandenburg, my mother told me. Frau Eckhoff had cried so hard. She couldn't keep her son. And they couldn't aim at all; they didn't even know how to hold the rifle. Unheard of.

And in Munich there would normally be a festival around this time of year. Everyone in traditional costume, the bars full, the people all drunk, yodelling and screaming, blaring from every house.

'When we went, of course, we didn't see the flower procession. Only happens once every ten years. Typical. Instead, we drove back home a week early. "We don't have any more money," your father had said. But then I saw that he'd completely forgotten about a whole wad of marks he'd squirrelled away in the desk drawer. Oh, I was so angry . . .

'Your father was unbelievably healthy, but his skin, and all that came with it, came from his crazy parents . . . They drove you mad! His own mother had even laughed scornfully in his face and said that he was a mistake. A strange woman, with no heart, and a strange family. Under those circumstances, with an upbringing like that, a person can't help but grow up slightly odd.'

'We've paid off the debts now, though. In the new era we'll go somewhere untainted. Now that the Nazis are gone. *We've* won the war, that much is clear.'

'What do you mean, my Gretelein?' my grandfather asked, as he put down his Rosegger and put his hand to his ear.

'I said: *we* won the war! The Church, and the forces of good!' That was a reason to celebrate! Cheers!

We'd heard nothing from Robert though, the sharp little guy. That was unnerving. Had he been taken prisoner? Or were things working out for him somehow? Maybe one day we'd wake up to find him standing at the door?

'"Oh, you arsehole," Robert used to say – the cheeky little guy. He's as sharp as he's short,' my mother said.

We'd been able to send off a packet to Ulla containing some of her old dresses.

'Lovely that she's safe. And Sven! Oh, I still remember our walk on the Weidenweg. I bet they're sitting in their garden, or whatever they have now, eating such nice Danish cake and drinking real coffee. Oh, how I'd enjoy that . . .'

'I believe they're here now.'

A few shots in the distance. I went back inside and looked down out of the window: a motorcycle with a sidecar, a Russian driving it. The sidecar was full of shoes from the cobbler next door. I quickly let the curtains fall and went back out on to the balcony.

'Yes, they're here now.'

Really we should run down and greet them. Shout 'Hurrah!' or 'Bravo!' But perhaps it was better to stay up here: they were probably incredibly angry at us, after all.

The shots came closer.

'Oh, heavens,' my mother said. She stood up and watered the tradescantia.

And now closer still: individual shots, probably shots of peace. One sailed through the pear tree and blossom rained down.

'I think we should go inside,' my mother said.

TRANSLATOR'S NOTE

About three-quarters of the way into *An Ordinary Youth*, the novel's protagonist, a boy named Walter Kempowski, is sent to stay with family friends in the countryside while Rostock, his home town, is bombed by the Allies. Clowning around with his provincial friends, Walter blurts out, '*Tadellöser & Wolff*!' His friends are mystified. '*Tadellöser & Wolff*? What's that supposed to mean?' someone asks. Walter isn't quite sure himself; it's simply something his family says – and the novel's original title. 'It means everything's perfect,' he explains. 'That's how people talk in the city.'

Here, Walter's friend gives voice to a question the reader has likely been asking since the title page, a question that contains all of the difficulties facing the translator of this famously untranslatable novel. The phrase, which plays on a cigar brand, Löser and Wolff – aryanised by the Nazis in 1937 – and which migrates from the vocabulary of his father Karl, to his brother Robert, and finally over to Walter throughout the course of the novel, would have been as opaque to the German reader of 1971 as it is to an English language reader today. Nonetheless, a German reader would be able to pick out the word *tadellos* – 'impeccable', 'flawless' – and from there, might intuit that the phrase is a playful, nonsensical expression of positivity. But an English reader can't be expected to make these leaps. How should the translator approach such a phrase? How best to render the novel's uniquely plastic relationship to language without sacrificing the immersiveness of its world by explaining too much or too little?

There are many points in the novel where a translator is sorely tempted to try, in the spirit of fidelity, to reproduce its distinctive opacity. Nonetheless, a translation lacks the primal linguistic connection to the reader possessed by the original, and for that reason, it also enjoys a much scarcer reserve of goodwill when it comes to matters of clarity and transparency. Given the choice, then, between a clear English translation and a faithful but off-putting rendering of the original, it has been my rule to opt for the former. In the case of the Kempowski family's unique jargon, like their repeated use of the phrase '*Goodmannsdörfer*', I have removed all but a few of the uses before Walter gives his explanation, and preserved all the subsequent ones. I kept all those unexplained expressions in the novel that could be directly translated, and struck those that could not. The novel's many uses of Low German and occasional bits of Bavarian dialect have also been translated directly into English.

Then, there is the matter of Kempowski's extensive and largely unclarified references to German history and culture, which run the gamut from high-, middle-, and lowbrow literature, to textbooks, popular culture, advertisements, and the Byzantine vocabulary of Nazi propaganda – which is something of a language unto itself. Here again, one hesitates. The very obscurity of the references is an essential component of Kempowksi's realism, which tries to capture a sense of the living world as a forest of historical signs, each clamouring to be deciphered. Part of this realism is the depiction of a racist society, and the necessity of retaining (rather than censoring or softening) the language used by this society, so as to portray the perspective that created the conditions for a genocide in which the bourgeois world depicted here was entirely complicit, despite its pretentions to the contrary.

To make the novel maximally accessible to the reader with no knowledge of German culture, I have added the names of authors and composers to the titles of books and pieces of music, and where I felt it would not interrupt the narrative, I have added a very brief in-text description. For those readers curious about the provenance of the novel's many interpolated texts, I have added explanatory endnotes where the source is not given in the text. There were a few references that rested on an untranslatable pun – Karl Kempowski's mention of a biography of the Social Democrat Louise Zietz after complaining about a room's draughtiness (*Es zieht*), for example – which I reluctantly deleted.

Lastly, and perhaps most difficult of all, was the question of what to do with the novel's near-constant use of reported speech. Unlike English, German uses the subjunctive mood to indicate that a person is being quoted, and Kempowski often employs this voice to inject ambiguity into the narrative. Each individual usage can be cleanly rendered in English; the cumulative result, however, is often so cryptic as to lose even the careful reader. As such, I generally chose to add quotation marks and to identify the speaker. By the same token, I smoothed out especially fragmented portions of the text by dropping in the presumptive subject or object of the sentence. And where the novel is especially cryptic or allusive, I have chosen to interpret, rather than transliterate.

All told, the result looks rather a bit more like 'a bourgeois novel' – to quote the German book's tongue-in-cheek subtitle – than does the original. Nonetheless, I am confident that a happy balance has been struck between Kempowski's inimitable style and accessibility for the reader unfamiliar with German culture and history.

An undertaking of this magnitude is always a cumulative effort. I cannot sufficiently express my thanks for the tireless editorial work of Dan Bird at Granta, as well as Bella Lacey, Susan Barba, and Vicki Harris. The richly detailed and researched annotations by Lars Bardram on the website of the Kempowski-Archiv in Rostock proved to be a life-saving resource. Cosima Mattner at Columbia University provided invaluable assistance with the portions of the text in Low German, and my colleague Franziska Schweiger at Hamilton College graciously helped me unravel some especially stubborn passages. This translation would never have been completed without their cumulative efforts, and for that I remain grateful.

Michael Lipkin

NOTES

CHAPTER 1

1. Lyrics from the German folk song 'How Gently They Rest, the Blessed', written by August Cornelius Stockmann in 1780, with the original title 'The Cemetery' and set to music by Friedrich Burchard Bencken. The song was especially beloved by the Freemasons – hence Grete Kempowski's calling it 'the Lodge song'. Note that Karl Kempowski morbidly changes the lyric.

2. From the popular poem of the same title by the religious poet Luise Hensel, published in 1816.

3. A song from 1830 by Franz Kugler, after a melody by Friedrich Ernst Fesca.

CHAPTER 2

1. From the 1938 hit 'Fraulein Gerda' by Erich Ewald Walter Plessow, with melody by Helmuth Wernicke.

2. Ibid.

3. Ibid.

4. The first verse of the song 'The Morning Has Rung' from the girls' songbook *Spinnerin Lobunddank*, with text by Georg Stammler and melody by Walther Hensel.

5. A Prussian general during the Napoleonic Wars and a philosopher of war best known for his treatise *On War*.

6. See chapter 2, note 1.

CHAPTER 4

1. The first line of an aria in Weber's 1812 opera *The Sharpshooter*. It likely jumps into Walter's mind because of the proximity of the family's sheet music to his father's World War One memorabilia.

CHAPTER 5

1. A hymn from the seventeenth century by Paul Gerhard.
2. Before 1934, students at technical school and at gymnasium (preparatory school for university) wore different caps. The Nazis abolished this practice in order to diminish class difference in the Reich.
3. From a 1939 hit song by Peter Igelhoff, 'In the Little Sky-Blue Limousine'.

CHAPTER 7

1. In *Home*, Kempowski's diary of the year 1990, published in 2006, he mentions that this practice was widespread among the Hitler Youth.
2. A poem by Walter Flex from his autobiographical book *A Wanderer Between Both Worlds: An Experience of the War*, which became a bestseller on publication in 1916.
3. From Erhard Wittek's World War One memoir *Breakthrough '18*, a book widely promoted by the Nazis.
4. From Goethe's likely most famous and certainly most anthologised poem, 'The Wanderer's Night Song'.
5. From a canon by Luigi Cherubini, an Italian composer of the Romantic era.
6. A typical fireside recitation for the solstice, common in

Germany in the first half of the twentieth century.

7. A widely circulated song from the Nazi youth movement.

CHAPTER 8

1. A popular song from the early twentieth century, whose best known version was by Louis Armstrong and the Mills Brothers – likely the one referred to here.

2. From the song 'Mr Paganini', written by Sam Coslow and performed by the Mills Brothers.

3. Walter is recalling verses his mother came up with spontaneously during a trip to Warnemünde in 1924, described in the sequel to *An Ordinary Youth, We're Still Golden.*

4. A song from 1830 by Franz Kugler, set to a melody by Friedrich Ernst Fesca.

CHAPTER 9

1. From the 1882 poem 'The Crypt' by Conrad Ferdinand Meyer.

CHAPTER 11

1. From the 1912 song 'The Violins Sing and I Lose My Breath' by Robert Stolz, with lyrics by Benno Vigny.

2. From Wagner's *Lohengrin.*

3. Philippians 1:21.

4. See chapter 1, note 1.

5. From the German hymn 'Christ the Saviour Is Here!'.

6. Iserlohn tobacco boxes were made during the Seven Years War (1756–63), a great-power conflict between England and France that eventually enveloped many of the other European states.

CHAPTER 12

1. An 1842 Christmas song by the theologian Johannes Karl with melody by Georg Eisenbach.

2. The Krauses sing the German lyrics of 'White Christmas', written by Irving Berlin in 1942 for the film *Holiday Inn*.

CHAPTER 13

1. From the 1941 poem 'The Time Is Hard' by Dr Julius Kober, a captain in the Luftwaffe.

2. From the 'Song of the Germans', Germany's national anthem from 1922, written by August Heinrich Hoffmann von Fallersleben in 1841, set to a melody by Joseph Haydn. It is forbidden to sing these lines of the song today.

3. A German folk song, author unknown.

4. From the book of German hymns *Set Off in Their Time* by Ulrich Sander, published in 1941.

5. From the 1934 poem 'Eternal Germany' by Wolfram Brockmeier, who would become head of the Reich's Chamber of Literature.

6. An original poem by Kempowski himself, to exemplify the type.

7. A dictation read aloud, to be copied in writing by the students. In the original German, the wording is meant to be difficult to spell out if one doesn't already know how to spell the words – for example, the double *l* and the identical-sounding *f* and *v* in *gefahrvollen*, dangerous.

CHAPTER 14

1. From the 1938 hit song 'You've Got No Clue' by Karl Berbuer.

2. From the poem 'Evening Breeze' by Friedrich von Matthisson, set to music by Beethoven as Opus 46.

3. Ibid.

4. A popular children's rhyme. In the original German, the rank referred to is *Unterarzt*, which corresponds to ensign or cadet, and after 1934 to senior midshipman.

5. From the song 'Up! Up to Battle!' Original from the workers' movement, it was rewritten by Adolf Wagner for the SA, the Nazis' paramilitary wing.

CHAPTER 15

1. The first lines of the poem 'The German Oath' by Rudolf Alexander Schröder, written at the start of the First World War.

2. A song from the *Jugendbewegung*, or youth movement – something akin to the Boy Scouts – from the early twentieth century.

3. A north German folk song with many lyrical variations.

4. A song from the Hitler Youth songbook.

5. The lyrics from the fourth movement of Mahler's Second Symphony.

CHAPTER 16

1. See chapter 8, note 1.

2. A song by Fats Waller, known to German audiences from the cover by Leo Mathisen in 1941.

3. Song of the same title, also by Leo Mathisen.

CHAPTER 17

1. See chapter 2, note 1.

2. Hit song of the same title sung by Peter Igelhoff in 1936.

3. From the song 'Oh Fraulein Grete', a tango by Juan Llossas with lyrics by Fritz Löhner-Beda, who died in Auschwitz in 1942.

4. Ibid.

5. See chapter 8, note 1.

CHAPTER 18

1. From the 1927 song 'That's When I'll Come Back to You' by Louis Armstrong and his Hot Seven.

2. See chapter 14, note 1.

3. One of the many untraceable rhymes and sayings common while playing skat.

4. See chapter 14, note 4.

5. The first lines of the 1812 poem 'Siegfried's Sword' by Friedrich Uhland.

CHAPTER 19

1. The beginning of the 1829 poem 'It Is He' by Eduard Mörike.

2. Song of the same title from 1937, recorded by Tommy Dorsey.

3. A quote from Hitler's opening speech at the 1933 Party Congress in Nuremberg that was printed on the edges of the stamps.

CHAPTER 20

1. From a 1561 Lutheran ballad by Johann Walter, intended to awaken Germany from sin.

CHAPTER 21

1. From the song 'Today the Whole World Makes Music for Me', lyrics by Bruno Balz and melody by Ernst Erich Buder, sung by Elfi Meyerhofer in the film *My Wife Teresa*.

2. See chapter 13, note 7.

3. A line from Theodor Körner's 1815 poem 'The Warrior's Night Song'.

4. See chapter 14, note 1.

5. In Latin: But as strength is lacking, is the will to be praised? From Ovid, *Letters from the Black Sea*.

6. 'If you'd kept silent, you'd still be a philosopher.'

7. See chapter 11, note 2.

CHAPTER 22

1. From the ballad 'The Glove' by Friedrich Schiller.

2. The opening verse of *The Song of the Niebelungen*.

3. A mnemonic for the cases in Latin.

4. From the nineteenth-century folk song 'Am I Not a Young Man?', author unknown.

5. A German children's song, composer unknown.

6. A canon by the twentieth-century German composer Christian Lahusen. The text is from a Swiss proverb.

7. Lines from a song composed for the film, a piece of Nazi propaganda about the importance of sacrificing personal happiness for the good of the country.

CHAPTER 23

1. From Psalm 42.

2. From Psalm 23.

CHAPTER 24

1. From the third act of the 1845 opera *Undine* by Albert Lortzing.

2. A march from 1813 by the composer and conductor Albert Methfessel.

3. The first lines of a children's poem by Victor Blüthgen, set to a melody by Franz Wilhelm Abt.

4. In an annotation to the novel, Kempowski clarifies that this

was printed on the box the model ships came in.

5. Two lines from the poem 'A Child's Questions', author unknown. The poem has many versions.

6. See chapter 11, note 6.

7. Sung to the tune of 'Frère Jacques'.

8. From the German Christmas song 'Something's Coming Tomorrow, Children'.

9. From the nineteenth-century Christmas song of the same title.

CHAPTER 25

1. See chapter 8, note 3.

CHAPTER 26

1. The first lines of the 1829 poem 'Day and Night' by Eduard Mörike.

CHAPTER 27

1. From the poem 'Love Song' by Rainer-Maria Rilke.

CHAPTER 28

1. From the song 'Girl, You Shouldn't Be Alone Here', sung by Lisa Lesco in the 1943 comedy *A Man With Principles*.

2. From the 1938 operetta *Anita and the Devil* by Theo Mackeben.

CHAPTER 29

1. A hiking song from 1915 by Hermann Claudius, with melody by Michael Englert.

2. From the 1883 poem of the same title by the Swiss poet Conrad Ferdinand Meyer.

3. See chapter 24, note 4.

4. From a provocative swing song of the time, author unknown. *Stenz* and *Louis* were slang terms for 'pimp'.

5. From an endlessly repeating bawdy rhyme.

6. A song from the 1943 comedy *I'm Entrusting My Wife to You.*

7. The boys are twisting a line from a song in the movie.

8. Dialogue from the 1943 film *The White Dream.*

9. A scandalous jazz number sung by Bully Buhlan and Detlev Lais.

10. 'The Song of Fritze Bollmann', a children's song mocking the eponymous Fritze, a barber who had told this story to his customers and so became, unwillingly, the subject of a popular song.

CHAPTER 30

1. Walter is citing the legend on a copper engraving by eighteenth-century engraver Martin Elias Ridinger.

2. A line from the 1903 poem 'Love Song' by Rainer-Maria Rilke.

3. A verse from the poem 'Korf's Enchantment' by Christian Morgenstern.

4. Ibid.

5. See chapter 7, note 6.

6. From the swing hit 'Lambeth Walk' from Noel Gay's 1937 musical, *Me and My Girl.*

7. The legend from a drawing by Wilhelm Busch depicting Silen, a satyr in the service of Dionysus, riding on a donkey. In Busch's 1878 pictorial narrative *The Bagwig,* Silen parts from a beautiful nymph and defends himself against an attack by Amor.

CHAPTER 31

1. An exhortation printed by the Nazis to save shoe leather.

2. A two-verse aphoristic poem by Theodor Fontane.

CHAPTER 32

1. From a folk song with often varied lyrics, titled 'The Hazelnut Is Brown'.
2. A saying attributed to Martin Luther.
3. A song from the *Wandervögel* youth movement.
4. From the national anthem 'Flags High!' by SA lieutenant Horst Wessel.
5. Refrain of the 1940 song 'Antje, My Blonde Child', with melody by Herms Niel and lyrics by Heinrich Anacker.

CHAPTER 33

1. A Latin inscription on Rostock's Stone Gate.
2. A quote from *The Great King*, a biopic of Frederick the Great. The Prussian Army was defeated at Kunersdorf in 1759, during the Seven Years War, by Russia and Austria.
3. See chapter 15, note 1.
4. See chapter 8, note 1.
5. A sixteenth-century Protestant chorale by Bartholomäus Ringwaldt.

CHAPTER 35

1. The first verse of the Nazi song 'Up, Raise Your Flag!'.
2. A catchphrase associated with the Winter Relief of the German People organisation.
3. Commonly circulated propaganda messages from this period of the war.
4. See chapter 32, note 5.
5. From 'Today on Board', a sailor song that the SS had appropriated for its songbook.

CHAPTER 36

1. A popular Nazi slogan.

2. An excerpt from Christian Morgenstern's *Steps*.

3. Germans credit Gottfried Leibniz, not Isaac Newton, with having mathematically proved gravity and invented calculus. Leibniz and Newton seem to have come to the same conclusions at the same time, independently of one another.

4. From the poem 'Paratroopers' by Walter Julius Gustav Bloem.

5. From the 1935 song 'A Young *Volk* Stands Up' by the writer and Nazi Werner Altendorf.

6. A quote from Christian Morgenstern's *Steps*.

7. Ad copy for Laxin, a laxative.

CHAPTER 37

1. From the song 'You're an Education', written in 1937 by Harry Warren with lyrics by Al Dubin.

2. From Psalm 37.

3. See chapter 14, note 2.

4. A nineteenth-century children's song by Friedrich Wilhelm Güll, set to music by Friedrich Wilhelm Kücken.